Praise for the novels of
LISA JACKSON

"Lisa Jackson is a real treat. She writes the kind of books
I like to read!"
—Kat Martin

"Provocative prose, an irresistible plot, and finely crafted
characters make up Jackson's latest contemporary sizzler."
—*Publishers Weekly* on *Wishes*

"Lisa Jackson takes my breath away."
—Linda Lael Miller

"Will keep you up nights . . . keeps you turning the pages
right up to the end."
—*The Daily Oklahoman* on *If She Only Knew*

"No one tells a story like Lisa Jackson. She's headed straight
for the top."
—Debbie Macomber

Praise for the novels of
ELAINE COFFMAN

"Coffman writes a smoothly milled romance. Her writing
is deft, capable, evocative."
—*Publishers Weekly*

Praise for the novels of
KYLIE ADAMS

"Say goodbye to cable TV—Kylie Adams dishes up
books so outrageously smart and sexy, you'll fall in love with
reading again."
—Stephanie Bond, author of *I Think I Love You*

"A talented and creative new voice has just joined the romance
genre. This debut novel by Kylie Adams is a funny, sexy and
slightly off-the-wall treat. Keep your eyes on Ms. Adams!"
—*Romantic Times* on *Fly Me to the Moon*

Praise for the novels of
LISA PLUMLEY

"Lisa Plumley creates charming characters. Her books
are a delight!"
—Rachel Gibson on *Reconsidering Riley*

"A romance you don't want to miss. Need a smile?
Grab this book!"
—Lori Foster on *Falling for April*

"Loaded with humor and fun, *Falling for April* is an endearing and
light-hearted read. Lisa Plumley has a knack for humor."
—*Romantic Times*

"I adored *Falling for April!* Lisa Plumley has penned a fast, funny
story, overflowing with characters you won't soon forget.
Lots of fun!"
—Elizabeth Bevarly

Books by Kylie Adams

FLY ME TO THE MOON
BABY, BABY

Books by Lisa Jackson

TREASURES
INTIMACIES
WISHES
WHISPERS
TWICE KISSED
UNSPOKEN
IF SHE ONLY KNEW
HOT BLOODED
COLD BLOODED

Books by Lisa Plumley

MAKING OVER MIKE
FALLING FOR APRIL
RECONSIDERING RILEY

Published by Zebra Books

SANTA BABY

Lisa Plumley
Kylie Adams
Elaine Coffman
Lisa Jackson

ZEBRA BOOKS
KENSINGTON PUBLISHING CORP.
http://www.kensingtonbooks.com

ZEBRA BOOKS are published by

Kensington Publishing Corp.
850 Third Avenue
New York, NY 10022

All Kensington titles, imprints and distributed lines are available at special quantity discounts for bulk purchases for sales promotion, premiums, fund-raising, educational or institutional use.

Special book excerpts or customized printings can also be created to fit specific needs. For details, write or phone the office of the Kensington Special Sales Manager: Kensington Publishing Corp., 850 Third Avenue, New York, NY 10022. Attn. Special Sales Department. Phone: 1-800-221-2647.

Zebra and the Z logo Reg. U.S. Pat. & TM Off.

First Printing: October 2002
10 9 8 7 6 5 4 3 2 1

Printed in the United States of America

CONTENTS

MERRY, MERRY MISCHIEF

Lisa Plumley

To Debbie Shade,
the only person I know who
loves Christmas as much as I do
and to John with much love—
meet me under the mistletoe!

Chapter One

When Katie Moore returned to her office at Brennan Homes late on the Monday before Christmas weekend, all she wanted to do was grab the pair of red stilettos she kept in her bottom desk drawer for cocktail-hour emergencies and scoot out the door. She didn't have time to waste.

The holiday party that was her ultimate destination was already in progress at her favorite downtown Phoenix hangout, and Katie didn't want to be late for the karaoke Christmas caroling. Or the peppermint martinis with candy canes on the rims. Or the dancing beneath strings of flashing multicolored lights. Christmas was Katie's favorite time of year, and this December she had every intention of making the most of it.

Starting with those stilettos. Snatching them from their protective nest of shredded, outdated "Your New Home" brochures, Katie smiled. Equipped with these, and minus the sensible suit jacket that had covered her close-fitting, spaghetti-strapped red sheath all day, she'd be sure to take the party by storm.

She clutched the shoes and her new red-sequined Santa purse (a fondness for cute handbags was her only real weakness), and careened down the short passageway between the vacated cubicles, wriggling out of her suit jacket as she went.

Halfway to the reception area, she glimpsed movement from the corner of her eye. A coworker who hadn't noticed it was already past quitting time and moving toward party time, probably.

Thinking she'd pop in with an invitation to the karaoke caroling, Katie headed toward him. After only a few steps, though, she recognized him. She stopped. The off-key interpretation of "Frosty the Snowman" she'd been humming died in her throat.

It was him. Jack Brennan.

Her heart knew it, and so did her body. Instantly.

Why him? Why now? Why here?

Well, the *why here* part was easy enough—Jack was the heir apparent to Brennan Homes, destined to assume leadership of the company when his uncle stepped down. And on second thought, the *why now* part was a slam dunk, too, since Jack pretty much defined "workaholic" these days. And now that she considered it, Katie realized the *why him* part was pretty obvious, too.

It had *always* been him, for her.

And now, just when she least expected it, here he was. Alone. With her. In exactly the circumstances they'd spent the past several months striving to avoid.

Even though his back was facing her, she'd have recognized him anywhere. His concentrated movements at his architect's drafting board were uniquely his own. So was his take-charge stance. And his aura of general authority . . . and his absolute, one of a kind, drop-dead hunkiness.

Had she mentioned the hunkiness? Jack Brennan personified yummy bachelor male—which was probably why Katie had thrown all caution to the wind seven months ago (an occasional impulsiveness was her only real weakness), and broken her ultimate rule: no flirty office flings.

Well, that had come back to bite her, now hadn't it?

All the same, she couldn't resist lingering. Jack couldn't see her, didn't appear to have heard her, and seemed to be deeply engrossed in whatever architectural plans he was working on. Drawn by a compulsion even more irresistible than the craving for eggnog latte and Christmas cookies that had required a desk-to-Starbucks hike at three-thirty that afternoon, Katie took a step nearer. She absently hugged her belongings closer. And then, even though she knew she shouldn't, she let go and allowed the longing she always felt for Jack Brennan to wash over her.

A rueful smile tugged at her Scarlet Surprise–lipsticked mouth. They'd had some good times together. Happy times. Sexy times. If not for—

Jack suddenly stilled. He glanced over his shoulder, his dark-eyed gaze going straight for Katie. The intensity of his regard shrank the thirty-odd feet between them to mere inches. Curious, *heated* inches.

Busted. Feeling her heartbeat kick into high gear, Katie lifted her chin. She looked back at him. They were supposed to be avoiding each other, and she knew it. So did he.

For the space of several scattered breaths, neither she nor Jack spoke. A connection spun between them all the same, though, a connection that was heady and spicy and meaningful, and laden with a sense that, if only things had been different . . .

"Did you lose your magic slipper, Cinderella?" he asked.

On that confusing note, Jack came toward her. Unable to move, even though she ought to, Katie unwisely savored the power of his strides, the width of his shoulders. She held her breath as he crouched a few feet to her right then retrieved one of her prized stilettos.

When he straightened and held it toward her, his height called to mind the way she used to tuck her head cozily beneath his chin, as though she'd been made to possess that niche. Katie blinked to dispel the memory. Christmas was a time for department store Santas and artificial snow in Tiffany's windows—not regrets. Never regrets.

Her fingers closed on the strappy shoe. It must have fallen from her arms while she watched him, she realized. She'd been too engrossed to notice (a secret sappiness was her only real weakness). And not noticing when one of your Manolos had gone missing . . . well, that was serious stuff.

She tried to give him a smile, so he wouldn't guess exactly how *little* she'd gotten over him since their split. "Thanks. I guess this makes you my own personal Prince Charming, doesn't it?"

Jack felt the shoe slip from his hand. Assuming what he hoped was a dispassionate air, he watched Katie arch and twist as she traded her workday shoes for the sexy, sassy glamour of Cinderella shoes.

It wasn't an easy task. Watching her, that is. Not if he wanted to remain sanely uninvolved and rationally untempted. Moving the way Katie did, especially in a nothing little slip of a dress, ought to be illegal. And he ought to be arrested for his own protection, for allowing himself to enjoy it. But he did enjoy it, all the same. *Too much.*

They'd been right to avoid each other all these months, Jack decided. No matter how he wished that weren't true.

"Prince Charming?" he repeated. "Not quite. Wrong

fairy tale. But I'd be willing to bet you're late for the ball."

She nodded. "Party. At Boondoggles. You want to come?"

What he wanted—what he *needed*—to do was work. "Brennan" had been at the top of the company letterhead for three generations. Because of that, the idea that Jack owed his success more to family connections than to effort or talent had dogged him for years. Despite having started at the bottom of the corporate career ladder. Despite having earned steady promotions. Despite having won a shelf full of design awards that decorated his same-as-everyone-else's cubicle.

During this slow week before Christmas, he'd planned to get a leg up on the new year's designs. He'd planned to take advantage of the quiet offices and really get some things done, including drawings for several innovative new subdivision elevations he'd come up with. But now, faced with Katie's indomitable appeal . . . well, strangely enough, Jack felt his resolve to get down to work double.

Maybe it was simply human nature kicking in. Survival of the stubbornest. Or maybe it was plain old self-preservation at work. Because when it came right down to it, stepping up to the life-is-a-party banquet that was being with Katie Moore hadn't meshed with what he needed.

What he *wanted* was another story.

Jack inhaled the cinnamon-spicy scent of her perfume and the fizzy-sweet energy surrounding her. For an instant, he closed his eyes. If only things had been different. . . .

"No, thanks," Jack made himself say. "I've got—"

"Work to do, I know. Haven't you heard that saying? Something about all work and no play?"

Her mischievous grin captured him as she glanced up from adjusting her shoe strap. Her soft, stylishly cropped hair, nearly as black as his own, seemed as cheery as her smile. Its shaggy ends whisked briefly over his forearm as she straightened.

"I *know* you have." She adjusted her discarded suit jacket over her arm. "So how about it? Sure you won't ditch your drafting table and come along? It's Christmas, after all."

Sure, Christmas. The only time of year when hard work wasn't its own reward, and the whole world exploded into some kind of tinsel-coated, red satin-beribboned, blinking-light-festooned fantasy land. The holidays were the most difficult time of year for Jack, and never-ending renditions of "Rudolph the Red-Nosed Reindeer" weren't the half of it. No matter what he did, he'd never been able to shake a feeling of discontent at Christmastime.

Spending the evening with the only woman he'd never *quite* gotten over—but definitely should have, given their disparate outlooks on life—probably wouldn't be the cure-all he needed, either.

"Nah." He mustered a smile. "But you go on. Have fun. Dance on a few tables for me, will ya?"

Katie nodded, her hazel-eyed gaze never quite meeting his. Not wanting to prolong a conversation that was undoubtedly uncomfortable for them both, Jack nodded, too. As he turned away, he touched her shoulder in farewell, the gesture automatic. Well intentioned. And unexpectedly sensual.

The warmth of her bare skin stopped him instantly. He thought of long nights and cool sheets, of whispers in the dark and shared laughter that went on and on. He thought of *her*. And of losing her. Like a fist, regret closed over him.

Their gazes met. Suppressed yearning tightened his muscles and shortened his breath. All he wanted, all he needed in that moment, was Katie. And him. Together. His hunger for it was as certain as the hammering of his heart, as inevitable as the Scotch pine tree-sale lots springing up amid the Arizona saguaros at Christmastime.

"Katie—"

"Well, sorry to bother you, then," she blurted. "I'll, um, see you around."

Her skittish expression made him want to comfort her with a caress. Her sudden wariness when he stroked his fingers over her skin—once—made him pull his palm away. Jack watched her.

"When a girl's deprived of her Prince Charming," she said lightly, fiddling with her things again, "there's only one thing to do, you know. Guess I'm destined to kiss a lot of frogs tonight."

At the impish, falsely rueful look on Katie's face, temptation flared again. Her feisty spirit attracted him like nothing else. *Don't do it,* Jack ordered himself as he thought over what she'd said and instantly formulated a reply. *Just don't—*

"Ribbit," he said.

Katie's eyes widened. Then, she laughed. "Don't tempt me, wise guy. I've got more lipstick in that bag"— she nodded toward her spangled Santa purse—"and I'm not afraid to use it. *Afterward.*"

She raised her eyebrows. He smiled. Hers was a challenge any red-blooded male would have been crazy to refuse. Never mind their shared history. Never mind the risks inherent in leaning forward to make sure she knew *he* could accept a dare as easily as she could issue one.

All at once, Katie's casually said words sparked something new and fresh between them. Jack could no more deny it than he could remember the correct order of the geese and the drummers and the lords a-leaping in the "Twelve Days Of Christmas" song.

He wanted to kiss her. She seemed interested in kissing him. And in the dimness of the deserted office, with

Christmas cards tacked on the cubicle walls and gold-foil garlands decorating the desktop PCs, it suddenly seemed entirely appropriate that they do so.

Which was how Jack knew he was in *way* over his head this time. And it was only likely to get worse, the more time he spent with Katie.

But this was only one moment. Nothing more. And because of that, he angled his body closer. Their clothes touched, vibrant red meeting shades of gray. She glanced upward, and the teasing intimacy between them expanded. How many times had they come together like this, savoring the breaths between nearness and contact? How many times had he kissed her, and not been able to stop?

"Not enough," she whispered, as though guessing his thoughts. Then Katie stepped closer, too.

Anticipation coursed through him, coupled with the familiar rush going toe-to-toe with her always gave him. Ruefully, Jack shook his head. Only an idiot came this close to tasting forbidden fruit . . . a hungry idiot.

"There must be some mistletoe someplace nearby," he said.

"*I* don't need an excuse." She raised her brows again.

At the implied *do you?* in her look, Jack felt his heartbeat quicken. He'd never been able to resist a challenge. Probably, that was part of the reason Katie appealed to him so strongly.

Probably, it was part of the reason he hadn't been able to put their brief affair behind him. Yet.

"Neither do I," he said, and lowered his head to kiss her.

Chapter Two

Hardly daring to breathe, Katie watched as Jack lowered his head. She wanted to touch him, to wrap her arms around him, to make sure he stayed with her for as long as she needed. But her arms were filled with her boring plain pumps, and her Responsible Accounts Manager suit jacket, and her adorable little Santa bag, and so she had to settle for watching. And waiting. And needing.

This was crazy; she knew it. They'd agreed things could never work between them, had mutually and amicably parted. But now . . . now all Katie wanted was Jack. At least for as long as a mistletoe-free holiday kiss would last.

Was that really so wrong?

If it was, she didn't care. Not while the promise of a moment's reconnection lingered within reach. Not while Jack brought his mouth nearer and nearer to hers, his arrestingly angled face and wicked dark eyes coming ever closer. In a perfect world, he was the Christmas gift Katie would have chosen. But since this world was ordinary and flawed and filled with things like disco-dancing display Santas and inedible plastic gingerbread houses, an early-evening kiss would have to do.

At the moment, it would do quite nicely, too.

The warmth of his mouth reached her, preceding the touch of his lips by a heartbeat. Wanting, *needing*, Katie rose on her tiptoes. The motion carried her the last half inch between them. Their mouths met, just barely. Jack drew in a breath—a gesture she recognized with giddy eagerness, since experience had taught her his hoarse inhalation meant their kiss was about to deepen—and Katie tightened her grasp on her things. *Yes, yes, yes*—

A loud knocking came from the reception area.

No, no—

Jack blinked like a man awakening from a long winter's nap, and raised his head.

Oh, hell.

The mood was broken. Unreasonably disappointed, Katie lowered until her stiletto heels touched carpet. The knocking continued.

"The door to the reception area is locked after five o'clock." Jack's voice was husky. He cleared it. "I'd better go see who that is."

She nodded. He cast her a reluctant look and ran a hand through his hair, calling her attention to the blunt, nimble shape of his fingers—and to the fact that those fingers *wouldn't* be tracing any of the familiar, fondly remembered paths her body seemed insistent on hoping for. Frowning, Katie tried to take comfort in the stick-your-head-in-a-wind-tunnel hairstyle his gesture caused. It didn't work. Even rumpled and frustrated, Jack looked incredible.

"I'll just slip out while the door's open, then." *Which will be a lot safer for both of us.* She strode ahead of him toward the reception area as though the devil himself were at her heels.

In a sense, he was, dressed in shades of uncertainty and packing the ability to make her lose her head over a simple kiss. Really, falling for Jack all over again would only lead to disaster, Katie reminded herself. Already, she'd nearly forgotten the party tonight. Her friends would be waiting for her at Boondoggles, drinks in hand and grins in place. They'd be the perfect remedy . . . for her stupidly susceptible heart.

"Uh-oh," Jack said from behind her.

"What's wrong?"

In the tastefully decorated reception area now, Katie looked past the front desk and upholstered client seating. Past the company's decorated artificial Christmas tree. And past the holiday greeting cards taped to the area's glass front wall and door. She glimpsed a woman standing on the threshold beyond.

Of average height and slender build, the woman was wearing a belly-baring tank top and ankle-length skirt in Army fatigue shades, with a gold arm bracelet coiled near her bicep. Her blonde dreadlocks framed a sweet, worried-looking face. As Katie watched, the woman raised her foot and aimed another combat-booted kick at the front door.

She had to. She didn't have a hand free to knock in the traditional way. Her arms were filled with a molded plastic baby carrier—and *it*, Katie could see, was filled with a wriggling, kicking baby, judging by the pudgy fists and tiny booted feet visible above the padded rim.

"That's not 'uh-oh.' " Wrinkling her brow, Katie glanced at Jack, who'd caught up with her. "That's the boss's nanny."

"And that's *my* baby cousin with her. What are they doing here at this hour?"

He punched the security code into the panel beside the door, then opened it with a greeting for the woman. Two minutes later, Jack was still carrying in assorted pastel baby paraphernalia: bags, blankets, a folded mesh

thing Katie recognized as a portable crib from the last
baby shower she'd attended. He stacked everything
against the reception desk while the nanny, Sierra,
rushed inside.

In a practiced gesture, she braced the baby carrier
against one hip, hurrying past Katie. The two women
passed in opposite directions: Sierra intent on whatever
had brought her to the office, Katie eager to leave Brennan Homes behind.

A babyish babble came from the carrier. Katie hesitated. She dropped her Santa handbag and things onto a
nearby chair. Intrigued despite the peppermint martini
she was probably missing at that very minute, she peeked
inside.

"Oh, what an *adorable* little outfit!" Fascinated, Katie
leaned nearer (an interest in fashion was her only real
weakness), examining the baby girl's clothes. Her dimin-
utive red corduroy jumper and Christmas green T-shirt
were embroidered with gingerbread people, holiday
stars, and Nutcracker figurines. "This is *so* Baby Gap.
How cute!"

"You think so?" Sierra reached into the carrier and
unfastened some mysterious-looking buckles and straps.
She lifted the baby—Belle was her name, Katie remembered—and cradled her against her chest. "Here. Have
a closer look."

Then she bundled baby Belle right into Katie's arms,
blankets, boots, teeny Gap clothes, and all, and went to
speak with Jack.

Hands on hips, Jack surveyed the pile of baby stuff
he'd created at the base of the reception desk. Someone,
somewhere, had to be experiencing a serious shortage
of pink plastic. There couldn't possibly be any left over
after the collection his Uncle Gil had amassed for his
one and only baby daughter.

He wondered if Amber, Gil's wife of eleven months and Jack's new step-aunt (if such a designation existed), ever got tired of living in a Bazooka-colored world. If she did, it hardly would have mattered. Uncle Gil doted on his only child and seemed determined Belle have the best of everything.

Apparently, "the best" only came in shades of Bubble Yum, Pepto-Bismol, cotton candy, and the aforementioned Bazooka.

Not that Amber suffered in any way. Gil Brennan was crazy about her, too. How else could a person explain hair implants, beer-belly liposuction, InstaWite teeth brightening, and not one but *two* Porsche Roadsters over the course of one man's fifty-second year? Jack was certain his uncle loved his young bride, and she, in turn, was a wonderful, enthusiastic mother. Which brought him around to . . .

"Jack! Thank God you're here!" Sierra tugged his shirt, her frantic energy leaping between them. Her dreadlocks whirled as she came to a stop. He saw that she no longer held the baby carrier. "I've been going out of my mind! Gil and Amber's flight's been snowed in, and mine leaves in just under an hour, and you know how insane Sky Harbor will be at this time of year, and I don't know how I'm ever going to make it!"

"Okay, slow down—"

"You're third on the emergency contact list, but everyone else has already left town for the holidays. You're it!"

"I'm it? What do you—"

From the corner of his eye, he glimpsed movement. Katie walked carefully across the room, headed for the office Christmas tree. Holding six-month-old Belle in her arms, she smiled down at the baby, gently cooing something about . . . nicely coordinated booties? Babywear trends? The wearability of red corduroy? Shaking his head, Jack refocused his attention on the nanny.

"Exactly what's the matter? Uncle Gil's flight got delayed?"

"Snowed in. In Switzerland." Sierra wrung her hands, flashing short, purple-manicured nails. "He and Amber went for a ski trip with friends. They thought they'd be back by now, but their flight's on hold until the storm lifts. And *I've* got a flight back to Austin to visit my family in"—she consulted her vintage Swatch—"fifty-six minutes."

"But what about—"

"Belle? That's where *you* come in, and not a moment too soon. I'm *so* glad you're here. I should have known I'd find you at work."

The wry, knowing twist of her lips niggled at him. So what if he was at the office a lot? It wasn't a crime.

But putting jingle bells on a baby's booties ought to be, Jack thought as Katie passed by again and the merry sound of Belle's "accessories" reached him. If Sierra had been listening to that all day, no wonder she was rattled.

"Someone needs to take care of Belle while I'm gone," the nanny went on doggedly, "and like I said, you're third on the emergency contact list. So you're it."

"I didn't even know there *was* an emergency contact list," Jack confessed. "Much less that I was on it." But he was prepared to step up to the plate manfully. "So how long before the number one and number two contact people get back? An hour or two? I can handle that."

Semi-doubtfully, he looked at Katie and Belle again. What he saw reassured him. Now the woman he'd almost kissed a few minutes ago was sticking out her tongue and making silly faces for Belle. She looked gorgeous, lighthearted and playful. The baby was probably more fun than he'd realized, if she could distract Katie from the soirée she was obviously (and sexily) dressed to attend.

"Not an hour or two," Sierra said. "A day or two. Everyone else has already left town for Christmas, and I can't stay."

"A *day?*"

"Or two. Maybe, *possibly*, three. At the outside. These winter storms can be pretty—"

"Three?" He swallowed. Hard. "I've never—"

"Arrgh!"

The nanny scrunched her dreadlocks in her hands, looking frazzled. Suddenly, Jack wondered if she'd been wearing that wild, twisted hairstyle at all when she woke up that morning.

"Please, Jack. *Please.* Please take care of Belle until Gil and Amber get back from their trip. She's a breeze, I promise. You'll hardly notice her at all."

"Well . . ." Jack caught sight of Katie and the baby again. He heard a murmured, "Very stylish holiday hair bow," and smiled in spite of everything. Visually, Jack measured Belle's size. Maybe two feet tall, he estimated. Probably pretty easy to handle. Sort of like a football.

He was pretty good with footballs. He played pickup games with his buddies every weekend.

No, this is nuts. "I haven't had much experience with babies."

"You're her older cousin. You have a natural aptitude," Sierra insisted. "Plus, I brought all Belle's stuff with me. Bottles, baby food, two jumbo packs of diapers, a portable crib, spare clothes, *everything.* You won't need so much as a can of Enfamil."

Good thing. Because Jack didn't know what the hell that was.

As though she sensed him wavering, Sierra picked up speed. "I have all the contact information right here." She pushed a pile of papers into his hands and started going over them. "Gil and Amber's itinerary, phone

numbers, flight info, hotel, you name it. Here's Belle's
schedule—just a rough estimate, of course. Babies don't
exactly punch a time clock."

She laughed, as though the very thought were uproar-
ious. Jack wrinkled his brow and set the papers on the
reception desk for safekeeping. Everything was happening so fast. All he'd wanted was a few days to get some
work done, away from the holiday craziness everyone
succumbed to at this time of year. Now he was . . . a
baby-sitter?

To his left, Katie began singing "Holly Jolly Christmas" to Belle. The soft sound of her voice soothed Jack,
too. He'd had no idea super-sociable party girl Katie
was so enamored of babies. Or so adept with them.

"So you'll do it?" Looking up at him, Sierra bit her
lip.

Her worried gaze penetrated the confusion surrounding him. Sierra really needed him, Jack realized.
More importantly, so did his tiny cousin Belle. Faced
with that fact, he didn't have the heart to say no. No
matter how out-of-his-depth this whole thing felt.

You'll be fine, Jack assured himself. He'd always been
good at whatever he tackled, had mastered challenge
after challenge during his thirty-one years of living. And
honestly how much trouble could one mostly toothless,
two-foot little person *really* be?

"Sure, I'll do it."

"You will?" Sierra whooped and hugged him. "Thank
you, Jack. You won't regret this, I swear."

Rapidly, the nanny reviewed a few more details with
him. Then she said good-bye to Belle, giving the baby
a fond kiss. With that accomplished, Sierra nodded
toward the Bazooka pink pileup, gave Jack an enormous,
grateful smile, and headed for the door.

There, she paused, a suddenly serious expression on
her face. "I wouldn't have asked you to do this if I didn't

believe you could handle it, you know. If you get stuck, just let your instincts guide you. You'll be terrific."

Jack wished he were as sure as Sierra. He nodded reassuringly, though, and raised his hand in farewell. "We'll be fine. I'll teach Belle how to play tackle football or something. We'll stay busy."

Frowning, the nanny hesitated.

"Kidding. Have a good trip."

Sierra scrunched her nose. She shook out her car keys and prepared to leave, blowing kisses to Belle.

"Merry Christmas!" Katie called. Smiling as she held the little girl, she encouraged Belle to uncurl her chubby baby fingers in a tiny good-bye wave.

Seconds later, the door closed behind the nanny. Silence fell, then was broken by the sound of Belle babbling. Probably, *"Oogoo, Oogoo"* was Baby for "good-bye." Or maybe it was Baby for "Help! This guy's an amateur!" Jack really didn't know.

Determined to think positively, he turned to Katie. At the same moment, she turned to him. Wearing a carefree look that could only be enjoyed by people whose plans went as they planned, she crossed the room. Carrying a baby, he couldn't help but notice, didn't strip any of the natural va-va-voom from her stride. She still managed to look like every fantasy he'd ever had, all rolled into one.

Before he could blink, his fantasy carefully slipped a cooing Belle into his arms. His infant cousin pushed three fingers into her drooling mouth and performed an aerial cha-cha with one foot. Jingle bells chimed. Babbling, Belle gazed up at him.

Charmed. Jack gazed back. *Hey, this could be all right. Fun, even. Yeah. Just him and Belle, together.*

"Well, I guess that's it." Nearby, Katie had gathered her things and was pulling a cell phone from her glittery Santa purse. She breezed toward the door, obviously intent on getting to the party she was dressed for. "Good luck, Jack. Byeee, Belle!"

She blew a kiss and opened the door. Panic swept over Jack. At the same instant, Belle scrunched up her face and let loose a foghorn-size wail.

Stricken, he held the baby at arm's length. For the first time in his life, he had no idea what to do. "Wait! You can't just leave me—*leave us!*—like this!"

Katie shrugged. "I don't see why not. I didn't agree to baby-sit, *you* did. Good luck, Jack. And Merry Christmas!"

Chapter Three

Katie made it all of four steps.

On the last, she paused outside the Brennan Homes offices. She gazed at Jack through the glass wall dividing them. His nervous expression as he awkwardly held Belle at arm's length was oddly endearing. Intriguing, too. Drawn by it, Katie squinted thoughtfully.

His expression looked nervous, sure. But it also held a bit of Jack's trademark determination. For that, Katie had to admire him.

The baby's opening wail had become full-fledged crying—crying Jack was obviously having trouble soothing. That didn't stop him from trying, though. Katie could see him earnestly speaking to his tiny cousin, probably telling her everything would be okay, the same way he'd reassured Sierra. Jack was a stand-up guy. And he was clearly out of his depth.

So, clearly, was Katie. Because if she was actually considering what she *thought* she was considering—

No, she told herself. There was a Christmas margarita with her name on it waiting a few blocks away. Red and green holiday tortilla chips with Boondoggle's special chipotle salsa. Friends by the dozen, to make her night as festive as it could possibly be. She didn't want, she didn't need—

Beyond the glass, Jack gingerly lifted Belle. His elbows crooked to the sides as he brought the baby nearer. With slow and reverent care, he kissed her forehead.

At the sight, Katie just . . . *melted*.

Okay, so there was something about a big, macho guy cradling a baby that got to her, she admitted to herself. Especially if that big, macho guy was the fella she was still secretly smitten with. Big deal.

For a moment longer, Katie deliberated. Then, decisively, she dialed up her friend Maya. Dismay twisted through her as the raucous sounds of Boondoggles in full holiday-gala mode crackled into the receiver.

She'd probably live to regret this. Her plans, since she'd decided *not* to brave the annual slog-through-the-airport Christmas craziness to visit her far-flung family, had simply been to spend the season with her *other*, self-made and very close, insta-family: her friends. Now, those plans were about to change.

A few minutes later, Katie had finished telling Maya to have fun at the party without her. She put away her cell phone and drew a deep breath. Then, with thoughts of that tender Jack-to-Belle kiss still whirling in her mind, she returned to the office.

At her entrance, Jack turned his head. Trying to seem as though she had no doubts at all about this hare-brained scheme, Katie slung her Santa bag, suit jacket, and spare shoes on a chair. Then she put her hands on her hips, surveying the out-of-control scene in front of her.

"All right, I'll help you," she announced.

Jack smiled. "We both thank you, I'm sure."

Seeing the relief in his face made Katie grin (a penchant for rescuing friends in need was her only real weakness). Seeing Belle turn her head—fat tears glistening under the fluorescent lighting—and perk up happily at the sound of her voice made her laugh out loud.

"After all," Katie continued, rubbing the baby's little back, "I figure you'll need *someone* around to make sure you don't zone out during 'Sportscenter' and try to give Belle the remote control for a teething ring."

Teething ring? asked Jack's blank expression. Shaking her head, Katie helped him hold Belle more like a baby and less like a potentially terrifying sack of potatoes. She might not know much about babies, but she did know nobody liked being treated like an Idaho Russet.

Murmuring a soothing comment about Belle's cute lacy socks, she wiped the tears from the baby's pink blotchy cheeks, then absently dried her fingers on her scarlet dress.

Jack gazed thoughtfully at the damp prints near her hip. "You'll miss your party."

Katie made a dismissive sound. "I've got more where that one came from," she said, waving her hand. "A holiday masquerade, two tree-trimming bashes, a cocktail party, one dinner party, a friend's December birthday, and a Christmas Eve brunch on Saturday. One event for every night this week, and two for Saturday. I figure it's practically a person's holiday duty to make the most of Christmastime."

In Jack's arms, Belle gave a shuddering sigh. She yawned noisily, her tiny mouth a perfect *O*. Without seeming to think about it at all, Jack rearranged his arms so he could stroke his fingers over her silky blonde hair.

"You make the most of everything, and you know it. It's one of your charms."

"And pointing out the obvious is one of yours." Katie grinned. "Holding babies, however, is not. Not *yet*. Here, let me show you."

With Jack's help, she eased the baby into her own

arms. "You have to hold on tightly enough to be secure," she explained, "but loosely enough to protect your fragile load. It's kind of like . . . holding a new Fendi bag while the salesperson is hovering nearby. You follow?"

"Not really. Who's Fendi?"

"Har, har."

"Really. You want me to hold Belle like a purse?"

"Well, that's how it was explained to me."

At the aforementioned baby shower, that is. One of her college pals had brought along her three-month-old son, and all the women had taken turns holding him.

When it came to the whole infant-cuddling routine, Katie had been a newbie. *Then.* But Jack didn't have to know that. And she sort of liked being an expert on something he valued. The glimmer of respect in his eyes made her secretly proud—and made up for the karaoke caroling she was missing, too.

Besides, Belle really was adorable. Her wispy hair, her long lashes, her tiny curled fists. Smiling, Katie nudged at one of those fists. The baby instantly grasped her hand, seeming to take comfort in the contact.

On a pleased breath, Katie glanced up. Jack was watching her . . . with a mysterious half-smile that stopped her in her tracks.

"What the heck is *that* look for?" she asked, feeling suddenly jittery. "What are you—"

"It's for *you,*" Jack said. "You—and Belle."

Jack couldn't help but grin wider as Katie shook her head.

"Oh, no. No, you don't. You're not getting any crazy ideas, are you? Like making *me* head baby-sitter? Because if you are—"

"Look at you," he insisted. "You're a natural. Belle loves you."

"I complimented her holly-berry holiday hair bow. Everyone likes someone who compliments what they're wearing."

"In that case . . . nice dress."

"Nice try."

"I mean it."

He did. They both looked at the racy length of scarlet hemline visible beneath Katie's armload of baby. Jack's gaze traveled farther, all the way down her remarkable legs to those look-at-me shoes. He nodded. "I really do."

"Okay, I believe you. Physical attraction was never our problem. But despite that fact—"

"Have I mentioned how grateful I am for your help? Because I am. Thank you for coming back. I know how much it means to you to miss a party."

Katie hesitated, as though unsure what to make of his remark. Then, she forged onward: "You're welcome. But if you think you can sweet-talk me into—"

"You must have some innate knack with babies," Jack continued. Just realizing it, he felt immensely cheered. "Maybe it's in your genes, or your double X chromosomes or something, because—"

"Hold on a minute, buster. Did Neanderthal Man just grunt his way in here, or did I actually hear you hypothesize that just because I'm a woman, I have some super-special baby-care ability?"

He shrugged. "Maybe you do."

Her glare gave him the distinct impression she was holding back a growl. Or possibly a Santa-bag wallop. *Whoops.*

Backtracking seemed wise: "Or maybe you've had some experience with babies. I mean, don't most teen-aged girls baby-sit? How else can they afford lip gloss and boy-band CDs and—"

"Oh, I don't know . . . maybe *jobs?* Just like the boys?"

"I didn't mean—"

"When I was a teenager," she persisted, "I was spending my weekends at the mall—"

Where lip gloss and CDs were sold. Jack couldn't help but think this helped his argument.

"—folding sweaters at the Gap and eating greasy food court lunches. I worked!"

"So the lip gloss and the CDs and the—"

"Not the result of baby-sitting," Katie confirmed. Her glacial look could have doused a flaming Yule log. The revelation behind it didn't do much for Jack's meager sense of baby-care confidence, either.

"But the Fendi bag baby-holding instructions," he protested, gesturing toward her very comfortable grasp on Belle. "The remote control teething ring thing. The—" He stopped and raked a hand through his hair, then squinted at her. "The general baby-style expertise surrounding you . . . I don't—"

At the word *expertise,* she brightened. Past the point of being misled by such a display, Jack continued:

"You mean to tell me you don't know *anything* about babies?"

Katie drew herself up. "So far, I know more than you."

"That's not saying much. *Everyone* knows more than me."

"Well, what did you expect?" she asked. "However, I *am* willing to help you. For tonight. So that's a start."

"For *tonight?*" This just got better and better. Sierra had said Gil and Amber's flight could be delayed up to three days. Maybe longer. "I might be taking care of Belle all week. Until Christmas Eve."

She glanced down, cooing to the baby. "Isn't he lucky, to have you all week? It'll be fun!"

Katie's smile, when she looked up at Jack again, was brilliantly cheery. She angled her body a little away from him. Through clenched teeth, she added, "Ixnay on the arguing, okay? It isn't good for Belle."

"*See?*" Frustration made Jack pace a few steps across the reception area, then back. "I didn't know *that!*"

"Okay, calm down. Just because I'm not an au pair in disguise—"

"A what?"

"—doesn't mean we can't handle this. Together."

He stopped pacing. Gave her a no-nonsense look. "Are you *sure* you don't know about babies? Didn't you have a—a doll or something when you were a kid?"

Wearing a patient look, she shook her head.

"We're doomed."

"I did have a Barbie," Katie ventured.

New hope rose within him.

"But of course, with Barbie the whole appeal is really just wowing Ken and the gang with fab new outfits, isn't it?"

He stared.

"It's not the same as pretend bottle-feeding a wee Baby Wetsalot. Not really."

Her blithe, knowledgeable tone sucked him in yet again. "What's the difference?" he asked cautiously.

"Well, cute pink plastic Barbie heels, for one thing. Did you know her feet are permanently on tiptoes?"

Jack gaped at her. She seemed perfectly content with the situation as it was. Confident, optimistic, even enthusiastic. Probably because caring for Belle wasn't *really* her responsibility. As he shook his head, Katie caught sight of the gesture.

"Come on," she said quietly. "What did you expect when you asked me to help? That I'd magically morph into Mary Poppins?"

He gave her a blank look.

"You mean you've never even *seen Mary Poppins?* Boy, is *your* cinematic history lacking."

Jack was reminded of those differences in perspective

that had precipitated the end of their interoffice fling. Forcing himself to concentrate on the issue at hand, he said, "We're getting off track here. I need a commitment from you—"

"Now *there's* a switch in the typical male repertoire."

"—to help take care of Belle this week, or this isn't going to work. I need to know I can count on you to help get the job done."

"*Sheesh.* All business, aren't you?"

He waited. There really wasn't any reply to that, anyway.

"But then I should have expected that," Katie muttered. Drawing in a deep breath, she gazed at the Christmas tree in the corner for a thoughtful moment. "Yes, I'll help you. Of course. Otherwise I wouldn't be here."

"You commit? All week?"

"What is this, the Inquisition? I said I'd help!"

"I'm not fooling around with Belle's well-being. I might not know much, but I know I care about my cousin."

Katie blinked. Her gaze, when she turned it on him again, looked suspiciously moist. "Do you mean that?"

Jack was aggravated she had to ask. " 'Course."

"*Awwww.* That's so sweet. I knew you were just a big mushball at heart. Now I've got proof."

"Don't go spreading it around. I know some things about you, too."

She gasped. "You *wouldn't!*"

Nodding, Jack gave her his most dangerous grin. "I *would.* Emergency party dress? Filed under "Optional Extras" in the Sierra Vista subdivision drawer. Spare nail polish? Tucked in with the exterior paint chips samples. Roster of favorite cocktail party guests? Culled mostly from the Brennan Homes client and subcontractor list."

"Okay, okay. So I network a little. I happen to be very good at socializing. Is that a crime?"

It wasn't. But he had her, and Jack knew it.

She sighed. A moment passed.

Katie shook her head. "We've got to be the two least likeliest people in the universe to take care of a baby."

Her words were less than encouraging. But they were a concession. She *was* going to help. He felt some of the tension ease from his shoulders.

"Maybe the second-to-last least likeliest. We're bound to be ahead of those people who glare at babies on airplanes."

A ghost of a smile quirked her lips. She smoothed a wrinkle from Belle's tiny dress with utmost care. Her voice was small when she spoke. "I hope we can do it."

"We can do it," Jack assured her. "Together, we can do anything."

Her head came up. A hint of sadness darkened her eyes—sadness it hurt him to see. He'd have bet anything in the world they were thinking exactly the same thing:

Anything . . . except stay together.

Their gazes held; deepened. Jack couldn't bring himself to look away. He and Katie were the same two people who'd loved . . . and lost, only months before. They were the same two people who'd been too different to *really* come together, for keeps. But now—now Belle had brought them together.

She was a tiny Christmas surprise, too small to understand the impact her arrival might have. Jack understood it, though. And in spite of himself . . . he *hoped.* Hoped things might be different, hoped some holiday magic might change things somehow.

Did Katie hope, too?

Looking at her, he couldn't tell. Even as the question crossed his mind, she blinked and looked away. Balancing Belle on one hip, she picked up the schedule Sierra had left.

"We'd better get going," she said. "According to this, it's past Belle's dinnertime."

"I suppose a nice thick T-bone is too much to hope for?"

"She's a baby, not a beagle."

With a shrug, Jack began deconstructing the Bazooka pileup for the drive home. "Hey, a guy's got to hope."

And that, he realized as he considered the days still ahead of him, was *exactly* what he was doing. He just couldn't help it. He hoped for him and Katie, together. *For keeps.*

Chapter Four

She still hadn't outgrown her hope—her *belief*—that Christmastime could magically make things happen, Katie realized as she wrestled with a jar of strained peas at Jack's bachelor digs later that night.

Despite being twenty-eight fun-filled years old, she still harbored a girlish belief that the holidays brought a special measure of goodwill and cheer and magic to ordinary life. And her recent trip between the office and Jack's place (fraught as it had been with differences of opinion) had done nothing to change her mind.

Even as he'd insisted it was *his* place they go to (because "cousin" trumps "fashion adviser"), Katie had felt herself weakening toward him. Even as he'd insisted she meet them there with a change of clothes and spend the night (dangerous as *that* was), Katie had wondered where—exactly—he planned for her to sleep. And even as Jack had insisted, upon her arrival, that they'd keep things strictly baby-based between them, Katie had begun hoping, secretly, this was their gift-wrapped second-chance-in-disguise.

Jack, however, didn't seem to be feeling any of the same mushy, gushy things she was. He sat on the family-room floor with Belle on a baby blanket in front of him, surrounded by pink-hued supplies and frowning at the opened bag of disposable diapers. While she watched (and answered her cell phone for the fourth time that night), he snatched a third folded diaper and deftly opened it.

He looked from the diaper to a squirming Belle. Sunnily, the baby gave him a two-toothed grin, her good cheer probably related to her relief at having gotten rid of the dirty diaper she'd produced upon their arrival. Now, bare-bottomed and filled with energy, she clapped her hands and babbled.

"I *knew* I should have looked closer at the original diaper before taking it off," Jack muttered. He looked at Belle. "Any hints?"

The baby kicked. Jingle bells jangled merrily.

"Right. Well, maybe if I don't unfold it this time."

He reached for another diaper, looking adorably perplexed and even more adorably determined. Really, pairing a hunky man with a cute, cuddly baby shouldn't be allowed. Especially around susceptible single women. Because while wearing his work clothes and ruffled-up hair, and while biting his lip in concentration, Jack was somehow more appealing to Katie than he ever had been before.

Still, she couldn't let him struggle. No matter how charming he might look while doing it. Refusing yet another party invitation, Katie hung up her phone and called to Jack.

"There are directions on the side of the bag," she offered. "Maybe you should read them."

He looked at her as though she'd suggested he gift-wrap himself and go caroling wearing nothing but a big red bow. Which actually, now that she thought of it, sounded kind of sexy. Would he look best in red velvet or green—

"I *don't* need to read the directions."

"Suit yourself." She shrugged. *Definitely green satin,* Katie decided with a wicked little tingle. It would coordinate so nicely with his dark hair. "I'll just be over here fixing up the portable high chair, uh, thingie."

His eyebrows raised. A smile crooked his lips. "Thingie? Is that the technical term?"

"It is as long as you're taping that diaper to your fingers."

"Touché."

Grinning, Katie successfully opened the strained peas. They were the color of a clearance-rack winter suit and would probably be just as hard to unload. She carried them at arm's length around Jack's pristine Scandinavian-style dining table, and then set to work hooking the portable infant seat to its edge.

Several minutes later, she'd wrestled the thing into submission. Proudly, she brushed off her hands and surveyed her work. As she did, Jack approached. Her awareness of him hadn't changed a bit. She could still detect his body heat at fifty paces. *Damn it.* Obviously her libido was a slow learner.

He cocked his head, studying the infant seat. Suddenly vulnerable, Katie braced herself for the inevitable teasing.

"Nice work," he said.

Her mouth dropped open. Before she could so much as quit gaping in surprise, he'd turned to fetch Belle. Jack returned with the baby in his arms. He effortlessly assessed the engineering of the infant seat and strapped his cousin in.

"You've got a knack for that," Katie told him.

He smiled over his shoulder. She felt an answering grin edge onto her own lips, prompted by the cozy feeling they shared. Maybe this would work after all, she thought. Maybe they *wouldn't* drive each other crazy by Christmas Eve.

Naturally, that was when she noticed it: The problem.

Jack had seated himself in a chair beside Belle and had coaxed the baby into opening up for her first bite of . . . well, it looked a lot like *mush,* when Katie spoke.

"Where are your Christmas decorations?" she asked.

Her tone was like that of a department store Santa who'd just realized his assistant "elves" had gone on strike. Amazement wrapped in dismay pretty much summed it up.

"Don't have any," he said, giving Belle another spoonful. She stuck out her tongue, making the primordial goo that passed for dinner squish onto her chin. "I usually spend Christmas Day with family at Mom and Dad's house. Believe me, *it's* got Christmas cheer to spare. A fake Santa and sleigh atop the gravel and desert landscaping in the front yard, strings of lights on the ocotillos, A/C cranked down to fifty degrees, roasted chestnuts on the gas fireplace—"

"But, but—*your* house—"

"No need to decorate." He shrugged. "I get all the holiday feeling a guy could want at Mom and Dad's. Besides, I like it this way."

Katie gazed around her, taking in his renovated Fifties ranch-style house. To judge by her expression, there was something seriously wrong with two bedrooms, a bath, picture windows overlooking a quiet central Phoenix neighborhood—and walls devoid of plastic Christmas wreaths. Obviously, she'd been hoping for *It's a Wonderful Life* and had gotten *Scrooged* instead.

She shook her head. "This simply won't do."

"What do you—*aaack!*"

Belle giggled over the baby raspberry that had just spewed strained peas all over his head and shoulders. As he wiped away the ooze, Jack spotted Katie purposefully carrying her Santa bag to the table. She rifled through it, her face determined.

A travel-size container of hair mousse emerged. He raised his eyebrows. Mostly goo-free now, he repeated, "What do you mean?"

"I mean this won't do. Not for you, and especially not for Belle. How's she supposed to have a happy holiday week, when your house looks like something out of *Architectural Digest*?"

He brightened.

She shook her head. "It's so minimalist in here, the entire Macy's Christmas department could explode in your living room and it would *still* look underdecorated."

"Hey!"

"It's not Belle's fault she's stuck here for her very first pre-Christmas holiday week. And it's not fair to penalize her with your festivity challenged idea of 'decorating.' "

Completely in earnest, Katie gave the baby a sorrowful look. "Don't worry, little Belle. You either, Jack. I've got a solution."

He glanced at the mousse. "What, you're going to style the place into submission? I've got news for you. I think my sofa's leather upholstery is past the point of achieving body, control, and fabulous fullness."

She pursed her lips. He couldn't help noticing they still looked luscious. *God help him.*

"Very funny." She plunked a pair of manicure scissors beside the mousse. "Have you got any plain white paper?"

"In the office." He angled his head toward the hallway, in the direction of the second bedroom he'd converted into a home work space. "First door on the right. Help yourself."

Katie was already on her way, answering yet another

cell phone call as she did. Bemused, Jack used Belle's spoon to corral some runaway peas and nudge them into the baby's mouth again. This time, she smacked her lips with apparent delight and swallowed the whole mess. Hey, that was progress.

Humming "Jolly Old Saint Nicholas," Katie returned, sans cell phone. Probably, she'd turned down yet another party invitation, he decided. Impressive. The sheaf of paper she'd retrieved fluttered as she set it on the table beside the mousse and scissors. With an air of complete absorption, she dragged a chair closer and got down to work.

Between offering Belle bites of chicken with noodles, Jack sneaked glances at Katie. The dining room light glowed over her as she folded and creased and cut. The house seemed to settle in to embrace her . . . all over again. Remembrances of other times at this table, other togetherness, reached out to Jack.

Self-protectively, he angled his shoulders. Still, the sounds of snipping shears competed with the gibbering conversation he and his baby cousin had. Belle could understand many more words than she could pronounce, he discovered as dinnertime progressed. And as the contents of the baby-food jars dwindled, he realized he felt more at ease with his new responsibility with each passing moment.

He'd spent time with Belle, of course. While visiting his family. But never alone; never for hours (or days) at a stretch. Getting to know Belle now was actually turning out to be fun.

She bashed her palms straight downward, sending a chicken noodle-covered infant spoon sailing into the air. It landed, naturally, on Jack's head. Okay, so make that *messy* fun. He plucked out the spoon. Scraped away a few squashed noodles. Made a goofy face at Belle.

She giggled.

His heart expanded. Awestruck by the sensation, Jack paused, his fingers still clutching the noodles.

At the same moment, he realized the *snick-snick* of the scissors had stopped. Slowly, he turned his head.

Katie sat motionless across from him, scissors slack. A half-clipped square of white paper dangled from her fingertips. She was watching him as though ... as though she were a poor little girl with a mile-long Christmas wish list and he were the grandest toy in the FAO Schwarz store window, all wrapped up in ribbons and bows. It was a look filled with a certain sense of revelation. A look so compelling, so *needful,* it was all he could do not to launch himself over the tabletop and explore the feelings behind it.

She blinked. Her expression changed. Moving carefully, Katie put the scissors on the table. Then she said the last thing he expected to hear from her:

"I'm not sure I can do this."

Belle turned her head, as though understanding something important had happened. Lamplight gleamed off the clump of smashed peas drying in her hair.

"Sure, you can," Jack said. He wanted to reach across the table for her hand, wanted to make Katie smile away the sudden downturn to her lips. "You have to. You agreed, at the Inquisition. One hundred percent commitment. Yes, sir!"

He mimicked a military salute. At that, she did smile. But wryly, like a woman who'd just strapped on her costume wings, only to spot *another* winter angel at the Christmas masquerade. There wasn't much real humor in that smile, but there was a tinge of worry.

"What's the matter?" he asked, seriously.

"You. Me." Katie waved her hands, making paper flutter around her. "Us, together. Are we nuts to even try this?"

"Possibly." His reply was punctuated with a Belle

babble. Keeping his expression neutral, he began post-dinner baby-cleanup duty. "But I'm glad you're here anyway."

"Really?"

"Really. Otherwise, I'd have no one to share these yummy leftovers with." He tilted his head toward the baby-food jars.

She snorted. Then she looked at him again, exactly at the same time as Jack looked at her. The smile they shared next started out slowly. Then, as Katie seemed to gather strength from it, it blossomed into a full-blown synchronized grin. One that, miraculously, chased away a teeny, barely noticeable, out-of-the-way corner of Jack's usual Christmas season discontent.

"Okay, enough waffling," Katie said. "Last-chance jitters are over with. I'm in, no matter what. No more second thoughts."

As if in demonstration of that new philosophy, she let her gaze rove over him, frankly appreciative despite his bedraggled business clothes and baby food–plastered hair. She raised her eyebrows. "After all, I always did like living dangerously."

So did he, Jack decided. Because heartbreak loomed on the other side of that come-hither look of hers—heartbreak he'd already experienced once. And he was still here, wanting more. More smiles, more togetherness, more Katie. Her companionship eased him in ways he'd rarely experienced . . . and wound him up in ways he couldn't help but feel again, now.

"Living dangerously, huh?" He rose to rinse the cloth he'd used to clean up Belle's cherubic, noodle-covered face. As he passed, he glanced down at the array of white shapes Katie had created. "That's good. Because if you're doing what I think you're doing, you're *dangerously* close to some major renegotiating. With me."

Chapter Five

"Renegotiating?" Katie asked. "What *kind* of renegotiating?"

She lunged upward from her chair and followed Jack to the kitchen sink. Behind her, Belle used her spoon to bang on the dining room table, but Katie couldn't concentrate on the exuberant rhythm. Instead, her mind was filled with thoughts of Jack—and what he could possibly have meant by that ominous, Scrooge-like *renegotiating* remark.

"Well, for starters," he told her offhandedly, "I think you should stop making those paper snowflakes."

Katie gaped at him.

"That *is* what you've been doing, isn't it?"

She nodded. Definitely Scrooge. Definitely. How could she be falling (all over again) for a Scrooge? She, a woman who loved Christmas trees and candy canes and stockings by the chimney and milk and cookies for Santa—

She nodded. Then folded her arms defiantly over her middle as she trailed him back into the dining room.

"Yes. Paper snowflakes. And the mousse is going to stand in for artificial snow in those big picture windows of yours."

His lips quirked. She frowned and straightened her spine.

"It's the best I can do until I can get to a store for supplies. And if you don't like it—"

Suddenly, Jack rotated to face her. Katie all but skidded to a stop at the table's edge, nearly nose to nose with him. Wearing an expression somewhere between amused and affectionate, he shook his head.

"I didn't mean I want you to stop altogether," he said. "I meant I want you to wait until you can show *me* how to make some snowflakes, too."

"Me? Show you? Paper snowfla—"

"Mmm-hmm."

"But I thought—"

"I know you did." And at that, he (to Katie's absolute amazement) actually burst into song.

"You're a mean one, Mr. Grinch," Jack sang in a deep cartoon-y voice. He pointed to himself, eyes shining with humor, as he went on. "You really are a heel—"

"Oooh!" Katie walloped him over the head with a snowflake-in-progress. Unfortunately, it didn't stop his singing.

Belle clapped her little hands and bounced in her infant seat, excited by her cousin's antics. Waggling his eyebrows at Katie, Jack sang as he finished cleaning up the baby, comically exaggerating every verse. When he'd finished, Belle was free to crawl across her living room blanket to await a bath, and Katie was more certain than ever she'd gotten in over her head.

She actually thought Jack looked charming as he sang.

He stopped beside the table, further rumpled by his exertions with Belle. He glanced at her.

"That was my favorite Christmas song as a kid."

"So I gathered."

"I can't believe I remembered all the words." He shook his head. "It's been years since I sang at Christmas. Don't know why I did now. . . ."

For an instant, he hesitated. He frowned, troubled.

"Belle seemed to enjoy it." Katie couldn't help but smile over the memory of big, tough Jack Brennan singing to his baby cousin. "So did I," she added under her breath.

"What's that?" He leaned nearer. Grinning now (her intention all along), he cupped one hand over his ear. "Didn't quite hear you."

"I said I enjoyed your singing!"

"That's what I thought."

Just like that he was back—the same sure, sexy, satisfied man she was accustomed to. For a moment there, Katie had wondered if he really *was* troubled by Christmastime. His hesitation, his frown. . . . But then she'd realized no one could possibly make it through an entire holiday season (much less several) without singing Christmas songs. Jack *had* to have been teasing.

She hoped. Otherwise, he needed some serious de-Scrooge-ifying. And he needed it fast.

"So will you? Show me how to make these?" he asked, nodding toward the paper snowflakes on the table. "I know I've done it before, but you've obviously remembered the technique better than I have. And it looks like fun."

He looked like fun. More lighthearted than Katie could remember. Less businesslike, more open. And that, more than anything else, was the reason she agreed.

"After Belle's bath," she said. It was time to roll up their sleeves (figuratively, in Katie's case) . . . and get wet.

* * *

Thirty minutes later, Katie and Jack were both drenched. They knelt beside the bathtub, Katie in her sodden red dress and Jack in his drippy shirtsleeves, staring in amazement at their tiny charge.

Belle splashed. They ducked, each retaining a now-practiced hold on the baby's soap-slippery body. As the bathwater slid across the vintage white honeycomb tiles behind them, they straightened.

"What was in that dinner?" Katie asked, wide-eyed. "She's super-powered!"

"Umm, *mush.* It shouldn't have had this"—he dodged a flying rubber ducky—"effect on her."

"The Grinch song, then?"

"Hey!"

"Maybe the mini shampoo Mohawk we made in her hair?"

Jack shook his head. "She liked it. Besides, we rinsed it out right away—"

"*After* taking that cute snapshot." Katie hadn't been able to resist. Belle had looked adorable with her wispy hair sticking straight up.

"—and I can't imagine a simple hairstyle affecting someone that strongly."

Katie could. Obviously *he'd* never gone for a desperate postbreakup shearing and emerged looking like Howdy Doody.

"Well, *something's* happened," she told him. "She hasn't been this wiggly all day."

Belle giggled and lunged forward like an Olympic diver going for a perfect ten in the Mr. Bubble Meter. Jack, who had one arm across her shoulders, caught her just in time.

"This baby," he said, "has no concept of her own inabilities."

"Neither did we, when we agreed to baby-sit."

But they were doing pretty well, Katie figured. They'd tag-teamed on the bathing, one of them holding Belle steady while the other washed, then switching. Now the whole bathroom smelled pleasantly of baby shampoo, and Belle was squeaky clean.

Whenever they tried to take her out of the tub, though, she cried. The baby's scrunched-up, disappointed face as she was lifted from the bubbles was the saddest thing Katie had ever seen—next to an unbedecked Christmas tree left on the curb for recycling pickup the day after New Year's, of course. She hated the end of the holiday season. Glimpsing those once-glorious trees laid out for the chop always made Katie feel gloomy, like—

"We'll have to distract her," Jack said, successfully distracting Katie from her postholiday thoughts, too. "I'll sing while you let out the bathwater. Once it's gone—"

"Uh-uh. She'll be scared. When I was a little girl, watching the water go down the drain terrified me. I was sure it was going to suck me right down with it."

"Maybe Belle has a better grasp of physics than you did."

"Har, har."

"Well, she's obviously too big to—oh, hell. Never mind. I can tell by looking at you. You'd sooner hammer nails with those stilettos of yours than risk scaring Belle."

Katie nodded. "So would you, and you know it."

"I generally stick to a sixteen-ounce wood-handled claw hammer for home improvement projects, but—"

"Be serious. She's getting pruney."

They thought about it for a minute, while Belle splashed happily—bolstered in their grasp—with the bath toys Sierra had left. Just when Katie had begun to think they'd have to risk another bout of loud baby misery, an idea occurred to her.

"I've got it," she said, snapping her fingers. Then

she left Belle in Jack's care and headed for the living room.

Left alone with Belle, Jack observed his baby cousin carefully. Then, experimentally, he grasped beneath her slick little arms and raised her a few inches from the water.

Her shriek reverberated from the walls with all the force of a jet screaming overhead.

Immediately, he lowered her back into the bathwater.

"It's all right, Belle. I didn't mean it."

She cooed and went back to playing. Holding her, Jack eyeballed the towels on the bar to his right. They looked wonderful. Fluffy, dry, thick, dry. And dry. Geez, what he wouldn't give to shuck off his soggy clothes and retreat to his home office for a few minutes' fortifying, *productive* work.

He tried sharing his views with the baby. "But wouldn't it feel nice to be dry? All cozy and warm and—"

"No dice," Katie said from the doorway, flipping her cell phone closed. Again. "If looking forward to future rewards *really* worked, nobody would need a Platinum card. We'd all have enough savings to buy everything we wanted. Including a cute new pair of slingbacks whenever we spotted them."

She looked momentarily dreamy, as though new shoes equaled nirvana.

"Interesting economic theory. So we're all just one pair of shoes away from financial solvency?"

"In a sense. It depends on the shoes." She grinned, rising up on her bare tiptoes. She must have abandoned her stilettos in the living room. "Now, back to Belle."

Smiling at the baby, Katie drew something from behind her back. Instantly, Belle quit splashing. Her infant gaze locked on the thing in Katie's hand, and she held out both arms.

"Agoo!" she squealed. *"Agoo!"*

Jack glanced backward to see what it was. Because without a doubt, *"Agoo"* had to be the coolest thing *ever* to have elicited such a reaction.

"It's a book."

Katie nodded. *"Pat the Bunny.* It was the rattiest-looking thing in Belle's bag. That means it's the most loved."

Awww, Jack thought. Obviously, despite what Katie had said earlier, he wasn't the *only* "big mushball at heart" around here.

"Agoo! Agoo!" Belle insisted.

Katie held it enticingly out of reach. "After you're all dried off, little Belle. Then we'll read a story."

It worked. Effortlessly—and without the waterworks this time—Jack pulled the baby from the bath. Katie helped him bundle her into a towel to dry off, then took over with a miniature soft brush to style Belle's hair. Within minutes, his tiny cousin was diapered and dressed in her candy-cane-print pajamas with her favorite blanket in hand.

"I can't believe that worked," he said.

Sitting on the sofa now with Belle in her lap and the *Bunny* book in hand, Katie shrugged.

"Bait and switch. It's what the designers always do to me, whenever I feel like I've finally got my wardrobe all set. I think it's good to go, completely classic, ready to wear. I'm happy." She gestured toward the lightweight sweater and jeans she'd changed into, postbath. "Just as happy as Belle was in that tub."

Ahh. So *that* was the connection.

"And then they trot out new designs, totally different from last season's," she continued. "And no matter how satisfied I was with what I had, I've just got to have them."

"Maybe." The intricacies of designers—*and* how they

related to babies in bathtubs—were beyond him. "But let's face it. You *bribed* Belle into getting out of the tub."

Katie made a dismissive sound. "Exactly what would *you* call a miniskirt revival after a season of below-the-knee lengths? Hmmm?"

He scrunched his forehead, thinking. "A leg man's lucky day?"

She rolled her eyes and opened the book. "Spoken like a true male. You wouldn't know fashion if it bit you."

"It can *do* that?" Feigning horror, Jack headed for a smashed-pea-cleansing shower. "In that case, I'm never getting dressed again."

"I should be so lucky."

He stopped. Looked over his shoulder. Raised his brows.

Katie waved her free hand. "Kidding, Mr. Nudist Wannabe. Your bodacious *un*bitten booty is safe with me."

Jack nodded and continued on his way. His thoughts, however, stayed with Katie . . . and all she'd said. Because while her official stance might be "safe," she was gradually veering toward "dangerous." He could tell.

Because so was he.

All of a sudden, he couldn't wait to find out what would happen when they got there.

Jack emerged after his shower with damp, finger-combed dark hair, a fresh shave, and killer abs that teased Katie for the briefest moment while he pulled on a clean T-shirt. Wearing it along with bare feet and a pair of casual cotton drawstring pants that rode low on his hips, he came toward the sofa. Upon spotting Belle on Katie's lap, though, he stopped.

"Is she asleep?" he asked, looking hopeful.

Katie nodded. "I think so. I'm afraid to move and risk waking her up."

The baby felt sweetly heavy in her arms, trusting and relaxed. The *Pat the Bunny* book lay on the sofa beside them, abandoned after much patting (of course) and giggling.

"Also," Katie added, "my left arm is asleep. It feels like it belongs to someone else. Someone in another time zone."

Jack grinned. At the sight, she felt her middle turn an excited somersault. In the dim room, with Belle peacefully settled, Katie suddenly felt all-too aware of her impending aloneness with him . . . and of her complete lack of a strategy to deal with it. She needed one, too (a susceptibility to charming, incredible-ab-endowed, joke-telling men was her only real weakness).

But before she could formulate anything to bolster her heart against the lure of his caring, his intelligence, his good humor, Jack went and did something that endeared him to her even more. He set up the portable crib, set up the baby monitor, arranged everything in his bedroom, and then returned to gently retrieve Belle from her arms. With an obvious tenderness, he carried the baby to bed.

Moments later, he returned. "She wiggled when I put her down, so I waited to make sure she was still asleep. If she wakes up later"—he raised the monitor's receiver—"we'll have this."

"Good." Think of something besides his naked chest, Katie ordered herself. Something besides his tight abs. Something besides the way he's looking at you right now, as though . . . as though he's thinking of you naked, too! She jerked upright.

"We'd better get busy," she said, getting to her feet.

"I was thinking exactly the same thing," Jack replied, stepping closer. "I've been looking forward to this all night. Our time. You. Me. Together. Alone at last."

Katie gulped. He *looked* so good. *Sounded* so good. *Felt* so right, as he drew nearer and nearer. If Jack decided to kiss her again, she didn't think she'd have the necessary bravado to pretend it wouldn't affect her. In the office earlier, her knees had nearly buckled when he'd accepted her dare, and they hadn't even gotten to finish their kiss!

She'd spent months trying to get over him. Months trying to convince herself they were better off apart. Now, after only a single evening together, her tough mental discipline had disintegrated to . . . to *this*. Faced with him, Katie felt like a dieter staring down the flashing Krispy Kreme "Hot Doughnuts Now" sign. When it came to her, Jack Brennan was the original glazed doughnut of temptation.

"Come on." He held out his hand. "We have unfinished business to attend to."

Chapter Six

Geez, Katie was skittish all of a sudden, Jack thought. He watched as she spritzed more mousse on his living room's picture window, then stood back to judge the effect against the paper snowflakes she'd already taped on. She hadn't sat still for more than two minutes at a stretch. Not since he'd held out his hand to her and mentioned their "unfinished business."

He'd been referring to the paper-snowflake-cutting lessons she'd promised him, of course. But Katie's shocked expression when he'd explained as much had sent him on another course. One of wondering what *she'd* been thinking of.

Could it be possible Katie had been hoping for . . . more? More closeness, more intimacy, more from the reunion they'd stumbled into? He didn't know, and he—

Her cell phone rang. With a practiced gesture she answered it. After a few seconds, Jack heard the same gentle refusal she'd been giving all night.

"Nope, sorry. I'm busy tonight. Out of commission."

A pause. "Probably all week, actually. Maybe I'll see you on Christmas Eve?"

A few more nods, some chitchat as she applied extra faux snow to the window. Then Katie said good-bye. This time, before flipping her phone closed and putting it away, she turned it off.

Jack stared. He'd never known party-girl Katie to deliberately cut herself off from potential socializing. In fact, her gala-a-day ways—and her refusal to do more than allow him a tiny corner in her life because of them—hadn't done their fling any favors. Now, seeing her voluntarily check out of her social whirl was like seeing Santa turn up clean-shaven and buffed-up: unthinkable.

Of course, he didn't have much room to talk, Jack recalled uncomfortably. He'd done his own share of backing away, of letting his career come first. Unlike Katie, he hadn't had time for shopping and brunching and dancing till dawn. Unlike Katie, he'd wanted to focus on working and planning and climbing the corporate ladder.

They hadn't been able to reconcile their two contradictory views of life. Despite the good things between them, their differences had loomed larger. They'd split, each vowing to avoid the other as much as possible so the pain would be minimal.

Except it hadn't been, Jack realized now. It had only been postponed. Seeing Katie now, so close and still so far away, made him realize how much he'd missed her.

She'd been wonderful with Belle. He still didn't understand some of her reasoning (the miniskirts, the shoe economics theory, the Fendi-bag baby hold and the Barbie philosophy all sprang to mind), but Jack couldn't dispute her surprising effectiveness. Katie unfailingly managed to cheer up his cousin, to comfort her and bring a smile to her face. Watching the two of them together was enlightening.

So was watching her transform his house.

A few feet away from his position at the kitchen table, Katie stepped away from the picture window with a flourish. "What do you think?"

He examined the mousse-turned-snow and the paper blizzard. "I think it's terrific. Very Christmassy."

She beamed.

"*And* I think you should come over here, like you promised, and help me." Jack raised the paper and scissors in his hands. "My snowflakes keep falling apart."

She bit her lip. She hesitated. Then she entered the dining room and cautiously took a seat.

He dragged her chair closer. Their shoulders touched. In response, Katie jerked. She laughed nervously.

"It's been a while since we were alone," she said.

"Believe me. *I know.*"

Her gaze lifted. Something sparked between them, something familiar and intoxicating. Something sweeter than Christmas cookies, spicier than cinnamon sticks, brighter than a star. For some reason, the song "I Saw Mommy Kissing Santa Claus," spiraled through his head. Jack looked around for some mistletoe.

Katie spoke. "I've been thinking. Since we're going to be together for the next few days, we should have some kind of a game plan. Something to keep us on the straight and narrow."

"The straight and narrow? Nah. It's overrated. I just decided."

"I mean, something to keep us apa—" She paused. Regrouped. "*Busy,* as much as possible."

"Busy." He waggled his eyebrows teasingly. "I like the sound of that. Busy doing what?"

Kissing leaped to mind. So did caressing, talking, laughing, snuggling beneath a nice toasty blanket, making up for lost time. . . .

"Making a really wonderful pre-Christmas week for

Belle," Katie said. "Showing her lots of neat holiday stuff, getting a Christmas tree, decorating your place—"

Confused, Jack gestured toward the picture window.

"A drop in the bucket," she assured him. "There are lots of Christmassy things we haven't even touched on yet. Holiday parades. Visiting Santa at the mall. Shopping for gifts."

She brightened, sitting up straighter. "I'll bet I can find just the thing for you!"

Gift shopping. Oh, no. Like a reindeer facing a foggy Christmas Eve without Rudolph, he froze. It wasn't that he didn't *want* to find great gifts for the people he cared about. He did. It was just that . . . well, he was terrible at actually doing it. And Jack hated doing anything he wasn't good at.

"Do you have"—he swallowed hard—"a wish list, or something?"

Katie waved her hand. "Oh, you don't have to get *me* anything!"

Oh, yes he did. No man was idiot enough to buy into that line. At least Jack wasn't. "I want to."

She smiled. Seeing her happiness, he really, *really* wanted to.

"Let's concentrate on Belle for now," Katie said. "Okay? While I was decorating the windows, I came up with a list of holiday things we could do together. Let's see . . ."

Forging onward with tinsel-bright enthusiasm, she ticked off one Christmas-related activity after another. Jack's head swam with visions of evergreens and flashing lights and fruitcake and stockings and—

"Pin the Nose on Rudolph?" he asked, raising his brows.

"It'll be fun! I promise. So, are we in agreement?"

"To give Belle the best pre-Christmas week ever?" She nodded, eyes shining.

"Sure. Why not?" Grinning, Jack picked up his paper

snowflake, which looked more like a deranged doily, and set to work again. "If we're lucky, I might even remember more Christmas carols to sing."

"On second thought . . ."

"Hey!"

"Kidding."

They both smiled, cozily together amid the drifts of paper scraps. Then, with a businesslike air, Katie grabbed a fresh sheet. Folding and cutting rapidly as she spoke, she said, "Here's how you make a snowflake. You cut here, fold here, cut some here, unfold, and— voilà!"

"Voilà?" But his hadn't even . . .

"Voilà." Covering her mouth with her hand, Katie yawned noisily. Her chair scraped as she stood. "Well, I'm bushed. It's off to bed with me. The couch? Yes? Here I go! I'll just get some linens and a blanket from the hall closet. No, don't get up. I remember where everything—I mean, everybody stores spare bedding in the hall closet, don't they?"

Her voice trailed away. She returned bearing an armload of sheets and a spare blanket. "Night, Jack. Sleep well."

He gaped after her. Before he could so much as stand to help make up her temporary bed, Katie had outfitted the sofa like a vintage four-poster and was rummaging through her overnight bag.

"I should have offered you the bed." Jack moved to the pass-through between the dining and living rooms. He pushed a hand through his hair, watching her. "But now with Belle sleeping in there—"

"It's okay. I don't mind the sofa." She straightened, something pink and flimsy in her hand.

At the sight of it, Jack's interest—and interested *parts* of him—perked up. "You can have the bed tomorrow night."

"Okay. Thanks."

He lingered, reluctant to leave. He imagined the slide of that delicate pink fabric against his skin as she came to him, imagined the wondrous impact of Katie's body joining with his as he stripped it away. She would smile when he looked at her, the way she always did. He would—

"Would you mind turning out the light for me when you leave, please? Thanks."

She turned away. Not quite smiling. Not quite naked. Not even wearing the pink thing. Disappointed, frustrated with his own inability to resist her, Jack did as she'd asked.

It wasn't until he reached the end of the darkened hallway—and heard Katie sigh—that he realized the truth: She wished he hadn't.

He smiled. Maybe, just maybe, there was hope for them yet.

Alone in the dark, Katie finished shedding her jeans and sweater. She cast them aside. Pulled her pink nightshirt over her head. And sighed. Two conflicting thoughts assailed her:

Whew! That was close.

I wish Jack hadn't gone.

Not that his leaving wasn't what she'd intended, all along. It was. After all, being alone with him would only make her want him more. It would only make her wish for more, only make her hope that Christmas contained enough magic to overcome their differences. And that was ridiculous, wasn't it?

All Jack was interested in was work. Work, work, work. Not her, not life, not fun. When she'd entered his home office to get the snowflake paper earlier, Katie had realized immediately his workaholic ways hadn't changed a bit. Architectural plans still littered every available surface, interspersed with drawing tools and cardboard carrying tubes. Design awards lined the walls, evidence of his dedication.

Signs of anything non-work-related had been nonexistent, and not just in Jack's office. His whole house seemed a testament to how little time he spent there—bare walls, spotless functional furniture, no embellishments save framed family photos and a few plants. Probably, Katie thought as she turned over in her solitary sofa-turned-bed, he'd hired a service to keep the greenery thriving.

He'd been amazing with Belle, though; she had to admit it. Caring, thoughtful, funny. With his tiny cousin, Jack had cut loose ("You're a foul one, Mr. Griiiinch!"). He'd worked to figure out what the baby needed. He'd made time to be with her.

To Katie's surprise, Jack had even arranged time off from the office for both of them, lasting until Christmas, if necessary. Listening to him make those arrangements with Gil Brennan over a crackling international phone line tonight, she'd hardly been able to believe her ears. Honestly, Jack taking time off was like . . . like Charlie Brown scoring the biggest, fanciest Christmas tree on the lot: highly unlikely.

She and Jack were so different from each other. So why, Katie wondered, did she still want him back?

You love him, her heart whispered. *You do.*

So? Smacking her pillow, Katie turned over again. *So what?* So what if without Jack, she felt like a Christmas ornament with no bough to rest on, like a festive wreath with no door to hold on to? That didn't mean she was just going to cave in.

Their breakup had hurt. Losing him had hurt. And losing him all over again would be even worse. Until she found some evidence he'd do more this time than squeeze her into his life between design meetings and drawings, Katie intended to do all she could to resist Jack, and all his charms.

Piece of fruitcake, she assured herself. After all . . . how irresistible could one man possibly be?

Chapter Seven

Jack was seducing her with Christmas, Katie realized when she awakened the next day. He *knew* it was her favorite season, and he was taking advantage of that fact. While she'd slept (whoa, was it really ten o'clock already?), he'd apparently zipped down to the nearest discount store with Belle in tow . . . and obliterated the Holiday Décor section.

Looking around, Katie elbowed herself upward against the sofa's armrest. She blinked groggily. Sure, the overall look Jack had achieved wasn't Martha Stewart. It wasn't even Martha Stewart Does Kmart. But the multicolored lights, buckets of candy canes, plastic plug-in-light-up Santa, cellophane-wrapped pots of poinsettias, and everything else he'd purchased and arranged did possess a certain hokey charm. Sort of like Jack himself.

And she *loved* it.

She smiled sleepily. As she did, a donut with red and green sprinkles drifted into her vision, held by Jack and bringing with it the intoxicating scents of sugar and at least four thousand calories. Katie wasn't entirely sure calories contained aromas, but in her imagination they did. The more enticing and forbidden—and more numerous they were—the better they tended to smell. So far, aromadieting hadn't steered her wrong.

"I absolutely shouldn't eat that," she said.

But of course, she was going to anyway. What good was aromadieting, if not to guide her toward the most delectable ways to treat herself? Party-hopping burned plenty of calories, Katie reasoned. And probably, so did resisting Jack, who'd brought the temptation and even now was seated on the coffee table to her left, looking irresistible himself.

Since she couldn't allow herself to have *him*, she accepted the donut in its paper bakery wrapping instead. It was a poor substitute, but it would have to do. Thanking him, Katie lifted the glazed-and-sprinkled sweet higher. She inhaled. *Mmmmm.*

Indulgences, after all, were meant to be savored. Otherwise, they were just routine diet infractions.

"I brought you one of these, too." Jack lifted a yellow-labeled bottle.

"Yoo-hoo!" Katie squealed with delight. She seized the bottle he offered, overcome with a sense of homecoming. The chocolaty drink was her secret treat, her nonsophisticated rejoinder to a world that sometimes let her down. She clutched its beloved coolness against her chest and gazed at Jack. *"Awww.* You remembered."

"Don't go getting all misty on me. It's just a drink."

"And an instant Christmas, to go with it." Refusing to let him downplay the importance of all he'd accomplished while she'd been logging beauty sleep, Katie gestured toward the haphazardly hung decorations. "You've really gotten into the spirit of things. I'm impressed."

He shrugged. "Just sticking with the plan. For Belle's sake."

Jack nodded toward the baby, who was happily playing a few feet away in her Mary Kay-colored bouncer. Then he looked back at Katie, a certain earnestness in his face, in the press of his palms between his knees.

"And for yours," he added quietly.

"Oh, Jack."

Awash in the warm feelings his confession aroused, Katie gave up on opening her drink. Her fingers wouldn't work. Neither would her sense of anti-Jack resistance. Evidently, it was susceptible to warmhearted Christmassy gestures, too.

Silently, she passed the bottle to him, as she'd done so many times in the past. Helplessly, she admired the flex of his forearms as he opened and returned it. Desperately, she slugged back some sweet Yoo-hoo, hoping it would clear her head.

It didn't. Because next Jack gazed toward the poinsettias, resplendently red in their baby-proofed hanging baskets, and nonchalantly said, "I thought we'd go to the mall today."

"Oh, Jack!" How was she supposed to resist *this*? A man who brought her breakfast in bed, remembered her secret childlike favorites, *and* voluntarily *shopped*? Boy, oh, boy. If only Maya and the girls down at Boondoggles could—

"It opened at ten," he went on, "so whenever you're ready—"

He understood Mall Standard Time. She'd never known that about him. With thoughts of caution fading, Katie flung back her makeshift sofa bed's blankets.

"I'll be ready in a jiffy," she promised. Still clutching her Yoo-hoo, she stuck the donut in her mouth and then grabbed her overnight bag. A quick shower, a date with the blow-dryer, a little lip gloss, and then—

She rose, bag in hand, to find Jack watching her. Hunger had darkened his eyes, straightened the sensual line of his mouth. He looked both languid and ready, open and unreadable. He looked . . .

. . . like everything she'd ever wanted.

His gaze met hers. A corner of his mouth lifted, as though Jack meant to pretend he *hadn't* just been ogling her like a starving man staring at sugared Christmas cookies.

"Nice legs," he said.

Her nightshirt. She'd forgotten she was wearing it. Its hem only came to the tops of her thighs. Its flimsy pink fabric didn't leave much to the imagination, either. Katie resisted the urge to tug it lower as she stepped toward him.

She bit off some donut, chewed and swallowed while she looked him over. A familiar heat curled between them, encouraged by memories of everything they'd shared. It had been so long. *Too long.* Both of them knew it.

"Nice . . . everything." Her reply echoed his, and so did the lingering look she allowed herself. "Did you put together that ensemble yourself, or does the Hunks-R-Us store deliver?"

His grin widened. "Actually, it's Garanimals for Guys. One pair of jeans plus one white shirt plus one pair of—"

"I can imagine." Katie advanced nearer. Her Yoo-hoo thunked on the coffee table near his hip, then was joined by the forgotten two-thirds of her donut. Her overnight bag landed near Jack's booted feet. "But I'd rather experience it for myself."

She leaned forward and took his mouth with hers. He tasted of coffee and donut, of desire and long-suppressed need. Groaning with pleasure, Katie deepened her kiss. This had *definitely* been the right move to make. Instantly, Jack's arms were around her, pulling her down.

They landed amid the blankets she'd discarded, Jack

beneath her and Katie thrillingly sprawled atop him.
Their mouths met, explored, withdrew for nothing less
than urgently needed breath. Their coming together
was old times melded with new discovery, longing joined
with abandonment. Rolling, seeking, caressing, they
remembered . . . everything.

She was falling, falling for him all over again. The
dizziness of his kiss, the warmth of his skin, the solid
press of his muscles against her . . . all combined to
leave Katie with the sweetest sense of déjà vu. *This* was
how they were meant to be. *This,* together. Eagerly, her
paltry resistance gone, she grabbed his shirt placket in
both hands and prepared to remodel Jack exactly as
she wanted him: naked, with her.

He beat her to it. His hands, big and familiar and
welcome, slid beneath her nightshirt. His palms cupped
her; his breath slid past her ear as he whispered how
good she felt to him. As though nothing had passed
between them, as though Katie and Jack had never
parted, they found every favorite rhythm, every sensitive
place, every pleasure.

Almost.

Because just as Katie prepared to throw caution—
and her nightshirt—to the wind, they both stopped.
Froze. Sniffed. They shared a puzzled look.

"Ohmigod!" Katie clapped her hands over her nose
and mouth.

Jack did the same. *"Uggh!* What *is* that?"

At the edge of the room, Belle babbled. With dawning
comprehension, they looked her way. She squealed. She
shook her baby bouncer with exuberant thrusts of her
tiny legs. She grinned.

And the odor of a baby who (really) needed a diaper
change grew even stronger.

"It's a miracle everyone isn't an only child," Jack
muttered, wincing.

"I guess it's shower time for me!" Katie said at the same moment.

Of course, it sounded like, "I duess dit's tower time for me," because she'd pinched her nose between her fingers to block the stench. But that didn't matter.

Their amorous intentions vanished. They parted with mutual speed, each headed in a different direction. And really, Katie reflected as she picked up her overnight bag and rescued her breakfast before it could be reverse-aromatherapied, there wasn't a damned thing new about *that*, now was there?

Over the course of the next few days, Jack realized several things. First among them was that Katie's kiss had triggered a craving for her unlike anything he'd ever experienced. Second, unfortunately, was that they might never get an opportunity to repeat it. Although Katie seemed suddenly open to the reunion he'd hoped for, baby Belle kept them on the run every minute.

They stopped at the mall on that first morning (visiting Santa, of course), and made the rounds of everything remotely Christmassy during the days that followed. They spent the daylight hours soaking up Arizona's December sunshine and mild sixty-degree weather, taking Belle to various holiday events. A parade (holding hands as the marching band passed). A crafts festival (cuddling behind the quilts). A Wild West holiday hoedown (laughing on a simulated sleigh). Then a Christmas train ride at the East Valley's Desert Breeze park, followed by Christmas tree shopping at a central Phoenix lot.

There they bought a spindly, four-foot, mostly needleless tree ("It just needs a little love!" Katie insisted when Jack speculated about evergreen-patterned-baldness), and then followed up their purchase by making red and green construction-paper chain garlands for it.

They strung popcorn and cranberries, hung foil icicles, and established a baby-proofed protective gate around the resulting masterpiece when Jack set it up on a table in his living room.

In the evenings, they walked through nearby neighborhoods with Belle in her stroller, oohing and aahing over the houses' elaborate Christmas light displays. They assembled homemade luminarias with paper bags and sand and stubby candles and arranged them along the sidewalk to Jack's house, where they glowed in the darkness like hope gone alight.

They feasted on gingerbread people ("Are you kidding me?" Katie had asked him when he'd suggested they bake, rather than buy, them. "In my world, baking your own cookies is like making your own shoes. Possible, but not advisable.") and hung knitted stockings on Jack's entertainment-center-turned-mantel: one big one, one smaller one, and one teeny one.

They joined together in ways they never had before. For Belle's sake, Jack and Katie somehow managed to put their ordinary priorities on hold . . . and their relationship flourished because of it. Katie abandoned her parties for the week. Jack donated his drafting table for use as command central in his house's ongoing Christmas makeover. His usual holiday unease faded, pushed aside by Katie's caroling, mulled-cider drinking, and jingle-bell ringing.

He was happy.

So was she.

He could tell. She smiled. She laughed. She greeted each day with boundless energy, a Yoo-hoo, and a new idea for how they could bring the holidays alive for Belle. Her generosity surprised him—and so did the realization, when it came, of exactly why Katie loved socializing.

They'd been visiting a local landmark, the East Valley's very own tumbleweed Christmas tree in Chandler.

Uniquely Southwestern, the forty-foot structure was made up of light-bedecked white-painted tumbleweeds atop a chicken-wire tree-shaped frame, and Katie had insisted they take Belle ("a native Arizonan, after all") to see it. While craning their necks to see the star at its tip, Katie had struck up a conversation with a group of tourists nearby. After the group had gone on its way, Jack glanced at Katie.

"You look happy." He nodded toward the departing tourists. "Friends of yours?"

"Not for long." Cheerfully, she gave them a wave. She helped Belle do the same. "Bye! Merry Christmas!"

He didn't get it. "Then why . . . ?"

"Because, Jack," Katie said as she turned to him, "it makes everyone feel good to chat for a little while. I like making contact with people. I like knowing our days are brighter for having talked for a few minutes, even if we'll never meet again." She shrugged. "That's all."

"That's all?"

She nodded and adjusted Belle on her hip.

"But that's . . . amazing."

Her gaze turned puzzled. "What is?"

Katie honestly didn't know, Jack realized. She didn't understand what was so special about reaching out to complete strangers and befriending them, if only for a few minutes. Watching her wrinkle her nose in confusion at him, he felt himself fall in love with her, all over again.

"You," he said. "You're amazing."

She ducked her head and grinned, making a fuss over Belle's latest holiday hair bow—a confection of snowy lace and stitched-on fabric ornaments. "Thanks. You're not so bad yourself."

They shared a smile. Belle *ooo-gooed*. And suddenly, Jack saw Katie's constant social whirl in a whole new light. Not as something taken, but as something given.

As something given freely, with only good thoughts behind it. He realized, in that moment, that he could never ask her to give it up—especially not to the extent he used to expect.

Things had changed. And now, so had he.

Unaware of that fact, Katie strapped Belle into her stroller, discussing the merits of wardrobe color therapy as she did. The baby spoke animatedly back, babbling as though she understood. And maybe, given that they were both females and thus perpetually mysterious, she did.

They waved good-bye to the tumbleweed tree and all its glittery "branched" glory, and then walked past the downtown Chandler shops to their car. That was when Jack spotted it: the perfect Christmas gift for Katie. With a hurried excuse, he handed the keys to Katie and promised to meet her and Belle in the parking lot. This was simply too good to pass up.

Jack slipped into his home office that evening, shortly after they put Belle to bed. He ducked beneath the garland draped in the doorway, picked his way through the jumbo rolls of red and green and gold wrapping paper Katie had left for safekeeping and moved aside a stack of holiday movies on DVD. Then he got down to work.

Pulling out fresh paper and pens, Jack let loose his feelings in the best way he knew: through drawing. He sketched and considered, examined, redrew, and then lettered. This was a Christmas card for Katie, and it had to be perfect.

He was halfway finished when a rustle in the doorway alerted him he wasn't alone. Jack froze, then with deliberate casualness drew a blank sheet of paper atop his design and turned to face Katie.

She blinked. "You're working?"

The disappointment in her face hurt him to see. "Not exactly."

"Yes, you are. You're drawing new plans or some-thing."

"Or something," he agreed. He put down his pen and went to her. "I can do it later. Let's go ... look through the Pottery Barn Christmas catalog again. You had fun doing that last night."

He tried to look enthusiastic about decorative throw pillows.

Katie wasn't having any of it. She folded her arms. "Why do you shut me out like this?"

"Like what?" There was no way he was showing her her Christmas card before it was ready. "I'm not shut-ting you out."

"I thought—" Her voice rasped. "I thought we'd moved past this. This week ... I thought this week was special."

Plaintively, she gazed up at him. Helplessly, Jack gazed back. How could he be hurting her, when all he wanted to do was make something special for her?

"This week *has* been special." He saw her lower lip quiver, and forged onward. "I thought you weren't interested in work, that's all. I'm sorry. I'll never do it again."

Just please, please stop looking at me as though I made a midnight snack of Santa's milk and cookies.

"Never do what again?"

She had him there. He was well-intentioned but, "Uh—"

"Oh, Jack."

"Never shut you out again?"

Katie's smile was wobbly, but it was there. He suddenly felt mighty enough to hoist the tumbleweed Christmas tree with one hand. Instead, he reached for the woman he'd dreamed of.

"Come here. I have some things to show you."

Chapter Eight

Watching Jack pull out plans and preliminary drawings, cover his desk with neatly-penned imaginings and
share them with her, Katie was struck by two things
that had never occurred to her before. First, that Jack's
architectural drawings were really *art*. Beautifully rendered, creative art. Second, that he loved creating it.
Really, truly loved it.

Jack unrolled his work with the enthusiasm of a kid
diving beneath the tree on a predawn Christmas morning, with the reverence of a hairdresser encountering
a natural blonde. He talked about it passionately, knowl-
edgeably, generously. Seen through his eyes, Jack's work
held meaning far beyond furnishing Brennan's home
buyers with inviting, beautiful places to live. His work
. . . *spoke,* for lack of a better word.

It spoke of Jack. His imagination. His precision. His
ability to see things in a way few others could. And
looking at it with him, Katie saw Jack in a way she never
had: as a man captivated by creating. His wasn't a world
of automatic ambition or endless corporate wrangling.

It was a world of giving of himself, over and over again, on paper.

All at once, those times she'd resented his decisions to work late, to put in overtime on a new project, took on new meaning. Suddenly changed, she *understood*.

Katie nodded as Jack took her hand. She trembled as he guided it across the paperbound pathways of a new house design, explaining how the rooms would feel to the people who'd one day occupy them. She ached as he paused, looked sideways at her, smiled.

She could never ask him to give this up, Katie realized. Not the way she'd always expected him to when they'd been together before. If she was to love Jack, she'd love him this way . . . exactly as he was.

And she did.

Turning, she cupped his jaw in her hand, savored the intimate prickle of his razor stubble against her palm. "Thank you for showing me this," Katie said. "I love . . . it."

Coward, her newly enlightened self said. *Tell him what you really mean!* But she couldn't. Not yet.

He looked surprised. "You do?"

"Mmm-hmm." At some point, he'd put his arms around her, Katie realized. They snuggled together automatically, with practiced ease. She could have stood in the warmth of his touch forever. "I do. You must be the best architect ever."

"Hey, I don't have to be." Jack's powerful shoulders rose on a shrug. "My uncle's the boss, remember? But thanks."

Katie narrowed her eyes. "Everyone knows you're at Brennan's because you're talented. Not because your last name's on the letterhead."

He shrugged again, then turned away to gather up the things he'd shown her. Watching him in astonishment, Katie learned the truth: Everyone knew that . . . *except* Jack.

"It's true," she said fiercely. "Really, really true."

He rolled a set of plans, slid them into a tube. Didn't look at her.

Katie touched his arm. "It's true." She kissed him. "You have a rare talent. We all see it."

"Katie—" He ducked his head, obviously uncomfortable. "You don't have to—"

"Oh, yes. Yes, I do." She grabbed his shoulders, turning Jack to face her. His pain, however buried, hurt her, too. She needed to make him feel better. "I'm telling you the truth. *Believe it.*"

"Okay, I do. Now quit manhandling me." With a cocky grin that belied the shadows in his eyes, Jack nodded toward his navy knit shirt. "You picked out this shirt yourself. You probably don't want to ruin it."

"Oh, I don't?" Katie raised her eyebrows. She grinned. Then she picked up the scissors she'd stowed with the wrapping paper and deliberately snipped his shirt's neckline.

"Hey!" Jack goggled at her. "What'd you do that for?"

"So it would be easier to do *this,*" Katie replied.

Then she seized both frayed edges she'd created, drew in a deep breath . . . and ripped Jack's shirt right down the middle.

"I've always wanted to do that," she said, giddily pleased with herself.

He stared, obviously unable to believe what had just happened. His shirt hung in two raggedly bisected halves. Between were revealed sculpted chest muscles, the lower edge of one shoulder, and those amazing abs, too.

While she watched, the sense of seductive fun returned to his eyes. "I think I've always *wanted* you to do that."

Katie smiled. If there was one thing she'd learned about men, it was that talk was cheap. Men like Jack understood action. In that spirit, she moved closer again.

"Now," she murmured, "I want you to believe me when I tell you this: I'm in awe of your talent as an architect. I *know* you're a star at Brennan's because of it, and not because of any currently skiing-in-Switzerland family connections. And if I have to hold you down and make love to you to prove it," Katie concluded with mock ferocity, "then I'm prepared to do exactly that. *Exactly* that."

Jack's grin widened. An unmistakable heat flared in his gaze, igniting a similar heat within her. They'd been down this road before . . . and this time would be even better.

His stance took on an obvious, teasing challenge. "In that case . . . I don't believe you."

She cocked a brow, anticipation whirling inside her. "Don't say I didn't warn you."

"Wouldn't dream of it."

"Hmmm." Katie advanced, then indulged herself in a hands-on examination of his newly bared chest. "*I'll* give you something to dream about."

His hands cupped her derrière, hauling her against him. Their hips made contact. "That goes double for you."

Geez, but she loved this man.

"I hope that's a promise," Katie said.

"You'd better believe it."

Those were loving words—and they were the last words Jack said that night . . . unless you counted the naughty ones.

Katie definitely *did*.

There was just something about the morning after, Jack decided as he made his way to the kitchen the next day. Something *amazing*. He felt better than he had in months.

Seven months, to be exact.

He'd awakened this Friday morning—the day before Christmas Eve—to find himself in bed alone, with Belle's crib empty beside him. His first thought had been to find her, and Katie.

Katie. After a night spent loving her, Jack knew he couldn't let her go. Whatever it took, they had to try again. Their time together would only last until Gil and Amber returned to pick up Belle, but that might still be days from now. Possibly not until after Christmas, Jack had begun to hope. Until then, he and Katie could be together.

A babyish squeal came from the kitchen. At the sound of it Jack picked up speed, looking forward to seeing his cousin—and the woman who'd left him to awaken with a smile.

A *big* smile.

All at once, the importance of the next few moments struck him. What if Katie had regrets? What if *he* did, when he saw her? What if things had changed . . . for the worse, somehow? Jack stopped abruptly at the end of the hallway.

Feeling inexplicably jittery, he glanced downward to assess the condition of his casual drawstring pants and T-shirt. He smoothed a wrinkle. Ran a hand through his hair. Checked the effectiveness of his toothpaste. Okay. At least he didn't smell like the Creature from the Black Lagoon. Things would probably be all right.

He rounded the corner. Katie's smile was the first thing he saw, and it was . . . beautiful. Just like she was, to him.

Relief filled him. " 'Morning. Sleep well?"

"Hardly a wink." Her smile widened as she passed some dry cereal to Belle along with a sippy cup. "You?"

"Barely closed my eyes." Jack kissed the top of Katie's

head. He stroked her hair, plucked out a rogue Cheerio. *"Somebody* kept me up all night."

"That sounds like a complaint."

"Only if we don't do it again. Soon."

He captured her cheek in his hand, turning her face upward to meet his. He smiled, then kissed her.

Okay, so his kiss quickly turned into a chair-straddling, hands-delving-into-her-hair, wanton wake-up free-for-all. And Katie quickly caught on to the morning's mood, fisting her hands in his T-shirt to hold him close and moaning her approval of their coming together. But did that really mean things had changed between them?

Sure it did, Jack figured. Until . . .

"Mmmm. Belle," Katie gasped, reluctantly pulling away. She gestured toward the baby, who was happily occupied in her hooked-on infant seat with the challenge of pinching Cheerios between her pudgy fingers and hurling them onto the floor. "We have to think about Belle."

"Okay." Jack waved to his cousin. " 'Morning, little Belle. I'll be with you in a minute. Just as soon as I finish telling Katie how beautiful she looks."

"Jack—"

"You look so beautiful."

She shook her head, laughing. "I have cereal decorating my bed-head do, apple juice spilled on my skirt" — she waved her hand toward her short skirt and matching red sweater—"and no recollection of how to apply eyeliner after having gone mostly au naturel all week. You're nuts."

No, I'm in love, Jack thought. *With you.* But he couldn't say it aloud. Not yet.

"I stand by my opinion," he said instead, kissing her again. He levered upward from his chair-straddling position and headed for the coffeepot. "You're just going to have to get used to it."

"Gee, I'll try. I may need some practice."

"Okay. I'll say it again: You're beautiful."

Katie smiled. "Very obliging of you. Thanks."

Jack returned with his cup of Christmas blend black coffee and settled across the table from her, on the other side of Belle. He sipped. "I aim to please."

"You *do* please."

"It's the company I keep." He raised his Santa mug in a salute to her. "It's easy to please the one you—"

She stilled.

Love! shouted his inner "mushball at heart." *Just say it!*

"—really want to please."

Lame.

Katie's mouth turned downward, as though she were disappointed. How that could be, Jack didn't know, because she couldn't possibly have guessed what he'd been about to say. And also because he was busy kicking himself for having wimped out.

All he knew for sure was that he wanted to make things better for her . . . yet he wasn't sure how. Something still held him back.

As it turned out, that something was Katie. Leaving.

"Well, this looks more like target practice than breakfast," Katie said to Belle. Briskly, she scooted back her chair and stood. "I think it's time for a bath. And some new clothes. Maybe that adorable Christmas-tree-print dress, huh?"

Gurgling, Belle squished two soggy *O*s between her palms. She smiled up at Katie when she gently pulled her from her infant seat and settled her against her hip. The two of them together made a wonderful picture.

All except for Katie's wobbly smile.

"Katie—"

"It's all right. Nobody said this week had to be perfect. Or perfect for *us*. So long as Belle's happy, we've done what we set out to do. Right?"

Then, before Jack could so much as disagree, she

turned, tugged Belle higher on her hip, and headed
for the hallway, disappearing from view.

Waiting for the tub to fill for Belle's bath, Katie sat
on the floor with the baby in her arms and tried not to
think of Jack. It was impossible, though. Last night had
changed things for her. For a minute there, she'd
thought it had changed things for him, too.

It's easy to please the one you . . .

"Love," she whispered now, quietly. "It's easy to
please the one you *love*. Right, Jack?"

That's how she'd felt, during their tender hours of
lovemaking last night. And afterward, too, while she'd
watched Jack sleeping. It hadn't been an accident that
Katie had been the one to get up with Belle. She'd
already been awake, trying to savor every minute of time
together with the man she cared about most in the
world.

"Ahhh gaaaa," Belle said, patting Katie's cheek. The
baby peered up at her seriously, just like a commiserat-
ing friend. *"Gaaaa."*

With a smile, Katie sniffed. She blinked back a tear.
Even females at opposite ends of the dating spectrum
could relate to each other. It had to be genetic. Sort of
like a fondness for holiday potpourri. Men didn't even
think about the necessity of holiday potpourri. When
every woman knew the proper blend of bayberry, evergreen, cinnamon and cloves was essential to a Christmassy ambiance.

Deliberately turning her mind toward topics both
safer and surer than her relationship with Jack (tinsel,
tree stars, silver dragees on iced sugar cookies, the "Reg-
gae Christmas" song she loved), Katie finished Belle's
bath. By the time she'd brushed her hair and dressed
the baby in a clean diaper and the aforementioned

Christmassy little dress, she was feeling just like her old self again.

Well . . . her old self minus a much-needed fresh manicure and a blow-out at the salon. But that was all right. She *felt* better, and Katie figured that was the important thing.

Naturally, that was when the other shoe dropped.

She carried Katie into the living room, looking for Jack as she helped Belle into her baby bouncer for playtime. Just as Belle gave her first exuberant jump, Katie spotted him. And knew instantly something was wrong.

"What happened?"

Blankly, Jack stared at the phone in his hand. He fisted the receiver, then blinked at Katie. "That was Gil. The storm broke yesterday. He and Amber just arrived at Sky Harbor. They'll be here to pick up Belle within an hour."

Chapter Nine

It was too soon.

That was all Jack could think when he heard the knock on his front door. It was all much, much too soon.

He hadn't told Katie he loved her yet. Hadn't explained to her that he understood about her parties. Hadn't, for that matter, mastered the deft flick of the wrist that meant Belle's diaper wouldn't sag to her chubby knees the minute she crawled away. He needed more time. His heart—and clearly, his tiny cousin's mobility—depended on it.

But time was one thing he didn't have. That much was evident when he opened the door to Gil and Amber, and saw their eagerness to be reunited with their daughter.

"Belle!" Amber cried, rushing forward in a swell of perfume to lift the baby from Jack's practiced Fendi-bag hold for a hug. She held her close, smiling. "Mommy missed you sooo much! Yes, I did!"

Gil was there, too, enveloping his family. He spoke gruffly

of having missed his tiny daughter, stroked her hair with his hand and tweaked the jingle bells on her booties.

"Thanks for helping us out like this, Jack," he said. "I don't know what we would have done without you. And you, too, Katie. We really appreciate this."

Katie stepped forward, lugging Belle's diaper bag. "It was our pleasure," she said as she held it toward Belle's parents.

Casually, Gil reached for it. Then he tugged. Finally, he pried Katie's fingers loose. He gave her a confused glance as the bag came free.

She laughed. "I guess I'm a little reluctant to see her go."

Katie's gaze darted toward Jack. In her eyes, he saw more than reluctance to see Belle go; he saw reluctance to end the togetherness the two of them had shared during this pre-Christmas week. He moved toward her.

Amber forestalled him. "Sierra said you'd be a natural with Belle," she said happily. "I guess she was right. And I guess we'd better be on our way, hadn't we? We've got a lot of family catching up to do."

Gil agreed. With well-rehearsed ease, he gathered Belle's pile of pink paraphernalia and began carrying things out to the car. Jack helped, along with Katie. Sooner than he'd have thought possible, Gil and Amber were back in their Lexus, with Belle strapped safely in her car seat behind them.

The sedan pulled out of the drive. Reluctantly, Jack and Katie waved. Belle's little face turned toward them through the window, then she pulled her fist from her mouth. She clenched and unclenched her fingers in her babyish version of a wave.

He realized how much he would miss her.

An instant later, Jack and Katie were alone, standing beside the unlit luminarias. It was over.

* * *

Surely it wasn't over just like that, Katie thought. She looked at Jack and saw him staring, inexplicably, at the luminarias along the sidewalk. They were unlit and cold; despite the sunshine overhead, the little candle-and-sand-filled paper sacks seemed bleak.

She stepped closer. Their eyes met.

In his she glimpsed a certain preoccupation. Probably, he was thinking of a new design, she realized, or of all the work he'd put off during their week together. Just like old times. Despite everything, disappointment stole through her.

Jack turned, hands in his pockets. He squinted up at the house's eaves, where they'd strung multicolored Christmas lights—now unlit, like the luminarias. His thoughtful expression seemed to shut her out, as though he had room in his mind for mid-Fifties architectural details . . . but not for her.

Any minute now, Jack would ask her to stay, Katie thought, biting her lip. He'd remember she was there, and shake his head and smile. He'd put his arms around her the way he had so many times over the past week, and suggest another game of Pin the Nose on Rudolph. He'd offer to serve eggnog in bed, to kiss her beneath the mistletoe . . . to love her.

A moment passed. Another. Finally, Katie gave herself a mental kick. *Quit being such a sucker. This isn't* It's a Wonderful Life. *Neither of you is going to change that much, just because it happens to be Christmas.*

Except she had, she thought. She had, because of Jack.

And he hadn't. Not if his inability to ask a girl for a simple RSVP for the immediate Christmas holidays was any indication. Heavy-hearted, Katie drew in a breath.

"Well, I guess that's that," she said, and fished her cell phone from her red-sequined Santa handbag.

She dialed. Maya answered on the third ring. Within minutes, Katie had checked back into her usual social whirl.

Jack followed the phone's return to her handbag with

something very close to animosity. Which didn't make much sense, really. What had her innocent social lifeline ever done to him?

"Big plans?" he asked.

Katie shrugged. "Same plans. A tree-trimming party. Brunch. Cocktails. The usual."

"Right. I guess you'll be wanting your things, then."

His stiffened shoulders all but begged for a hug. Katie stepped nearer, but Jack turned at the same moment. He went into the house, politely holding open the front door so she could follow him. She did.

There was nothing to say as she gathered her belongings from the bathroom vanity, plucked her half of the matching Santa mug set they'd bought from the kitchen counter, stuffed everything into her overnight bag. What could she say?

Please, ask me to stay came to mind.

So did *good-bye.*

Katie had trouble with both (a smidge too much pride was her only real weakness). So instead she stood tall in the house's foyer beside the opened front door, holding her bag, and gazed up at Jack.

"We did pretty well," she said. "With Belle, I mean. Who woulda thunk it?"

His unexpected grin disarmed her further. It was brief but potent. Damn, but she wished he'd *do* something!

"All thanks to you," Jack told her. "You were wonderful."

She wished this didn't have the feeling of a long good-bye. "So were you . . . Mr. Griiiinch."

He laughed, just as Katie had intended. *Always leave 'em smiling.*

With forced cheerfulness, she held out her hand. "Well, I guess this is good-bye. See you around, Jack. Take care of yourself."

* * *

Jack stared at Katie's outstretched hand, unable to believe this was happening. Again. How had it come to pass that he was letting her go . . . just when he'd vowed they should stay together?

He hesitated. He should have been glad, a part of him knew. After all, this was, ostensibly, what he'd wanted all along, wasn't it? To be left alone, with plenty of time for work. With Katie on her way to her round of holiday parties, Jack would be able to finish the projects he'd had in mind. He'd be able to really make his mark at Brennan Homes.

Except last night, he'd *believed* Katie. He'd believed her when she'd said everyone knew his abilities were the base of his business success, not his family connections. And because of that, he was changed today.

Sure, it had taken a few kisses (okay, a lot) and some creative (okay, sensual) persuasion . . . but in the end, Katie's Christmas gift to him had been an end to Jack's uncertainty about his work. In light of that fact, spending the holidays cozying up to his computer's CAD software to perfect new architectural plans seemed wrong.

He and Katie had had a wonderful week. A magical week. He didn't want to let her go. On the other hand, looking at her now with her cell phone back in business and her bags in hand, she didn't seem changed by their time together at all.

Evidently, he'd been the only one to feel the deepened connection between them—the only one to fall in love over paper snowflakes and a semi-bald Christmas tree and a bunch of mousse-turned-snow.

Maybe it had all been a product of caring for Belle, Jack thought. Maybe it was baby-induced temporary togetherness that had rekindled their relationship, and not genuine feelings at all. Maybe he and Katie had gotten carried away with jingle-bell gaiety and luminaria-lighting closeness, and their love was only a holiday illusion.

Maybe he'd never know.

He took her hand. Savored the warmth of her skin against his, probably for the last time. Forced himself to speak, in a voice turned suddenly rough. "Let's get together in a few days."

Katie bit her lip. She nodded.

"This has been . . . a crazy time. The holidays—"

"I know, they're nuts." Still nodding.

"—and with Belle—"

"Sure." She waved her free hand. "Of course."

"In a few days," Jack went on, "after Christmas, maybe we'll know how we really feel. Without the baby. In a few days, maybe we'll be able to say—"

A honking car horn cut off his words. Katie turned her head toward the sound. She waved to the dark-haired woman behind the wheel, who pulled up at the curb alongside Jack's house.

"That's Maya. We're caravanning to the tree-trimming party I told you about." Katie adjusted her Santa purse, checked the position of her overnight bag, then used her grasp on Jack's hand to rise on tiptoes. Her lips brushed his, faintly. "I'd better run. Merry Christmas, Jack."

The warmth of her kiss faded slowly. In a flurry of cheery red clothes and a clatter of high heels, she strode down the walk and got into her car. After blowing a kiss—and giving him one last lingering look from behind the wheel—Katie drove away.

Jack gripped the doorjamb, watching her car follow Maya's down the street. It disappeared around the corner.

"Maybe by then," he finished saying quietly, "we'll be able to say 'I love you' . . . and know it's true."

Then he closed the door, and did his best to close his mind to all they might have shared . . . if only she had stayed.

Chapter Ten

At the tree-trimming party that Friday afternoon, Katie accidentally dropped and shattered an angel-shaped ornament. She burst into tears, right in the middle of "Jingle Bell Rock." Everyone said they hadn't realized how sensitive she was about holiday home décor.

At cocktails on Friday night, Katie kicked back one too many peppermint martinis and lurched onstage in her party dress and stilettos for a soulful solo rendition of "Please Come Home for Christmas." She burst into tears, right in the middle of happy hour. Everyone said they hadn't realized how powerful a performer she was.

During brunch on Saturday, Katie shocked the entire crowd by turning down her usual Bellini and requesting a Yoo-hoo instead. Then when the waiter brought it (via special delivery from the Circle K on the corner), she burst into tears, right in the middle of the banana-stuffed streusel French toast. Everyone said they hadn't realized how much she appreciated retro-chic nostalgia beverages.

Katie knew better. It was missing Jack that had gotten her so off-kilter. Nothing—not even the holiday joviality she usually loved—felt right without him. She needed Jack, needed him the way Dasher and Dancer needed Donner and Blitzen. The way a gift-wrapped package needed a festive bow. The way gingerbread men needed gumdrop buttons. And he . . . well, he *didn't* need her.

She could wait until after Christmas, Katie told herself. She could stick to the arrangements they'd made, hold out to feel Jack's arms around her again, to hear his laughter in her ear and feel his warmth all around her. She could.

But *damn it,* she didn't want to.

Hopping on one foot while she removed her post-brunch slingbacks on Saturday, Katie wrenched off her shoes and dropped them in her apartment's living room. She grabbed her trusty cell phone. To hell with being miserable. It was practically a modern woman's holiday duty to make the most of Christmastime, she reminded herself. And unrequited love definitely did *not* make for the merriest Christmas Eve.

Impatiently, Katie waited while the phone connected. She held her breath, thoughts of what she'd say to Jack whirling in her head. Maybe she'd tell him she finally understood his dedication to work. Maybe she'd tell him she thought they should try again.

Maybe she'd tell him she loved him.

His line was busy.

Rats. Foiled again.

Alone in his living room, Jack shot a baleful glance toward his phone. He'd taken it off the hook almost an hour ago in an attempt to evade his well-meaning relatives' calls, but the damn thing still bothered him. Its steady dial tone had devolved into an annoyingly monotonous mechanical voice message urging him to "hang up and try again." By now he was ready to hang up and disconnect his phone service. Permanently.

But then he realized he'd never be able to order a pizza for delivery again, and reconsidered.

Leaning sideways, Jack snatched the receiver. Sunshine bounced from its slick surface, moving on a late-afternoon slant through the window. The glowing lights on the runty Christmas tree nearby were reflected, too. They reminded him of the family get-together he'd bailed on this morning, and the reasons behind his leaving, and his purpose in having taken the receiver off the hook.

He could have unplugged the phone, he realized. But the resulting incessant (and unanswered) ringing would have made his family worry. So he compromised. Instead, he buried the receiver beneath the sofa cushions to muffle its squawking.

Mistake. Nose to cushion as he stuffed in the phone, Jack caught a hint of the cinnamon-spicy scent of Katie's perfume, a remnant of her sleepovers there. His heart clenched. In a moment he considered utterly and embarrassingly unmasculine, he buried his face in the leather upholstery and inhaled. Deeply.

Hell, but he missed her.

His family had known something was up the minute his brother had caught Jack moonily watching *A Christmas Story* on TV . . . and not even cracking a smile at the mom's reaction to Ralphie's longing for a Red Ryder BB gun: "You'll put your eye out!"

They'd become increasingly curious when Jack had flubbed a pass in the usual family touch football game because he'd glimpsed a dark-haired, stiletto-heeled, red-wearing woman walking through the park. A woman who *hadn't* (damn it) been Katie.

But when he'd gotten misty while joining in a family sing-along of "You're a mean one, Mr. Grinch" . . . well, that was when all hell had broken loose. The questions had begun, the bets had been laid, and the "who's the lucky woman?" predictions had been proclaimed. Apparently, the whole Brennan clan found the idea of Jack rendered sloppily sentimental over love absolutely fascinating. And they all wanted to talk about it, too.

Talk about it. Who in their right mind would want to do *that?*

It had all been too much for Jack to take, especially given how raw his feelings were about having lost Katie. Amid the matchmaking chatter ("Does she have a sister? Your cousin Rupert could stand meeting a nice girl."), the pooh-poohing of relationship bumps ("I could've killed your Aunt Marta when she sold my golf clubs on e-Bay. But we're still together!"), and the insanely optimistic urgings to sign up for a postholiday wedding gift registry ("Pottery Barn does a nice one!"), he'd slipped away. Now he was here. Alone. Missing Katie.

He should have found a way to tell her he loved her, Jack told himself as he splayed his hands on the sofa cushions and straightened. He should have explained that he understood about her social life, that he thought they could make a go of it if only they tried.

Instead, he'd remained silent. Stoic.

Stupid.

After all, what possible reason could justify letting your dream woman walk out the door?

Unless you were Bogie's character in *Casablanca,* Jack couldn't think of a single one. And even Rick and Ilsa would probably have made an exception for Christmas. Sam would have played something nice on the piano, "I'll Be Home for Christmas" maybe, and Captain Renault would have served fruitcake in the café, and the happy couple would have . . .

Enough. Christmas was a time for togetherness, and the plain fact was, Jack wasn't together with Katie. Without her, the season lost all its sparkle. Without her, nothing felt right . . . and never would.

Decisively, he excavated the phone. He pressed the receiver button to restore service. Then, before anyone could call and delay his connection with a slew of potential proposal ideas ("Popping the question via Jumbotron at Bank One Ballpark is awfully cute!"), Jack dialed Katie's number.

He only hoped he wasn't too late.

Carrying the packages she'd assembled on her way out, Katie paused outside her open apartment door. She bit her lip. Carefully, she pulled her cell phone from her sequined Santa handbag. Looked at it. Then, deliberately, she leaned inside and set her phone on the small table just inside her apartment. Bravely, she left it behind when she leaned out again.

Katie closed the door with a clunk.

For an instant, panic struck her. She thought of her trusty cell phone, its built-in microbrowser silenced, its enhanced digital phone book temporarily out of commission. She remembered how it had looked so alone on the table, so forlorn and abandoned.

But she had to be strong. She had to go on with her plans. Her entire Christmas season depended on it. So she did.

Several steps toward her car, Katie thought she heard her phone ringing. She stopped, cocking her head. *Jack. Jack could be calling!* At that moment, a truck drove past, burying the sound in a grinding of gears. Disappointed, Katie shrugged and continued onward. More than likely, she'd only imagined that cheerful ring.

That was what came, she guessed, of wishing for Jack so hard. And of giving up a perfectly good, social-life-enhancing cell phone on Christmas Eve, no less.

The snow-free Phoenix streets were gaily festooned as Katie drove resolutely across town. Holiday decorations hung from light posts and stretched across intersections.

Landscaped saguaros and palm trees sported Christmas light strings; wreaths of glossy chili peppers adorned neighborhood front doors. Amid all the decorations, a few last-minute shoppers rushed to beat the stores' closing times.

Seeing them, Katie patted the packages on the seat beside her. Steering one-handed, she smiled. This year would be her best gift-giving season ever. No doubt about it.

She reached her destination, drove in, parked. As Katie got out of the car with her packages and purse in tow, an uncharacteristic burst of uncertainty struck her. Maybe this wasn't the right thing to do. Maybe she should really—

Get moving, she ordered herself, and started walking. After all, if there was one thing she was good at, Katie figured, it was making decisions.

Even if they might be (*especially* if they might be) wild and crazy, out-of-the-blue, Christmas-hopeful ones.

Jack had a system worked out.

It went something like this: He'd try calling Katie. Then he'd listen to her recorded "leave a message" request. Then he'd do something Christmassy to give Katie time to actually answer her phone (since what he had to say wasn't exactly message material). Then he'd repeat the process as necessary.

One, two, three. Simple. Logical. A genuine guy-tested, bachelor-approved *system.*

But by the time he'd called, put on a holiday music CD, called, strung small white Christmas lights all over his living room, called, lit enough wreath-wrapped bayberry candles to toast s'mores over, called, and memorized Katie's upbeat cell phone voicemail message (down to the tone of the starting chirp), Jack had realized the truth.

His system was crap.

If he wanted Katie—and he really, really did—there was only one thing to do: Go out and get her. Wherever she happened to be. And really, given Katie, that could be just about anywhere that featured people, music, or dancing. The possibilities were endless. But Jack meant to sift through every one of them, if necessary, to bring Katie back to him.

So what if he'd been the one spouting "let's get together in a few days" platitudes? So what if it had taken him a while to wise up to the fact that, without Katie, there was no way *any* Christmas could ever be merry? Jack had wised up now, and that was what counted. Someone had to make the first move, and it was going to be him.

Decisively, he picked up the holiday card he'd made for Katie and the wrapped gift that went with it. He smiled, imagining her face when she opened it. This year would definitely be his best gift-giving season ever.

Grabbing his car keys, Jack went to the door. He opened it and made ready to step outside, never expecting the sight that greeted him there.

Katie.

She stood on his front porch wearing a red felt Santa hat, one arm laden with packages and the other raised to knock on the door, looking beautiful and determined and (possibly) as surprised as he felt. At the sight of her, Jack's pulse kicked up. His heart lurched. His smile broadened, hugely.

For an instant, he didn't move.

Only an arm's-length distance separated them, but it was enough. Enough, apparently, to remind them both of their mutual agreement to wait a few days before seeing each other. Jack could read the remembrance of his knuckleheaded suggestion in Katie's eyes, could feel it in the taut hesitation that strung between them.

She drew a breath. He fisted his hand on the door,

needing to go to her . . . and wanting to know she had come to him. He'd never seen anyone more welcome, more needed, more *beloved*. Just looking at her, Jack knew his entire lifetime wouldn't be enough to spend with her. Eternity would come up short.

Lowering the hand she'd poised to knock, Katie looked at him. A certain hope filled her eyes, a certain Christmas magic Jack felt sure hadn't been there before.

He made his decision. Apparently, so did she.

"I couldn't wait," they said in unison.

Katie smiled. As one they stepped forward, united in semidefiance. They met in the doorway. "I love you," she said.

"I love you," he said, and kissed her.

No mistletoe hung there above them. No Christmas carol urged their coming together. It was love alone that prompted it . . . love, and a particular holiday second chance, begun with jingle bells on a baby's booties and ended with two changed people.

Katie moved nearer in his arms. Her Santa hat fell to the floor, and their combined packages were squashed between them. But as the moments swept past and their kiss went on, neither of them cared. Holiday trimmings and cards and Christmas-wrapped packages were only temporary. Gifts, *real gifts*, were forever.

Their kiss ended. "I tried to call," they both said.

They laughed, with all the good cheer of two people whose plans went *exactly* as planned. Smiling, Jack pulled Katie inside. He kicked the door closed and gestured for her to speak first.

"I tried to call," she said again as she set aside her packages, "but your phone was always busy. Jack, you've got to know—I was wrong. I was wrong before to expect you to give up so much of the work you love, and I'm sorry. I understand now, and I think—"

"If we just talk about this stuff—"

"—then it'll be okay, from now on."

He nodded as he put down his own packages. Overcome with relief and emotion, Jack borrowed time by retrieving the fallen Santa hat and putting it back on Katie's head.

"I'm sorry, too," he said gruffly. "I'm different, because of you. I get it now—why you love going out so much—and I never should have expected you to give it up."

"Well, for *you*"—she grabbed the waistband of his low-slung jeans and hauled him closer—"I'll give *some* of it up. A compromise, if you will."

"And I'll cut back on work," Jack vowed. "After all, it's not as though I have something to prove at the office."

"No, you definitely don't."

"And maybe, now, I have something better to come home to."

"Yes, you definitely do."

The smile they shared was broad, wiser than before, grateful. Lowering his head, Jack claimed the woman he loved in a kiss as fierce and sweet as he could muster—and Katie kissed him back, with every indication of feeling exactly the same kind of love. Fierce. Sweet. Undeniable.

"I love you," she said again when they'd parted. "That's why I got you *this*."

Waggling her eyebrows, she showed him the wrapped package she'd picked up from her stack. She waved it enticingly.

"You're not the only one." Jack grabbed the gift and card he'd set aside, and carefully held them up. "I love *you*. And that's why I got you *these*."

Katie laughed. She looked on the verge of clapping with glee. "You *shopped* for me!"

Her gaze made him a hero for having done it. Jack felt suddenly nervous. "It's, uh . . . well, I hope you like it."

He rubbed the back of his neck. Katie captured his hand and squeezed. "I'll love it. Because it comes from you."

Ribbons flew. Paper rustled. Bing Crosby sang about a "White Christmas" in the background. And moments later . . .

"Awww, Katie." Jack turned over the set of vintage architectural drafting tools she'd given him. Contained in a leather-bound case, they were technically cool *and* sentimental. "Thanks. I love them."

Glancing up happily, he saw her holding his gift, now unwrapped, in her palm. She examined it with an air of utter absorption.

His spirits sank a notch. "No matter how long you stare at it, I'm afraid it won't turn into something from Tiffany. It's not that kind of gift."

"I don't want something from Tiffany," Katie said gamely. She smiled at it. "I want . . . *this!*"

He admired her spirit, her joie de vivre, her willingness to make him feel good. But given that his gift for her was a Christmas-themed plastic snow globe . . . well, Jack could understand her befuddlement.

"Maybe next year I'll manage the Tiffany gift," he said, wondering about engagement rings, wedding rings, what the heck the difference was, and whether Tiffany could help him sort it out. He raised his hand to cradle hers, so their palms were stacked facing upward beneath the snow globe. "But this year . . . this year, there's this."

Katie squinted. "Is that . . . a tiny version of the Chandler tumbleweed Christmas tree inside the snow globe?"

Jack nodded.

"Complete with some of the surrounding scenery?" she went on. "And little people?"

Again, Jack nodded.

"It's . . . cute."

"It's a remembrance of a moment," he said seriously.

Their eyes met over the top of the snow globe, and he sensed Katie holding her breath. "A remembrance of the moment I fell in love with you beside that Christmas tree. And I knew I had to have it, for you. To have *you* with me, forever."

Katie blinked. She sucked in a gulp of air. He had the impression she was trying not to cry.

"Merry Christmas," Jack said as he kissed her again. "From here on out, we'll always have each other. And it doesn't get any merrier than that."

"Oh, Jack!"

Then Katie did cry. But they were happy tears—the kind, as she helpfully explained later, that didn't smear your eyeliner or turn your mouth all blubbery. Wedding-guest tears, she said. So that was okay. And as she and Jack unwrapped the rest of their gifts and cards, and snuggled beneath their partly bald Christmas tree, they learned together that Christmas brought many things to those who opened themselves to its magic.

Things like peace. Love. Goodwill. And, if you were really lucky, someone who didn't mind when you accidentally pinned the nose on *him*, instead of the cardboard Rudolph.

Now, as Katie shared with him the last slice of fruitcake (an appreciation for the stuff, they agreed, was their only real weakness), Jack smiled and realized something else for certain, too.

Next year would definitely be a Tiffany Christmas. *No doubt about it.*

Dear Reader,

Between shopping, celebrating, cookie baking, and trying to find that elusive last roll of scotch tape for gift wrapping, Christmas can be a crazy time of year—but I love it! I'm so glad you decided to spend a few of your holiday moments with me, and I hope Jack and Katie's story was a fun (and *funny*) diversion for you.

My next full-length Zebra Books contemporary romance, *Reconsidering Riley*, is on bookstore shelves right now. It joins my previous romantic comedies *Making Over Mike* and *Falling For April*, and I can't wait for you to try it. I hope you'll look for it.

Until next time . . . I'd love to hear from you! Please write to me c/o P.O. box 7105, Chandler, AZ 85246–7105, send e-mail to *lisa@lisaplumley.com*, or visit my website at *www.lisaplumley.com* for previews, reviews, my reader newsletter, sneak peeks of upcoming books, and more.

In love and laughter,
Lisa Plumley

HOLIDAY STUD
Kylie Adams

Acknowledgments

I'm dedicating this book to me. Why not? I wrote it! So I want to thank myself for getting off the phone when I could have blathered on another hour and for turning off *The Real World* (I hate those people, but I can't stop watching) to bang out more pages.

Also, in the spirit of the season, I want to send a special message to the big guy with the sleigh. Hey, it never hurts to ask. Years ago he brought me that pink banana seat bicycle with the white flower basket attached. Here's hoping he can deliver at least one of these things . . .

KYLIE'S GROWN-UP CHRISTMAS LIST

1. George Clooney
2. George Clooney in a Santa suit
3. George Clooney in an elf costume
4. George Clooney dressed up like a reindeer
5. George Clooney covered in chimney soot

Chapter One

A healthy sex life. Best thing in the world
for a woman's voice.
—Leontyne Price, Opera diva

Bacara Resort & Spa
Santa Barbara

"He gave me the best sex of my life."

Audra Jarecki shifted her position to listen in. This
was the kind of conversation made for eavesdropping.

"It was amazing," the woman continued. "This guy,
George, was like a machine. He came four times in one
night. And I was wild, too. I mean, there's no point in
being inhibited when you're paying for it."

Audra wondered if George was on the property. Perhaps one of the many services? It stood to reason. Everything else was offered here. Her skin still tingled from
the citrus and avocado body scrub, and her muscles
ached in a strange but glorious way from the morning
hike through the Santa Ynez mountains. Now she was
poolside, sipping cold cucumber water and dangerously
close to interrupting to get this man's contact information.

"I couldn't do that," the other woman said. "Living with the guilt would drive me crazy."

"I don't have any guilt. Dan's either away on business or on the golf course. I can't help it if I've got a high sex drive, and I'm not going to apologize for it. Anyway, since I'm paying George, I don't feel like an adulterer. It's just a personal service. Like a massage or a facial."

Audra rose up to take a sip of water. "You've convinced me. Is he available on Saturdays?"

The women looked at each other, then back at Audra.

"Come on. It's too good a conversation to pretend not to overhear." She smiled. "I'm Audra."

"Rena," the satisfied one said. "This is Amanda. Are you here by yourself?"

Audra nodded. "I drove in from L.A. Friday night. Bad breakup. Exhausting business deal. I heard this was the perfect place to refuel."

Rena shook her head enthusiastically. "I come at least twice a year."

Audra's lips curled into a sneaky smile. "That's all? With this George in your life, you have to be coming more often than that."

Rena cackled. "You are wild. What kind of loser let you get away?"

"A male model," Audra said, getting an instant mental picture of Ollie in his Calvin Klein underwear ad.

"Figures." Rena clucked knowingly. "Let me guess. He met a female model, and it was love at first pout."

Audra giggled. "You're close. A flight attendant named Mandy. She told him to put his carry-on in the overhead compartment, and he was a goner."

Rena made a face. "I hate girls named Mandy."

Audra lifted her cucumber water in salute. "Me, too."

Amanda huffed in her lounge chair. "Hey, I went by Mandy when I was younger."

Rena rolled her eyes. "Don't say that so loud." She

turned back to Audra. "Have you had the stone massage?"

"No."

"It's heaven."

"Maybe I'll indulge later."

"Hey, you should join us for dinner tonight," Rena said.

Amanda appeared less than thrilled by the suggestion.

Audra accepted anyway. After all, Rena seemed like a kindred spirit to mix it up with.

Rena glanced at her watch, then back at Amanda. "You have a pedicure in five minutes. Better run."

Amanda hesitated a moment, as if leaving meant losing her status as Rena's first and best spa buddy.

Rena moved her chaise closer to Audra's and waited until Amanda was just out of earshot. "You *must* join us for dinner. She is so boring. If I don't have a buffer tonight, I might stab myself with a fork."

Audra smiled. "Don't worry. I'll be there. Just don't leave *me* with her."

Rena stretched and gazed up at the twin palm trees towering over them. "I shouldn't be so mean. Amanda's one of those peripheral friends. You know, in a group she's not bad, but one on one is pure torture. The third member of our party had to cancel at the last minute, so I got stuck with her. All she does is talk about decorating her house. I blame Martha Stewart."

Audra returned a knowing nod as she thought about her two sisters, Judith and Reese. All together, they were fine. But Audra and Judith had never done well as a solo pair.

"You mentioned a big business deal," Rena said. "What do you do?"

"I'm a fashion attorney."

"Sounds better than a divorce lawyer."

"It's primarily corporate stuff, only all of my clients are in the fashion industry."

"I used to be in the fashion world. Before I got married. I did PR for Giorgio Armani."

"Really?"

Rena nodded. "At least that's what they called it. Technically, I was just a sales associate for rich and famous clients. That's how I met my husband. I sold him six new suits for a European business trip."

"Which category does he fall in?"

"Rich. He's a venture capitalist. So what kind of big deal chased you here? Is the Gucci family at war again?"

"Nothing that complicated. I represent Jacqueline Cosmetics and negotiated a deal for their first spokesmodel."

"Interesting. Anyone I know?"

"I really can't say." It was Tiko, the Asian pop star, but Sofia Estes, Jacqueline's CEO, had a major press event planned to herald the announcement.

Rena groaned. "I hate confidentiality. It ruins all the fun. I have a psychiatrist friend who sees lots of Hollywood people, and she won't tell me shit. I guess you'll just have to give me all the gory details on this idiot model who dumped you."

Audra laughed. She liked Rena's no-nonsense attitude. "Well, if I do that, then I want a play-by-play on your night with this George person."

Rena extended a well-manicured hand adorned with a diamond so large it probably equaled the national debt of Chile. "Deal. You go first."

Audra shook firm and fast. "His name's Ollie Brinton. We met in New York. He was doing runway modeling for Matt Nye's spring collection."

"Oh, my God!" Rena cut in. *"Ollie Brinton?* Isn't he the new Calvin Klein underwear guy?"

Audra nodded. "It's tough to rid yourself of ex-boyfriend evidence when he's staring at you from the pages of every major magazine. Not to mention billboards all over L.A."

Rena leaned in to half whisper, "Tell me the truth. Is that bulge real?"

"Yes," Audra said. "And it's fabulous. If only the son of a bitch had a big heart and a big brain to go with it."

Rena laughed. "How long did you go out?"

"About a year. But we were never in the same city. To see each other three times a month was a lot." Audra shrugged. "It's not the best feeling in the world, but it's not a romantic tragedy either. At least I don't have to worry about lockjaw or soreness anymore."

Rena gasped. "He was *that* big?"

Audra laughed. "I'm kidding!"

"Oh," Rena murmured, disappointed. "Do you miss him?"

Audra considered the question. "I miss the idea of him. Even though we rarely saw each other, I had a *boyfriend*. That was a comfort in and of itself, despite the fact that our relationship was going nowhere. But I had my poor pitiful me day with Dove bars and Joni Mitchell CDs, and now I'm over it. Of course, it sucks to break up around the holidays, no matter how wrong for each other you are."

"Ugh!" Rena covered her face in mock horror. "I'm only in a semi-happy marriage, but I prefer that to being single on Christmas. I think it's worse than Valentine's Day. You can always find a love stinks crew to hang out with in February. But Christmas? How many people are you going to find who think Santa is a fat bastard?"

Audra giggled. "Not many, I hope."

Rena sat up cross-legged. "Do you come from a big family?"

"Two sisters and a brother."

"Lucky you. I'm one of six. All my siblings got married and had kids before I even met Dan. I used to stand out like neon at holiday gatherings. Pathetic, lonely, single, miserable Rena with the twitching ovaries. Whenever I held one of my nieces and nephews, my mother would run over and hug me."

Audra sat up, too, adjusting her big white Chanel sunglasses. "I can top that. My mother thinks I'm a lesbian. In fact, she even joined a parents-for-gay-children support group. And this was *before* my brother came out. I still get the occasional brochure in the mail. She also sent me the Chastity Bono, Melissa Etheridge, and Rosie O'Donnell books."

Rena completely lost it. In fact, she was beating the lounge chair with her fist. "No offense," she began, finally able to speak, "but your mother sounds worse than mine."

"Oh, none taken. She probably is."

All of a sudden, Rena stood up. "Let's do something."

"Like what?"

"I don't know. Take the hiking trail along the beach!"

Audra winced. "Rain check. I'm all hiked out from my mountain excursion this morning."

"What about shiatsu?"

Audra loved the idea. "A massage sounds great."

Rena dashed over to the guest phone, barked out a few demands, and rushed back. "They can take us now!"

Minutes later, Audra and Rena were in the couples massage room, listening to Enya and being tended to by expert hands. Periodically, Audra drifted in and out of sleep, but Rena managed to keep her awake.

"Wouldn't it be great to wake up here on Christmas morning?" Rena said.

Audra moaned her agreement. That idea sure beat her plans, which were to go home to Texas for a very dysfunctional Christmas. The obligation filled her with dread. Granted, she loved her family, but more often than not the hype of the holidays stood no chance against the actual outcome. Close quarters, old resentments, petty jealousies, bad gifts, passive-aggressive tendencies. Maybe she could spike her brother-in-law's punch with a heavy tranquilizer. Audra wondered how many times her mother would remind her about turning thirty this year. Avoiding that alone was ample reason to stay away.

Suddenly, an even more depressing realization hit Audra. The original plan had been for Ollie to go home with her. They were to fly into Dallas on Christmas Eve and escape the morning of the twenty-sixth. Now, of course, she was on her own.

The masseuse did her work, kneading Audra's body, at times painful but ultimately fabulous. If ever there was a time to ruminate over messy family matters, it was during shiatsu. Remarkably, it made everything less stressful.

"What are your Christmas plans?" Rena asked.

"I'm going home. To Texas," Audra murmured. "You?"

"To Greece."

Audra threw her a glance. "No fair."

Rena sighed. "One of the perks of marrying a fifty-four-year-old man who doesn't want a family. Well, a *new* family I should say. I have a stepdaughter who's older than I am."

Audra couldn't imagine. "That must be strange. How old are you?"

"Guess."

She gave Rena a studied gaze. "Twenty-nine."

Rena's face contorted into a portrait of horror. "I'm twenty-seven!"

"The light is really bad in here," Audra said, applying a verbal kiss to the psyche damage.

"I don't care. I'm getting Botox injections as soon as I get back to L.A."

"Relax. It's not like your husband can trade you in for a younger model yet. You've got that locked up for at least five years."

Rena rolled her eyes. "Ain't that the truth." She

craned her neck to address the massage therapist. "Will you *please* work on my poor feet? I wear four-hundred-dollar shoes, but not a dime of that pays for comfort."

The woman nodded quietly and dutifully focused her attention there.

Rena moaned her appreciation. "You know, I think that I cast out my wire for the big fish too soon. I love Dan, but the age difference is harder than I thought it would be. He's got a mild heart condition, so his doctor won't let him take Viagra. And from what I can tell, he's stopped thinking about sex altogether. His whole life is business and golf."

"Have you thought about cutting your losses?"

Rena snarled. "I'd be giving up too much. He made me sign a bitch of a prenup. Anyway, that's why I have George on speed dial."

Audra perked up. "That's right! It's your turn to spill the details."

Rena licked her lips. "Okay, this is a great story. September Moore is a friend of mine."

"The actress?"

Rena nodded. "She prefers *Oscar-winning* actress, but yeah. Anyway, she was one of my best customers when I worked for Armani. We got together for lunch a few months after I got married, and she looked fantastic. I mean, her skin just *glowed*. I thought she'd just had a chemical peel or something. Turns out she'd just had *George.*"

Audra shook her head in disbelief.

"It took me a long time to work up the courage to call him. Finally, I did, and I had to email a recent photo before he'd agree to a date."

"Seriously?"

Rena nodded. "And he was so cocky about it. He was, like, 'I only take on certain types of clients because I aim to satisfy.' Anyway, I did what he asked, we set up a time, and it was the best fifteen hundred dollars I've ever spent."

"Wasn't it—"

"He's a *professional,* "Rena cut in. "I never felt uncomfortable. Not once. And he did two things that were so incredibly hot."

Audra lay there, dying to know. "Tell me!" she hissed.

"Okay, the first thing was, he asked me if I could help him in, which I thought was really sexy. And the second thing was, after he was all the way inside me, he took a rest without disconnecting. He just stopped and kissed me for a long time. Oh, God, that drove me insane. I mean, it was such a relief from all the endless pounding that most guys think they have to do."

Audra sighed with longing. "I want a George."

Rena laughed. "Take the original. You could make him a Christmas present to yourself." Suddenly, she yelped and propped herself up on both elbows. "Oh, my God! You should take him home for the holidays!"

Audra stared back as if Rena's head carried the snakes of Medusa.

"I'm not joking. George is nobody's boy toy. He's really smart. I think he used to be an air force pilot."

Audra started to laugh. "That is a wicked idea." It would almost be worth the money to see her mother's reaction. The bedroom time didn't sound bad either. She felt a surge of bad-girl vibrations. "Do you have his number?"

"In the words of September Moore, 'Honey, it's like American Express. I never leave home without it.' "

Chapter Two

Beverly Hills

Continued chaos in the Middle East.

Another security breach at an airport in the U.S.

More financial woes for the nation's major airlines.

"Screw you, Matt Lauer." Colby Douglas zapped off the television and attempted to go back to sleep. He tossed. He turned. As if he stood a chance in hell. Finally, he gave up and bounced off the bed, out of the guest bedroom, and into the kitchen.

A black cat called Ice Man pounced onto the counter and immediately began meowing demands.

Colby knew the drill. He opened a can of Fancy Feast and spooned it into a silver bowl.

Ice Man chowed down, purring as loud as a small motor.

Colby stroked the feline's back, then poured a glass of white cranberry juice and wondered how he was going to fill the day.

Suddenly, George McCall burst inside, all heaving

breath, sweat, and running gear. He headed straight for the refrigerator to grab a bottled water and pointed disapprovingly at Colby's choice of beverage. "You know that's thirty grams of sugar per serving, don't you?"

Colby shrugged and drank up.

George shook his head. "Wasted calories, man."

"I've never counted."

"You should. I keep track like a man obsessed." He slapped his rock-hard stomach. "I'm down to eight percent body fat."

Colby lifted his Tommy Hilfiger T-shirt to pop his equally firm midsection. "I'm not far from that and don't count a damn thing." He laughed. "You've been living in L.A. too long, dude. You're starting to sound like an actress."

George took the hit in stride. "I should kick your ass out on the street for that one. But I couldn't do that to my washed-up air force buddy."

Colby downed the rest of his juice. "Of course not. I've always been the one to kick *your* ass."

"Oh, yeah?" George taunted him, pivoting back and forth like Oscar de la Hoya.

Colby indulged him in a minute or two of playful sparring, then surprised with a light gut punch, not enough to hurt, just enough to drive the message home: Even on the downhill slope, Colby Douglas still had the moves.

George surrendered. "You always did play dirty."

"Still a sore loser?" Colby teased. "I thought you would've matured by now."

George took a seat at the kitchen table. "Some things never change, I guess." He knocked back the water and chucked the bottle. "So what's on tap for you today?"

"Oh, the usual. Oprah, Maury, Judge Judy, Montel, *The View.*"

"You're killing me," George said lightly. "Get a job. Any job." He gave Colby a faux once-over. "You're kind of cute. Maybe you could stand around with a bottle of cologne at Neiman Marcus.''

Colby shook his head. ''You can't take me on physically, so you pull this shit. It's a very girlish way to show aggression. Did you know that?''

George dropped his mouth open in a show of exaggerated interest. ''Really?''

''Lucky for you I need a place to crash.''

George stood up and squeezed Colby's shoulder. ''Yeah, lucky for me. I don't stand a chance against a tough bastard like you.'' He started for the master bedroom. ''I've got clients until late this afternoon, but tonight we party.''

''I don't really feel up to—''

''The mission is to get you laid.''

Colby took instant offense. ''Come on, man. I'm not that pathetic.''

George had vanished but reappeared in the doorway to answer. ''You're out of work, and your fiancée just dumped you for your younger brother. That's *hall of fame* pathetic. Normally, I would insist on dangerous amounts of liquor and a three-way to get a man like you on the road to recovery. But I'll let you slide with a regular one-night stand. Provided the girl is really hot.''

''Have I told you lately how much I appreciate the way you're willing to meet me halfway?'' Colby said.

George looked puzzled. ''Sometimes I can't tell if you're serious or not.''

''Take a shower, asshole.''

George pointed at him. ''Now that was hostile. I'm deeply hurt.''

Screw the calories, too, Colby thought. Once George ambled off, he poured a bigger glass of white cranberry juice and upped the ante by tossing a Pop-Tart into the toaster oven. It was all a wash. Since being pink-slipped by East/West Airlines, he'd been putting in an hour at the gym almost every day. And ever since Natalie had called off the engagement and announced her interest in his kid brother, Mikey, he'd added an extra hour to his routine. Serious sweat. Major stress relief.

Colby glanced around George's posh digs. This two-bedroom high-rise in Beverly Hills had to be expensive. The place was top of the line: crown molding, marble floors and countertops, plush carpet, high ceilings, great views, even a uniformed doorman and a concierge. Not bad for an air force goof-off who spent six years in college but never earned a degree. Obviously, *personal consultants* did very well in L.A. Only Colby had so far been unable to pin down George on exactly what the hell a personal consultant did. Besides consult. Personally.

From the guest bedroom he heard the faint ringing of his cellular phone. Could be an airline about a pilot opening. He hustled to pick up before it rang over to voice mail. But it was his father's name on the ID screen. Should have moved a bit slower. "Hello?"

"Hi, sweetie. Did you find a job?"

"Hey, Mom. No, I would've called if something had happened."

"Well, now's a bad time with Christmas so close. You'll have lots of offers at the first of the year." She paused. "Do you need any money?"

"No, Mom. I have a six-month emergency fund for situations like this. I'm fine."

"I wish your brother would handle his money like you do. We're getting calls from creditors again. He told us that he closed those accounts your father co-signed on, but apparently he's over the limit and behind on payments again." She let out a frustrated sigh. "We had to put his tickets to Vail on our American Express."

Colby remained silent.

"Sweetie, are you there?"

"I'm here."

"Since nothing's happening on the job front, maybe

you can get to Vail early. Think of it as a vacation. We have the lodge booked from the twenty-third until New Year's."

"I'm not coming this year, Mom."

"Oh, stop talking crazy. What are you going to do? Spend Christmas alone?"

Colby said nothing. The truth was, he'd given no thought to how he was going to spend the holidays— only how he *wasn't*. "It's better that I not be around Mikey and Natalie right now. I can't decide which one I'd like to push off the ski lift the most. That's where my head is."

"One day you're going to thank Mikey."

"Oh, yeah? Well, that won't happen before Christmas."

"If Natalie is flaky enough to take up with Mikey, then thinking she was marriage material was a mistake all along."

Colby sighed. There was a certain motherly logic to that. It made him out to be the smart one with a temporary lapse of judgment and, in typical fashion, absolved Mikey, the perpetual screw-up. Basically, the story of his life.

"Your father thinks they'll break up before Christmas anyway. I do, too. I've kept a quart of milk in the refrigerator longer than Mikey's kept a relationship intact."

Colby laughed. "That was a good one, Mom."

"Does that mean you'll come?"

The eagerness in her voice did a number on his resistance. "I'll think about it."

"Good." She brightened. "I hate to see a girl come between my two boys. Especially a twit like Natalie."

Colby smiled. "Did you think she was a twit when I was engaged to her?"

"I thought so when you first introduced us."

"Mom!"

"Colby, please! She's spent the last few years trying

to get on one of those stupid reality shows. *Survivor, Big Brother, Real World*—none of them will take her."

"It's too bad they canceled *Temptation Island.*"

"I think Mikey was an alternate on that one. His new plan is to get out of debt by going on that *Fear Factor* show."

Why doesn't he do something really scary like finish school and get a job?"

"I worry about him sometimes. A woman in my book club has a forty-year-old son who delivers pizzas, and whenever she complains about him, I think of Mikey. Is that terrible of me?"

"No, it's realistic. But if air travel doesn't pick up fast, I might be delivering pizzas, too."

"Stop that. You can do anything. Mikey's different."

"Mom!" Colby began hotly. "It's not like he's Corky from *Life Goes On*. Mikey's just a lazy bum. Except when it comes to women. He can work fast when he wants to."

"You only have one brother."

"Yeah, I know. And last time I checked I hadn't taken up with his fiancée." Colby heard a beep and checked the screen to see a low battery message. "Listen, I have to go. My cell's running out of juice."

"Think about Vail!"

"I will. Promise."

"Love you."

"Love you, too."

"Merry Christmas!"

"Yeah." He signed off.

"What about the one at the end of the bar?" George asked.

Colby looked, trying to determine which girl he meant.

"Brunet, pink shirt . . . oh, she's turning this way . . .

I don't know who the doctor was, but I'd like his name, so I can compliment him on a great pair of t—"

"You can't tell from this distance."

George shot up his eyebrows. "Buddy, I can tell over the phone. That's how good I am." He gave the woman an appraising stare. "She could snap me out of a funk. Go over there and buy her a drink."

Colby sat statue-still.

"Come on. She *wants* you to hit on her. Otherwise, she's in the wrong place in the wrong outfit."

Colby shook his head and knocked back some beer. "I'm not up to it tonight."

"Oh, I see," George said, his voice taking on a mocking grave tone. "You're not even thirty yet. Have you seen a urologist?"

Colby shot him an annoyed look. "Physically, I'm fine. Mentally, I'm just not there yet."

"Promise me that you'll stop watching *The View.*"

Colby laughed. "I'm serious, man. It's not as simple as you make it out to be. Do I think that girl's attractive? Yes. Would I like to have sex with her tonight? Of course. But where my head is right now, I don't even feel like going through the conversational games to get to that point."

"So cut through the bullshit. Tell her what's up."

Colby gave George an incredulous look. " 'Hello, I'd like to have sex with you, but you'll have to leave as soon as it's over, and there will be no exchanging of phone numbers.' What kind of woman would accept those terms?"

"More than you realize. But you'd have to change your name to Ben Affleck."

Colby managed a half grin. "Besides, Christmas is just a couple days away. The holidays are a depressing time for a lot of people. I don't want to prey on some-one's loneliness."

"Okay, I'm serious now. No more daytime TV for you.

And I'm blocking the Lifetime channel. Want another beer?"

Colby glanced at his watch. "I was thinking about catching a movie. The new James Bond is playing."

George shook his head. "You're hopeless."

"Stay here and party. Bring a harem home. I don't mind. It's your world."

George's pager zapped his attention. He stood up abruptly. "Don't go anywhere yet. I've got to make a quick call."

Colby took in the scene at the Standard Lounge in the Standard Hotel, a guaranteed Hollywood hot spot, according to George. The guy knew his VIP haunts. Colby recognized Luke and Owen Wilson, John Stamos, and Vince Vaughn hanging out together and eyeing the go-go-booted waitresses. The retro/futuristic vibe left Colby cold, but his friend loved to be part of the trendy scene.

George returned a few minutes later, a rare look of worry on his face.

"Something wrong?"

"Not really. Just a scheduling snafu. A new client booked me over Christmas, but one of my regulars had a change of plans and wants me for the same time."

Colby finished his beer and shrugged. "Can't be in two places at once. But now that the subject's on the table, would you please tell me what the hell a personal consultant does?"

There was a long stretch of silence before George answered. "That depends on the client. Some women just want to talk. They need someone to listen to them. Some want a date to a big event or to a restaurant. And some just want sex."

Colby waited for the punch line. It never came.

George simply stared back at him.

Colby experienced a strange feeling, followed by a

disturbing realization. This guy was serious. "You're a gigolo?" He practically choked on the last word.

"Gigolo is a seventies term. I think of myself as a personal consultant. Honestly."

"If women are paying you to have sex with them, then you're a gigolo, whether you call yourself a personal consultant or the milkman." He paused a beat. "Okay, that last one was a bad example."

George laughed.

So did Colby. "Forget James Bond. I need another round."

George fetched two more beers from the bar. "Don't let this freak you out. I'm still the same guy. It's just that I found a way to get paid for doing something I love." He winked. "God bless America."

Colby held his face in his hands. "I can't believe it, man. You're a prostitute."

"Like hell I am," George snapped. "I don't lean against lampposts. I don't advertise on the Internet. I don't have a pimp." He nudged Colby with his elbow. "Unless *you're* interested. I could be your bitch and bring you back all my money. You'd like that, wouldn't you?"

"You're sick."

George cracked up. "I didn't chase after this line of work. It came looking for me. I was having dinner at Chaya Brasserie. A friend had stood me up, and I'd waited too long to try the place, so I just ate by myself. So there I am eating dessert, and this woman—late thirties, nice looking—sits down at my table all of a sudden." He looked around conspiratorially. "Are you ready for this?"

Colby nodded, leaning in closer.

"She says, 'If you can eat me like you're eating that chocolate cake, then there's a thousand dollars in it for you.'"

Colby was stunned. "You're bullshitting me."

George bit down on his lower lip and shook his head back and forth. He held up his right hand. "I swear, man. It's the truth. Turns out she's a big player at one of the studios. A real power chick. The weird thing was this: Once she got me back to the hotel—Chateau Marmont, by the way, very swanky place—she wants me to be in control. I guess she just wanted a guy to *take* her, you know? And she loved sex talk. I pumped her full of it, and she went wild. Practically scratched the skin off my back. Anyway, she paid me in cash and asked if she could give my name and number to a friend of hers. That's how it all started. By word of mouth."

Colby could hardly believe it. "This is crazy."

"And *lucrative.* I'm stashing away as much as I can. I don't plan on staying in this a long time. Just until I have enough saved up to start my own business."

"But doesn't it make you feel . . . "

"Dirty, cheap, used?" George filled in.

Colby gave him a brief nod.

"Not at all. These are high-class women. And I require a photo in advance from first-timers." He reached into the inside pocket of his leather jacket. "This is my newest client."

Colby was stunned at the sight. "She reminds me of Ashley Judd."

"I thought the same thing."

He couldn't take his eyes off the photograph. "I don't get it. Why would this woman need to *pay* for a date?"

"You'd be surprised. Take the girl who referred her to me. Rena's about my age and married some rich guy in his fifties who can't take Viagra on account of a heart condition. She hires me because I get the job done, and I'm not complicated. Not sure what Audra's story is. That's the girl in the picture. She looks like a corporate type, though. Probably a workaholic, never makes time for fun. You know the drill. Her family must be hounding her to get married because she wants me to play her boyfriend on a trip home to Texas for Christmas. Too bad I have to cancel on her."

"Why?"

"Because she's new and sounds like a one-time client. The woman who paged me is a regular. I don't want to piss her off. Her business alone pays for that condo we're living in."

Colby kept staring at the photograph of Audra, trying to figure her out. "Do you mind me asking how much she was going to pay you?"

"Five thousand," George said easily. "Fifteen hundred for each overnight and an extra five hundred for holiday pay. Plus all expenses."

Colby took a swig of beer and shook Audra's picture in George's face. "To spend time with *her*? That's easy money!"

George's eyes went wide. "Hey, I hate to leave this woman in the lurch. Why don't you fill in for me?"

Colby laughed. "Now who's the pimp?"

"I'm serious, man. I've never met Audra. And the two of us look enough alike so that if Rena gave her a detailed description, she'd think you were me."

"Are you insane?"

George sighed. "No, I'm a resourceful problem solver. What's the harm? Audra needs a pretend boyfriend. You could use five thousand dollars to replenish your savings. The way I see it, this is more meant to be than Rachel and Ross."

Chapter Three

"I've never regretted paying for it. Not one time," September Moore said. "And men who don't charge have always cost me much more one way or another. Relax. You're in very good hands with George."

Rena's collagen-pumped lips curled into a secret smile. "Good hands, good thighs, good ass, and a *great* . . ."

Audra laughed and sipped on her martini. "You two are a bad influence. I say we get together more often."

They were at Houston's in Century City, not the most glamorous choice, but Rena had a craving for the restaurant's fantastic spinach-artichoke dip.

Several diners had approached the table for September's autograph, and each time she'd graciously complied. Audra knew many celebrities whose personal policy was to refuse such requests while they were eating or with their families, but September didn't seem to mind at all. Clearly, she loved being a star.

"Oh, how I envy you," September went on. "The first time with George is the best. Not that it's downhill after that. Don't get me wrong. The man holds his value. But the first time is unforgettable. I remember having one big orgasm and then lots of little ones that just stretched on and on. I think I even had a delayed climax a few days later.''

Rena laughed. "Whatever you do, don't let your sisters get their paws on him. He's yours.''

September looked confused.

"She's taking George home with her for Christmas,'' Rena explained. "It's Texas, right?''

Audra nodded.

"Home for Christmas?" September shrieked. "What a waste. You should get a room at Shutters on the Beach in Malibu and not come up for air until New Year's.''

Audra and Rena laughed.

September didn't. "I'm serious. Nothing will kill a sex drive faster than a family holiday.''

Audra had to give her that point. "For me, this really isn't about sex.''

The *X* in sex had barely dropped before Rena and September doubled over.

"Let me guess,'' Rena managed to blurt out. "You want to get to know him as a person.''

Audra lengthened her spine. "His primary purpose is to pose as my boyfriend and take some of the pressure off. I hope it'll save me from my mother's lesbian fears and my sister's warnings that I'm waiting too late to settle down and therefore will be forced to adopt a child from overseas.''

"You don't need *George* for an assignment like this,'' September scoffed. "That's like calling in a trauma surgeon to look at a paper cut. The guy who parked my car at the Ivy last week could step in for this job.''

Rena bobbed her head but still gave Audra a supportive smile. "She's right, you know. There's no point in hiring George if you're not going to let him do what he does best. It'd be like hiring Marc Anthony for a big event and then telling him not to sing. Why bother?"

Audra shrugged. "We'll just have to make time, I guess."

September grabbed her purse and fished out two pills, washing them down with what remained of her martini. "Don't squeeze him in between Christmas carols and tree trimming. George takes his time with everything, unlike so many guys who think the bed will self-destruct if they don't finish in two minutes."

A few tables away, there was an eruption of laughter and squeals.

Audra turned to see a large party of coworkers engaged in what looked to be a riotous gag gift exchange.

September sniped a derisive look in their direction. "God, I hate this time of year. Which reminds me. I need to find a new personal assistant to get out there and buy my family presents."

Rena moped a little. "Dan refuses to let me decorate the house. He says it's a waste of time and money. How did I come to marry such a grumpy old fart?"

"The fact that he made the cover of *Fortune* might have something to do with it," September said.

Rena dipped a tortilla chip with half interest. "All I can say is this: be careful what you wish for. Right now I wouldn't mind a guy stuck in middle management who loved cranberry pie and wanted to take me to see *The Nutcracker.*"

Audra grew quiet. Rena was generally fun and upbeat, but the more Audra got to know her, the sadder and lonelier her new friend's life seemed to be. And as for September, to hire an assistant to buy family gifts? Lack of time didn't appear to be her problem. She just didn't give a damn.

The air of cynicism prompted Audra to rethink this hired boyfriend plan. But everything was set up. Ian St.

Claire, a designer client, had offered up the small jet he leased as a Christmas gift, and George was scheduled to meet her at a private air strip in the morning.

"Who wants another martini?" September asked.

Rena quickly indulged.

But Audra begged off. "I haven't packed a thing and should really be going." She reached for her handbag and searched for cash to cover her part of the tab. "This was fun. We'll have to do it again sometime."

September waved a dismissive hand. "Let me treat. I need to spread a little Christmas cheer to erase some bad karma. I hit a Salvation Army guy on the forehead with his own bell. It was clanging in my ear. I just couldn't stand it."

Audra gave her a strange look. "Thanks."

September flashed a wicked smile. "You have quite a stocking stuffer this year. Better make the most of it."

Audra grinned and stood up to leave.

Rena rose to embrace her. "I'll call you when I get back from Greece. *Enjoy.*"

Audra shook her head. "I hope he can live up to all this hype. I'm half expecting the earth to move."

"Oh," September said. "Here's one tiny drawback you should be aware of: George has a habit of cheering his own name when he comes. Some women are put off by it, but it's actually kind of cute."

Audra wished them both a happy holiday and walked out, the doubts piling up with each step. On the drive home she promised herself that she would at least meet him, but if for any reason she felt uncomfortable or uncertain, then she would call it off.

"Hi, I'm George McCall."

Yes, you are. He looked nothing like Audra expected. In her mind she carried an *American Gigolo* image: tight pants, shirt buttoned down to there, club stud vibrations. But this guy wore beautiful Italian boots, dark jeans, a starched white Oxford, a leather bomber, aviator sunglasses, and a Jack Spade weekend bag slung over a broad shoulder. The whole package smacked of neatly ordered confidence.

"Audra Jarecki." She shook his hand fast and filled the silence with a nervous laugh. "This is all new to me. I have never—"

"Don't worry," he assured her. "I've never met you, either, so this is like my first time, too." He removed his glasses and whistled, stepping back to admire the King Air. "I'll say one thing. You really know how to travel. LAX security's a nightmare. If we were going commercial, we'd be stuck in the terminal for hours."

"It's not mine. It belongs to a client. His way of saying Merry Christmas."

"Sure beats a fruitcake."

She smiled. "I take it you have a thing for planes."

George nodded. "It's more of a full-blown affair."

The pilot appeared on the top step. "We're free to take off, Ms. Jarecki."

Audra waved. "Thanks, Mason. We'll be right up." She turned to George, struck by his intelligent eyes. "Shall we?"

He made a gallant gesture. "After you . . . "

George buckled into the seat directly opposite Audra.

"I should probably tell you now that you'll be earning every penny of your fee," she said.

George's handsome face actually flushed pink. "Just . . . just say when."

Suddenly, Audra realized the impact of her words and covered her face in embarrassment. "I didn't mean it that way. I swear. I was actually referring to my family. They're insane. That's where you'll earn your money."

Remarkably, George seemed relieved. "No problem. I've got a lot of experience with crazy families. I was born into one."

She grinned. "Since I'm bringing you home as my *boyfriend,* I suppose we should create some sort of personal history."

He nodded as if to say the suggestion was reasonable. "How long have we been together?"

Audra thought about it. "Three months. That's long enough to be serious but short enough to still not know things about each other."

"How did we meet?"

"I'm a fashion attorney, so it would stand to reason that we met through work." She paused to think. "Maybe you're a designer."

He winced. "I don't know anything about fashion."

"Okay . . . maybe you're the manager of a modeling agency." She left the idea to hang in the air for a moment. "You obviously know something about women."

George gave a brief nod.

"At least that's what Rena Farrell and September Moore tell me."

His stare was blank.

Audra figured that everything must be true about this guy *in* bed because out of it left something to be desired. She sighed deeply. "I guess it's only fair that I let you know what you're getting into. Family Christmas at Barbara and Samuel Jarecki's house. Here's the lowdown. My mother thinks I'm a lesbian. My father watches television all the time. If we hear so much as three syllables from him, that's considered talkative. My oldest sister is Judith. She and her husband Dennis are personal injury lawyers and star in their own commercials. Their office number is 495-I-SUE. Need I say more? Oh, they have a child, Josh. I think he's fifteen now. Overweight, bad acne, sullen—a total mess. But a sweet kid deep down. My younger sister is Reese. She's married to Nick. We'll never see him because he's always playing golf. We'll always see her because she'll always be around to complain about it. And then there's Max, my younger brother. He's recently out and is a bit of a conspiracy theorist about other guys in the closet. I'm sure he'll be convinced that you're gay. Just ignore him. Let's see . . . is that everybody? I think so."

George smiled wryly. "I should be getting time and a half for this." He gave her a penetrating stare. "I'm kidding, of course. But I can't imagine why a woman like you would need the services of . . . a man like me."

"I just broke up with someone, and the idea of going home single and alone . . . well, let's just say I haven't been singing 'Winter Wonderland' over it."

"I recently broke up with someone, too. We've got great timing, don't we?"

Audra was surprised to hear that he'd been involved. "It must be hard to stay in a relationship."

"Relationships are hard for everybody."

"But given the nature of your business, it must be especially difficult for you."

"Oh . . . my business . . . uh . . . you're right. It doesn't make things any easier."

Audra eased back in her seat and observed him for a moment. George came off more like a nervous blind date than an experienced escort. But she found this quality charming, especially coming on the heels of Ollie, who had an ego bigger than his billboard images.

George unfastened his seat belt and slipped into the seat next to Audra, leaning in close to say, "We'll be cruising at this altitude for a while, so it's safe to move around a bit."

She couldn't get over how good he smelled—sweet breath, subtle aftershave, shower-fresh skin.

"Any P.D.A. rules I should know about?"

Audra did a double take. "What?"

"Public displays of affection. For instance, if we're in the kitchen talking to your mother, is it okay to do this?"

He reached out, threaded his fingers through hers, and squeezed tight.

Audra swallowed hard. His hand was warm and strong. "I have no problem with that."

"What about this?" He let go of her hand to place his on the back of her neck, kneading it with his fingers, slowly, sensually, occasionally using his fingertips to play with her hair.

"No problem there, either." All she could think about was what else those hands might be able to do.

"We can make up a history," George said softly. "But body language can't be faked. Three months means we're at that stage where we can't keep our hands off each other, right?"

She managed a dumb nod.

"That means we should be kissing a lot. We need to be able to make out and have it look like we've been doing it every day for weeks. Tell me if this gets you hot." He kept that hand on the back of her neck and tilted her head toward him, cradled her cheek with his other hand, and kissed her.

As kisses go, it was good. She wanted it to continue. But then his tongue moved in, and Audra took leave of her senses. *Ohhhh*. Not fair. He had a drug on his tongue, some kind of erotic narcotic that made you want to ... *mmm* ...

All of sudden, George drew back. "Are you comfortable with the way I kiss? Does it feel awkward?"

This pleased her. A man who took his work seriously. "I'm not sure exactly. Let's try it again."

Chapter Four

The plane was landing. But the passion was just taking off. What a great way to make a living.

Colby took a moment to watch Audra's face and listen to the rush of her breath. "I think we'll be able to convince anybody that we're hot for each other."

"I couldn't agree more."

Colby had made a quick decision somewhere in the sky, and it had been this: Stop acting like a lab geek and start acting like a sex god for hire. After all, Audra was paying good money. He had an occupational duty to deliver excellent service.

He still couldn't quite believe that George had talked him into this. The only reason it had been possible to pull off was the fact that Audra had secured the use of a private plane. Otherwise, no matter how much Colby resembled George physically—matching age, height, and weight, similarly styled short blond hair, the same deep dimpled smile—commercial airline security would have busted this scheme wide open at the ticket counter.

You're not George McCall. Guard!

Of course, it wouldn't be just one guard. Given the state of the world, it would be twenty. Flights delayed. Terminals closed. Maybe the entire airport shut down. And Colby would be investigated to the nth degree. Eventually, of course, they would learn that he wasn't a terrorist threat but instead merely an out-of-work pilot who had nowhere to go on Christmas, a freshly dumped loser who let his dumb friend talk him into an equally dumb thing. But by the time all this was discovered, thousands would have missed their flights, ruining their holiday plans, and he would be targeted for death by an angry mob. Man, a pilot shouldn't think this way, but it's really not safe to fly.

"I arranged for a shuttle to take us to my parents' house," Audra was saying.

"Not a limousine?"

Audra looked at him.

"I'm afraid the private plane has spoiled me."

She smiled. "Well, better you should get used to the real world again. I thought we could stop in first and visit for a few hours. That way checking into a hotel will be a great reason to escape."

He nodded. "Sounds like a plan." Colby's guilt about the deception continued to erode. The truth was, he never expected this crazy trick to feel so liberating. But being someone else, even for two lousy days, was precisely what the doctor ordered. He was George McCall, manager of a successful modeling agency, lover to Audra Jarecki, and right now, that sounded much better than his own life.

They boarded a van already jam-packed with other travelers and luggage. The shuttle made several stops before depositing them outside a nice two-story home in a well-manicured cul-de-sac in Plano, a suburb of Dallas.

After the driver rescued their bags from the rear of

the vehicle, Audra tipped him twenty dollars. "Merry Christmas."

"It is now! Merry Christmas to you, too."

As he drove away, Audra murmured, "When we leave, we're taking a cab to the airport. All those stops were killing me." She smoothed her cheek. "And don't get me started on that old woman who dropped her Samsonite on my face."

Colby grinned. "Maybe your designer friend has a Rolls Royce he can let us borrow."

Playfully, Audra hit him with her Louis Vuitton hanging bag. "It's not my fault that I'm spoiled." She stepped onto the driveway and lingered there for a moment, staring lasers at the five parked cars.

"Something wrong?" Colby asked.

A long stretch of silence. "Everybody's here."

"That's good. Otherwise the next person who arrives will have to park in the yard."

"Stop teasing me," Audra whined. She turned to him in faux distress. "We could leave. You know, just go to a hotel and live on room service and say that we missed our flight."

He went along, arching his brows lasciviously. "And do what?"

"Audra!" a voice screamed from the front door.

"Never mind," Audra muttered under her breath.

"Sam, Audra's here! Quick! Put on the Indigo Girls CD!"

Colby laughed. "That has to be your mother."

"Ding, ding, ding. You win the toaster oven." Audra dropped her bags and embraced her mother on the front lawn. "Mother, you look great!"

"Oh, stop! I need to lose five pounds." She kissed her daughter on both cheeks, then stole a glance at Colby. "Who's this?"

"My new boyfriend, George." Audra paused a beat. "Surprise."

Her mother pumped his hand hard and fast. "Barbara Jarecki. Merry Christmas and welcome to Texas."

"Thank you," George said. "It's nice to be here."

Barbara turned back to Audra. "Now is he your boyfriend or your *boyfriend*? I've been reading about how gays like to create surrogate families." She touched Colby's arm. "I go to PFLAG meetings every week. That's short for Parents for Lesbians and Gays."

Colby gave her a supportive nod. "Good for you."

"He's my *boyfriend,* Mother. My lover in sin. We can't keep our hands off each other. Look." Audra yanked Colby toward her and kissed him ferociously, as if entire civilizations were hanging in the balance.

"That's nice, dear," Barbara said.

Audra came up for air.

Colby wondered if he still had a tongue.

"But you don't have to pretend with us," Barbara said. "We love you for who you are." She shook her head and smiled. "Now come inside, and let's get the two of you settled. You'll never believe what happened. Judith's water heater exploded, and the first floor of her house is flooded."

Audra looked alarmed. "That's awful."

Barbara nodded. "Josh is a mess. His PlayStation was on the floor of the living room. Completely ruined. Anyway, they're staying with us until it all gets sorted out. So are Reese and Nick."

"What happened to their house?"

"They're building near Judith and Dennis, but all the rain we've been having has delayed construction. Then they got a great offer on their old house, so they sold it and moved in with Judith until the new one's ready."

Audra shook her head. "Well, don't worry about trying to make room for us. We're staying at a hotel."

"Over my dead body!" Barbara said.

Audra turned to Colby. "George, close your eyes. I'm going for the gun in my purse."

Colby chuckled.

"It's Christmas!" Barbara exclaimed. "There's plenty of room here. Why stay at some smelly hotel?"

"We have a reservation at the Four Seasons."

Barbara dismissed the luxury chain with a wave of her hand. "Too expensive and too far to drive." She turned to Colby. "George, what's going on here? Are you too *California cool* to spend a few days in a modest middle-class home?"

Colby had to hand it to her. The woman was good. "We'd love to stay here. All I need is a blanket and a spot on the floor."

Audra kicked his ankle. *Hard.*

Barbara beamed. "We can do better than that." She took Audra's hand and led her to the door. "The two guest rooms are already spoken for, but you can take the sleeper sofa in the library, and we'll set up George to bunk with Max and Josh in Max's old bedroom."

"Mother, no," Audra protested. "We have reservations—"

"Enough of that nonsense." Barbara shouted into the house, "Sam! Call the Four Seasons and cancel Audra's reservation! The cordless is right next to your recliner. You don't even have to get up. Use directory assistance."

"No, Mother, I really—"

"Audra! If you're home for Christmas, then you're home for Christmas. End of discussion."

Audra sighed and seemed to accept defeat. "Well, George sleeps with me."

Suddenly, Barbara halted and gave Audra a pious stare. With a severe shake of her head she said, "Not with children in the house. The two of you aren't married."

"Josh is fifteen, Mom."

"Still an impressionable age. I'm sure George understands my position," Barbara said, fixing an expectant gaze on him.

"Of course," Colby quickly agreed. "I have no problem bunking with the guys. It's just for a few nights."

"There," Barbara said, pleased with herself. "It's settled. Now, your sisters are busy in the kitchen. Let's go join them." She moved ahead.

Audra looked at Colby as if he were street vermin.

"What was I supposed to say?"

"Anything but that."

The moment they stepped inside, a heavy man beached on a recliner shouted, "Baby girl!"

Audra rushed over to hug and kiss him. "Merry Christmas, Daddy."

"The whole litter's here!" He turned his attention back to the television. The tornado thriller *Twister* was on. "I'll visit with you in a few, baby girl. I don't want to miss the part when the cow flies through the air."

Barbara whipped past and slapped him on his bald head. "Oh, honestly! Sam, you watch that stupid DVD three or four times a week."

"Daddy, this is my boyfriend, George."

Sam tossed a quick glance backward. "Got a job, son?"

Colby cringed. Of all the questions to ask. "Yes, sir."

Sam flashed the thumbs-up sign and turned back to the objects taking flight on the screen.

Audra gave her father an affectionate pat on the shoulder and hooked her arm through Colby's, leading him into the kitchen. "Two down, six to go," she whispered.

"I think he likes me," Colby said.

Audra withdrew her arm and, with exaggerated petulance, put both hands on her hips. "I hope you saved a dish for me!"

One sister spun around from the sink, her face bright with glee. "Audra!" She started over with a chopping knife, then realized the gaffe and tossed it behind her. The steel clattered in the sink this way and that as she embraced Audra and stole a lingering glance in Colby's direction. "You look fantastic." One beat. "And so does he." She cut the hug short and made a beeline for him. "I'm Reese, the *younger* sister."

"George, the new boyfriend."

The other sister, busy making what looked to be a pie crust from scratch, turned around with vague interest. "The only dish left is canned cranberries, Audra. Shall I assign you a helper?" She punctuated this with a half-affectionate, half-bitchy smile.

"No, Judith, I think I can deal." Audra scooted over to brush her lips against her sister's cheek. "No hug, please. I don't want flour all over my blouse. I'm sorry about the water heater. How are you otherwise?"

"A wreck. Josh has put on another twenty pounds and has no friends. But my gynecologist gave me an anti-anxiety drug that works wonders. It's the only reason I haven't run off to Mexico."

A worried look skated across Audra's face. "Where is he?"

"Probably upstairs eating Oreos and listening to that rap singer named after the candy."

Audra grinned. "You mean Eminem?"

Judith shrugged. "Maybe. I can't keep those thugs straight." She zeroed in on Colby. "Hi, I'm Judith, and in case you're wondering, we're always this neurotic."

Colby smiled. "There's no place like home."

Judith glanced at Audra. "This one's smarter than your last boyfriend."

Colby's brow furrowed.

"He was a model," Judith explained. "You've probably seen a billboard of his crotch."

"You know, there's a rumor going around on the

Internet that he stuffs his underwear before every photo shoot," Reese put in.

Audra bristled defensively. "I can assure you there's no truth to that rumor."

Reese moved in closer on Colby. "You must be a very confident man to follow in Ollie's footsteps."

"Who's Ollie?" Colby asked.

"She hasn't told you about him?" Reese gave Audra a look of shock. "How long have the two of you been going out?"

"Three months." Colby and Audra announced this in unison.

"Is there a dance that goes with that routine?" Judith cracked.

"Again," Colby said, "who's Ollie?" He was surprised by how badly he wanted to know.

"Ollie isn't a secret," Audra began, a slight edge to her voice. "Just like *your* recent ex isn't one." She directed her words to Judith and Reese now. "We've decided not to burden the early stage of our relationship with old emotional baggage. Too much wasted energy—"

"That can be spent having hot, wild, uninhibited, crazy sex," Reese finished.

Colby, Audra, and Judith merely stared at her.

"An exact quote from that audio book I sent you— *The Husband Project: How to Say 'I Do' to Mr. Right in Six Months* by Dr. Barbi Bambi!"

Audra was horrified to learn that she was reciting anything verbatim by a person named *Barbi Bambi*. But it was true. She'd listened to that drivel while pumping away on the StairMaster at Sports Club L.A. Apparently key sections had seeped into her inner psyche.

"Ah, yes," George said, looping an arm around Audra's waist and pulling her close. "The wonderful Dr. Barbi Bambi. Where would we be without her? Not together, that's for sure." He kissed Audra on the cheek with a loud smack.

Audra reached around, ostensibly to affectionately scratch Colby's back but instead she surreptitiously dug her nails deep into his skin.

Reflexively, Colby arched his back, laughing a little. "Not now, honey. We're in your parents' house, remember?" He gave Judith and Reese a shrug. "She can't seem to get enough of me."

Barbara emerged from the laundry room with a distressed look on her face. "Who started a new load of wash?"

"I did," Reese said.

"We have to go through Josh's pockets. Another candy bar went through the machine."

Reese chewed on a nail.

Judith threw up her hands. "Where are my pills?"

Suddenly, yet another Jarecki (same eyes, same mouth) crashed onto the scene through the kitchen door, decked out in form-fitting biker gear, a helmet under his arm.

"Max!" Audra said, hugging him sweat and all.

"I probably stink, but what the hell." Her brother responded with deep affection and checked Colby out in much the same way that Reese had. "What happened to Ollie?"

Audra sighed. "If you all must know, Ollie met a flight attendant named Mandy."

Max put a supportive arm over her shoulder. "Oh, that sucks. I bet you miss his big—"

Audra elbowed him in the gut. "Don't you dare!"

"Smile," Max coughed.

Reese giggled.

"Oh," Audra murmured, embarrassed. "Sorry." She gestured to Colby. "Max, this is George McCall."

Her brother shook firmly and gave him a suspicious look. "Are you a model, too?"

"No," Colby said. "But I'm in the business. I manage a modeling agency." That's all he was prepared to say. Hopefully, there would be no follow-up questions.

"Which one?" Max asked.

Shit. He thought fast on his feet. "McCall Management." Hey, he liked the sound of that.

Max narrowed his gaze. "Never heard of it. Who's the biggest name on your roster?"

Who was this guy—modeling's answer to Matlock? He shot a HELP ME! glance to Audra, but her face registered blank alarm. "Uh . . . you wouldn't know them. I specialize in hand and foot models. We do a lot of lotion advertisements. Jewelry, too. Some footwear. Mostly sandals, of course." He laughed. "Don't need a pretty foot for a sneaker commercial!"

"Max," Barbara began, "why don't you help George get settled into your room. He's going to be bunking with you and Josh."

Max grabbed a bottle of Gatorade from the fridge. "No problem. Follow me, *George.*" He started up the stairs.

Colby moved fast to catch up, following him up to a spare bedroom where a sullen teenage boy with bad skin was slumped in the corner, eating from a Whitman's Sampler.

"Josh, George. George, Josh," Max said.

The kid barely nodded. He looked miserable as hell.

Colby's heart went out to the guy. Fifteen was a rough place to be, even if things were going well for you. He decided to reach out. The kid could use more than a paranoid uncle. "Mind if I hang out up here with you for a while?"

Josh shrugged. "I don't care."

Max wrestled a sleeping bag, extra blankets, and pillows from the closet, dropping them at Colby's feet. Then he fixed a penetrating, assessing gaze on him.

"What?" Colby asked.

"Nothing," Max said. "Just trying to figure you out. Something's not quite right."

"I don't know what you mean," Colby said. He tried to weather Max's stare, but the intensity was driving him crazy. "So . . . I hear you came out recently. How's the gay thing working for you?"

Chapter Five

"George is *hot*," Reese said. *"Yum, yum, yum!"* She crunched down on a carrot. "I bet he makes you scream the dirtiest things in bed."

Audra was appalled. "Reese! My God!"

Judith rolled her eyes. "Forgive this poor child. If it's not a golf club, Nick doesn't have his hands on it."

Now Audra understood. "Ah, a dry spell."

Reese let out a frustrated groan. "I should be living with a gay man. At least I'd have more fun and better conversation."

Judith sipped her wine. "Just wait until he discovers Viagra. One day you'll wonder why you ever complained about this."

Audra giggled. "What's wrong? Is Dennis too much man for you to handle?"

Judith stared back without a trace of amusement. "I hate that drug. All it does is allow a mediocre lover to keep you bored longer and more often."

Audra cackled. Exclusive sister time like this was fun,

especially after a little bit of wine, which always loosened Judith's lips.

"We're too young a couple to be having sexual problems," Reese whined. "It hasn't even been three years yet." She frowned. "Maybe he thinks I'm ugly."

"Don't do that," Audra scolded. "I hate to hear women bash themselves about their looks. Nick is *lucky* to have a wife as beautiful as you. I mean, face it, you're not waking up to Brad Pitt every morning."

"You don't think Nick's handsome?" Reese asked.

"Of course, I do," Audra said. Actually, he reminded her of David Spade, the man-boy on *Just Shoot Me,* only shorter. But she couldn't tell Reese that. "My point is, don't start thinking about a boob job if he's not thinking about pectoral implants."

Judith topped off everyone's glass, finishing the first bottle of Merlot. "I'll drink to that. Dennis dropped hints about me getting an enlargement once. I said, 'How about you adding two inches to your willy, asshole.' "

Audra and Reese laughed so hard that they practically fell on the floor.

"Speaking of willies," Reese began once fully recovered. "How does George stack up against Ollie?"

"I have no complaints," Audra said.

"Did I mention how hot he is?" Reese asked.

Judith nodded wearily. "Yes, you got that point across."

"You've outdone yourself this time, Audra. Damn you! You've always had the best-looking boyfriends. Hasn't she, Judith?"

"Yes, but Audra can never seem to find a man who's the total package. Invariably, they're either great looking and dumb or great looking, reasonably intelligent, and unsuccessful."

"That's not true!" Audra protested. But too soon.

She speed-searched her brain and couldn't think of a single guy to refute Judith's assertion.

"Okay, prove me wrong," Judith challenged her. "Name one significant ex who doesn't fit in one of those categories."

Audra knew she was in trouble when she accessed her elementary school mental file. No matter, she took a shot in the dark and blurted out, "Donny Pickles." Senior year. Her last big high school romance. It was amazing what two people could do in a Honda Civic with the seat all the way back.

"Great looking, reasonably intelligent, and unsuccessful." Judith grinned. "I rest my case."

"He took over the family business!" Audra argued.

"And ran it into the ground," Judith said. "Dennis handled the bankruptcy."

"Oh."

Judith, pleased with herself, drank up. "I take it George's McCall Management isn't setting the world on fire. Otherwise, you would've mentioned his name."

Audra brightened. "Actually, I was too busy revisiting my questionable past to think of the present." She held up her wineglass in smug salute. "I take back Donny Pickles and raise you one George McCall. Ha! The vicious cycle is broken."

Judith looked skeptical. "Not so fast. I need to see a balance sheet first."

"Who cares about that?" Reese asked. "I just want to see him naked. Let me know when he takes a shower, so I can accidentally walk in on him."

Audra giggled. "You are impossible! Mother has forbidden us from staying in a hotel, but maybe we should—for safety reasons."

"Oh, please," Reese said, gulping the last of her wine and scouting around for another bottle. "I'm harmless. Remember—he's sleeping in Max's room. That's where the real danger lies."

"Don't tell me that," Judith blurted. "Josh is in there, too. My son's got enough problems. The last thing he needs is to learn how to be gay."

Audra grinned. "Don't join Mom at her PFLAG meeting just yet. It's not something that you *learn*. God, you make it sound like needlepoint."

Reese laughed. "Speaking of PFLAG, I saw one of your stocking stuffers. It's a Christmas CD recorded by the local lesbian choir."

Audra's mouth dropped open. "No!"

Reese nodded yes.

Judith laughed the laugh of the delighted. "If you're not a dyke, it's not for Mother's lack of trying. She *wants* this for you."

Audra slapped the kitchen table. "What is the deal? I don't understand. She's got a gay son. Will her world not be complete without a lesbian daughter?"

"I think it all started with Greta Hatcher, the swimmer you were friends with that summer," Reese said. "Remember her? She was kind of butch."

Audra shrugged. "Well, I don't know what it will take to convince her. I basically swallowed George's tongue in the front yard for her benefit, and she still thought I was pretending."

"Maybe *I* should kiss George," Reese suggested.

Audra gave her an odd look. "How will that help?"

"You could walk in on us and pretend to be really jealous and angry."

"I would be really jealous and angry."

Reese sighed. "Just an idea. You know, Ollie was hot, but Ollie was hot in that way that made women jealous of him. You know, because he was prettier than most women. Those lips, those long eyelashes, that skin. And don't get me started on that long, shiny hair. But George is hot in that other way where women are jealous of you. Wanting to know what he's like in bed, how he smells, how big his—"

"That's it!" Judith cut in. "I'm slipping two of Dennis's Viagra into Nick's sweet potato casserole." She glanced at the clock. "Everybody accuses Dennis of cheating on the green. I thought they would be in an argument and back by now."

"Maybe they went shopping," Reese said hopefully. "You know, to buy us really expensive presents for all the hell they put us through this year. I bet George got you a great gift. He seems like a romantic guy. Last year Nick bought me a new iron. I threw it at his head. I missed him. But it hit the wall so hard that they had to replace the Sheetrock. Mom and Dad just repainted, so I hope I got my point across."

Audra felt an instant's pure panic. Christmas presents! She'd completely forgotten. What kind of couple three months into dating didn't exchange gifts?

"What did you get George?" Reese asked.

"I still have some shopping to do," Audra said. And she did. For George, for her parents, for poor Josh— he definitely needed a boost. "I had one free weekend to shop, but I was too drained to do it, so I went to a spa instead."

"Ooh, fun," Reese cooed. "I've never been to a real spa. I got a massage once at my gym, though."

"This is the Bacara Resort in Santa Barbara. The two of you should come to L.A. for a weekend. We'll all go. It took the owner twenty years to build it because the land he bought was not only on a sacred Indian burial ground but also a protected habitat for a rare species of frog."

"Wait a minute," Reese cut in. "I've heard about that place. Debra Messing spent her wedding night there." She turned to Judith. "Oh, let's go visit Audra next month."

"I'm serious. You should come. Nobody in the family has ever visited me in L.A."

Judith warmed to the idea. "What about Mom?"

"She can come, too," Audra said. "It'll be an all-girl retreat. There's an avocado and lemon farm on the property. The food at this place is fabulous. You'd never know it was healthy eating."

"Do you really think we could get Mom to come with us?" Reese asked. "You know how she is about going out of town."

"I'll handle her," Judith said confidently.

"Where is she anyway?" Audra asked.

"She took some cookies next door to Mrs. Townsend," Reese said. "She's probably giving Mom a rundown of all her ailments. I don't expect her back for at least another hour."

Audra pondered opening a second bottle of wine.

Judith shared a secret smile with her. "Are you thinking what I'm thinking?"

"Oh, what's to think about?" Reese shot out of her seat, grabbed another Merlot, and set about freeing the cork. "We need all the help we can get. Dad bought new home theater speakers, and he wants everyone to watch *Titanic* tonight."

Audra groaned. "Oh, God. How many times have we seen that?" She gestured for Reese to hurry up. "Come on with it. I need a buffer for this news."

Reese sloshed more wine into everyone's glass.

"I want to do something special for Josh, Judith," Audra said. "Mom says his PlayStation was ruined in the flood. What do you say I buy him a new one?"

Judith was visibly touched. "He would love that."

Audra nodded. "Consider it done. Assuming I can find one. It's not, like, a Tickle Me Elmo nightmare, is it?"

"No, no," Reese said, talking a bit too loud, feeling no pain. "I saw a whole stack of those things at Target last week."

"So . . . Audra," Judith began, taking a moment to

throw back a serious hit of wine. "Are you and this George guy serious?"

Audra hesitated. "Maybe. But it's only been three months."

"If you don't think he's husband material, then move on," Judith said severely. "Time is not on your side."

Audra smiled. "How do you figure that? I turn thirty this year. I'm where you were *seven* years ago. That's practically a decade. Almost two presidential elections."

"Don't get cocky," Judith warned. "I see it all the time. A woman finally meets the right guy. Six or nine months later she gets a proposal. Planning the wedding takes about a year. A few more years of wedded bliss."

"Wedded *what?*" Reese demanded, turning up her glass. "Ain't that a crock!"

Judith ignored her. "Then she starts thinking about a family. These aren't colonial times, Audra. Women don't get pregnant at the drop of a dime anymore. Especially highly successful career women. Plan it right, or you could be spending a month in China trying to cut through red tape at an orphanage."

"I think I'm ovulating," Audra joked. "Say, why don't I go in the other room and stick my legs up in the air? Someone can go upstairs and tell George to come on down."

Reese's laugh turned into a snort.

Audra and Judith traded worried looks that translated, "No more wine for her."

"I'm serious about this," Judith said. "The longer you wait to have a family, the more complicated things can be. Get me George's social security number. I can get a complete credit history. We'll see how he stacks up."

"Judith! That's a total invasion of privacy."

Her sister waved off the charge. "If I were dating today, I wouldn't go on a third date without one."

Audra raised her glass. "Well, luckily you're married to the *love* machine."

"Yeah, luckily," Reese echoed. She giggled. "I want to see George naked." She giggled again.

Audra looked at Judith. "I would say put her to bed, but it's still early afternoon. I think we're in for it."

Audra gave a low chuckle. "A little too much wine, muttered, working fast for a save.

"Reese, you're not making . . ." Audra might buy to back out but would have . . . sense for it.

Chapter Six

Reese gave George a red-eyed leer. "Do you model underwear?" Her voice was slurred.

George shot Audra a worried glance. "I'm afraid not."

Reese wobbled a bit. "How big? Come on, you can tell me."

"She's had a little too much wine," Audra muttered, working fast for a save.

Suddenly, Reese dipped and swayed. "I'm so sleepy." She held her arms out to George. "Take me to bed."

Audra smiled apologetically. "Would you excuse us for just a moment? Thanks." She grabbed Reese's arm in a snake-bite grip and yanked her back into the kitchen. "Are you on something?" Audra hissed. "We all had about the same amount of wine."

Reese's eyes rolled up, down, and all around, finally settling on Audra. "You've got Donny Pickles. Let me have George."

"Reese, you're not making any sense."

"I feel better now. Thought I had a cold coming on. But I took some Nyquil."

"How much?"

Reese's expression drooped. "Um ... enough, I guess. It was a family-size bottle." She giggled and peeked around the corner at George. "I can't believe you're dating another Calvin Klein model."

"He's not . . . oh, forget it. You're going to bed. Right now."

Judith stepped over to check Reese's eyes. "She's almost in a coma. She'll probably sleep for three days."

"I have to finish making my dressing!"

Audra steered Reese away from her *Bon Appetit* project. "Sweetheart, you're too looped to operate a toaster, much less follow a complicated recipe. Let's go take a rest."

George stepped into the room and offered his immediate assistance, taking one side of Reese as Audra struggled with the other. "What's wrong with her?"

"Enough wine and Nyquil to inebriate Mötley Crüe."

Reese's neck rolled over to the shoulder on George's side. "Audra is ovulating," she mumbled.

George grinned. "Good to know."

"It's Christmas!" Reese shouted. "You should give her some of your best swimmers!" Then, just as quickly, she slumped into oblivion. Thank God.

They carefully carried Reese into one of the bedrooms and covered her with a blanket.

Audra stepped into the adjoining bathroom to check her makeup. She sighed at her reflection. One casualty already. They'd only been in the state a few hours.

George leaned against the door frame.

Audra found it difficult not to stare. This guy's DNA had definitely been blessed. There was something else, though, a refreshingly unstudied air about him. He was centered, at home in his own skin, unaware of how potent his good looks could be.

"There's something I've got to do," George said.

"What—go up on your fee? Sorry. There's no combat pay."

George shut the door, closing them inside the tiny room. *"This* is what I've got to do." He took her face in his hands, inclined his head, and placed his mouth softly over hers.

Audra shut her eyes tight, sealing in the beauty of the moment. In record time she relearned the feel of the shape of his mouth. It was fuller than she remembered on the plane.

He kissed her with varying speeds and pressures: from long to short, from soft to hard. His hands moved to her head, cradling it gently, his fingers combing through her hair.

She hooked her fingers into the belt loops of his jeans and allowed her tongue to touch his as his kiss thundered on, more brazen, more forceful, his tongue on a delicate exploration. A soft moan escaped her, and she felt him draw back, just mere millimeters from her mouth. His warm breath rained against her crushed lips, and slowly, Audra opened her eyes.

"We can't just stay in here making out," George said.

"Why not?" Audra murmured, amazed that he could kiss like that and talk so sensibly, too. "There's water in case we get thirsty, and the lock on the door will protect us from those loons. I mean, my family."

George smiled and landed a kiss on her nose. "What do you say we go downstairs and watch television with your father?"

She brought her hands up to his chest and began tracing the definition of his chest. "I hate *Twister*. I wish Helen Hunt would blow away."

He brushed a tendril of hair from her eyes with his fingers and planted a brief, tender kiss on her lips. "It's over. He's got *Gladiator* going now."

Audra couldn't get over how soft his touch was. As

he'd cupped her cheeks moments ago, as he'd skated across her forehead just now, his fingertips felt like the finest satin.

A sudden pounding on the door speed-crashed the mood, startling them. "Audra? Are you in there?" Judith demanded. "Reese's head is pounding, and she needs some aspirin." *Bam! Bam!* Her sister's fist continued to wage war on the door. "Is somebody in there?"

"We'll be out in a minute," Audra hissed.

George reached around Audra to open the door.

Judith stood on the other side. "Oh, sorry." She checked her watch. "If you two are going to get any shopping in, then you better leave now. It's three o'clock on Christmas Eve."

"Can we borrow your car?" Audra asked.

"Dennis and Nick have it." She shot a glance to Reese. "Take hers. She'll never know."

"What happened to her?" It was Max, standing over Reese as if he were inspecting road kill.

"The dangers of mixing wine and Nyquil," Audra said. "George and I are going shopping. Do you need any last minute gifts?"

Max zeroed in on George. "Do you like to shop, *George*?"

George whispered to Audra, "Why does your brother choose to speak my name in italics?"

Audra whispered back, "He's a homosexual conspiracy theorist who thinks everybody's gay—Tom Cruise, Richard Gere, Ricky Martin, even Bill Clinton."

George addressed Max now. *"Bill Clinton?"*

Max held his ground. "The whole Monica scandal was a hoax. Somewhere out there is a hot male intern. My guess is that he's a strapping corn-fed boy from Oklahoma with lots of stories to tell."

"I see," George said. "Well, good luck with that."

"Are you sure you don't need anything?" Audra asked Max again. "Besides a good therapist, of course."

"You laugh at me now," Max said ominously. "But the truth will come out." He looked at George as he said this. "No pun intended."

Audra laced her fingers through George's and led him downstairs to fetch the keys to Reese's Ford Explorer and make a quick escape.

Her mother was still being held hostage by Mrs. Townsend, and her father hadn't moved, though his hearing had obviously gotten worse, since the television blared louder than ever.

George stole a look and did a double take. "Hey, isn't that your sister, Judith?"

Audra gasped.

Judith filled the fifty-inch screen, standing next to a demolished Chevrolet and holding an oversized check, one of those gargantuan numbers that lotteries trot out for big winner press conferences. "Somebody crashed into me at a restaurant drive-through. I called 495-I-SUE, and Dennis Taylor told me not to worry. He'd fight to get me my check. That's exactly what he did."

Audra cringed.

Next, Dennis appeared on the screen, seated behind a massive desk with a plastic smile on his face. "I'm a man of my word. Call 495-I-SUE. I'll do everything in my power to get you a check."

Audra turned her face into George's chest. "I can't watch anymore."

He laughed and stroked her hair. "It's over now. But very effective. I already have the number committed to memory."

Audra found Reese's keys, and they started out through the kitchen door.

Judith walked back in to finish Reese's dressing.

"I hope you didn't suffer whiplash," George said.

Judith gave him a strange look.

"In the drive-through accident," George explained.

Audra started to laugh. "We just saw the commercial. Judith, sweetheart . . . *why?*"

"I'm not going to pay some bad local actress good money for something I can do for free." She maintained her composure, but there was a slight blush of pink in her cheeks.

Josh came loping down the stairs. "Hey, Aunt Audra."

"Josh!" Audra erupted, rushing over to give him a warm hug. She was alarmed at the sight of him. He'd gained a considerable amount of weight in the last year, and his acne had taken a turn for the worse, too. "I was about to come looking for you. George and I are heading out for some last-minute shopping. Want to come along?"

"No, thanks." He stepped over to the pantry, grabbed a fistful of Heath Bars and poached a carton of chocolate milk from the fridge. "Kind of tired."

It broke Audra's heart to see him this way. "Are you sure? Come on, it'll be fun."

Josh shook his head no. "Don't feel like it."

Audra looked to Judith, who gave her a hopeless shrug. "We'll bring you back something cool."

Josh said nothing and left to go back upstairs.

Audra saw the misery and helplessness in Judith's eyes. "I know it must be hard for you to see him like this."

Judith blinked back tears. "I don't know what to do. Josh hates to go to the doctor. He refuses to see a psychologist. He won't even let me make an appointment with a dermatologist about his skin."

Audra instantly thought of Sofia Estes and Jacqueline Cosmetics, one of her major clients. The company had just launched a men's line called, simply, Ben, named after the founder's dreamy husband, a successful pop singer. The products had received rave reviews from skin care experts, especially the solutions for troubled skin, which were being called near-miracle workers.

"Don't worry," Audra told Judith, squeezing her hand tightly. "We're going to turn him around by Christmas."

Judith didn't appear convinced. "Christmas is tomorrow."

"I know. I've got a plan."

Audra had the steering wheel in a white-knuckled grip as she careened down the highway. "It's a tragedy! Josh has no self-esteem, no sense of joy! Well, I just can't sit back and do nothing like my sister."

"The kid's got a natural athletic build," George said. "With a little more exercise and a little less chocolate, that weight would come off fast."

She turned to him with optimism. "Do you really think so?"

"Absolutely."

"Would you show him some things while you're here?"

"Sure."

Audra reached over and patted George's knee. "Thank you."

"We could get him a set of free weights and a bench. I could design a routine for him and take him through it over the next few days."

"You would do that?"

"Why not?"

Audra smiled, thinking him more sweet and less self-involved than Rena and September had described. "What about your own family?"

"They're in Vail. It's kind of a tradition."

"Wish you were there?"

He answered right away. "No. I'm happy being with you."

She wondered if stud school had taught him such a winning line. "You're good."

George seemed to catch on to her meaning. "I mean that. I needed some space from my brother. It's a long story. So I took a break from my people this year."

Audra believed him.

"It's weird," George went on, shaking his head, "but this doesn't feel like an escort situation to me. More like a very long, very strange ... *date.*" He paused a beat. "Where the girl pays, of course."

Audra laughed.

George reached over to massage her neck. His fingers were like magic. "But if I'm stuck upstairs with your brother and nephew, when are you going to get your money's worth?"

Chapter Seven

They were parked in an underground garage at Northpark, a major retail mecca in Dallas, and Barbra Streisand's "It Must Have Been the Mistletoe" blared from the speakers, courtesy of a station playing Christmas music exclusively.

Audra shifted in the backseat. *God, he's so sexy,* she thought, *he's practically . . . liquid.* She fought against the urge to touch his torso, to test the firmness of his sheet-flat abs.

"It's been a long time since I've made out like this in a car," he said in a thick, breathless voice. "What about you?"

"High school," Audra whispered. "His name was Donny Pickles."

His gaze cut into her like the slash of a knife. "I hope you remember *my* name in ten years."

She felt a shock go through her body. Oh, how she wanted him. Right now. Desperately. "I have a feeling you'll stand out."

"I want you to imagine something, so do me a favor and shut your eyes."

Audra caught her breath and did as she was told. George moved closer, so close that she could feel the heat emanating from his body. Imagining his mouth inches from her own, she trembled, nearly overcome by desire.

"Pretend we're seventeen years old," he said softly into her ear, cradling her waist with hands so hot they seemed to sear through the fabric to scorch the skin of her hips.

Involuntarily, she responded, brushing against him.

"It's way past curfew, and we're at make-out point. There's nobody around, and except for the moonlight, it's dark."

Audra opened her eyes, only to get lost in the intensity of his gaze, in the beauty of his lashes, in the sensual curve of his mouth.

"Does that turn you on?"

Her heart picked up speed, and she relished the sensation of his creamy voice, the intoxicating fantasy of his words. "It has a certain appeal."

"I'm the new guy at school. A rebel. And you're the popular—"

"Stop," Audra cut in. "Why can't I be the bad girl and *you* be the golden boy?"

"Works for me," George murmured. "Is that how it was back then?"

She paused a beat. "No, I was always good."

"Not tonight." His hands moved up, skating languorously under her shirt and across her navel.

Audra swallowed hard, her gaze fixed on him. "I'm going to get you grounded, Mr. Goody Two-shoes."

"It'll be worth it."

The role-play filled her with a brash sensual confidence. "Damn right."

Barbra Streisand gave way to Diana Krall's smoky reading of "The Christmas Song."

Audra was glad he didn't speak again. There was no need to. Instead, George just pulled her to him and smothered her mouth with kisses. Her body shook a little, and her heart beat very fast, just as it had on the plane and in the bathroom of her parents' house.

When George came up for air, she stirred, expelling her breath in a sigh. His hands reached for the waistband of her jeans and stealthily, gently, began to loosen them, hesitating, looking at her, his lips curving into a slow smile.

Audra felt poised, as if at some incredible height, ready to dive down. The moment throbbed, the tension smoked, and she reached up to touch his handsome face. She could sense his hardness, feel his fingers slip under the elastic of her panties, the burning breeze of his breath against her face. Meeting his eyes, Audra got lost in a wave of erotic heat, of what he wanted, of what he knew she wanted, too.

Passion.

Now.

Audra caught her breath, afraid to move, whirling inside the hurricane of desire, temporarily lost in the mystery, in the strangeness of it all. Inside her head, Rena's rave reviews hummed. But now it was her turn.

George gently parted her thighs, and in one smooth movement, touched her . . . *there*. Audra moaned softly. Her shirt was open now, one breast partially exposed, the other loosely covered by the Sea Island cotton. She arched her back to proffer her breasts to him, wanting to feel his hands and mouth all over her.

And then came the riotous pause when his eyes bore into hers, and he moved his lips to say, "Merry Christmas, baby."

She reached out and pulled him toward her, his back so strong and muscular beneath her fingers.

"Shut up," she murmured. "And give me my present."

Laughing, George touched noses with her. "You *are* a bad girl."

Audra groped for the waistband of his jeans and began to wrestle with the five-button fly. Where were simple zippers when you needed them? He was hard and hot and straining for release.

"Remember, I'm the golden boy," he teased. "I'm saving myself for marriage."

Boldly, she met his gaze. "Not anymore." The top two buttons were history.

"Be gentle."

Button number three was a goner.

"And no hickey, please. I sing in the choir on Sunday."

"Then save your voice." With a violent rip, she deep-sixed buttons four and five, pushing his jeans down. Her eyes widened. There he was in white boxer briefs that left nothing to the imagination. Besides, her imagination had never been this good.

George merely sat there, waiting for her next move.

There was no turning back now. Audra leaned over, released him from his boxers, and prepared to feast. Suddenly, her lips parted, as if of their own volition. And then her mouth locked itself around him. The taste of his flesh triggered an overpowering hunger. She wanted more.

A soft mewl of ecstasy escaped him.

She reached out to stroke him as she sucked, feeling the most vital part of him twitch and jerk and stiffen to the point of steel. Sliding her tongue up and down and all around, she opened wider, eager to show how much she wanted him.

Suddenly, there was a flash of light and a loud knock on the window.

Audra jolted violently.

"Oh, shit!" George screamed. "Your teeth!"

"Sorry!" Audra whispered.

He groaned in agony.

She closed her shirt and peered outside to see two security guards laughing and driving off in a golf cart. "Those idiots scared me half to death!" She let out a deep sigh. "Can you hear my heart pounding?"

George sat there, immobile.

Audra looked down. That glorious thing protruding so assertively just moments ago, was, well . . . fading . . . fast. "Did I hurt you?"

"I think you bit me."

"I didn't *bite* you."

"We'll work out a name for it later. Your teeth knocked against me pretty hard. My dick hurts like hell." George shut his eyes. "I can't look. Is it bleeding?"

Audra pawed at the roof until she found the interior light switch. "I don't see anything."

"Look closer."

She practically had her nose in his crotch. "I see a tiny little red mark. No big deal."

"No big deal?" George said hotly. "That is a *very* sensitive area."

"Okay, I'm sorry. It was an accident." She reached out to stroke his cheek. "Forgive me."

George managed a smile. "I guess we better get out of here before those rent-a-cops circle back around."

They put themselves back together and tumbled into the front seat.

Audra sighed and started the car. "Well, choirboy, I guess you'll still be pure on your wedding night."

"Funny. Will you be here all week?"

Chapter Eight

"That stuff is for girls," Josh mumbled. "People will think I'm a fag."

"It's called *Ben,*" Audra said, all but exasperated. "And it's a product made for men. By the way, don't use that awful word. Besides, there's no way you could be homosexual. A true fag would've raced to the Clinique counter at the first sign of a blemish."

Josh stared at his Sketchers.

"Look in the mirror."

He didn't budge.

"Look in the mirror."

Slowly, his gaze traveled up.

"Are you happy with what you see?"

He seemed to be close to tears.

"This acne is not going to go away unless you work at it. You have to start taking better care of yourself. Okay?"

Josh gave her a reluctant nod.

"Normally, I don't bribe people. But I only get to see you a few times a year, so I figure, what the hell, right?

I bought you a brand-new PlayStation to replace the one ruined in the great water heater disaster.''

Josh flashed her a broad smile.

"There's also a stack of new games."

Suddenly, he hugged her. "I love you, Aunt Audra."

She held him tightly for a long time. "There's a catch, sweetie."

He drew back suspiciously. "You're not going to make me go on a liquid diet, are you?"

Audra laughed. "No, Josh. Relax."

"My mom tried that once."

"Here's my deal: You give me some time to show you how to improve your complexion, and you give George some time to show you a workout plan that will help get you into shape. After that, you can play all the Pac-Man you want."

Josh laughed. "That is *so* eighties."

"Donkey Kong?"

Josh shook his head.

"I give up."

"George is pretty cool," Josh said. "He hung out with me earlier. We listened to my new P. Diddy remix CD. Uncle Max never does that, and Dad and Uncle Nick are always gone to play golf."

"He's thinks you're pretty cool, too."

"Really?"

"In fact, it was his idea to buy you a weight bench and all the neat stuff that goes with it."

"Awesome."

"But first there's the matter of your Ben products, which *I* picked out for you." Audra ran her hand across three chrome containers. "Wash your face twice a day with this one. After you wash, wipe this one on with these cotton squares. And every night before you go to bed, apply this drying lotion to all your zits. See, not so bad. Just takes a few minutes. I bet you'll look like a movie star in a few days."

Josh grinned. "No way."

"I'm serious. And once you start building up those muscles, oh, my God, it'll be like Justin Timberlake came to town."

He picked up the cleanser and scanned the instructions on the back. "Can I try it now?"

"Sure!" Audra chirped. "Let me know what you think. I'm going to see how George is coming along with the weight equipment."

Audra left Josh to his routine and checked in on Reese, who was completely zonked out. She met Dennis coming up the stairs and embraced him right away. "Merry Christmas, stranger."

"You, too." He grinned. "Nice boyfriend you've got there. Judith says he's a keeper."

"Judith says?" Audra laughed. "Well, he must be, then. How was your game?"

"Nick destroyed me out there. He could play professionally."

"I think he does, in terms of sheer hours on the green." With that, she floated down to the kitchen to find her mother and Judith rummaging through old cookbooks and recipe files.

"We're trying to find your Aunt Hilda's recipe for gravy," Barbara said. "Have you seen it?"

"I think Mrs. Townsend borrowed it."

Her mother looked horror-stricken. "We'll just have to make do with another one. I'm *not* going back over there. This time she took off her shoes and socks and actually pointed out every corn and bunion."

Audra laughed. "I'm kidding, Mom. I have no idea where Aunt Hilda's secret to lumpy gravy is."

Distracted, Barbara began tearing through a junk drawer. "Still that smart mouth. Go see about your friend, Audra. He's all alone in the garage."

Audra peered into the living room first. Her father hadn't moved. Max had joined him. *Gladiator* was over.

Now *The Sopranos* played at deafening volume. She turned to Judith. "Where's Nick?"

"He dropped Dennis off and went back to the golf club." The expression on Judith's face that followed this translated, "Don't ask me."

Sometimes Audra wished that Reese would just cut her losses and start over. Nick Klam was piece-of-shit-brother-in-law personified.

When she entered the garage, Audra stood back and watched George for a few minutes. It was pretty sexy to watch a guy who was totally caught up in a task he did well. "Hey, can I get you something to drink?"

George made a final adjustment and looked up. The weight bench was fully assembled now. He reached for a bottle of Miller Lite and drank deep. "Your mom brought me a beer."

Audra sat down and smoothed her hand along the bench's leather padding. "Josh is so excited about this." She smiled. "He thinks you're cool."

"I am cool. Didn't you get the memo?" George grinned.

"You know, I might actually miss you when we get back to L.A. and go our separate ways."

George hesitated. "Me, too."

Audra felt the sting of humiliation before she could sort if out logically. She kept forgetting that this guy was a *professional* date. He wined them. He dined them. He made love to them. Being missed was part of his master plan. It meant the promise of more bookings. "You must think I'm so pathetic."

George's face registered real alarm. "Why do you say that?"

"Because. I'm probably crossing all sorts of lines here. You're obviously trying to think of all the right things to say to keep our *magic* going." Right now she regretted the entire arrangement. "You know, I could probably do this if it were only for a few hours. You know, *wham, bam,* thank you, *sir.* But this is my home. This is my family. It's become so intimate so quickly, and I don't like the way it's making me feel."

"How is that, exactly?"

At first, she just stared at him. "Like a girl who's with a guy because of the way they feel about each other and not because of money exchanging hands." Audra compressed her lips, angry at herself for speaking her heart.

Just as George opened his mouth to answer, Josh came bounding into the garage. "Aunt Audra, look! I think my face has cleared up some!"

"I think you're right," Audra lied. The truth was, Josh's complexion hadn't improved a bit, but he wasn't the only one around here fooling himself.

Her nephew picked up a free weight and raised it over his head.

"Ready to get buff?" George asked.

"Yeah," Josh said.

George clapped his hands and winked at Audra. "Then let's do it, man!"

"Come on, Josh. One more. You can do it."

There was grunting and straining, but the fifteen-year-old lifted the bar once more, then collapsed in satisfied exhaustion.

"Good job, buddy. Good job," Colby said. "That's it, man. You finished your first workout. How does it feel?"

"Can we do it again tomorrow?"

"Hell, yeah. No workout, no Christmas dinner."

Josh, panting hard, wiped the sweat off his brow with a towel.

"Allow me to preach a little. You should be drinking lots of water and cutting back on the candy."

The kid gave him a dutiful nod, saluting him like an army general. "Yes, sir!"

Colby shook his head. "Wiseass. Get out of here!" Playfully, he lurched toward Josh, and the turnaround teen bolted.

It had been tough to give the kid one hundred percent because another issue was stamping around in Colby's brain demanding attention. He had to tell Audra the truth. There was no other way. Besides, he had no intention of accepting her money, so why not drop the act? Oh, man, he wanted to just forget all defenses and circumlocutions and tell her, "I like you. You like me. Let's start the new year off together in L.A. and see what happens." His heart was thrumming now at the prospect.

Colby dashed upstairs, stripped fast, and jumped in the shower. He was determined to get clean and come clean. In that order. He finished up, wrapped a towel around his waist, and headed back to Max's room. What he saw next lit a quick fuse.

Max was hunched over Colby's weekend bag, rifling through his things.

"Hey! What the hell do you think you're doing?" Colby shouted.

Max stood up defiantly.

Colby noticed his wallet in the snoop's right hand. "That's mine."

"No, it's not, *George McCall*. I believe this wallet belongs to a Colby Douglas."

"Give me the wallet, Max."

"But it's not yours, *George.*"

"I would hate to kick your ass right here in your own room. But I will. Now give me the wallet."

Max shook his finger accusingly. "I know what you're up to."

Colby's patience was running out fast. "Oh, yeah? This should be interesting. What?"

"You're using Audra to get close to Ollie."

"Her ex-boyfriend? That's ridiculous."

"No, it's not. Actually, it's quite clever." Max began to pace the room imperiously, as if he were super-sleuth Hercule Poirot at the end of an Agatha Christie who-dunit. "Like any red-blooded American gay male, you find yourself drawn to the powerful homoerotic imagery of Calvin Klein's underwear campaigns. But you're dangerous. You're a man obsessed and willing to take any measure necessary to get close to the most downloaded male model in history . . . *Ollie Brinton.*" Max raised a triumphant fist in the air. "I knew you were gay! I knew it!"

Colby stared back at him in disbelief. "You're insane."

Suddenly, Max dashed out of the room and started down the stairs. "Audra! There's something you should know!"

Colby bolted after him but lost ground when his towel slipped, leaving him buck naked.

At that precise moment, a groggy Reese appeared. She was staring directly into his crotch. "This must be a dream."

"It is. Go back to sleep."

Chapter Nine

Audra stared at the Illinois driver's license, reading the name and casting her eyes on the photograph over and over again.

Colby Alan Douglas.

She could no longer hear the world around her. A rushing sound, like steam, filled her head. Glancing at the staircase, a sudden sense of stark, transfixed fear overwhelmed her. Who *was* this son of a bitch?

Max recounted his colorful theory of a gay fatal attraction.

Judith started for the phone. "I'm calling the police."

For some inexplicable reason, Audra stopped her. "No, not yet."

"But we don't know who this man is!" Judith screeched.

Barbara stepped in. "Yes, we do, dear." She glanced over Audra's shoulder. "His name is Colby Douglas."

"You know what I mean, Mother," Judith snapped.

"I really don't. To be honest, I feel like I know this

young man better than I know Reese's worthless husband."

Audra could hear the synapses firing in her own skull. What the hell was going on? For a moment, she wondered if this was some sick joke being played on her by Rena and September. Or worse, if this Colby Douglas had in some way harmed the real George McCall.

And then the man formerly known as George appeared at the bottom of the stairs half naked, draped only in a towel.

It drove Audra crazy that her first rush of thoughts had everything to do with how sexy he looked. *Concentrate!* But now she was suddenly feverish and experiencing a mounting panic. She would be calm. She would be cool. She would deal with this in an intelligent, rational manner. *Later.* Right now she wanted blood.

Audra grabbed a rolling pin and plunged forward, chasing after him as fast as her legs would go. "You lying bastard!"

But he moved fast, taking several steps at a time, easily outdistancing her, making it to Max's room and locking the door before she even came close to reaching it.

Frustrated and out of breath, Audra shook the knob violently. "What have you done with George McCall? Did you kill him? Is Max right? Are you trying to get to Ollie?"

"Hold on! Stop talking crazy! I can explain!"

Colby pressed his ear to the door, listening intently. He could sense Audra on the other side. Maybe she would hear him out. "Calm down and put the rolling pin away."

"You're in deep shit, aren't you, dude?"

Colby spun around to see Josh slumped near the stereo. "Something like that." He glanced at the kid once more, then turned his palm up. "Give me the candy."

"What candy?"

"I saw the Heath Bar, buddy. Hand it over."

Josh sighed miserably and surrendered the forbidden snack.

Colby slipped it under the waistband of his towel, then refocused on the crisis at hand. "Audra, are you out there?"

She said nothing, but he could hear her breathing. "George McCall is a friend of mine from the air force. He had a scheduling conflict, and I took this booking for him on a lark. I'm sorry. I should've fessed up a long time ago. I fully intended to tonight, but Max beat me to it." He laughed a little. "It's actually kind of funny, when you think about it. Turns out, I'm not an escort. I'm a commercial pilot. I was recently laid off from East/West Airlines, though, so I'm currently unemployed. Listen, if you hear of anything . . ."

Audra cleared her throat and spoke in an exterminating hiss. "I'm going to take a scalding bath and wash off any evidence that you've ever touched me, and when I come out, I want you gone."

And then nothing.

Nervous as hell, Colby tore open the Heath Bar and took a big bite. He glanced over at Josh. "Not bad. A little tough on the teeth, though."

There was the sound of a slamming door. Followed by running water.

Colby looked at Josh again. "I guess she is taking a bath. If only she would talk to me face-to-face. We have a connection. I really believe that I could reason with her."

Josh's eyebrows shot up. "I know another way to get in that bathroom."

"You mean pick the lock?" Colby shook his head. "I couldn't do that."

"No. There's a secret passage. I used to play CIA all the time as a kid. But then I got too fat. Once I got stuck. No one knew where I was for four hours."

"Sounds traumatic. But let's get back to the present."

Josh opened the closet door and pointed to an opening in the back just wide enough for Colby to squeeze through. "Crawl through there and loop all the way around. You'll end up in the linen closet where Aunt Audra's taking a bath."

Colby smiled. "I can do this. It's just weird enough to make me feel okay about it. Could be that I don't know where I'm going. I'm just crawling around and *oops*—stumble upon Audra while she's taking a bath." As he bent over, the Heath Bar dug into his skin. He tossed it to Josh. "Here, take the other half. You've earned it."

The crawl space was cold and dusty and his towel kept slipping, but other than those annoyances, no complaints. Finally, he reached the linen closet and dug through a heap of towels to find the inside door handle. Just as he touched it, Colby lost his balance and went crashing into the bathroom.

Audra screamed. Naturally. It's not every day that a man falls out of a linen closet without warning.

"It's okay. It's okay. It's just me." He stood up and brushed himself off. "Did you know about that passageway? Pretty cool. Josh gave me the heads-up."

"I should have you arrested!"

"Now hold on a minute . . . for what, exactly?"

"Fraud!"

"Easy. Right now you've only got me on a free one-way flight, the shuttle ride here, and a cookie in the mall. I just want to clear the air. I don't expect you to pay me anything."

"Good!"

Her tone bugged him. "Now why is that *good?* I'm well worth the fee we talked about."

Audra snorted. "Do you have any references to back up that claim? Because I have it on good authority that *George McCall* is tops in his field."

"George is adequate. But I've always been better. At everything. Flying, sports—you name it."

"Excuse me, are you forgetting a certain incident in the parking garage?"

"That doesn't count. You bit me."

"I *grazed* you with a tooth. I've popped balloons that went down slower than your—"

"That's it. I want another shot at it. Right here. Right now." He could feel the sexual tension between them. It crackled like a hot wire. Going on pure instinct now, he moved in on her . . .

Audra's mind was still alert with poisoned thoughts of erotic stranger danger. She tried to equalize the noise in her head, eventually giving herself up to this notion of Colby proving the George hype was just that—hype.

"It's time to set the record straight." His voice sliced into the moist air.

Heart in her throat, she watched him, the one she thought had been George McCall, the one she knew was Colby Douglas. For long seconds she tried to focus, all the while thinking this bizarre, deliciously hilarious situation nothing more than a dream.

But it wasn't a dream.

Audra's heart pounded in a familiar rhythm, sending emergency signals to every nerve ending. Somewhere in the silence, doubt began to grow. Was she crazy for doing this? Shivering slightly, hovering on the edge of fear, chilled by alarm in the closed room bathing them in steam heat, she narrowed her eyes, beaming a gaze straight through him.

Obviously certain of his ability to come out on top,

Colby covered her mouth with his lips and pressed his groin against her thigh to announce his proud erection.

She made a weak attempt to push him away, but the hands that pushed became the hands that caressed. Her pulse raced as she assured herself, *This was right. Yes. It had to happen.* She knew Colby's mouth, the way his tongue plundered, the perfect stroke of his touch, the shape and size of his hardness straining against her.

Fear gripped her in a pleasure vise. She had to admit that there was an illicit thrill to the fact that the man whose fingers were buried in her flesh was some phantom lover who had stolen his way into her life. The drums beat in her stomach. It was all a game. He had played it to the hilt. So would she.

Stabbed by desire, Audra moaned. Her towel was rucked up, almost exposing her as he ground himself into her thigh, his hands feeling the shape of her breasts under the thick, plush cotton. She stopped breathing, her stomach muscles clenched tight, her fingers working without hesitation, to peel the towel away from his waist, to expose him totally.

In response he gave the top of hers a fast yank, his hands cupping her bare breasts with immediate need, teasing their distended tips with the warm wetness of his tongue and gentle nips of his teeth.

Against her thigh Audra felt it. He had reached the point of no return, the split second that separates desire from everything else in the world. No risk, no consequence would supersede his need to enter her, to be enclosed by her tightness and warmth. She was the absolute focus of all his wanting, and the realization filled her with an intoxicating power.

Her towel no longer served a purpose. It was pushed down at the top, shoved up at the bottom, and the only thing that saved it from a fast trip to the tile under their bare feet was Colby's flat torso pressed against hers, trapping it. Audra felt for his hair, already damp with sweat, and yanked it up, pulling his mouth away from her breasts.

She took his lower lip between her own and sucked greedily, then bit down, hard enough to deliver a little pain, but soft enough to make him love it. His grunt was all the proof she needed that he did—love it, her aggression, her sense of sexual adventure, her willing body. But the one question clamping down on her pleasure, amidst the mad, wild groping and thirsty kissing, was a simple one. Was this *real*?

Because Audra had a feeling about Colby Douglas. If they said good-bye tomorrow, there would always be that gnawing question deep inside her mind. What if he had been the one?

Let's go for it.

She wanted to cry out the words, but she bit down on her own lip this time to keep them locked inside.

Lost to all tenderness, Colby flung her worthless towel down to the floor next to his own and cupped her buttocks in a steel grip as he entered her in one fast, fluid movement. He was rough and ruthless and impatient and for one heart-pounding, dangerous second she wondered if everything he told her had been true.

Audra's practical mind told her to stop, to demand that he leave, but instead she succumbed to the need spiraling through her and jackknifed her legs around him, pushing away the tiny terror of the unknown.

Colby wrapped his arms around her, burying his head between her neck and shoulder, thrusting into her with relentless, hard-driving strokes almost criminal in their raw need.

She breathed in his craving, her mouth open in an unuttered plea of gratitude for the primitive act. Her own brutality shocked and amazed her as he pounded into her wanting, welcoming body.

With a buck and a shudder, Colby let out an animal cry. She felt him bursting inside her, the relief of his tension, the triumph of his ecstasy. It all flooded through him at the end of his final thrust.

At that moment Audra let herself go, bracing herself for the eye of the body storm, clawing at him as he baptized her with the milky gift of his desire, panting into the misty silence as peace descended.

Colby said nothing. His arms gripped around her and his face out of view, he just held her, still inside, forever silent. Nothing but heavy, satisfied breathing. Finally, he spoke. "Still wondering about George?"

"Who's George?" Audra whispered.

Epilogue

A turgid remix of Cher's "Song for the Lonely" thrashed from the state-of-the-art JBL speakers at Cardio Barre in Studio City, California.

"Lift those knees!" The instructor, a beautiful black girl with the abs of Janet Jackson, the face of Halle Berry, and the lungs of Jessye Norman, barked the orders from a headset mike.

Audra, drenched in sweat, pumped hard, determined to punish herself for all those Christmas calories.

Rena, a formally trained dancer who once spent a year on tour with the Rockettes, kicked like a showgirl, making it look all too easy.

Poor September had stopped altogether. "This bitch wants to kill us!"

When the torture ended, they huddled together, downing big bottles of Propel Fitness Water and chatting up former *Beverly Hills 90210* star Tiffani Theissen, who kept up better than anyone else and had the body to show for it.

"I've never seen the class this crowded," Tiffani was saying.

"It's the week after New Year's, honey," September explained. "Most people will abandon their resolution next month. Like me."

Everybody laughed.

Tiffani moved on.

"Who's up for lunch at Eat Well and then a little shopping?" Rena asked.

September signed up right away.

Audra begged off. "Sounds like fun, girls, but I've got just enough time to shower, change, and make it to the airport."

"That's right. You *really* work for a living," Rena said.

"At least finish your story," September insisted.

"I did. That's all there is to it. He never called."

September let out a frustrated groan. "Christ, doesn't it always work out that way? The losers you don't want to hear from become instant stalkers. The great ones fall into a well like Baby Jessica. You know, a therapist once told me that a man's emotional voice will atrophy by the time he's five years old. If you don't hook them in preschool, it's hopeless. So don't beat yourself up."

Audra shrugged. "There's always the real George McCall."

"Not anymore," Rena said. She sighed wistfully. "He retired on New Year's Eve."

A look of panic flashed across September's face. "What do you mean he *retired?*"

"He's starting his own business," Rena said. "But the other night he gave me a farewell session to celebrate my divorce. Took me to dinner at Balboa, too. And he wouldn't let me pay. It was like a real date. Very romantic."

September huffed. "Well, he owes me a freebie, too. With all the referrals, I'm the reason that bastard can start his own business. I should sue him."

"Call my brother-in-law," Audra said. "He's an attorney."

"Is he any good?" September asked. "Because my guy is really sleazy."

Audra laughed and started for the parking lot. "Better stick with him." She tumbled into her car and checked her cell phone. Two missed calls. Both from Reese. Worried, she dialed home right away.

Her sister picked up on the first ring. "Guess what? I got a job!"

"Congratulations!"

"It's just answering phones right now, but if things work out, I'll be groomed as a junior publicist. Of course, the pay sucks."

"Hey, you have to start somewhere," Audra said. "And you're welcome to stay with me for as long as you need to. There's plenty of room, and I travel all the time."

"My boss is awesome. Her name's Kitty Bishop, and she tells everybody where to go. She doesn't care who they are. While I was there this morning, she screamed at Katie Couric. Can you believe that? God, I'm so excited! I haven't thought about Nick one time today. Well, until now."

"This is a whole new life for you, Reese. I'm so thankful you didn't have kids with him."

"Me, too. Kitty doesn't hire anyone with kids or pets. I'm on probation just for liking houseplants. Anyway, I'm off to shop for work clothes. Kitty says a publicist should look like a million bucks."

"Take my Saks card. It's in the top drawer of my desk in the study. Don't spend a million, though. I'll see you when I get back from New York. Be careful."

"Rena's taking me to Spago tonight. We're going to swap stories about why we left our jerky husbands."

"Sounds cathartic. Have fun." She signed off, thrilled that Nick was out of Reese's life for good. He simply didn't deserve her. Everything had reached a boiling point on Christmas Day when Reese opened Nick's gift to her—a fondue set. It wasn't as heavy as an iron, so the wall damage was minimal.

Audra was sitting in total gridlock now. Some dope had run out of gas on the freeway. People were honking, screaming, and making obscene gestures. At first, she got tense, then realized that she had plenty of time and just relaxed.

Besides, her Mariah moment had happened on Christmas morning, before Reese had flung the fondue set and after opening her mother's gift—a collection of lesbian erotica. Actually, it was pretty hot. She'd read some on the flight back and intended to make a certain section required reading for the next guy she dated. At the time, though, receiving it had pushed her over the edge, considering the fact that Colby had left abruptly to join his own family in Vail and Max had just cornered her to share his suspicions about Batman's relationship with Robin. Though it hadn't been a total meltdown, she had been given a brown paper bag to breathe into at one point.

Her emotional crisis was helped along by the fact that no one in her family really cared that she had hired a male escort to play holiday boyfriend. With Reese's breakup, Josh's improved skin and commitment to working out, and Max's new theory about President Bush and Dick Cheney, her scandal had been all but ignored.

Movement at last! Audra made it home, showered quickly, grabbed her prepacked travel bag, and found herself back in the car, racing toward LAX. A former protege was suing designer Ian St. Claire, and depositions had been scheduled early tomorrow morning in Manhattan.

The King Air was on the tarmac. But no sign of the flight crew. Audra boarded the aircraft anyway, buckled herself in, and began combing through the complaint papers against St. Claire. This was a bogus case. Everything added up to sour grapes. The ex-employee in question had been through three rehab programs in a single calendar year (all generously paid for by the company) before finally being pink-slipped.

She was deep into her reading and hardly noticed the pilot and copilot take their positions. It was only after takeoff that Audra came up for air. Grabbing an orange juice from the half-fridge, she knocked on the thin cockpit door.

A man she didn't recognize answered it. "Everything okay, Ms. Jarecki?"

Hello. Audra was taken aback. The copilot was drop-dead gorgeous. "I'm fine. Just wanted to say hello to Mason."

"He's flying another aircraft today. I'll let him know that you asked about him."

Audra nodded her thanks and returned to her seat, still swooning a little. But then she scolded herself. A slide show featuring Ollie and Colby flashed in her mind. Great-looking men were a pain in the ass. Next time out she wanted a pudgy average guy who wouldn't give her any headaches.

Suddenly, the cockpit door opened.

She glanced up and was instantly abloom with heat and anxiety, heart pounding beneath her breastbone.

There stood Colby Douglas. He wore creased black slacks and a crisp white pilot's shirt, and he was smiling at her. "Happy New Year, Audra."

Okay, forget that crap about pudgy average guy. She'd take her chances on the troublemakers any day. "What are you doing here? I don't understand."

"I'm the new owner of this leasing company. By the way, the guy you just met is the real George McCall. He's my business partner."

Audra couldn't believe it. She merely sat there, too stunned to speak.

"I'm sorry about leaving so abruptly on Christmas. Remember that issue with my younger brother that I mentioned?"

She nodded, already feeling a sense of giddy elation.

"He needed me. The same girl who did a number on me dug her high heel into his heart, too. He was torn up about it real bad. I've never heard him sound like that before."

"Who is this girl?"

"Natalie. She's an aspiring reality TV star. Just hasn't found the right show. If anyone decides to produce *Who Wants to Marry the Antichrist?* . . ."

Audra laughed.

"Mikey's an idiot ninety percent of the time, but I've only got one brother, so I can't be choosy."

"When it comes to family, we have to play the hand we're dealt."

"Nicely said."

Audra looked at him, feeling like her eyes were lit up with a thousand watts. There was an uptick of adrenaline, and after five or six seconds, the silence seemed to sizzle. She wondered what would happen next.

Colby loosened his tie. "Want to hear something funny?"

She nodded, teetering on the precipice of an animal urge to ravish him.

"With all the flying I've done over the years, I've never made it into the Mile High Club . . ."

Audra unhooked her seat belt and rushed into his arms. "Captain Douglas, you are cleared for landing."

Darling!

Happy Holidays! I hope you had fun with this naughty little novella. I certainly had a blast turning *Pretty Woman* on its ear. Enough stories about the hooker with the heart of gold. There must be plenty of studs out there hoping to find their *Princess* Charming.

Did you know that there's a very famous actor who early in his career made a living just like George McCall? I swear! But I can't name names, darling. I'd get sued within an inch of my life. All I know is this: There are some women in Hollywood who still have smiles on their Botox-perfect faces. Okay, I've revealed too much.

If you want more of the wild September Moore, check out my second full-length novel, BABY, BABY, released a few months ago. She'll have you howling for more in that one. And for the origin of Audra's clients Sofia and Ben Estes, you simply must read FLY ME TO THE MOON. That was my first book. I'm kind of sweet on it.

Anyway, here's wishing you a healthy holiday season and a new year that brings all your dreams full circle. I'll be back next summer with EX-GIRL-FRIENDS. So prepare yourself, darling! It's going to be a wild and crazy trip.

Air kisses,
Kylie

P.S. Visit me on the Web at www.kylieadams.com and join my VIP section to receive my e-newsletter. Or write c/o Zebra Books, 850 Third Avenue, New York, NY 10022.

Under the Mistletoe
Elaine Coffman

Chapter One

Holly Winter always did everything right.

She was a WASP, a Southern Belle if there ever was one, and she always did everything in the proper way. It was something she had learned early, a sort of woman's tradition taught from birth and passed down, mother to daughter, generation after generation.

Because it was expected of her, and sanctioned, she was a popular girl who graduated from high school at the head of her class. In college, she spent four years as a cheerleader. As expected, she was also a sorority girl—Kappa Kappa Gamma, since Mama and Aunt Gracie had been Kappas—a debutante, and a Peach Blossom Princess.

Even before she graduated and became a member of the Junior League, Holly knew one never, ever wore white before Easter, velvet after Valentine's Day, or patent leather after Labor Day. She knew which fork to use, and which spoon, too, and sitting at a table with five wineglasses flustered her not in the least.

At home, she had the acceptable china pattern, silver

napkin rings monogrammed with her grandmother's initials, and traditional furniture. She always wrote thank-you notes, hung seasonal wreaths on her front door, wore David Yurman jewelry with casual wear, and owned a long denim skirt. As her mama had long been fond of saying, "The first thing little Holly learned to read was the Neiman-Marcus catalog."

There was no denying that Holly Winter was just about as Southern and proper as a body could be. There was never a time in her life when she could recall not doing things in the time-honored and traditional way. In fact, it could be said she never, ever did anything that went against the grain of her Southern upbringing.

With one exception, that is, and that was the big M.

The big M. It stood for a lot of things, but mostly it stood for marriage—an area Holly had tried often, and just as often with poor results. It was sad to admit and sorely true. When it came to marriage, Holly Winter failed. Miserably.

Here she was, thirty-five years old and she had three marriages under her belt.

She didn't understand it. *Marriage* was such a noble word, a time-honored word. "The union of beauty and blood," as her Aunt Gracie liked to say. Well, if she was traditional and marriage was traditional, then why did the two of them mix like oil and water? What a disappointment she must be. Here she was, the only woman in her family for generations who did not succeed at marriage, and they had tried it only once. Married for a lifetime to one man? Holly didn't know how they did it.

"Your father and I were married for fifty-six years before he died," her mother loved to remind her.

"I know, Mama, but times are different now."

"Posh! Times aren't different. It's you that's different. I honestly don't understand what happened to you, Holly. Such a beauty, and our family saturated with fine

Southern blood. You were always such a sensible girl. You never gave me a moment's worry. I would have thought you, of all people, would make a stable, long-lasting marriage. I don't understand it. Here your sister was as shallow and flighty as they come, and what came of it? Ruth has been married for ten years."

"I was married for eight years, Mama."

"A *total* of eight years . . . and not to the same man, I might add."

"The same man? Gee, I didn't realize that was one of the rules."

"Don't raise your eyes to heaven. God won't help you. And I didn't raise you to be sassy, Holly Noel. As for the other, of course you didn't realize that was one of the rules, because you allowed that artsy crowd at the university to make a Bohemian out of you. There was a time I was certain you were going to throw tradition out the window and succumb to their influence. I'll never understand why you wanted to major in art any more than I'll understand where that rebellious streak in you came from. Lord knows, I did the best I could. An angel could have done no better."

"Some people were destined not to be happy. I guess I was one of them."

"So who's happy? Cows in the field are happy. You don't have to be happy to stay married. It was majoring in art that started you off on the wrong foot."

"I don't think my problems are all related to my being an art major, Mama."

"They are, and don't contradict your mother. Lord knows I did everything I could to convince you to major in home economics or English. Why, I would have even settled for a schoolteacher. But an artist? There has never been an artist in the Carpenter family and for good reason."

"I minored in English."

"And a lot of good it did you. Look at you . . . three

marriages and not one of them took. I thought I'd never hear myself say this, but I wish we'd been Catholics— then you could become a nun. But we aren't Catholic, so perhaps you should just give up on marriage altogether.''

"I have, Mama. Believe me, I have."

When Holly said that, she was being truthful. She had decided some time ago that marriage was not for her. Although she would have to admit it was beyond her, just why was it that she failed so miserably in something she had tried so often?

Didn't practice make perfect?

Heaven only knew it wasn't because she didn't try to be the perfect wife, or keep the perfect house, raise the perfect 2.5 children, belong to the right clubs, or cook Martha Stewart meals. It wasn't because she wasn't pretty, or didn't keep herself trim and well-groomed. She did all of these things, but even then, perfection always seemed to be just beyond her grasp.

Perhaps her mother was right. Perhaps she was a Bohemian. She was an artist, and in her mother's book, the two were synonymous. "It comes from your father's side, you know. No one ever did know anything about your father's great-grandmother, on the maternal side. On every family tree, her background is as blank as an idiot's face. She could have been a gypsy, for all we know. They say blood will tell." Then she would look at Holly, shake her head, and sigh. "Blood will tell."

Blood must have told, and because of the streak of Bohemian in her, the free spirit in Holly was sometimes at war with her conservative Southern upbringing. But even then, when the artist and the Southern belle seemed to be at cross-purposes, it was breeding and tradition that won out. At least, most of the time.

Chapter Two

Stanley Levine was not a married man. He had never been married. And he never wanted to be married.

He might have been married . . . if he had grown up around women. But he did not. He was raised in an all-male, Jewish household, where women were as mysterious as outer space and just about as accessible.

Stanley was a psychiatrist, but he didn't know anything about women. It wasn't that he had anything against women, or marriage either, for that matter. It was simply that Stanley knew very little about either one of them. To him, women were like Tibetan monks: He knew they existed, but he had no first-hand knowledge. As for marriage, most of his dealings with that had been with broken ones. He rarely saw the reasons why people marry, only the reasons why they didn't want to stay that way.

Stanley's mother died when he was born and he had been raised by his father, grandfather, and bachelor uncle, so it seemed the natural thing to him to remain single. So far, he hadn't met the woman who made him want to change his mind.

Stanley had been born Jewish some forty years ago, but he wasn't much of anything now. What he was, was Ivy League to the core—Rhode Island born, educated at Yale and Johns Hopkins, where he graduated with honors. His family was fairly poor, and he had attended college on scholarship. He had almost married once, when he was in medical school, but that had ended bitterly, and after that, Stanley considered himself a bachelor. His one disastrous relationship left him with a determination to avoid women. Seeing what marriage did to people made him avoid that as well.

Stanley went out of his way to avoid them. He did not like talkative women, or pretty women, or short ones, and he especially did not like flashy blondes.

Five years ago, he was a successful psychiatrist in New York, but he wasn't happy. He knew something was missing, but he didn't know just what. He only knew that his life was artificial and phony, that he felt less human and more plastic as the days came and went. Until one morning when that all changed.

Stanley received a phone call from an attorney in Charlottesville, Virginia. "I've got great news for you, Dr. Levine. Your great-aunt Sylvia has died."

"You call that great news?"

"I mean she has died and left you her entire estate."

"Which is?"

"A small sum of money and a lovely house in Georgia."

The house, the lawyer went on to say, was in a small town not far from Atlanta, a place called Peach Orchard, Georgia. The more Stanley thought about living in a small, quaint town with a tranquil name like Peach Orchard, the more he thought there wasn't a plastic sounding thing about it. So, he decided to move there.

He sold his medical practice. He resigned from all

his boards and clubs. He sold his apartment on East Fifty-seventh Street. He bought a Range Rover, loaded up his mastiff, Plato, and left everything else to United Van Lines.

He never regretted that move. Not once. His life in Georgia was peaceful. Here he was finding the thing he had searched for. Life had meaning. It had purpose. And he hadn't given up a thing.

He still had his psychiatry practice, but now he had time for a lot of other interests, too. He taught a couple of courses at the local junior college, and he had taken up gardening. Life was good. He had a beautiful yard, a housekeeper who was deaf, and a dog who knew better than to set foot in one of his flowerbeds. His life was just the way he liked it—predictable, orderly, and serene.

Until *she* moved in next door.

Chapter Three

Holly Winter was born thirty-five years ago on Christmas Day. In honor of the occasion, her father had insisted upon naming her Noel. Holly's mother wasn't about to stick her daughter with a foreign name, so she held out for "Holly" and threatened to chain herself to the hospital bed until she got her way.

In the end, they compromised and named their daughter Holly Noel. In the beginning, Holly's full name was Holly Noel Carpenter. Now it was Holly Noel Carpenter Alexander Nichols Winter, although that wasn't her mother's doing, or her father's either. It was the marriages.

All three of them.

When Holly entered the University of Alabama, her name was Holly Noel Carpenter, but by the time she graduated, she was Holly Noel Alexander. That was because she married, just two weeks before graduation, the Crimson Tide's All American and first-round draft choice for the Houston Oilers, Buck Alexander. That

If the Free Book Certificate is missing, call 1-800-770-1963 to place your order. Be sure to visit our website at www.kensingtonbooks.com.

To start your membership, simply complete and return the Free Book Certificate. You'll receive your Introductory Shipment of FREE Zebra Contemporary Romances. Then, each month as long as your account is in good standing, you will receive the 3 newest Zebra Contemporary Romances. Each shipment will be yours to examine for 10 days. If you decide to keep the books, you'll pay the preferred book club member price of $15.95 – a savings of up to 20% off the cover price! (plus $1.99 to offset the cost of shipping and handling.) If you want us to stop sending books, just say the word... it's that simple.

BOOK CERTIFICATE

Yes! Please send me FREE Zebra Contemporary romance novels. I only pay for shipping and handling. I understand I am under no obligation to purchase any books, as explained on this card.

Name _____

Address _____ Apt._____

City _____ State _____ Zip _____

Telephone (___) _____

Signature _____

(If under 18, parent or guardian must sign)

Offer limited to one per household and not valid to current subscribers.
All orders subject to approval. Terms, offer, and price subject to change. Offer valid only in the U.S.

Thank You!

CNHL2A

THE BENEFITS
OF BOOK CLUB
MEMBERSHIP

- You'll get your books hot off the press, usually before they appear in bookstores.

- You'll ALWAYS save up to 20% off the cover price.

- You'll get our FREE monthly newsletter filled with author interviews, book previews, special offers, and MORE!

- There's no obligation — you can cancel at any time and you have no minimum number of books to buy.

- And – if you decide you don't like the books you receive, you can return them. (You always have ten days to decide.)

lll.ı.ıı.lll....lll.ı.l.l.ıl..ıl..ll..ıll..lll..l

Zebra Contemporary Romance Book Club
Zebra Home Subscription Service, Inc.
P.O. Box 5214
Clifton , NJ 07015-5214

marriage lasted two years, producing a set of twin girls and a divorce decree.

The twins were nine months old when Holly was offered a job as a graphic artist with a small printing company in Birmingham, Alabama. Before making the final decision, Holly called her lifelong friend, Heather.

Heather Landry had been Holly's best friend back in Peach Orchard, Georgia. They had been friends since kindergarten. After college, Heather, who was now a veterinarian, returned to their hometown to open her practice as the only vet in Peach Orchard.

Because Holly and Heather were still best friends, it was only natural that two years after moving to Birmingham, Heather was the first person Holly called to break the news.

"Heather, guess what! I'm getting married."

"Oh, Holly, that's wonderful. I'm so happy for you. Is it anyone I know?"

"No, but you'll love him. I've told him all about you. Please say you'll come to the wedding. I want you to be my maid of honor."

"I don't know. Maybe that would be bad luck. I was your maid of honor when you married Buck. Isn't there a rule against having the same maid of honor twice?"

"Don't be silly. I don't think there is such a rule, but even if there was, it wouldn't matter. You're my best friend. I couldn't get married without you. I want you there."

"Okay, but do me a favor."

"What?"

"This time, don't wear a veil."

"Why not?"

"You need to see what you're getting."

Holly didn't wear a veil when she married Edward Nichols, a successful Birmingham attorney. Ed had a lucrative practice, a half-million-dollar inheritance, and an ex-wife. Holly's marriage to Ed produced a daughter,

Maudie, born three months before Edward discovered his divorce from his first wife wasn't legal. By the time he had all the mess cleared up, he and his first wife decided they wanted to be together again. By this time, Holly decided they deserved each other.

She told Edward he had to marry her in order to give Maudie his name, agreeing to a divorce as soon as the marriage was legal. She kept her word and they divorced. Holly always wondered if she insisted on the marriage for Maudie, or if she did it for spite. Perhaps it was both.

After her second divorce, Holly decided it was time to forget men and concentrate on her career. While working for Southern Star Graphics, she illustrated a children's book for a college friend, and a new career was born. It was something she loved and because of the children, perfect for her. She made more money than she did as a graphic artist, and even better, it was something she could do at home. With three children, two of them twins, home is where she was needed.

A year or so later, Holly was reading an article about the death of Jacqueline Kennedy Onassis to Heather over the phone one afternoon. In the article, Jackie was quoted as saying, "You marry the first time for love, the second for money, and the third for companionship." She paused, then went on. "My marriages might not have worked out, but at least I can say I did them in the right order. I have only one of the three left. Companionship."

"Are you trying to tell me something?" Heather asked. "Do I need to dig out my maid of honor outfit?"

"No. Keep it put away . . . at least for now."

"I thought you'd sworn off men."

"I have, but if I ever do marry again, it'll be for companionship, nothing more."

"I don't know, Holly. If I were you and I wanted companionship, I'd get a dog."

Holly got a cat instead—a calico Persian with a harelip and crossed eyes. She named the cat Sweetie Pie.

It was a full year later when Holly made another call to Heather and asked, "Do you know where the maid of honor outfit is?"

"Oh God, I knew you should've gotten the dog. You aren't going to get married again, are you? It isn't fair. This is your third and I haven't had *one.*"

"Don't say a word until you hear who I'm going to marry. You simply won't believe it, Heather. Who's the last person in the world you'd expect me to marry?"

"The President."

"Be serious."

"Okay. I can't imagine who you're going to marry, so you'll have to tell me who it is."

"Remember Bill Winter?"

"Bill Winter . . . You don't mean little Billy Winter . . . down the street from us? That Billy Winter?"

"The same."

"Well, wonders never cease to amaze me. Where did your two planets collide? How on earth did the two of you ever get together? Billy's been history for so long, I'd almost forgotten him. Tell me how this came about."

"At our high school reunion. Oh, Heather, it was simply wonderful. I'm ever so happy I went. I wish you could have been there. It's a shame you weren't, especially since you live right there."

"No one in their right mind would turn down a month in Europe to go to their high school reunion. At least, not *our* high school reunion, or Billy Winter, either. There were only thirty-five kids in our whole graduating class. I didn't like thirty-four of them."

"I thought you liked Bill."

"You know I always liked Bill. I hated you for two years, just because he liked you better than me. Remember?"

Holly remembered and smiled. It had been such a long time ago that Bill and his family moved down the street from Holly's family. Bill was seven at the time. Holly was five.

Heather, Holly, and Billy were always close friends and together constantly—save the two years Heather hated her. By the time they were in junior high, Billy and Holly were going steady. She wore his basketball on a chain around her neck for years. They dated all through high school, then broke up after graduation, when Bill couldn't talk Holly into going with him to Dartmouth. Instead, Holly did as her family wanted. She went to their alma mater, the University of Alabama.

Holly hadn't seen Billy for years, not since high school. She might not have seen him this time, either, if she hadn't decided at the last minute to attend her high school reunion. Once she saw him, that was it. One look was all it took. They married two months later.

Happier than she could ever remember, Holly and Bill were elated when they were blessed with another addition to their family. Their daughter, Genny, was ten months old when Holly found out she was pregnant again. Five months into her pregnancy, Bill was killed in a plane crash.

It happened just before Thanksgiving. Holly and Bill flew their Cessna to Savannah to pick up Holly's sister and brother-in-law and the four of them flew back to Atlanta for a football game. After the game, on the way back to Savannah, Bill's plane crashed during a thunderstorm. Bill, Holly's sister, Ruth, and Ruth's husband, David, were all killed. Only Holly survived. Miraculously, she had only a few scratches and a broken collarbone, but the worst thing that happened to her was losing the baby she carried.

When they were children growing up, Holly and Ruth had always been close. Out of this closeness came the promise that if anything ever happened to one of them, the other one would raise their children together. Naturally, taking Ruth's children to raise with her own children wasn't something Holly had to think twice about. Ruth was her sister. Her only sibling. It was the natural thing to do. The day after she was released from the hospital, she went to Savannah to get her sister's children. Ruth had three daughters, April, Erin, and Katie. Their ages were eight, six, and four.

That made seven girls for Holly to raise: seven little girls whose ages were two, four, five, six, eight, and the twins, who were nine.

That was a lot of girls and they drew a great deal of attention wherever they went. From time to time, someone would ask Holly if she wanted any more kids. To that, she would always reply, "I wouldn't give you a nickel for another one, and I wouldn't take a million dollars for the ones I've got."

Holly adored her children. All seven of them. Raising seven kids wasn't easy, but thankfully, Holly had her housekeeper, Ernestine, and the children's nanny, Esmeralda. Ernestine and Esmeralda, the two Es, whom the kids started calling ER and ES.

Seven kids, a housekeeper and a nanny, plus Holly, made ten women. Even Sweetie Pie, was a female. So for the Winter household, there was nary a male in the place. And that was the way they liked it.

A few months after the plane crash, Holly's mother died. Holly put the family home in Peach Orchard, Georgia, up for sale immediately, but people didn't move to Peach Orchard in great numbers, and so her family home remained on the market.

It was about a year later, when her mother's home was still on the market and not a buyer in sight, that Holly's grief became bearable and her head began to clear. One of the first things she did was to make some important decisions.

Holly's home in Birmingham was large, but it wasn't

large enough. Soon, she realized that with a bigger family, she needed a bigger house. That was when she struck upon the idea of taking her girls back to Peach Orchard. Somehow it seemed fitting that Ruth's daughters be raised in their mother's former home. Besides, it was a good business decision. Holly's house in Birmingham was easier to sell.

It was the perfect idea, to raise the children in a small town and to live in the house where she had grown up.

The house was wonderful, a huge, roomy place where she and Ruth grew up, loved and nurtured, a haven with three floors and eight bedrooms. It was on the corner of the street, on a beautiful, tree-shaded lot. It had been a plantation at one time, and had been in her mother's family since before the Civil War. The land had been sold off bit by bit over the years, until a little less than two acres remained, but that was more than enough for Holly and the girls.

As soon as she made the decision, Holly called Heather. "I'm coming home. The girls and I are moving into our old house on Orchard Street."

"You don't mean it. You're moving home? Really?"

"Really and truly. We're going to live in our old house. Can you think of anything better than that?"

"Your mama's place? Oh, Holly, that's perfect. And you're right. I couldn't think of a better place. That's a grand idea. We'll be together again, just like we were when we were growing up. I can't believe it. You, living here . . . just half a mile from me!" Suddenly, Heather fell silent.

Holly wondered what she was thinking. "What is it?"

"Oh, nothing. I was just wondering."

"About what?"

"You don't think you'll get bored living in a small town, do you?"

"No, and besides, I need a vet for Sweetie Pie—one that won't laugh whenever I take her in for her shots."

"Holly, I can't promise I won't laugh. I don't see many harelipped, cross-eyed cats. It's difficult to keep a straight face around her."

"She's a pure-bred Persian. Her mama and daddy were champions."

"Her mama and daddy were probably first cousins and that's why she's harelipped and cross-eyed, but if that's the only way I can get you back here, then I'll promise not to laugh. When are you coming?"

"As soon as I can make arrangements. Do you think Peach Orchard is ready for ten unattached females to descend upon it?"

"Sure. As long as you don't plan on getting married and adding more."

"Oh, don't worry about that. I'm definitely through with marriage. No more men for me. After three strikes, I'm out."

"You mean I can retire the maid of honor outfit?"

"Burn it. Shred it. I don't care."

"Gosh, I don't know. I've sort of gotten attached to it. After all, I've worn it enough. I think I'll hang on to it, just for sentimental reasons."

"Oh, Heather, why don't you get rid of it?"

"Because I think I'll make you wear it when *I* get married."

"You wouldn't dare! It's horribly out of style."

"You didn't say that when *I* had to wear it."

Two months later, Holly moved back home. At last, she and her children could live in peace on Orchard Street, far away from the haunts of single men and the threat of marriage.

And that was the way Holly wanted it.

Chapter Four

Stanley was standing in his front yard, watering his flowers, his faithful mastiff, Plato, lying nearby. Stanley was conversing with Merv Arnold, his neighbor from across the street.

Merv had been there for a while, watching Stanley water, making small talk, when he stopped talking and studied the yard next door. "When did they take the sign down?"

"What sign?"

"The 'For Sale' sign that was in the yard of old Mrs. Carpenter's place."

Stanley glanced toward the yard next door, searching the overgrown lawn for the spot where the sign had been. He gave the petunias another squirt. "I don't know. I hadn't noticed it was gone until you mentioned it."

"I suppose that means we'll be getting some new neighbors pretty soon." Merv wiped the beads of sweat from the top of his bald head, turning his red, round face toward the light, like a sunflower following the sun. "I know you must be happy to see the place sell."

"Why is that?"

"The yard, man. I've never seen it looking so seedy. Living next door to that eyesore, I'd think you'd be hoping the new owner would do something about it. You've gotta admit that next to your well-kept yard, it looks pretty lethal. Needs a good shot of fertilizer, a couple of mowings, and a whole lot of water."

Stanley gave the yard a critical going-over this time, not that he needed to. It had been a source of irritation to him to have his beautiful flowers humiliated by that hideously kept yard next door. "It's pretty dismal-looking, all right."

"Who do you suppose bought it?"

Stanley shrugged. "I don't know, but I know one thing."

"What's that?"

"I hope they don't have any kids."

A few days later, on a sunny Saturday morning, Stanley stood watering that same flowerbed, his jaw slack as he watched the van from hell pull into the driveway next door.

Plato noticed it, too, and came trotting over to Stanley. He barked a couple of times, but when Stanley said, "No," he quieted down.

When the minivan came to a full stop, the driver's door opened and a woman got out. A short woman. A short, pretty woman. A short, pretty, blond woman. He disliked her instantly.

She was everything he did not like in a woman. She was tanned, with medium-length hair, streaked blond and turned under in that Junior League style. She had on a pair of shorts—he had to admit she had nice legs—and Chanel sunglasses. She reminded him of that

German model, Claudia something-or-the-other, who was indefinitely engaged to that magician with the original name, David Copperfield.

He sized her up again. Yes, she had all the attributes he abhorred in a woman. He had been right to dislike her instantly.

She turned around and spoke to someone in the backseat and Stanley cringed, his head drawing down between his shoulders, much in the way one does when fingernails have been scraped across a blackboard. She had a syrupy Southern drawl that was so pronounced that even after she finished talking it seemed to linger heavily in the air. It reminded him of the scent of cheap perfume that clings to an elevator long after the wearer has departed.

One by one, the doors of the mini-van opened and women began to pile out. They kept on coming— women of all ages, nationalities, sizes, shapes, and colors. He had never seen so many females in one vehicle. He had never seen so many kids. Surely to God they weren't all hers. He tried counting them, but they were milling around so much, it was impossible. He looked around for a man. Where was her husband? *Oh God, don't tell me she's divorced.*

And then he saw the cat.

The cat. It didn't look like a cat exactly, but it was a cat. Definitely a cat. He didn't know how he knew it was a cat. But he knew. It sure didn't look like anything Stanley had ever seen. It was one of those flat-faced cats, the kind that look like someone slipped up behind them and slapped them in the face with a shovel. Only this cat was unbelievably ugly—an orange color with brown and black mottling. When it looked up at him, its eyes were also orange, but what made him laugh was the fact that they were as crossed as hell.

He couldn't concentrate on the eyes for long, for there was something peculiar about the cat's face—

something beyond the fact that it was flat. He had to study it for a minute before he realized what it was. The cat's tongue stuck out, even when its mouth was closed. Harelipped? A harelipped cat? Was there such a thing? Stanley narrowed his eyes and looked again. Apparently there was.

The blonde was holding the cat. She looked at him and smiled. "Hello," she said.

Stanley nodded. "Hello."

She looked like she was about to say something, then changed her mind. She put the cat down to take a little kid from a Hispanic woman. The Hispanic was talking up a blue streak, but since Stanley did not speak Spanish, he had no idea what she was saying. He didn't get a chance to observe anything further, for about that time all hell broke loose.

Stanley knew the exact moment Plato saw the cat, because he tore through the flowerbed, barking and running straight toward the cat. Stanley grinned, then turned his head, looking innocently in another direction. He squirted water over the periwinkles, whistling a little ditty, keeping watch out of the corner of his eye. Plato would make fast work of that damn ugly cat.

About that time, Merv crossed the street and walked toward Stanley. In the midst of all the barking and hissing, Merv said, "Looks like Plato has found a new playmate. Are these the folks that will be moving in?"

Stanley didn't take his eyes off Plato, who was barking in earnest now. "I'm afraid it looks that way."

Merv chuckled. "Looks like Plato has the cat cornered. Things are about to get interesting."

"It won't take Plato long to make dog food out of that obese cat." Merv laughed outright, but Stanley chuckled to himself as he watched Plato run around to the front of the mini-van.

Plato went down, lying flat in front of the van with

his head just under the bumper. Just a few feet from him, the cat was bristled.

Without warning, the cat suddenly shot out from under the van, arched its back, hissed, and charged Plato. Everything was a blur after that and for a moment, it was difficult to see just where Plato left off and the cat began. Stanley had never heard such a ruckus. The cat was meowing and hissing. Plato barked and howled in pain. Two of the kids were calling for the blond to do something and the little one in her arms was bawling its head off.

Tufts of fur floated about the air. Unfortunately, most of them were the same color as Plato. Stanley frowned. This wasn't going exactly as he planned. Suddenly, Plato let out a loud, painful howl and to Stanley's mortification, tucked his tail between his legs and came tearing home, dashing through the flowerbed, throwing up clods of dirt as he went. He picked up speed when the obese cat took up the chase.

Merv busted out laughing. "When do you reckon Plato's going to show him who's boss?"

It was too humiliating for words. It was also the first time Stanley had ever walked into the house and left Merv collapsing with laughter on the front lawn, the hose going full blast, water running down the driveway and into the street.

Once he was inside, Stanley went to the window and peeked out. The woman was holding the cat again, petting and soothing it as she talked to a tall black woman. The two of them kept looking toward his house. The kids were running all over the place, so it was still difficult to get a head count. Unless he counted some of them twice, Stanley counted ten kids. He prayed some of them were just visiting. He knew the old house next door was big, but it wasn't that big. He saw his orderly and tranquil life slipping away right before his eyes.

Just then, one of the kids threw a ball. It hit the side

of the driveway and rolled into his yard. Stanley stared in horror as three of the girls gave chase, running through his flowerbed, trampling his flowers.

That was when Stanley's mind formed the articles of war.

Chapter Five

Still thinking about the strange man next door, Holly put Sweetie Pie into one of the bedrooms upstairs and scolded her for being so naughty, then went next door.

She rang the bell and heard the dog barking inside. A few seconds later the man she'd seen watering the yard opened the door. He stared at her with stony recognition and said nothing. Holly could not help but notice he looked provoked.

"Hi, I'm Holly Winter. I wanted to apologize for the way my cat behaved. She isn't accustomed to being around other animals. I hope she didn't hurt your dog."

The moment she said those words, Holly knew she had said the wrong thing. She saw the man's mouth tighten as he glanced down at the dog sitting beside him. Holly glanced down, too, and saw the drops of blood on the dog's nose. "Oh, I am terribly sorry," she said, reaching out to pat the dog on the head.

"He'll survive."

"I feel terrible about this. It isn't exactly the right foot to get off on, is it?"

"No, it isn't."

She glanced down at the dog again. "He's a real sweetheart. What's his name?"

"Plato."

At the sound of his name, the dog stood up, looked at Stanley, and wagged his tail.

She smiled. "He's so big."

"Mastiffs are a large breed."

"Yes, I know. We ... that is, I had a mastiff when I lived in Houston, but I had to give him to a friend when I moved."

"If you had that militant cat when you had the dog, I can understand why you had to give him away."

She laughed. "No, I didn't have Sweetie then. I acquired her later."

"Tell me, are all of those children yours?" He almost spit the words at her.

Holly gave him an odd look. This man wasn't bad looking in a rumpled sort of way, but he was definitely a strange egg. She tried to give him a vocation; judging from the way he looked, she decided he was either a teacher or a man who repaired clocks. But his personality belonged to an undertaker. "The children are all mine ... that is, they aren't exactly *mine*, per se, but they all live with me."

"I don't believe you're allowed to take in boarders in this neighborhood."

She felt the desire to be neighborly slipping away. It was replaced with the desire to tell this man what she thought of him. She was on the verge of doing just that when she recalled the words of advice that she had been taught: *Never lower yourself to act like the opposition.*

She forced herself to be nice. "They aren't boarders. Four of the children are mine, the other three are my dead sister's. Do you have something against children?"

"Only when they create a disturbance."

"They're good kids, and they're girls, so I don't think

they'll be causing you any difficulties. If they should bother you, please let me know."

"You can count on it."

Holly tried to see his eyes so she might have some clue as to what made this man tick, but the glare on his glasses prevented her from doing so. You could tell a lot by looking at someone's eyes. He had to be the most unaccommodating man she had ever had the displeasure of meeting. She wondered what his wife looked like and if she was as unaccommodating as he was. "Do you have children?"

"No. I'm not married."

"Oh." She gave an insecure little laugh and could have kicked herself. "I didn't mean to pry, Mr. . . . I'm sorry, I forgot your name."

"I didn't tell you my name, Mrs. Winter. I'm Stanley Levine."

"It's nice to make your acquaintance, Mr. Levine, even under such adverse circumstances. I didn't think I'd meet my first neighbor when I was offering my apologies."

"It's *Dr.* Levine, and unless you keep that cat locked up, you may be meeting all of your neighbors that way. This is a very quiet, orderly neighborhood."

Her temper, which had been simmering on the back burner, was coming to a slow boil. "Yes, I know all about this neighborhood, Dr. Levine. I grew up here. I was raised in that house and my mother and grandmother before me. It's been in my family for generations . . . since the 1830's, I'm told. My mother was Mrs. Carpenter."

"The former occupant?"

"Yes, did you know her?"

"No. When I moved here, the house was vacant and up for sale."

"I listed it with a realtor shortly after my mother's death. When did you move here?"

"About eight months ago."

"Where did you live before?"

"New York."

"Is that your home?"

"I was born in Rhode Island."

"How do you like living in the South?"

"Until today, I liked it fine. I moved here by choice."

She could hear her mother's voice in the back of her head, telling her she would get more with honey than with vinegar. She forced a smile, but it was hard. "Well, if it'll make you rest any easier, I don't think we'll have trouble with Plato and Sweetie for very long. Once they've established their territories and had a few run-ins, they'll learn to avoid each other."

He did not make any observations about her comment.

She let that pass. "What kind of doctor are you?"

"I'm a medical doctor."

"Oh? My father was a doctor. He was a pediatrician. What's your specialty?"

"I'm a psychiatrist."

Those four words explained everything. A psychiatrist. A head shrinker. Just her luck to move next door to him. *Won't he have fun when he finds out I've been married three times?* "And you moved your practice here, to Peach Orchard?" She was aware that she could not keep the tone of amazement out of her voice.

"I did. Do you find that strange?"

She shrugged and rubbed the side of her sandal across the sisal doormat. "In a way, yes, I suppose I do. Peach Orchard is such a small town. I guess I thought we wouldn't have enough problems here to keep someone like you in business. I declare, the closest thing we've had to a psychiatrist was a fortune-teller by the name of Madam Zolta. She used to live in a trailer out on Highway 67."

He ignored the part about Madam Zolta, but she

could tell by the way he gripped the door that it hadn't set well with him. "You'll probably be surprised to learn I stay quite busy. There are plenty of problems here." He gave her a direct look. "And more moving in every day."

She wasn't sure if she should say *touché* or *ouch. He's quick, Holly,* she reminded herself. *You won't be able to let your guard down around him for a minute.* She laughed. "Well, I daresay my little brood is a bit young to be giving anyone severe emotional problems."

"How many kids did you say you had?"

"Seven. Four of mine and three of my sister's. The oldest two are nine-year-old twins."

"And you care for them by yourself . . . without a husband?"

She really laughed at that one. "Dr. Levine, can you imagine anyone in their right mind wanting to marry a woman with seven kids under the age of nine?"

"No," he said rapidly.

"As for help, I have ER and ES."

"ER, as in emergency room?"

She laughed again. "Good analogy, but actually, ER stands for Ernestine and ES stands for Esmeralda. They're my housekeeper and nanny."

About that time, Plato nuzzled Dr. Levine's hand. Holly looked down at the dog and saw his poor nose. "Do you have anything to put on those scratches?"

"Yes, I was just about to put a little ointment on Plato's nose when you came over." He held up a tube of cream. "So, if you'll excuse me . . ."

"Oh, of course. I'm sorry. I didn't mean to take up so much of your time. It was nice to make your acquaintance. Once again, I apologize for the scratches on Plato's nose."

"I think our . . . er, *his* self-esteem suffered the most damage. Good day, Mrs. Winter." He shut the door, leaving her standing there.

Good riddance, Mrs. Winter. Drop dead, Mrs. Winter, and take all your brats with you, Mrs. Winter.

Holly turned away from the door. She might have thought him and his behavior went beyond rude if he had not informed her he was from New York. She had visited New York enough to be familiar with their abrupt ways and lack of gentle breeding.

She crossed the yard and walked home to wait for the moving van to arrive with her furniture, wondering as she went if she and Dr. Levine would learn to politely avoid each other or if they would eventually lock horns again.

ER was standing on the front porch holding two-year-old Genny when Holly came up the steps. "You'll never believe what our neighbor does for a living," she said.

"Undertaker," ER said.

"That's what I thought, too, but as it turns out, he's a psychiatrist."

"Which means he spends most of his time trying to figure out why people behave the way they do when it would be far simpler just to ask them."

"It gets worse."

"How?"

"He's a bachelor and it's obvious he doesn't care for women or kids."

ER raised her eyebrows. "You don't suppose he's one of *those* kind, do you?"

Holly shrugged and glanced back at the house next door. "I don't know. He doesn't look like he is, but you can't always tell by looking."

"Only thing you can tell by looking at him is that he's a first-class sourpuss. We sure got his goat, though. Did you see the way he went on when he saw that big old dog of his come running over here? He was thinking that chicken-livered dog was going to have Sweetie Pie for lunch. I guess she showed him."

"I hope this dog and cat thing doesn't become a bone

of contention. Maybe we should keep Sweetie inside as much as possible, at least for a few days until we get settled.''

''Won't do no good. He'll just find something else to be unhappy about.''

''Well, I don't know what he could find to complain about.''

Chapter Six

Those damn kids were driving him crazy.

He found bubble gum stuck to his doorbell, a pacifier on his front porch, assorted silverware in his flowerbed, banana peels on the hood of his car, a tube of toothpaste in the driveway, and a pair of tennis shoes in his mailbox. He had been called upon to pry a foot from a bicycle wheel, asked for his opinion of what to do when a child has bitten a rectal thermometer in two, fished English peas out of nostrils, extracted an eraser from an ear, and called in the middle of the night to be asked, "Maudie swallowed a nickel. Should I take her to the emergency room?" It was enough to make him give them candy laced with Valium.

Stanley was sitting at the desk in his study, trying to concentrate over the noise of the kids from next door playing hopscotch in his driveway. He had "The Three Tenors" CD on loud enough to drown out the kids, and almost didn't hear the phone ring.

He picked it up. "Hello, Dr. Levine here."

"Dr. Levine, this is ER. Someone left the door open

on the gerbil cage and they're all gone. I just wanted to tell you that if you see any gerbils around your place, please call us."

"What do gerbils look like?"

"Fat mice."

"All right. If I see any fat mice, I'll call you."

"Thank you. Erin is crying her heart out. She's afraid Plato will find them and eat them."

"Tell her Plato isn't into gerbils."

He heard a car door slam and looked up just in time to see Holly get out of her Jeep wearing a color-coordinated outfit and enough silver jewelry to open her own shop. She had her car keys in one hand and a potted plant in the other. She stopped for a moment to talk to the kids, then handed one of them her keys and plant and proceeded to hopscotch up the driveway and back.

Over the sound of the blaring CD came a child's voice. "Mama, Genny has been holding her breath until her face turns red."

Holly went to Genny and picked her up. "Look at Mommie. Let me see your eyes."

Stanley couldn't tell if Genny looked at her or not, but she must have, for Holly said, "Just as I thought. She's constipated." She handed Genny to ES. "Take her in the house and give her some Castoria."

Ten years of medical education, and he didn't know you could tell someone was constipated by looking at their eyes. Was there something mystical about mothers, or was she crazy?

He buried his head in his hands. Two months of this and it seemed like two years. It gave the term "terrible twos" an entirely new meaning. He felt like he was living next door to a trauma unit.

As for Holly, he had never seen anything or anyone like her. What kind of woman hand-painted her mailbox with tulips, staked her flowers with red bows, painted all her garbage cans yellow, and put a cup of vodka in the water when she boiled lobsters. "To relax them," she said. "Wouldn't you want a drink if you were about to be boiled?"

Early the next morning, Stanley heard something hit his house with a thump. A few minutes later, he heard the sound of shattering glass.

He threw back the covers and jumped out of bed. Without thinking, he slipped his feet into his slippers, yanked his robe off the chair, and looked at Plato. "Stop that infernal barking."

Thankfully, Plato stopped. Stanley had a blistering headache. Last night he had stayed up late, trying *her* remedy for boiled lobsters. It would be a long time before he could drink vodka again. He put the robe on and tied it as he walked to the bedroom window and looked down into the grassy expanse between his house and the yard next door.

Five or six of the brats were running toward their house. Little devils. They had broken another window. He left the bedroom in a hurry and headed for the stairs, his house slippers slapping against his heels as he went. Stanley knew, even before he walked into his dining room, that he would find a broken window.

He wasn't disappointed. It was broken and there was glass glittering on the hardwood floors. That was the second window in as many months. He looked at his watch. It was seven-fifteen on a Saturday morning, and already his window was broken. He began to mentally calculate just how long it would be before all the kids next door were grown. Hell, the youngest was not yet three. There wasn't a way on earth he could survive. Something had to be done about those little monsters, and there was no time like the present.

Without bothering to dress, he went outside in his

robe, running his fingers through his unruly hair. He glanced up and saw the truck for Green Pastures Dairy down the street, then looked down at the spot where Chester Ledbetter always put Stanley's two quarts of skim milk. The milk was gone, but it had been there. Stanley could see the wet rings. Damn kids—they had stolen his milk again.

By the time he reached his driveway, that six-feet-tall housekeeper they called ER was heading toward him and Stanley was beginning to have second thoughts. He had tangled with that Amazon before, and came away feeling like he'd engaged a wildcat. There was no way he'd win at verbal sparring with her.

However, he was here, and he couldn't very well turn tail and run. That feat was reserved for Plato. Speaking of Plato, he noticed the cat he silently referred to as Sourpuss was following ER. What was she doing, bringing reinforcements?

Behind him, Stanley heard Plato whine. He looked back, intending to tell the dog to go back to the house, when Plato tucked his tail and slinked away, going as far as the flowerbed, where he slithered behind the holly bush. Damn cowardly dog. Intimidated by an overweight, cross-eyed cat. It was too humiliating for words.

Stanley shook his head. If he didn't know better, he would swear that Plato was losing his self-esteem—to the point of becoming neurotic.

"Well, Doc, what brings you out so early? Must be something mighty urgent to bring you out in your undies."

The kids giggled.

ER had stopped at the edge of their property, looking for all the world like she was daring him to step over the border. She crossed her arms and waited.

"The kids broke my dining room window."

"So I heard."

"You'll have to call the glass company and have them come out to put in another one."

"I've already done that. They'll be here before you can get your rompers on."

Stanley had never encountered anyone so mouthy . . . not even in New York. "You need to tell these kids to play in their own yard."

"They *were* playing in their own yard."

"Then they need to keep their balls in their own yard, as well. I can't go on replacing windows all the time."

"Mrs. Winter pays for it."

"I was speaking of the inconvenience. If I wanted children to destroy my property, I would have had my own."

"It ain't that easy, Shrinker. You'd have to find somebody willin' to marry you, first."

"My single state is by choice, not default."

"Humph! Tell that to somebody who'll believe it."

"Is Mrs. Winter at home?"

"She's home, but she ain't in."

"What does that mean?"

"It means she's out jogging, as in exercise."

"I know what jogging is."

She looked him over good and proper. "Doesn't look like you do much in the way of exercise, Doc. Your body doesn't have much definition. Your arms are scrawny."

"Just tell Mrs. Winter I'd like to see her when she comes back. We need to reach some kind of understanding about these kids."

"Only understanding that needs to be done is on your part. Everyone over here understands each other perfectly."

"Just tell her I'd like to see her. Can you do that?"

ER turned away. "Sure. I'll be glad to tell her . . . if I don't forget."

Stanley stood there in his robe and slippers, knowing in no uncertain terms that he had been dismissed by his neighbor's outspoken housekeeper. God, how he wished he'd bought the house next door while it was still up for sale. If he'd had any inkling that this would happen, he'd have stayed in New York. Traffic wasn't this much trouble. Not by half.

He turned and marched back to the house. He went into the kitchen and took out a bowl, spoon, and a box of Grape Nuts. He went to the refrigerator and opened it. No milk. He wasn't certain if he was angrier because the kids had taken his milk, or because he had forgotten to mention it to that Amazon housekeeper.

He ate his cereal with orange juice poured over it instead. It was awful, but he was hoping his stomach wouldn't know the difference. Then he went upstairs and dressed, slipping into his corduroy pants and button-down shirt. He did his routine in the bathroom, then came out and grabbed his favorite sweater—the brown tweed with the suede patches on the elbows.

As he went down the stairs, he glanced out the window and saw his neighbor jog up her front walk in a pair of shorts. A moment later, she went into her house. Good. She was home. Without another thought, Stanley headed that way.

When he rang the bell, ES answered the door. She had a kid in one arm and another hanging onto her skirt.

"I'd like to speak to Mrs. Winter."

ES hurled a barrage of Spanish at him, ninety percent of which he was certain were expletives.

"Tell him to come in," Holly called.

She stood back and opened the door wider, her black eyes looking at him with suspicion. Stanley stepped into the house and saw Holly coming down the stairs. She had changed into a pair of jeans and a short sweater that showed part of her midriff. He could not help noticing that in spite of her four kids, it was flat.

"Hi, Stanley. You're out making house calls early. Had your coffee yet?"

"No. I didn't have time or milk."

"Well, I haven't had my coffee yet, either. Come into the kitchen. I'll get us both a cup."

"I didn't come over here for . . ." Holly disappeared around the door and Stanley's words trailed off to nothing. He followed her into the kitchen.

"Oh, my God!"

Stanley paused in the doorway and looked in the direction of Holly's horrified stare. There, sitting on the floor next to the cat's bowl was the two-year-old with blond curls and pink cheeks. The one they called Genny. She was eating cat food. Her mouth was full and she clenched an equal amount in both hands.

"Genny, no! You don't eat the cat's food! Nasty! Yuk! No! No!" Genny started crying. Holly hurried to the child and scooped her up, carrying her to the sink. She put her fingers in Genny's mouth and scraped out the cat food. "ES," she called, "Genny is eating cat food."

She finished fishing the brown bits out of Genny's mouth, then opened the little girl's fingers and shook their contents into the sink. She pointed at the cat food and said, "No! Bad girl. This is nasty. You mustn't eat Sweetie's food."

ES hurried into the room. She wasn't holding Katie, the four-year-old, anymore, but the five-year-old, Maudie, trailed at her heels. "Genny likes cat food," Maudie said.

Genny started crying again and ES started speaking rapid-fire Spanish to her. Genny must have understood what she said, for she stopped crying.

Holly filled a glass with orange juice, then gave Genny a few sips before she turned and handed her to ES. "Take her upstairs and change her clothes. She's got cat food all over her. Don't forget to wash her hands. I'll clean up this mess."

Stanley was staring at the cat food scattered across the floor. It made a crunching noise as ES carried Genny from the room.

Holly grabbed a broom and gave him an apologetic look. "Sorry for all the confusion. I haven't forgotten about the coffee I promised you."

"That's all right. I had cereal with orange juice on it this morning."

She made a face at that, but didn't say anything about it. "I'm sure this all looks pretty strange to you, since you don't have children."

About that time, ER walked into the room and took the broom from Holly. "Here. I'll do that." She glared at Stanley.

Stanley ignored her and said to Holly, "It may be commonplace to you, but I would think the sight of a child eating cat food would startle anyone, whether they had children or not."

"If you had children, Dr. Levine, you'd understand that things like this happen. Not that you plan for it to, but there are always surprises."

"Yes, and it's some of those surprises that I want to talk to you about."

Holly glanced at ER. "I heard about the window. ER said she called the glass company." She poured him a cup of coffee. "Cream or sugar?"

He took the cup. "I'll take it black." He took a sip. Surprisingly, she made good coffee.

"Was there something else you wanted me to do . . . about the window?"

"There's nothing you can do about it now. What I'd like is to find a way to prevent that sort of thing from happening again. I'm a strong believer in prevention."

"I'll just bet you are," ER said, sweeping across the tops of his shoes.

Stanley stepped back and noticed that Holly was smiling at him. He felt himself go warm all over. He had no explanation for what was happening. Must be the vodka, he told himself, and dismissed it. He followed Holly into the garden room.

He hadn't been in here before. He had to admit that the room was stunning with its brick floors and wall of windows that let in a stream of fall sunlight. The wicker furniture was painted white and the fabric a green and pink floral that Stanley at first thought matched the rug. He wasn't into decorating, of course, but this room spoke to him. He could see himself sitting here in the mornings, reading his paper and having a cup of coffee.

He could see himself needing analysis if he kept thinking things like this.

She indicated a chair and took one across from it.

Stanley sat down. "Mrs. Winter . . ."

"Holly. I've lived next door to you for almost three months now. It's time you called me Holly."

"We need to discuss your children."

She sighed and put her cup down. "What do you want me to do, Stanley? Drown them?"

"Is that the only choice we have?"

She ran her fingers through her hair. "I know this must be upsetting to you, especially since you've always lived alone, but there are going to be times when children do things we would all rather they did not do. There's simply no way to control that. I do everything I can. I have ER and ES here to keep an eye on things while I'm working."

"You work?"

She drew her brows together and gave him a puzzled look. "Of course I work. How do you think we live?"

He looked at a huge schefflera plant in the corner. "I figured your husband gave you child support or alimony, or something."

That seemed to anger her. "I'm capable of taking care of myself. I don't have to depend on anyone. I got nothing from my first two husbands. They were deadbeats. My last husband was killed in a plane crash, so there was some insurance money. However, I like working and am fortunate to have a fulfilling career. Does that surprise you?"

"Yes. I never noticed you going to work ... or returning, either."

"I work at home. I'm an illustrator for children's books."

"An artist," he said.

"You sound remarkably like my mother when you say that. Do you have something against artists?"

"No, I was just thinking that explains your fondness for color. I couldn't help noticing all of your rooms have a great deal of color in them. Your trash cans, too."

"Yes, I love color, and sunlight." She rose to her feet.

Stanley followed her lead. "Well, I've got to be going. I've got a lot to do today."

"I'll make a concerted effort with the children. Honest."

"I'd appreciate that, Mrs. Winter."

"Holly," she reminded him.

"Holly," he said, noticing how easily the word rolled off his tongue.

Stanley made his departure, then went outside and down the sidewalk. Just as he turned up his driveway, he saw the twins huddled over something on the sidewalk. "What are you girls doing?"

Amy looked at him and squinted at the sun. "We're making a kite."

Stanley looked at the trees. Not a leaf moved. "There's no wind."

"That's okay," Beth said. "We're making the kite now, then we'll save it until it gets windy."

Stanley looked down where the girls were working so diligently, thinking he would make an effort to be nice. The girls were making their kite out of newspaper and small, round dowel sticks. Something about those dowel sticks looked familiar.

He glanced toward his flowerbed, where he had spent the good part of last Saturday afternoon staking some gladiolas. The glads were lying on their sides, the sticks gone. Stanley was about to say something when his eyes zeroed in on the newspaper. He had another thought. "Where'd you get the newspaper?"

"Out of your yard," Beth said.

"Did it ever occur to you that I might want to read my paper?"

"It was just laying in your yard, so we thought you weren't going to read it."

"Don't touch my paper again, and stay out of my flowerbeds. Better yet, stay off my property altogether."

What happened next might have shocked him, if he had understood a word of what was being said.

Stanley's last words had hardly left his mouth when a barrage of Spanish adjectives came flying toward him. He turned to see ES, her rotund frame hurling down the sidewalk with a target in sight, much like a guided missile with nothing but seek-and-destroy on her mind.

She stopped between him and the girls, who seemed to be taking no notice, and began to blister him with a whole new set of Spanish adjectives sprinkled with a few verbs. The only option left to him was to retreat.

Without a word, he turned toward the house, thinking there wasn't much difference between his retreat and the one he had chastised Plato for. They were both fleeing in the face of the enemy: He, because he did not understand Spanish; Plato, because he obviously understood cat.

About the time Stanley opened the front door, Plato came howling around the corner with that obese cat after him. He shot up the steps and before Stanley could get through the door, Plato dashed inside, knocking Stanley back against the screen door.

The militant cat stopped on the step and fluttered its tail, then turned and walked slowly down the walk to join forces with EL Curso, the nanny from next door.

Shaking his head, Stanley went inside. It took him two hours to coax Plato out from under the bed.

Chapter Seven

Holly heard a commotion outside and went to her bedroom window. She parted the curtain and looked out. Since her bedroom was on the corner on the second floor, she had a good view of both her yard and Stanley's. She saw him talking to the twins, then she saw ES charge down the sidewalk like a woman with a mission.

A rash of colorful expletives reached her ears and she reminded herself to speak with ES. One day the girls would learn to speak Spanish and Holly shuddered to think what their first words would be.

She stopped worrying overmuch about what ES was doing. It was enough that she was such a guard dog when it came to the children. That put to rest, her interested gaze rested upon Stanley. Nerdy Stanley, as she had come to think of him. Pity, she thought. He wasn't that bad looking, if one could get past that awful haircut which was way too long and made him look like a cross between a chrysanthemum and a rocket scientist. The horn-rimmed glasses she remembered from a YSL ad some ten or twelve years ago—too heavy and too square for his face, and they hid one of his best features. His eyes.

He had a nice build, in a lanky, Gary Cooper sort of way. How she would love to take him shopping. There was nothing a Southern woman loved more than a lost cause. Stanley obviously liked corduroy, flannel, and tweeds. His entire being screamed Ralph Lauren. She could also picture him in a gray flannel Brioni, double-breasted. She wondered if he had ever heard of *Gentleman's Quarterly.*

Oh well, she told herself, *Stanley's appearance is Stanley's business and I've got more than I can handle at my own house.* So much for lost causes. She dropped the curtain back and turned away from the window.

The following Sunday afternoon, Holly and the girls were in the kitchen making cookies. The nine-year-old twins, Amy and Beth, were doing the measuring, while the younger ones were all standing in chairs around the big island in the center of the kitchen, waiting for Holly to assign tasks.

"Let's see. Erin, you can operate the mixer."

"Erin is only six," April said. "I'm eight. Why can't I do the mixer instead of Erin?"

"All right. April will operate the mixer and Erin will pour the ingredients in."

"But I want to operate the mixer," Erin whined. "You told me I could do it. Why does April get to do everything? It's not fair. It's not my fault she's older than me. Nobody asked me if I wanted to be the youngest."

April cleared that matter up. "You aren't the youngest. Genny is."

"What can I do?" four-year-old Katie asked.

"Hmmmm." Holly looked around the kitchen. "I know. You can grease the cookie sheets." Holly opened a cabinet and pulled out four large, stainless cookie sheets and placed them in front of Katie. She shoved the can of Crisco next to the cookie sheets and handed her a pastry brush. "All set?"

Katie nodded and Holly gave her a kiss, then looked around the room. Genny, who had been eyeing the cat food again, climbed off her chair. Holly hurried toward Sweetie's bowl, picked up the cat food, and carried it into the utility room where Ernestine was folding clothes.

"Let's keep this bowl in here and keep the door shut."

"Is Genny eating it again?"

"No, but she would've been in a couple of shakes."

Holly returned to the kitchen and scooped Genny up into her arms and whirled her around. "Now, Miss Mischief, what kind of job am I going to give to you?"

"She can taste the cookies when they're done," April said.

"That sounds like a wonderful job. Genny will be our official taster. Now, come here and I'll let you wash the plastic spoons and spatula while you're waiting for the cookies."

Holly filled the sink with warm, soapy water and pulled a chair up, depositing Genny there. While Genny played in the water, Holly opened a drawer and took out a few plastic utensils and placed them in the water. "Now, wash those nice and clean. Okay?"

"Okey-dokey," Genny said, washing.

"Mother, we don't have enough sugar."

"Want me to run to the store?" ER asked from the other room.

"No, go ahead and finish what you're doing. I'll go . . ."

"Why don't you borrow some from Stanley?" Amy asked.

"That's a great idea," Holly replied.

ER expressed her doubt about that. "I doubt that shrink has any sugar."

Holly smiled. "He might surprise us."

"I bet you my next day off that he doesn't."

"And I'll bet you double wages for one day that he does."

Holly heard ER chuckle and then she said, "It's a deal."

Holly picked up a cup and started from the room. "I'm leaving now. Will you keep an eye on the kids?"

Holly went next door to Stanley's house. As she passed the flowerbed, she glanced at his roses. They looked better than hers. She rang the bell. She could hear Plato barking in the distance, then Stanley opened the door. He glanced down at the cup in her hand.

She smiled brightly. "Hi, Stanley. I'm making chocolate chip cookies and I'm out of sugar. Could I borrow two cups?"

He stood back and she entered the house. The moment he saw her, Plato whined and dashed up the stairs. "What's wrong with him?"

"Overdose of the neighbor's cat. I guess he recognized you."

"Poor Plato. Stanley, I'm so sorry. Is there anything I can do?"

"Short of drowning your cat, no."

"I've been trying to keep Sweetie inside."

"You've been failing."

She sighed. "I know. It's just that she loves to be outside. Every time someone opens the door, she darts through it. How can you keep a cat in the house when it's digging tunnels under the door?" Holly paused just inside the door and looked him over. "I like your apron, by the way. What are you cooking?"

For a moment Stanley stood there looking at her strangely, and she was wondering if he was psychoanalyzing her.

"Chili," he said at last, removing the apron.

"I love chili. Do you make it spicy and hot?"

"No."

"I learned to love it hot when I was living in Houston. When I first moved there, the chili was so hot it almost burned my taste buds off. Now, I can't get it hot enough."

Stanley had a look in his eye that made her wonder if he was considering making a bowl of "special" chili just for her and lacing it with a couple of bags of those hot little peppers.

She put the thought out of her mind and followed him to the kitchen.

He went to the cabinet and took down a canister. "How much sugar did you say you needed?"

"Two cups."

"You should feed your kids something besides sugar. They don't need any more energy."

She laughed. "I meant to ask you if they got the windowpane in all right."

"Yes. He offered us a discount if we want to buy a dozen panes and just keep them here for the next time. He seemed to think this wouldn't be the end of it."

"I'm hoping there won't be a next time."

"Are you locking up all the baseballs?"

"No. I just figure the girls will lose interest in baseball before long. Then they'll take up something else."

"As long as it isn't BB guns."

He poured the sugar into her measuring cup and set it on the counter near her. "Two cups."

"Thank you." She made no move to pick up the sugar or leave. "You're uncomfortable around me, aren't you?"

"I'm accustomed to being left alone."

She seemed surprised. "And you like that?"

"Of course. Why wouldn't I?"

She shrugged. "I'm surprised you haven't tried to

analyze that, seeing as how you're the psychiatrist. Why are you asking me?''

"Why would I analyze it? Preferring your privacy isn't considered a mental illness in any of the books I studied. Do you have some advanced research I don't know about?"

"No, of course not. I just find it strange that you aren't very neighborly. Of course, I understand about the kids . . . their rambunctious natures, and all."

"Holly, you asked if you made me uncomfortable and I believe in being honest. Yes, you do, for the simple reason that I'm not accustomed to having women poking around in my house."

"I am not poking. Why don't you have women here?"

"It isn't the way I was raised."

"You mean, with women around?"

"Precisely."

"And here I've been thinking all these years that everyone had to have a mother. Where did you come from, Stanley, if you didn't have a mother?"

"I didn't crawl out from under a rock, if that's what you're asking. Of course I had a mother. I just never knew her. She died when I was born. I was an only child and I was raised by my father, grandfather, and uncle. I went to boys' schools until I entered college. Now, is there anything else you'd like to know about me?"

"Why did you never marry?"

"Because I never wanted to."

"You aren't . . . that is, you don't prefer . . . what I mean to say is . . ."

"I am heterosexual. How about yourself?"

Holly busted out laughing. "After three marriages, I'd say I definitely have no worries in that department."

He looked down at the sugar. "Are you sure two cups will be enough?"

"What? Oh, the sugar . . . yes, thank you. Three cups is plenty."

"Three? You wanted three cups? You asked for two."

She put her hand to her head and knew she looked confused for a moment. What was happening to her? Every time she was around him, she acted ridiculous or said something stupid. He made her so nervous, she couldn't remember what she came over here for. What an exasperating man.

"Are you all right?"

"Yes, I'm fine. I don't know what came over me. I meant two cups, of course."

He pushed the sugar a little closer to her.

She picked it up, hoping that one act would put his mind at ease. What did he think? That she was going to stay here indefinitely? "I do appreciate it, Stanley. I'll bring it back tomorrow after I go to the store."

"Don't bother. I have plenty."

"It's no bother and I insist. I always repay anything I borrow." She remembered then that she had borrowed several things from him that she had not returned, so she said, "Sooner or later."

"Why make such an issue out of it? Forget it."

"I can't. It's the way I was raised."

"You were raised to repay anything you borrowed, even if the person you borrowed it from said it was all right?"

"Yes."

"Why?"

For a moment she drew a blank. She knew he was committing every shred of this conversation to memory. She felt like a specimen under a glass. She couldn't help wondering if he had a notebook with her name on it and after she left he would go write notes about this conversation. "I don't know why. It's just that we've always done things that way."

"Ahhh, tradition, something you can't buck ... the pressure of all of those who went before you. Having ancestors can be such a burden. There's nothing more stubborn than dead people, is there? You can't threaten them, or frighten them, or even reason with them. You can kick them, shoot them, or hack them into little pieces, but they won't change."

She understood now just why he was a shrink. If you were crazy, it was cheaper to do your own counseling, and this man needed all the counseling he could get. She started from the room. "I'll send one of the girls over with your sugar . . ."

Stanley scowled.

She corrected herself. "That is, I'll send ER . . ."

He scowled again.

"ES?"

He just stood there looking at her.

"Okay. I'll bring it over tomorrow evening."

She turned and walked back into the entry hall. "Thanks again, Stanley. You're a peach."

Holly walked home thinking about Dr. Stanley Levine, reflecting on her flustered feelings when she'd said three cups instead of two. It was because he was a psychiatrist. It had to be. There was no other explanation.

Chapter Eight

On the thirty-first of October, Stanley made his rounds at the hospital, then drove straight home, deciding not to stop by the office. It was Halloween, and he wanted to put some stakes and string around his flowerbeds in the front, or his chrysanthemums would be trampled by all those kids tromping up to his front door.

He made one stop at the grocery store. He bought a bag of miniature Hershey bars, one of Three Musketeers, one of Snickers, and one of Peanut Butter Cups. He wasn't into this Halloween thing, naturally, but he had tried it both ways. If he had his light on and passed out good candy, there was a minimum of damage to his yard. If he turned his light off and stayed in a dark house, he bruised his shin bumping into furniture and the kids demolished his yard.

When he reached his house, he got out of the car and carried the bag of candy inside, still wearing his white hospital coat. Once inside, he put the candy in a bowl and set it on the entry table, then went down to the basement to let Plato outside.

Plato went as far as the doorway and sat down.

That damn cat next door made Plato so nervous that Stanley had taken to leaving Plato in the house, but even then, the dog would sit at the window for hours, only to whine and dart under furniture the moment he spied that cat.

"Go on."

Plato took one last look at him. "Go on outside. You can't stay in forever. Out!"

Stanley watched Plato step through the door cautiously, then he closed the door and went upstairs to change his clothes. When he finished, he started back down the stairs. It had become a habit to check out the yard next door each time he passed the window on the stair landing. This time was no different, but when Stanley glanced briefly at their yard, he stopped and walked to the window to get a better look.

Holly was in the backyard, taking advantage of the unseasonably warm weather by firing up the barbecue grill. The back door opened and ER came out carrying a tray of hamburger patties. At first, Stanley was surprised to see so much hamburger, but then he figured with ten people to feed, you had to make a lot of patties.

Holly stood there talking to ER as she put the patties on the grill, then the two of them walked into the house. Stanley turned away and went on down the stairs.

A few minutes later he was in the kitchen when he happened to get a whiff of something that smelled awfully good. He knew it was Holly's barbecue, but he glanced out the window anyway. He saw ER turning the hamburger patties over. A moment later, she went back inside.

Stanley was about to go back to what he was doing when he caught a glimpse of Plato. He watched with interest, wondering what Plato was doing slinking around in the Winters' yard. Was he crazy? Had he forgotten about that killer cat? All of a sudden it hit him. The smell of food superseded the fear of the cat. Plato never could resist barbecue.

Stanley was about to go to the door and call Plato when suddenly Plato trotted up to the grill and yanked a patty off. One by one, he pulled the patties off, eating each one the moment it hit the ground, not mindful that they were hot.

Stanley felt his spirits soar. He grinned from ear to ear. There was nothing like the feeling of getting even. He could not remember when he had felt anything akin to pride, but he was feeling it now.

Plato was wolfing down the last burger when ER came outside and screamed. Soon, the entire household was giving chase to poor Plato. It was a rather colorful sight, for the kids were all in various stages of putting on their Halloween costumes, from the twins who were completely dressed as a pair of dice, to the youngest one, Genny, who waddled around in something that looked like it might end up being a duck.

Stanley started to go over to Holly's and apologize, but decided to wait a bit, just to see if anyone came over to report the dastardly deed.

Whistling a tune, he went into the garage and got his stakes and string, then went outside to work on his flowerbeds. That done, he came back inside. It was getting dark now, so he switched on the porch light.

The phone rang and Stanley picked it up. "Dr. Levine, here."

"Hi, Stanley, this is Holly."

"I suppose I owe you some hamburgers."

"You know about the burgers?"

"I saw what happened. I was going to give you time to cool off before I came over to apologize."

She laughed. "Forget it. I don't suppose I can say anything about Plato eating those burgers, seeing as how we've given you so much grief. Besides, you can't chastise a dog for behaving like a dog any more than you can condemn a cat for acting like a cat. However, that isn't why I called. I was wondering if you observe Halloween.''

"If you mean do I wear a costume, the answer is no.''

She laughed again. "No, not even I would expect that of you. What I meant was, do you hand out treats?''

"Only because I'm afraid of what will happen if I don't. Why?''

"The girls are putting on their costumes and clamoring to come to your house first. If you didn't like trick-or-treaters, I was going to steer them in another direction.''

"I've just turned the porch light on. That's a sign I'm open for business.'' He paused. "Aren't you afraid to send your kids over here?''

"Just don't try giving them candy that isn't wrapped.''

"You're in luck, then.''

"Great. We'll be over in a little bit.''

Stanley hung up the phone, then went into the living room to turn on more lights. He glanced out the window and didn't see any sign of them leaving their house. He folded up the paper and put the ottoman back in front of the chair. He glanced out the window again. The yard was vacant.

He berated himself for appearing anxious, then went into the kitchen. He made himself a cup of coffee, then spilled it all over his alpaca sweater when the doorbell rang. They were here.

Why did that make his heart beat a bit faster?

Fear, probably.

He hurried into the living room and picked up the bowl of candy. He opened the door and his heart seemed to drop down to his feet. Standing at the door were a couple of kids from down the street.

"Trick or treat!''

Stanley paid them off and they went scampering down

the sidewalk. He put the bowl in its place and went to sit in his chair. He picked up a book on Jung and tried to read, then closed the book and stood up. He straightened a couple of pillows on the sofa, then heard Plato whining at the back door. He let Plato in and returned to the living room. He parted the curtain and looked out. Four kids from across the street were coming up the walk.

He opened the door and thrust the bowl of candy at them, then closed the door when they left. He checked his watch and then he realized what he was doing. What was happening to him? He couldn't actually be looking forward to that brat factory next door descending upon him.

He started from the room when he caught a glimpse of something out of the corner of his eye. He looked toward the window and saw the faces of the twins, Amy and Beth. Good God! They were peeking at him through the window. He pretended not to see, and walked from the room.

He was just putting a Healthy Choice frozen dinner in the microwave when the doorbell rang. He went to the door and opened it. There stood all the brood from next door, Amy and Beth included, each of them with their faces painted and costumes on, thrusting empty plastic pumpkins toward him.

"Trick or treat!" they clamored in unison.

Stanley made each one of them show him their costume, then he held out the bowl of candy, instructing them to take as much as they wanted, which was a mistake, since they emptied the bowl.

Holly was standing on the sidewalk a few feet away, wearing a pair of jeans and a jean jacket. Her hair was in a ponytail. Big gold loops in her ears reflected the porch light. He stared at her for a moment, then realized what he was doing. The fact that she had caught him staring at her left him flustered.

"Hello," he said, trying to think of something neighborly to say. "You certainly had your work cut out for you, trying to find different costumes for each one of them."

"It's not so hard, really. I just let them decide what they want to be, then I make their costumes."

"You sewed these?"

She nodded.

"All of them?"

She nodded again. "All of them, although I must confess I used a pattern."

"I'm impressed. I really am."

She looked surprised. "Why, Stanley, that's the nicest thing you've ever said to me. Thank you."

The kids had finished and were starting to leave the porch. Maudie had been the first to leave, obviously trying to get ahead of the others, but when they all began to run after her, Maudie was bumped. She lost her balance and fell against the string Stanley had staked around his flowerbed. She went crashing into the chrysanthemums.

A split second later, she let out a loud wail.

Stanley's heart raced. He was terrified she might have fallen against one of the stakes and hurt herself. He started running and reached her about the same time Holly did.

Holly took her in her arms. "What's the matter, sweetheart? Are you hurt? Show Mommie where you're hurt."

"No." Maudie sniffed, then looked at Stanley and started bawling in earnest. "I *bwoke* Stanley's *thanthemums* and he won't like us anymore."

"He doesn't like us now, dimwit," Beth said.

Holly glanced at Stanley and he felt the heat of seven pairs of little eyes upon him. God, he never knew kids could make a person feel so guilty. He had egg on his face now. He could never remember feeling so rotten or so helpless. He dropped down beside Holly and Maudie, who was dressed as Little Bo Peep. He ruffled her curls and took out his handkerchief to blot her face, careful not to smudge the red circle on each cheek. "Don't worry about the chrysanthemums. They'll grow back. And you're all wrong. I do like you. I just don't know how to show it."

Later that night, after Stanley had given out all his candy and turned out the light, he thought about his next-door neighbors. Nothing in his medical education had prepared him for something like this. Holly wasn't like anyone he had ever known. The children irritated him one minute and got under his skin the next. How could a person form an attachment for something that was such a source of irritation?

And then there was Holly. She was forever coming over to borrow something, whether it was his tools, which she never remembered to return, or something from the kitchen, which she never returned, either, or his "strong arm" as she put it, using that syrupy drawl of hers that made him want to do asinine things.

He went to sleep that night, trying to figure out just what it was that made Holly Winter tick and why it was that he even cared.

Chapter Nine

Heather came over on Saturday morning.

"My God, it's so quiet in here. It's like a tomb. Where is everybody?"

"ER and ES took the girls to the mall."

"I saw your neighbor puttering around in his flower-beds like a little old maid. Ye Gods! I couldn't stand to live next door to a man who had better-looking roses than I did."

"You noticed?"

"How could I not? His roses are right out of *Southern Living*. I didn't think people puttered in their flower-beds in the fall."

"He's probably repairing his chrysanthemums. Last night, Maudie fell and crushed one horribly."

"What did he do? Order you to pay for another one like he did the window, or did he string her up for forty lashes?"

"No, surprisingly enough, he acted positively human."

"Stanley?"

"Yes. Isn't that bizarre?"

"What did he do?"

"He told Maudie it was okay, that the flowers would grow back, and when one of the kids said he didn't like them, he said they were wrong. Then he said the strangest thing."

"What was that?"

"He said he did like them. He just didn't know how to show it."

"What do you make of that?"

"A great deal. We all have our fears and we all try to hide them. Some people just do a better job. That one remark changed things between us, or at least it changed the way I see him. You know, life is a funny thing. You can live by someone—for years, even—always having a strong dislike for their arrogance and conceit. Then they can reveal a bit of themselves by letting one little comment slip out and it shows us a whole other side, another person, actually, one who has been there all along and we just never saw him for what he was: a man unsure of himself, uncertain about life, and living life the best he can, just like we are."

Heather, who looked enough like Jamie Lee Curtis to be her twin sister, looked dumbfounded. "Stanley Levine, you old rascal, you're just full of surprises. Wonder what other surprises he has up his sleeve?"

"Not much. He'll be more careful next time. I think that admission just slipped out. He looked terribly embarrassed after he said it."

"Stanley embarrassed? Will wonders never cease? Stanley acting human. Who would have thought it?"

"Yes," Holly said absently, "who would have thought it."

The room grew strangely quiet. Holly was aware of it and aware, also, that Heather was aware of it, too. But she couldn't seem to shake away thoughts of Stanley.

At last she told herself she simply felt sorry for him, just like she felt sorry for his dog.

Heather turned her head to one side, her dark brown eyes studying Holly thoughtfully. "You aren't taking a sudden interest in our resident shrink, are you?"

"I wish everyone would quit calling him a shrink . . . including me. He's really a very nice, decent sort of man. He acts strangely with women and children because he's never been around them."

Holly went on to tell Heather about Stanley growing up in an all-male household. As they talked, Heather said, "That still doesn't answer my question. Are you becoming interested in Dr. Levine?"

"Stanley isn't my type."

"After three marriages to three very, very different men, I'm not certain you have a type. Are you sure you don't find him attractive in any way?"

Holly drew her knees up and put her arms around them, thinking. "I don't think Stanley is so bad-looking. He's like an old car that just needs a coat of paint. When you get to know him, he's attractive in a northern, tweed-and-corduroy sort of way. Sometimes I find myself wondering what he would look like without those awful horn-rimmed glasses."

"Have you ever seen him in a suit?"

"No, but I saw him in his white hospital jacket once."

"And?"

"And he didn't look bad. Not bad at all. In fact, he looked pretty good."

"Holly, doctors' coats are like military uniforms. You could put one on a broom and it would look good. I'm worried about you."

"Why?"

"You don't sound very neutral on the subject of Dr. Levine."

"Am I supposed to be neutral?"

"There are only three possibilities. Dislike. Neutral. Or love."

"Oh, posh. You know I decided after Bill died that three marriages were enough for anyone. You couldn't hire me to risk my heart again. Believe me, there's nothing to worry about . . . especially where Stanley is concerned. He has as much personality as a speed bump."

Heather laughed. "He does, doesn't he?"

They both laughed and made a few lighthearted comments. Then Heather took a sip of her coffee. "You know, back to you and Stanley . . ."

"Will you stop saying it in the same breath, like we're joined at the hip or something? He's my neighbor. Nothing more."

"People have started with less."

"We have no common ground, Heather. My cat raises his ire. The children irritate him. Sometimes I think he'd like to choke ES, and I know he'd love to get inside ER's head. He complains about the noise, the toys in his driveway, broken windows, trampled flowerbeds, missing milk cartons, confiscated newspapers. The other day, the kids took his mail."

"You're joking."

"No, I'm not. I walked in the kitchen and April was sitting at the table reading a letter to ER."

Heather scooted to the edge of her chair. "What did it say?"

"I can't believe you asked me that."

Heather laughed and came to her feet. "I can't, either."

"I didn't read his letter, if it makes you feel better."

"A missed opportunity is a missed opportunity. Thanks for the coffee. I've got to get back to the office. Pearlene Simmons is bringing her cat in to be spayed and I must say, it's about time."

"I can't believe she's doing it, either. What made her change her mind?"

"I think it was because I volunteered to do it for free."

"That was nice of you, Heather."

"Listen, that cat has had at least a dozen litters and every one of them is running wild. There are more cats than there are trailers out there. None of them has had shots. I'm terrified one will get rabies and bite some kid."

Holly shuddered.

Heather gave Holly a hug. "Have I told you how happy I am to have you here?"

Holly smiled. "Yes, about five times a week."

"Wanna go to the movies Saturday night? Brad Pitt is on."

"What movie?"

"Does it matter? I'd pay money to stare at a poster of him for two hours. Brad baby looks soooo good on film. Have I talked you into going yet?"

"Yes."

After Heather left, Holly went up to the third floor where she had her studio. She was illustrating a book called *Ten Little Turtles*. Holly had a pet turtle in a dish on her desk. She picked it up and studied it for a minute, then fed it and moved to the drafting table.

She looked at the picture she had started, where a log had fallen over a creek. On the log she had drawn eight turtles. She picked up her pencil and began to sketch two more.

She heard a car drive up and what sounded like a dozen doors slam. She wondered who it could be, since the van's doors slid back and made a different noise. Then she remembered ER had driven Holly's Jeep and left the mini-van in the garage. She heard ES rattle off commands in Spanish and knew the kids were home. She looked out the window and saw them piling out of the Jeep. They followed ER and ES into the house . . . all except Erin and Maudie.

Holly watched with interest as the two of them crossed over into Stanley's yard and walked up the driveway toward his garage.

Her interest peaked now, she watched them go to one of the windows. She was horrified to see them pull a step stool out from behind a bush and stand on it. Oh, my God! She could not believe her eyes. Five and six years old and they were window-peeping! She was properly horrified at what her children had done, but her thoughts were on Stanley.

Poor Stanley. It was little wonder why he never looked at her with anything but irritation. She could not blame him. She knew the kids were a nuisance. Before this window incident, she had thought they were getting better. Obviously, they were not.

It was just that it was so difficult for all of them to adjust to their losses and living together as a family. It was difficult for April, Erin, and Katie, having lost both parents and having to adjust to living with their aunt and cousins. It was equally difficult for Amy, Beth, Maudie, and Genny. They were having to learn to share not only their possessions and home, but their mother as well. Jealousies flared. Feelings were hurt. It wasn't easy for any of them.

She knew the kinks were starting to smooth out somewhat, and they were settling into something that looked remarkably normal, at least to her way of thinking. All it took was time.

She thought about the way things had gone after she moved in. She knew Stanley had gotten tired of her borrowing his tools and never returning them, not that she didn't intend to. That's why he offered to do little odd jobs for her whenever she asked to borrow a saw or drill. Poor Stanley. Better to go with his tools, to do the work for her, than to risk loaning them and not getting them back at all.

She remembered, too, the afternoon just a week or so ago when he came over as she was trying to teach one of the girls how to shoot baskets. Holly had never been much of a basketball player, even when she was young. It was hard sometimes to teach children something you knew. It went beyond difficult to teach something you had absolutely no skill at.

That afternoon, Beth was playing basketball and wanted to practice and Holly had done the best she could with her. But even she would have to admit it was pretty dismal. Evidently, Stanley had seen it as dismal, too. He must have seen she was doing it all wrong, so he came over and gave them a few pointers.

And there was the afternoon she decided to plant some fall flowers. The soil was rock-hard and she had already bent two spades and broken a third when Stanley came over. He showed her what the soil in Georgia needed, then went to the nursery with her to buy mulch and bark and to help her pick out ornamental cabbages and pansies. She glanced at the flowerbed. Even now, the purple cabbages and the yellow pansies looked as good as the day she planted them.

With a heaviness in her heart that was unusual for her, Holly left the room and went downstairs to find Maudie and Erin. It was time for a scolding.

Chapter Ten

Stanley came home from the office one afternoon, just like he always did. He went to the basement and fed Plato, then opened the door for him to go outside. Plato wouldn't budge. After numerous tries, Stanley had to take his collar and lead him outside.

Less than half an hour later, he heard a commotion in the yard. He saw Plato and the cat in his driveway, going at it again. Plato let out a loud yelp and came running home with his nose bleeding again.

Later that night, Stanley was watching the news with Plato curled up at his feet. A commercial came on advertising cat food. When Morris the Cat flashed on the screen, Plato jumped up with a whine and crawled under a chair, leaving a tuft of hair scraped from his back. Stanley couldn't coax him out and it was several hours later before Plato came out on his own. Stanley was getting concerned. In a human, this type of behavior would need treatment.

He heard a noise on his front porch, then the doorbell rang. When Stanley got to the door and opened it, no one was there. He knew it was the kids next door. They thought this sort of thing was fun.

He was praying for a blizzard, hoping that when cold weather came, he would see less of them. They had taken to inviting him over for dinner. He always declined, but that didn't seem to matter. Every week or so, one or two of them would come traipsing over to invite him to dinner. In fact, they had made such a habit of it that he began to hide out whenever he saw one of them head his way. When they rang the bell, he wouldn't answer.

It was a week before Thanksgiving when Stanley answered the door and saw Holly standing there. She was all muffed up in a short fur jacket. She looked warm enough, but he did the neighborly thing and invited her in.

"I came over to invite you to have Thanksgiving dinner with us."

"I don't celebrate Thanksgiving."

She seemed taken aback by that. "You don't celebrate Thanksgiving?"

"No."

"Why?"

"Why should I?"

"Because it's a holiday. A very important holiday."

"Not to me, it isn't."

"Stanley Levine, how can you say that? This country was founded upon the principles of Thanksgiving. It was the first holiday celebrated on these hallowed shores. Americans have been celebrating it ever since."

"Oh yes, I forgot about tradition. You're still having trouble with all those dead people, aren't you? Ancestors can be a troublesome lot."

"I think you're a hypocrite. No, worse than that. You're Scrooge."

"I believe you have your holidays confused. Doesn't Scrooge belong with Christmas?"

"Yes, well, you probably don't believe in that holiday either," she said, then turned and left his house.

He saw that when she opened the door, several of the kids were waiting there on his porch.

"Is he going to eat with us?"

"No, he's too busy being boring."

He watched her march home with her children clustered around her.

The next afternoon, Stanley was cleaning leaves from his gutters. He was on the ladder when the mini-van pulled up. Holly and the kids got out, then went to the back and began unloading pumpkins.

He wondered if she was going to make pumpkin pie, but decided she probably wasn't when he watched them stack the pumpkins on the front porch. They were getting into the spirit of things, for they had some cornstalks that they put to one side of the door, then stacked pumpkins around the bottom.

Holly and a couple of the kids went inside, then came back a few minutes later. Stanley moved his ladder to a new spot and watched them carry some wooden figures of two Pilgrims and an Indian. Before long, they had arranged a scene with a backdrop of cornstalks. Then she set about decorating the door with a wreath. This woman was amazing. Did she go around looking for work to do?

The younger kids were busy hanging pictures of Pilgrims and Indians all over the windows. What a mess that would be to clean up. He was thinking how glad he was that he didn't have a mess like that to clean up when he heard them laughing. He glanced over in time to see Genny and Katie put leaves down Holly's back.

Holly chased the two of them, catching them next to a pile of leaves in the front yard. The three of them rolled in the leaves and were soon joined by the other five kids. He had never heard so much laughing and shouting in his life.

When it was over, Holly hugged Katie and Genny and gave each of them a swat on the pants and a kiss. He heard Katie say, "I love you, Aunt Holly."

"I love you, too, Katie mine."

"I love you, too, Mama," Genny said, climbing into her lap and giving her a kiss that sounded wet, even from where Stanley stood.

"And I love my little Genny," Holly replied. Soon it was a free-for-all with more declarations and wet kisses.

For some time, Stanley did not move. Even after they had all gone inside, he stood there on the ladder, thinking. It occurred to him that while he didn't have all that mess to clean up, he didn't have any love like that in his life either. Since she had moved in next door, he had seen more love and closeness than he had seen in his entire lifetime. He saw how women of all ages and nationalities and color managed to live together with love and respect.

By the time he finished cleaning the gutters, it was getting dark. He carried the ladder around the house and toward the garage. As he passed by her house, he saw the light on in Holly's kitchen. The kids were all crammed around the table, looking like they enjoyed being there. He saw Holly bustling around, bumping into ER, the two of them putting the children's plates on the table. The fragrance of something spiced with cinnamon reached his nose, and for just a twinkling, Stanley remembered a time when he was a young boy and his grandfather had taken them all to visit his grandfather's sister, Rachel. After their visit, Rachel invited them to stay for dinner. Stanley had never eaten apple pie before, but he had some that day. He remembered going home and thinking how nice it was at Rachel's house, with her warm, cozy kitchen that smelled of cinnamon and apples, her ready laugh, and the way he felt all soft inside when she hugged him and invited him to come back.

But they hadn't gone back. Rachel died the next year and Stanley spent the rest of his life trying to forget the smell of cinnamon.

He put the ladder away and shut the garage door, then walked rapidly to his house. Once inside, he slammed the door behind him, as if by doing so, he could shut out the memory of a time he wanted to forget.

Although he had several invitations to dinner with friends, Stanley spent Thanksgiving Day at home, alone. He was watching the University of Texas play A&M. At halftime the commercials came on. Morris the Cat was back. So was Plato's neurosis. The moment he saw Morris, Plato whined and shot under the armchair. Stanley knew he would stay there for the rest of the afternoon.

To take advantage of halftime, Stanley left his easy chair and headed for the kitchen. After rummaging around the refrigerator, he couldn't find much in the way of food. He had stopped by the grocery store on his way home yesterday, but when he pulled into the parking lot and saw the crowd there to shop for Thanksgiving, he left.

He rummaged some more. He threw away some green cheese, a piece of molded apple, two wilted carrots, a few mushy stalks of celery. There were two slices of bologna left that didn't look too bad. The head of lettuce was ruined, but he managed to salvage a couple of leaves. The tomato had black spots all over it, but he peeled it and ended up with three small slices.

He spent some time looking for bread that wasn't molded. When he found some, it was a little on the hard side. He sprinkled a little water over it to soften it up a bit, but realized it was soggy in places, so he popped it in the toaster, thinking that might dry out the soggy spots. He was looking for a jar of mustard when the doorbell rang.

He left the refrigerator door ajar and went to answer the front door.

Holly was standing there with a tray in her hands.

"Hi, Stanley. I decided to bring Thanksgiving dinner to you, since you wouldn't come over to eat it with us."

"Thank you for your kindness, but I've just eaten." He rubbed his stomach. "I don't think I could eat another bite."

She looked at him like she didn't believe a word he said. "That's all right. You can eat this later. I'll just leave it in the kitchen."

"Here, I'll take it in there for you," he said, trying to head her off, but Holly held on to the tray. Without another word, she stepped around him and headed for the kitchen.

"You don't have to do that, really. I don't want you to go to any trouble."

"No trouble. I'll just leave it on the counter in case you get hungry later. What you don't eat tonight, you can refrigerate. It'll still be good tomorrow."

He followed her into the kitchen, trying to get a word in edgewise without much luck. She walked to the counter and put the tray down. She pulled the cloth cover off of the tray and Stanley felt his mouth water. He had never seen such white, succulent slices of turkey next to a heap of steaming dressing and buttery mashed potatoes covered with giblet gravy and cranberry sauce on the side. The aroma of warm yeast reached his nose and he saw a plate of hot monkey bread. There were little bowls of every vegetable he had ever heard of, and one of fruit salad. A larger bowl held a slice of pecan pie which sat next to a slice of fudge pie, both of them warm and topped with vanilla ice cream. His stomach growled. He could hardly wait for her to leave. He had never seen food like this.

Holly turned toward him, her gaze going to the open refrigerator door. She checked it out, then closed it.

She turned toward him and wrinkled up her nose. "I smell something burning."

"My toast!"

They noticed the smoke coming out of the toaster at the same time. Both of them made a dash for it. Holly got there first. She unplugged the toaster, then carried it to the sink. Upending it, she dumped the two blackened slices of bread into the sink where they lay smoldering, looking like two charred turtles.

"Looks like they got jammed in there when the sides curled in," she said, staring at the bologna lying on the counter. "What is that?"

"Bologna."

"Bologna is brown."

Stanley glanced at the bologna. It was sort of brown in the center, gradually turning to green at the edges. "This is the imported kind."

"It looks like the dangerous kind to me. I'd throw that out, if I were you." She stopped and looked at him. "I thought you said you had just eaten."

"I have."

"Then what is all this?"

"I was making dessert."

"Dessert. Green bologna for dessert?"

"It's a Jewish delicacy. Do you find that strange?"

She looked at him like she was trying to connect the dots in her head that would give her a picture of what was going on here. "No, I don't find that strange at all. It's exactly what I would expect from a psychiatrist." Without another word, she picked up the cloth and threw it over her tray, then turned and carried it out the back door.

Stanley was sorely tempted to mug her and take the tray. Even after she had gone, the aroma of the food stayed in his kitchen, a tortuous reminder of the consequences of pride and hastily told lies.

Hungrier than he could ever remember being, he

went back to the football game. After it was over, Plato stayed under the chair so long that Stanley decided he had to do something.

A few days later, Stanley went into the kitchen and took out the phone book. He called Heather Landry. He knew Heather was a friend of Holly's, but she was the only vet in town. He called her out of desperation. He figured professional courtesy would keep her mouth shut.

"Dr. Landry's office."

"This is Dr. Levine. I'd like to speak to Dr. Landry."

When Heather came to the phone, she sounded surprised to hear from him. "Hello, Stanley. What can I do for you?"

"I'm having problems with Plato."

"Why don't you schedule an appointment and bring him in?"

"I'm not having that kind of problem."

"Oh? What kind of problem are you having?"

"Emotional problems."

"Emotional problems?"

"Yes."

"Plato is having emotional problems?"

"Yes."

"What kind of emotional problems?"

"The cat kind."

"Oh."

"Listen, Heather, it's quite involved and I don't want to take up your time. I was just wondering if you could give me the name of a dog psychologist."

"I'll have to think about that one for a minute. You know, of course, that there isn't one in Peach Orchard."

"I don't want one in Peach Orchard. I'd rather take him out of town."

"I think I've got the name of one in Atlanta."

"That would be perfect."

"Hang on a minute, Stanley. I'm looking through my

Rolodex . . . here it is. Patricia Silvestre. Her office is on Peachtree." She gave him the address and telephone number.

"I really appreciate this, Heather."

"Think nothing of it. Is there anything else I can do for you?"

"No, that's all. Thank you."

"Oh, Stanley?"

"Yes?"

"I almost forgot. I'm having a Christmas party on the seventeenth of December. Jot that down on your calendar. I'm telling you early because I know you don't have a damn thing planned that far in advance and I won't take no for an answer."

"I'll have to check and . . ."

"Stanley, you didn't come to my Fourth of July swim party and you didn't come to my Labor Day barbecue. My feelings are going to be severely trampled if you beg off this time."

"All right."

"You'll come?"

"I'll come."

"Promise?"

"Yes. I'll be there. I'm writing it down on my calendar now."

"Seven o'clock."

"Gotcha."

"See you then. And Stanley?"

"Yes?"

"Thanks for coming. You won't regret it."

Stanley wasn't so certain, but he thanked her for the invitation and hung up. Then he called Patricia Silvestre in Atlanta.

Chapter Eleven

Stanley went outside one crisp morning late in November and saw Holly hanging out clothes on the clothesline, which he thought peculiar, since he had never seen them hang clothes outside before. When he stepped off the porch, Holly saw him and yelled over the hedge, "Hi, Stanley."

"Good morning." He walked to the hedge that separated their yards. "When did you start hanging out your laundry?"

"Since the dryer went on the fritz this morning. We've called a repairman, but he can't come until Wednesday."

"You can use my dryer."

"Why, thank you. That's sweet of you. I'm almost finished here, but I'll take you up on the offer with the next load." She hung the last pair of jeans, picked up the laundry basket, and walked to the hedge. "I didn't realize what back-breaking work this was. I have a whole new appreciation for my grandmother."

He thought she looked particularly pretty this morning, sort of like a peach when it's still on the tree and frosted with early morning dew.

"I can't believe it's going to be December in a few days. I'm taking my decorations out of the attic this evening."

"Rushing the season a bit, aren't you?"

"No. I like to decorate right after Thanksgiving, and then take everything down after Christmas. I can't stand looking at the tree after all the presents are gone. It's sort of like looking at a turkey carcass after it's been picked clean."

"I see."

"When are you going to decorate?"

"What?"

"Decorate. When are you putting your decorations up?"

"I don't put up decorations."

"None?"

"None."

"Not even a tree?"

"No tree, no nothing."

"Why?"

"This is beginning to sound like Thanksgiving."

"I'm sorry. I don't mean to sound like I'm grilling you. It just seems so strange."

"Most Jewish people don't celebrate Christmas. It is, after all, a Christian holiday."

"Oh ... yes, of course. I didn't realize you were Jewish."

"I am, and I'm not. I was born into a Jewish family, so that makes me a Jew. However, I'm not really much of anything."

She changed the subject. "I'll do enough decorating for both of us. You'll probably be sick of Christmas long before it gets here. I've decided to have an ethnic Christmas this year."

Stanley was wondering: *What in the hell is an ethnic Christmas?*

By the first of December, he was getting a pretty good idea. This woman went at Christmas with profane enthusiasm. He bet her oven didn't cool until the twenty-sixth of December.

Soon, she had enough lights on her house, strung in her trees, and over the bushes to light up the whole of Manhattan Island. Her front door was decorated, and three deer made out of grapevines stood on the lawn, wearing big red collars and covered with twinkling lights. There was a big bow on the chimney, greenery wrapped around the mailbox and the yard light, both of them topped with red velvet bows. There were even bows on those yellow trash cans when she put them out on collection day. The brass lights on either side of the door were decorated with greenery and red bows. Hell, everywhere he looked, he saw red . . . bows, that is.

He had never seen anyone "do" Christmas. He thought it was something you watched happen. But Holly was a doer.

The day she brought her Christmas tree home, she said she was sorry he wasn't going to have one. The way she said it made him think that his not having a Christmas tree really, really bothered her. For some strange reason, he took perverse pleasure in knowing there was something he could do to get under Holly's skin.

Holly was in the kitchen one afternoon, decorating a cake, when Amy walked in. She took a seat on the bar stool across from Holly and began dragging her finger around the perimeter of the cake, scooping up chocolate icing.

"Keep your mitts off the cake or you won't get any for dessert," Holly said.

Amy licked her finger, then said, "Mom, do you know Stanley watches TV in his boxer shorts?"

Holly jabbed the spatula into the bowl of icing so hard she snapped the plastic handle in two. "Amy Winter, what did you say?"

"I said Stanley watches TV in his boxer shorts."

For a moment, Holly stood there with her mouth open, the broken handle in her hand, staring at her daughter. Her daughter. Her nine-year-old daughter talking about boxer shorts and window-peeping. Had she raised a colony of Peeping Toms? "How do you know Stanley wears . . . how do you know that?"

Amy looked a bit sheepish. "We saw him."

"We . . . as in you and Beth?"

"And April and Erin."

"I'm surprised you didn't have Genny and Katie along with you."

"It was Genny and Katie who started it."

"Are you trying to tell me that a two-year-old and a four-year-old instigated window-watching?"

"Well, they did."

"I have told you children to stop spying on him. It isn't polite to peek in another person's windows. Don't you understand that?"

"Then how will we know what he's doing?"

"You aren't supposed to know. What a person does within the confines of his house is his own private business."

"Then he ought to close his curtains."

"No, you ought not to spy on him. You're going to stop spying and you're going to stop now."

Chapter Twelve

Stanley carried the last sack of groceries in the back door and put them on the kitchen counter. He pulled the ice cream out first and carried it to the freezer. He should have waited to buy ice cream. Two hours in the car was too long. It was probably all melted.

He shrugged and put it inside and closed the door. It would just have to get cold again. Going to the grocery store in Atlanta had been a good idea, and it was certainly a great way to while away the two hours Plato was at the dog psychologist.

He finished putting away the rest of the groceries, but kept the package of lightbulbs lying on the counter. One of the kitchen lights had burned out, so he went to the garage for the ladder.

He positioned the ladder under the light and climbed up as high as he could go. The kitchen ceilings were high and the old wooden ladder wobbled. He made a mental note to get a new one, then removed the bulbs from the lamp one at a time, climbing back down the ladder to place each one of them on the counter.

As he worked, he kept thinking about the way the house next door looked when he drove home tonight, with lights blazing all over the place and the sound of Christmas music coming from the piano.

He heard Plato come into the room and began thinking about what the dog psychologist said. He was afraid the woman was a bit too optimistic. He couldn't believe Plato would be back to normal after five or six sessions.

Outside, the five oldest kids were gathered in the flowerbed. They whispered among themselves as they took turns peeking in the window.

"Is he in his boxer shorts?" Erin asked.

"Shhh," said April. "Don't talk so loud. Do you want him to hear you?"

Erin shook her head and whispered in a lower tone, "Well, does he have his boxers on?"

"No. Not yet," Beth whispered. "He's putting light-bulbs in the lamp. We'll have to wait until he goes upstairs—that's when he puts on his boxer shorts. Then he'll come back down to watch TV."

The kids kept watching as Stanley removed each bulb. They were growing restless; after all, nothing the least exciting was happening.

Suddenly, Amy noticed the new lightbulb on the counter near the door and had an idea. She turned and whispered something to Amy, who whispered to April, who told Erin, who told Maudie. As the children watched, Amy slipped along the house until she reached the back door. Holding her finger to her mouth to indicate absolute silence, she quietly opened the back door.

She waited a moment, and when nothing happened she opened it a bit more. When it was open wide enough to get her arm through, she slipped it inside and reached for the lightbulb.

Everything went fine, until Sweetie hopped up on the porch behind her and darted inside.

A split second later, all hell broke loose. The moment she went into the house, Sweetie spotted Plato and charged. Plato, who had been dozing at the base of the ladder, was taken off guard. Hearing Sweetie hiss, he leaped to his feet and made a dash for the dining room, bumping the ladder. The ladder wobbled, just as Sweetie cut him off. He whirled around and took off in the other direction, Sweetie in hot pursuit.

"What the hell . . ." said Stanley.

Suddenly, Plato saw the back door was partially open and he darted toward it, taking the shortest path, which led him beneath the ladder, which was still rocking. On his way out the door, Plato hit it again, harder this time. The rickety old ladder swayed one way and then another before it crashed to the floor, throwing Stanley off as it went.

Stanley hit the floor with a loud thud, but not before his head hit the sharp corner of the kitchen cabinet. Unconscious, he lay as he had fallen.

Outside, the kids stared in horror, but when they saw the blood seeping out from beneath his head, they turned and ran screaming toward home.

Holly met them at the front door.

"What happened?" she asked, looking each of them over, trying to see if one of them was hurt or bleeding.

Amy, who was crying violently, screamed, "We killed him. We killed Stanley. He's bleeding. There's blood all over the place."

"Where is he?"

"He . . . he . . . he's ly-lying on the k-k-kitchen floor."

"Did he get up?"

"No. He hasn't moved. He's dead. I know he's dead."

ER came up about that moment, and Holly turned to her. "Call an ambulance," she said, then took off for Stanley's house.

She ran to the front door and found it locked. Without wasting a moment, she picked up the wicker chair on the porch and hurled it against the window, shattering the glass. She climbed inside.

By the time she reached the kitchen, the kids were there, crowded around the open back door. Stanley was lying on his back, a huge pool of bright-red blood spreading beneath his head.

Holly grabbed a towel from the counter and ran to the freezer, grabbed a few ice cubes, and wrapped them in the towel. She returned to where he lay and rolled him to his side, cradling his head in her lap. She searched through his hair, wishing he had gotten it trimmed, until she found the large L-shaped cut. She put the towel and ice against the cut and pressed hard, praying this would slow the flow of blood.

The EMS arrived quickly and Holly moved out of their way, her clothes covered with blood, her hands trembling as she watched them bandage his head, then load him on a stretcher. A few minutes later, the siren running full blast, the EMS vehicle pulled out of the driveway and headed for the hospital.

Holly gathered the crying children about her. "Stop crying. He is going to be all right. Let's go home. I need to change clothes and then I'll go to the hospital to see how he's doing."

"Is he going to die?" Amy asked.

"No," Holly said, praying that was so.

"I'm sorry. I didn't know something like this would happen," Amy said, throwing her arms around Holly and crying, not minding that Holly's clothes were covered with Stanley's blood.

Holly dropped down to a squat in front of Amy. "Oh, Amy, Amy, what have you done?"

The children all began talking then. In spite of it, Holly was able to piece together what happened. She felt sorry for Amy, of course, but thought this was a good lesson for her to learn. It wouldn't hurt the others to benefit from it, either.

Holly left ER to clean up Stanley's place, and ES to get the children fed and put to bed.

She drove to the hospital. When she inquired about Stanley, her knees almost buckled beneath her when the nurse said he would be okay.

"He lost a lot of blood . . . head wounds always bleed a lot. Dr. MacAllister said he didn't know how you found him so fast, but it was a good thing. He could easily have bled to death."

"May I see him?"

"Not tonight, but you may come again in the morning. He's in room 102."

As she drove home, Holly thought about what had happened . . . what *might* have happened if the children had been too frightened to tell her.

What if they had left him lying there on the kitchen floor, to bleed to death?

The next morning Holly dressed to go to the hospital. She still could not believe what had happened. This morning, after breakfast, she'd had a good talk with the children. They told her what happened and seemed truly remorseful. But somehow, that didn't seem good enough. She wished there was something she could do, something that would make them realize the graveness of what they had done. Suddenly, she had an idea.

She found ES in the playroom on the third floor. "Find ER and come to the girls' rooms. I want each one of them dressed . . . with the exception of Genny."

ES followed her down the stairs, then went to find ER. By the time the two of them returned, Holly had the girls' clothes laid out. "I want you to change clothes.

We're going to the hospital to see Stanley," she told them.

"I don't want to go," Amy said.

"Well, you're going, and before we go, we're going to write Stanley a note and each one of you is signing your name to it."

Not one of them spoke a word.

At the hospital, they walked quietly toward Stanley's room, each one of them carrying a plant for him. The note they had written was tucked inside the fern Amy carried.

Holly opened the door, then stood to one side as the children filed quietly into the room, clustering around his bed. Holly looked at Stanley. He was lying on his side, his head bandaged. His face was pale, his eyes closed.

"Is he dead?" Katie whispered.

"No, he's asleep."

"Are we going to stay here until he wakes up?" Erin asked.

"No, we'll leave our flowers and the note, then we'll go."

"Will we come back?" asked Maudie.

"If you'd like."

"I don't want to come back," Beth said.

"Why not?"

"He's going to hate us."

"No, he won't. When you tell him what happened, he'll understand. Stanley won't hate you. He's a nice man."

"I wish he was our daddy," Erin said.

"He wouldn't want to be *our* daddy," Beth said. "Not after what we did."

"Put your flowers down on that table," Holly said. "Katie, let me have yours. I'll put it in the window."

"Will he see it when he wakes up?" Katie asked.

"Yes, he will."

"Will he know it's from me?"

"He will when you tell him."

One by one, Holly led the children, who walked on tiptoe, from the room. There was little doubt that what they had seen left them shaken. She hoped it would be a long, long time before they thought about doing mischief again. She closed the door behind them with a click.

Chapter Thirteen

When he heard the door shut, Stanley opened his eyes. His head ached abominably, but he had heard every word they said. He wasn't certain what it was that the kids had done, but somehow, it involved letting Sweetie Pie into his kitchen. Stanley didn't remember anything after that.

When he returned home the next day, Stanley discovered not only that something profound had happened to his house—it was wonderfully clean from top to bottom—but something profound had also happened to him.

Somehow, some way, Stanley had changed. He blamed it on the blow to his head, the kids, that damn cat. Even Holly. Regardless of who he blamed, he couldn't deny he had changed.

He didn't have much time to think about it, for Holly and the kids kept coming over to see him, checking to see if he was okay. Even ES and ER were coming over, fussing over him, bringing him something to eat and stocking his refrigerator with treats. They even did his laundry and washed his car.

He thought about how nice they were being and then he remembered what the kids had said about wishing he were their daddy. That shook him up. There was little doubt that they did need a daddy . . . but not *him*. His chest puffed out. Not that he wouldn't make a good one.

Wait a minute. What was he doing? A daddy? Him? The thought scared the ever-living hell out of him. He suddenly felt trapped, like everyone next door was out to get him. Their being nice had a motive behind it. They *were* out to get him. He was suddenly convinced Holly was looking for a husband and he was it. He already had proof the kids wanted a daddy. He cringed at the thought.

He was still shaking when Holly came over.

"How are you feeling?" she asked.

Stanley laid the book he had been trying to read facedown in his lap. "I'm feeling fine, and do you know why I'm feeling fine?"

She shook her head.

"Because there's nothing wrong with me. I had a cut on the head. I had it sewed up. The stitches come out in a few days. I went back to work yesterday. I worked today. I'll go to work tomorrow. My life is back to normal. My neighbors are not."

"But you had a nasty cut."

"Which I have fully recovered from."

"You spent the night in the hospital."

"For observation, nothing more. Believe me. There's nothing wrong with me, save the fact that I have a bald patch in the back of my head where they shaved it."

Holly started crying. "I'm so sorry, Stanley. This is all my fault for moving here."

"What's your fault?"

"Your accident."

"It doesn't matter. It wasn't that severe. I'll grow more hair and manufacture more blood. There's nothing to worry about."

"Yes, there is. The children want to come over and apologize, but they're afraid you hate them."

"They haven't done anything for me to hate them."

"Yes, they have."

Stanley just looked at her.

"The night you fell, they were watching you through the window. When they saw the lightbulbs on the counter, they thought it would be funny to snitch them and watch you look for them. Only when Amy opened the door to take the lightbulbs, Sweetie ran into the house."

"Well, don't be too hard on them. I have a feeling they've learned their lesson."

"Oh, they have."

"Then forget it."

"May the children come over to apologize?"

"Tell you what," Stanley said, rising to his feet. "I'll come over to your house and they can apologize there."

He followed Holly over to her house and waited in the living room while she rounded up the girls. One by one, they came into the room, hands folded in front of them, quiet as mice, innocent as angels.

Stanley sat on the sofa next to Holly as the girls took turns telling him they were sorry. Only Genny escaped the torture by sitting in her mother's lap. Stanley listened, yet all during the time the older girls were speaking, he couldn't get those words that haunted him out of his mind. *I wish he was our daddy . . .*

When the last of them had finished, Holly told them they could go back upstairs. They departed, much in the same manner they had entered. When they were gone, Holly put Genny on the floor and told her to join her sisters.

Genny put her thumb in her mouth and toddled toward the door, then turned around and came back to Stanley. She pulled her thumb out of her mouth with a pop, then pointed her finger at him and said, "Stanley hurt." Then she climbed into his lap and pulled his head toward her and gave him a big smack on the head. "There," she said, "feel better?"

Stanley smiled. "Much better."

She climbed out of his lap and left the room as Stanley and Holly stared at each other.

"What was that all about?" he asked.

Holly smiled. "I always kiss their hurts and then I ask them if it doesn't feel better."

Stanley went home after that. He didn't sleep well that night, or the next night, either. He was troubled. He was even more troubled when he went out to get the paper a few days later and found Plato asleep on Holly's front porch with that contentious cat, Sweetie Pie, curled up just a few feet away.

He didn't know what to do. Should he give up, as Plato apparently had done, or sue that damn dog psychologist?

Once Plato made peace with Sweetie Pie, he began spending a great deal of time away from home. All of a sudden, Stanley couldn't keep Plato in the house. He was always next door. He had lost his dog to the enemy, and the enemy seemed to be too busy with Christmas to think about anything else.

Stanley didn't know why they had bothered to give him all that attention if they didn't intend to keep it up.

Things seemed to get even more miserable when he realized that Holly's life was simply too full for her to be hunting for a man to fill it. He found that more of a disappointment than a relief.

He saw so many things going on next door that reminded him of what he never had. He decided he wanted those things in his life, only he wasn't certain how one went about getting them. What would it take to make a forty-year-old psychiatrist happy?

A Christmas party?

Chapter Fourteen

It started snowing the morning of Heather's Christmas party. She called to complain. "Can you believe my luck? Everyone will have to schlepp over here in their snow boots, wearing their Armanis and riding in a four-wheel drive. Damn weather."

"Not everyone. I'll be wearing my McFadden and driving a minivan," replied Holly.

"You're wearing Mary McFadden?"

"I went to Atlanta yesterday and found the most divine cocktail suit on sale at Neiman's."

"A McFadden marked way down would still set you back eight or nine hundred dollars."

"It did, but I decided I was worth it. It's my Christmas present to myself."

"Speaking of Atlanta, did I tell you that your neighbor is taking his neurotic dog to a dog psychologist?"

"Stanley?"

"The same."

"He's taking Plato in for counseling?"

"All the way to Atlanta."

"Poor Stanley. I guess Sweetie was giving Plato a harder time than we thought." Holly paused a moment. "You know, I think the therapy must be working. Yesterday, when I came home, I saw Plato asleep on our porch and Sweetie was lying just a few feet away.

"Yes, I heard about that. Now he thinks the psychologist has overdone it, so he's taking Plato back for more therapy." She shook her head. "If only we could work out our problems as easily. Do you think Stanley's coming tonight?"

"I don't know. I thought you said he was."

"He told me he would when I invited him, and after the invitations went out, his office called to say he'd be here. But that doesn't mean he won't get cold feet at the last minute. He's never come to one of my parties, you know."

"No, I didn't know. Well, maybe this will be a first."

"If he shows up, it will definitely be a first."

Holly and Heather chatted a few more minutes, then hung up. It was half past three. Holly was having a manicure at four and her hair cut and styled at five, then she had to come home, shower, and dress. Squeezed in between all of that was the girls' evening ritual of prayers, hugs, and kisses. That wouldn't give her much time to dress and drive to Heather's, and Heather wanted her to come early.

The manicurist was running thirty minutes late. The hairdresser was half an hour behind. Holly was supposed to be at Heather's at seven, and it was almost seven when she arrived home.

She hurried into the bathroom. Someone had left the shower lever up and the moment she turned on the water, it sprayed her new hairdo. Holly was on the verge of tears, but thankfully, it was only one side of her hair that was wet, but it was another delay. She called Heather to apologize, telling her she wouldn't be there early to help.

"Don't worry about it. Mary Anne and Fred came over early. Everything is done. We're sitting here having a glass of champagne, waiting for everyone to arrive. Take your time, Holly. Don't get stressed out and have a wreck on the way over. Thank God it stopped snowing."

"How are the roads?"

"The snowplows came through a couple of hours ago, so the snow isn't deep, but it can be slick. Are you bringing the mini-van?"

"No, I think I'll drive the Jeep."

"I thought you were having trouble with the Jeep."

"It was hard to start a time or two, but it seems fine now. I'll feel safer in the four-wheel drive."

"Okay. See you when you get here."

By the time Holly arrived, the parking places on the street were all gone, so she parked the Jeep in Heather's driveway, then took off her snow boots and slipped her feet into a pair of red Manolo Blahnik evening sandals. She didn't bother to ring the bell, but let herself in. She removed her coat and carried it down the hall to Heather's bedroom. She gave herself the once-over in the mirror. She had to admit it. This dress was a killer. All gold and red brocade—short, tight, and looking good.

She left Heather's room and walked toward the party, following the sound of music and conversation. When she reached the family room, she saw it was packed with people. She also saw Stanley. He was standing in the open archway at the top of the stairs that led down to the family room.

She stopped next to him. "Hi, Stanley. Are you coming or going?"

"I haven't decided."

"You've come this far—you can't leave now."

"Why can't I?"

"Because everyone has seen you. To leave now would be past rude."

He turned and allowed his gaze to travel over her slowly, not that Holly minded. One did not wear a suit like this if one did not want to be looked at.

"Is that written somewhere in the Pi Phi's Primer for Proper Southern Behavior?"

"Probably, but I was a Kappa."

He was still looking her over. She decided he must like the color. "Do you like red?"

"I like that red."

She smiled. "It's my Christmas present to myself."

"You should give yourself gifts more often."

"Are you two going to stand there making eyes at each other, or are you going to get with the program?" John Fedder shouted.

Suddenly, John's wife, Madge, shouted, "Look! They're standing under the mistletoe."

The noise level dropped as everyone in the room turned to look. "Kiss her," they shouted. "What are you waiting for?"

Holly made a mental note to kick John Fedder's fender when she left. Her face grew warm and she glanced at Stanley to see if he was as mortified as she. His expression was what she would call tolerant.

Ray Sebastian shouted, "Come on, man. Kiss her! Don't you know what mistletoe is for?"

Then everyone joined in, shouting and calling for Stanley to kiss her.

Holly glanced at Stanley again. He was positively flustered. "That's what we get for being late," she whispered.

"Do we have to do this?" he whispered back.

"Oh, come on, Stanley. It isn't like you're being asked

to kiss the prize pig at a country fair. I don't have anything contagious."

"I wasn't worried about that."

"You should be worried about what everyone is thinking. Look. Everyone is staring at us. In a minute they're going to be wondering which one of us is strange. I mean, we're both attractive people, and if we don't join in the spirit of things and get this thing over with, we're going to be talked about." She paused and gave him a contemplative look. "When was the last time you kissed someone?"

"Four or five years ago."

"Geez, Stanley. Do you think you remember how?"

Stanley started to say something, but Holly went up on her toes and aimed for his mouth. She was ready to get this absurd kiss over with so she could join the others and get on with the evening. She did not want to stand here all night trying to figure out the best way to overcome Stanley's insecurities. One peck, that's all . . . just one quick, innocent, and chaste kiss.

Her mouth touched his. His lips were warm and soft. It wasn't so bad. Really. Everyone cheered, and she was about to withdraw when suddenly, Stanley got into the spirit of things.

Suddenly his arms came around her and he crushed her against him with a passion she would have thought belonged to Senator Packwood, not Stanley.

His mouth opened. Hers did likewise. He kissed her deeply, and the feeling it evoked shook her. She heard the whistles and the catcalls, then everything seemed to fade into the woodwork. *This was Stanley kissing her.*

Stanley, her next door neighbor. Stanley with the eccentric ways. Stanley with the rumpled Ivy League clothes and glasses. Stanley, the nerd psychiatrist who hadn't kissed a woman in four or five years.

Well, ole Stanley might not do much kissing, but he

was one hell of a kisser. She knew then that things would never be the same.

When he broke the kiss and released her, Holly stumbled backward, thankful that a pillar was there to support her. She stared up at Stanley, knowing there was a confused look upon her face, wanting to see if he was as stunned, as dazed as she was.

His psychiatrist expression was unreadable and for a moment she envied him that. But as she looked deeper, searching behind the guarded look in his eyes, she saw a tense control there, a control that said he was every bit as shaken as she.

Blessedly, everyone began to crowd around them, offering congratulations on the way they had gotten into the spirit of Christmas. The men were clapping Stanley on the back, telling him that in spite of the fact that Holly had initiated the kiss, he had done the manly thing by taking control of the situation.

Holly glanced at Stanley. Much to her surprise, he seemed to be taking all of this in stride. Judging from the way his chest puffed out, he seemed quite pleased with himself.

Merv gave his shoulder a squeeze and said, "That's what I like, a man who takes control of things. Bless my soul, if that wasn't about the best mistletoe kiss I've ever seen."

Stanley chuckled. "A man does what he has to do."

Holly's mouth dropped open. Stanley had a personality? Stanley actually had charm and wit? And she, who prided herself on always having command of her faculties was at a total loss? How dare he recover, when she was so unsettled. She was nothing but loose ends. She prayed no one would notice.

"I do believe this is the first time in my life that I've seen Holly speechless," Heather said.

Every eye in the room was suddenly upon her. Holly looked at Heather like she couldn't believe what she had just heard. Heather was her friend. How could she say something like that?

Of course, Holly would have to admit it was the truth. She couldn't have spoken if someone had stuffed her mouth with the words. She just couldn't get over it. Stanley a kisser?

She simply could not believe it. What was worse, she couldn't believe she had enjoyed it. What was wrong with him, grabbing her and kissing her like that?

What was wrong with her, kissing him back? She was a grown woman, for heaven's sake . . . with children . . . and three marriages behind her. This wasn't supposed to happen to her. Not here. Not now.

And most assuredly, not with Stanley. He wasn't even her type.

She ignored the doubtful feeling that thought produced, and without a look in his direction, left him standing there in the doorway relishing the extolling of his prowess.

The party went on and it was obvious everyone was having the time of their lives. Everyone except Holly, that is. She was having a miserable time. No matter how hard she tried, she could not get into the groove. There was little doubt that Stanley's kiss changed everything, and to what extent, she was uncertain.

From time to time, she would glance in his direction, just to see if he was as disturbed by what had happened as she. Frequently, when she looked, she would find him looking at her. Other times, she would feel as if someone was watching her, and when she would look, Stanley would be looking at her like he was probing her psyche. He probably knew more about her than she did. It gave her the willies and she vowed to ignore him and his analyzing gazes.

It didn't work.

All evening they kept exchanging glances. She went out of her way to avoid him and had a miserable time.

She wished with all her heart this hadn't happened, for now she wouldn't ever again feel that wonderful nonchalance, that indifferent feeling around him. Now, anytime she saw him, she would remember that kiss. She would worry about the way she looked, or the things she said. Her casual passive regard would be forever replaced by acute awareness.

From this moment forward, she would be aware of him, not as her nerdy neighbor, not as a sloppy dresser, or even as a stodgy eccentric. Now she would always be aware of him as a man.

"You haven't said a word to me all evening," Heather said. "I'm sorry if I made you mad."

"You didn't make me mad, you just made me the center of attention when I was desperately trying to blend in with the wallpaper."

"I'm glad you aren't upset with me, but you're being awfully quiet. Kissing Stanley really shook you up, didn't it?"

"I feel like I've been sacrificed to a volcano. Things are getting hot and there isn't anything I can do about it. I've never had a more miserable time. It's a lovely party, but I just can't get in step with the music." She glanced at her watch. "It's eleven-thirty. I think I'll go home."

Heather took her arm and the two of them walked to Heather's bedroom and Holly put on her coat. "I don't know how I'll ever be able to look him in the face. I'll be a prisoner in my own home. This is awful. Just awful."

"Holly, I think you're getting too worked up over this. It was just a friendly Christmas, under the mistletoe and under a lot of pressure, kiss."

"It isn't *what* it was. It's the *way* it was. He kissed me good and proper, Heather."

"So, that's *his* problem. He's the one who won't be able to look *you* in the face."

"Heather, I kissed him back. I mean I really, really kissed him back."

"Oh, dear."

"He probably thinks I've got designs on him. I bet he's paranoid that I'll try to make him husband number four. I lay you odds he's in there right now, trying to think of ways to avoid me."

"Well, you could always move."

"That's what I like about you, Heather. You always did come up with such simple, workable solutions."

"I'm sure Stanley is just as mortified as you are. The best thing to do is to forget it ever happened. The two of you will keep your distance for a few days, then when you do encounter each other, you'll go on like before, never mentioning this at all."

Holly picked up her purse and the two of them walked to the front door. "I hope you're right."

"Don't worry. Stanley has enough to keep him busy worrying about Plato. He's probably forgotten all about you and the kiss."

"I hope so."

Holly kissed Heather's cheek and thanked her for the party, but as she walked out the door, she somehow doubted Stanley was the kind of person who ever forgot anything.

Chapter Fifteen

The first thing she noticed was that it had snowed again. Holly picked her way to the car, staying close to the house to protect her shoes as much as she could.

When she reached her car, she saw the windows of the Jeep were covered with snow, so she brushed the worst of it off with her gloved hand, then unlocked the door and climbed inside.

She was shivering by the time she put the key in the ignition and turned it.

It clicked.

She tried again.

Click . . .

Just click, nothing more.

Click . . . click . . . click . . . Great. Wonderful. Now she was sitting out here in a snowbank in freezing weather and was going to have to trudge back into the house and call AAA.

She pounded the steering wheel in frustration. "Damn . . . damn . . . damn . . ."

Someone tapped on her window.

She looked up. It was Stanley.

Great! The one person she did *not* want to see. He was bundled up in a heavy overcoat with a beaver collar. A thick scarf was wrapped around his neck. His glasses were gone and his hair was blowing. He looked absolutely, positively wonderful.

She hated him. She couldn't even curse in private, damn him.

He tapped again and she rolled down the window.

"Don't ask me for a ride."

"I wasn't going to. I was just curious as to why you were beating an innate object. Steering wheels can't fight back, you know. Are you all right?"

"I'm fine, Stanley, simply fine and dandy. I've never been better in my life. In fact, I'm having such a great time, I thought I'd stay right here enjoying myself until I freeze and turn into a block of ice."

The corners of his mouth looked like they were struggling to remain where they were. *If he laughs at me, I'll stuff his ears with snow.* How dare he come out here looking better than a tropical vacation, making her think about things she had no business thinking about.

Great kisser . . . Great kisser . . . Great kisser . . .

She wanted to tell him she wouldn't kiss him again no matter how great he was, that he could take that great kisser of his and have it bronzed. She sighed heavily. She couldn't be getting a crush on this man. She simply couldn't. It was not part of her plan. He was not her type. She didn't even like him. And yet, he was making her heart pound by just standing there. "It isn't my steering wheel. My car won't start."

"What's wrong with it?"

"I don't know, Stanley. If I knew the answer to that, I'd be an automobile mechanic. I don't have any idea why it won't start. I put the key in the ignition. I turn it. All I get is a click."

She demonstrated it for him, just so he would know

this wasn't some contrivance on her part to spend more time with him. Well she knew, after three marriages, that men could read all sorts of screwy little innuendos into things. With Stanley, she wanted all her cards on the table. Face up.

She tried one more time to start the Jeep, just for good measure. *Click . . . click . . . click . . .*

"It might be the starter. Or your battery. It could even be something wrong with the electrical system."

"Why don't we just hope for all three?"

"That isn't very likely."

"Whatever it is, I don't need this to happen tonight." She opened the door, reached for the keys, and got out, locking the door. "I don't know why I bother. I wish someone would steal this piece of junk." She dropped the keys in her purse, then turned to go. Stanley was blocking the way. She looked up at him. "I have to go back inside and call AAA."

He took her arm. "Come on. I'll take you home."

"No! I mean, that's all right. Really. I don't mind calling AAA. I like to call them, actually. I don't want to put you to any trouble. I'm a member of AAA. They're supposed to come out if I have any trouble. That's what I'm paying for. They expect their members to call when they have car trouble. It says so in all the brochures. It makes them feel needed. If AAA members don't use their services, then they'll be forced out of business. I wouldn't want that on my conscience. Putting AAA out of business would make me feel terrible and I feel terrible enough already. I'll just go in and call them and they'll be here in a . . ."

"Holly, will you shut up for once in your life and stop trying to take control? Can't you let things happen instead of making them happen?" His gaze searched her face.

There went her heart again, turning flips and acting crazy.

"I'll take you home. It won't be any trouble. You live next door, so you're right on the way. However, if it will make you feel better, when I get to your house, I'll slow down to fifteen or so, open the door, and roll you out onto your driveway as I pass by. That way, I won't even have to stop."

She found herself laughing in spite of her determination not to. She couldn't believe it, but it was true. She was actually laughing at something Stanley said. It was the first time she had ever heard him say anything funny, or anything that even remotely resembled a joke. "Why, Stanley, that was funny."

"I have been known to be entertaining upon occasions."

She glanced back at the house. "Well, if you're sure you don't mind . . ."

"I don't mind. Tell you what. You wait here. I'll bring the car."

She watched him go, liking the sound of his whistling.

A few minutes later, he pulled into the driveway. He was out of the car and had her door open by the time she reached it. Once inside, he backed out and drove down the street.

She snuggled down into the seat. "The person who invented car heaters should be decorated. "It's freezing out there."

"A common occurrence in December."

"Don't get practical with me, Stanley. It's Christmas. I feel like being festive and jolly. I want to believe in Santa Claus and miracles, even if it's just for a little while. I don't want serious. I don't want practical. I don't want to be analyzed. And above all, I don't want to listen to my stuffy, critical neighbor being his customary pragmatic self."

He turned the corner and drove out onto the main thoroughfare which was cleverly named Main Street. He still hadn't spoken.

"I haven't made you mad, have I?"

They stopped at a red light, but he did not turn to look at her.

"No, why should speaking your mind or the truth make me mad? You're entitled to your opinion."

"I don't want to hear about my entitlements right now, Stanley. I don't want to hear about normal behavior. Christmas is a time for being abnormal, for stepping out of character and doing something reckless and perhaps, just a little bit foolish. It's a time for pinning all your hopes and dreams on a star." She stopped and turned a serious face on him. "Do you know what scares me about you?"

"No, what?"

"I see you as the kind of man who could eat dog food when he gets old."

He chuckled. "Plato wouldn't let me. Besides, that shouldn't bother you. Genny eats cat food." He turned onto Orchard Street and gave her a grin so charming she wanted to slap him. She had had enough of charming for one evening.

"Eating cat food isn't something Genny does on a regular basis."

He pulled up in front of her house and turned into the driveway. "Eating cat food is eating cat food. It's the deed, not the number of times it's performed."

"And an opinionated, old-before-his-time bore is a bore. Good night."

She didn't give him time to put the car in park, but hopped out quickly. Her feet sank into snow over her ankles. She didn't care. All she cared about was getting away from him. "Thank you for the ride," she called back to him.

She didn't give him time to respond. She slammed the door and whirled in a theatrical manner, then marched up the driveway. She was beginning to feel the snow on her feet and remembered her boots back in the Jeep. She looked down. Her lovely red satin shoes were buried in snow.

They were also slick on the bottoms—something she discovered when she started sliding and her feet went out from under her. She landed smack on her butt. Before he could get his door open and out of the car, she was on her feet, but not for long.

She slipped again and went down a second time. Two more times she tried to get up, but she was too mad, too confused, and too humiliated to think about what she was doing. Finally, she quit struggling and simply sat there, feeling the cold, wet snow soak through the red McFadden suit, through the pink satin slip and what lay beneath, to her goose bumps. This was going to be the worst Christmas ever. She just knew it.

She heard him coming up behind her and readied a fistful of snow. If he so much as said a humorous word, she would let him have it.

"Are you ready to let me help you, or would you rather sit there melting like the polar ice cap?"

She gave him a go-to-hell look and realized instantly it had been a mistake—not the go-to-hell look, but looking at him. There he was, standing in front of her, big as Dallas, a grin on his face, looking for all the world like he had already analyzed her and come up with *childish behavior* as a diagnosis.

She let fly with the snowball, but he ducked it effortlessly.

He leaned forward to give her a hand up. "Feel better?"

She hated psychiatrists. She really did. She slapped his hand away and struggled to get up by herself and failed miserably. She slumped back into the mushy hole she had made. Her entire backside was wet. Her dress was probably ruined. Her shoes definitely were. She wanted to cry, but she would be damned if she would do it in front of him.

He dropped down in a squat beside her. "Do you want to talk about it?"

She rolled her eyes. "Oh Lord, I'm going to be psychoanalyzed while I'm sitting here, completely helpless, with my ass frozen to the driveway. No, I don't want to talk about *IT* or anything else . . ." She tried to get up again, struggling as she talked, which made her words come out in a breathless manner. "And if I did feel like talking, it wouldn't be with you."

"I find that interesting."

She was on her knees and felt her hose rip. His face was inches from hers. She struggled in earnest now. "I'm sure you do. It's your job to take morbid interest in other people and their misery. No wonder psychiatrists are so warped. They wallow in other people's dirty laundry. You're always so proper, so correct. Now I understand why. You exist in a state of alertness, watching for clues to a person's happiness—or lack of. You're like a vulture sitting on a fence, waiting for something to die. Do you ever do anything besides be critical and appraising? Do you have to know *all* the answers to *all* the questions *all* the time? Don't you ever live for the sake of being alive? Have you ever laughed at yourself, or taken chances?"

"I've been known to take a risk now and then."

She slipped again and was back where she started from, but she paid that no mind. She was more interested in the question she had to ask. "When? I'd really and truly like to know when."

"I believe the last time was tonight."

"Tonight? What could you possibly have done tonight that was risky? Driving your car across town in the dark?" Suddenly, she gave him a knowing look. "Oh, I forgot. Of course. You offered me a ride home. Was it a big, scary risk to be in the car, alone with a woman?"

"No, that was no risk. I knew you'd let me take you home before I asked you."

"I hate you. I really and truly do. I've never hated a neighbor in my life, but I hate you." She stopped for a breath, suddenly curious. "What was the risk you took tonight? Tell me. I want to know. Just what did you do tonight that was so risky?"

"I kissed you, didn't I?"

"And you call that a risk? A kiss? One measly little Christmas mistletoe kiss?"

"Of course. I didn't know what your reaction would be. You could've slapped my face, or insulted me, or bolted in the opposite direction. You could've even been a good sport about it. But you didn't do that, either. What you did was kiss me back."

"I did not."

"Holly, I kissed you and you kissed me back, and something happened between us, something you spent the rest of the night avoiding. And that's how I knew you'd let me take you home."

"That's no proof."

"It is. You let me take you home because you wondered if I'd try to kiss you again, and if I tried, you were going to let me."

She opened her mouth to hotly deny that, but he put his fingers over her mouth and went on talking.

"And do you know why I knew you'd let me? Because you wanted to know if it was really the way you remembered. When I offered you a ride home, that provided the perfect opportunity to find out."

"So now you think I'm enamored with you? That I'm throwing myself at your feet? I suppose you're even so swellheaded that you think I did something to my car just so I'd have the opportunity to go home with you."

"No, I think you're so shocked and so dumbfounded over what happened between us that you're terrified. You've been hurt by those you cared for, more than once. You don't want to care about anyone. It's safer. You don't want to love again. You don't want to be hurt again, so you're afraid to take another risk. For a long time I was nothing more than your nerdy neighbor, someone you looked upon as completely harmless, totally safe. You felt no risk around me."

"And I don't anymore? Is that what you're saying?"

"That's exactly what I'm saying."

"And you could tell all of that from one little, insignificant kiss? My, my, you *are* astute."

"It wasn't an insignificant kiss."

In spite of the fact that her fanny was frozen, she studied her fingernails. "It was insignificant to me."

"Like hell it was." He brought his face closer and she could feel the warmth of his breath against her face. "Some people are quite adept at lying. You aren't one of them." He drew closer still.

He was so close, she had to lean her head back, so far back that she had to brace herself with her hands.

Every time she drew back, he came closer. His lips were almost brushing hers. "Stay away from me," she warned. "Get off my property."

"Let's settle this thing, once and for all."

"I don't want to settle . . . What thing?"

"The answer to the question we've both been asking ourselves all evening."

"And what question is that?"

"If there was really something to that kiss we shared, or were we just imagining it."

He didn't give her time to think about it. All he had to do was move his head a hair's breadth to put his lips against hers. She leaned back and would have fallen if his hand had not come around to support the back of her head.

Her heart began to pound and the blood seemed to run too thick and too slow to reach her brain. She felt warm and groggy, as if she were drugged. This couldn't be happening to her again. It couldn't be. A person did not fall in love sitting on her butt in a pile of freezing snow in the middle of the driveway. It simply wasn't done this way.

She had another thought on the way, but it got side-tracked somewhere between the feel of his body against hers and the warm taste of his kiss. All those years in college, she had avoided nerds. What a waste. If she had only known then that nerds could kiss like this. And to think how much time she'd wasted kissing football players.

He broke the kiss and looked down at her, his voice unbelievably soft and sincere. "We seem to have a definite problem here. Question is, how are we going to deal with it so that we both come out getting what we want?"

"I don't know the answer to that," she said, "because I don't know what I want."

He was hypnotizing her. That's what psychiatrists were good at. She gave her head a shake, collecting her senses. "I'll tell you what I think we should do about it. Of course, I don't know about you, but I'm going inside before I get too cold to be mad at you for the rest of my life."

He laughed and reached for her hand. Finding it, he rose to his feet, then tugged her upward until she was standing. He looked down at the red satin shoes. "No wonder you were falling all over the place. Where are your boots?"

"In my car, and don't you dare tell me they're doing me a lot of good there."

He caught her and lifted her into his arms, then walked toward her porch.

It was too much. Now he was being chivalrous. Dear God, what would he try next? She was too speechless to speak. What had happened to him? Where was the man who lived next door? This man looked like Stanley, but it wasn't Stanley. This man could make conversation.

He could laugh. He could be charming. He could be chivalrous and understanding. He could even kiss.

But he still didn't know the first thing about how to dress. Yet, even as she closed the door behind her and went up the stairs to her room, she was thinking that it was far easier to teach a man how to dress than it was to teach him how to kiss.

Chapter Sixteen

Stanley woke up a few days later, a new man.

After dressing, he fed Plato, then himself, then went to the hardware store. After leaving there, he stopped by Bradley Brothers Nursery.

Once he was back home, he unloaded his car and went to the garage for his ladder. When he came out of the garage, he saw Maudie standing there, all bundled up in a snowsuit and looking like a round little munchkin.

"Hi, Stanley."

"Hello, Maudie. Are you going to play in the snow?"

"Our snow is all mussed up. Can I play in your snow?"

"Sure, go ahead." He carried the ladder down the driveway.

Maudie ran around the corner of the house and Stanley saw that ES was standing at the end of the driveway waiting for her. He put the ladder in position, then said, "Good morning, Esmeralda."

"Good morning, Dr. Levine. Maudie wants to play in your snow. It's okay?"

"Okay by me," he said, then climbed up the ladder. At the top, he pulled a nail out of his pocket and began hammering.

His hammering woke her up.

Holly looked at her clock. Seven o'clock. She put the pillow over her head and murmured the same Spanish curse word ES loved to use. She could still hear the hammering, so she threw back the covers and crawled out of bed. She opened the door and yelled downstairs, "Who is doing all of that infernal hammering this early in the morning?"

ER yelled back, "It's Dr. Levine . . . and it isn't early. It's almost eleven o'clock."

"Eleven? But my clock says seven."

"Your clock is wrong. I bet you forgot to reset it last night when the electricity went off."

"Blast and double blast." She went to the window and looked out. Stanley was on a ladder, hammering the dickens out of a nail. What was he doing? She moved closer, pulling the curtains back to get a better look. She could see that he had something looped around his shoulder and as she watched, he took one end and held it against the house and started hammering again. Her vision was clearing now, and she could see he held a string of lights.

Christmas lights? Ebenezer Scrooge was hanging Christmas lights? He was nothing but a hypocrite. How dare he celebrate Christmas.

She turned away from the window. She would not give him the satisfaction of noticing his lights. He could light up the whole state of Georgia and she would not notice.

She dressed, ignoring the furious hammering going on next door, then went downstairs. She was just pouring milk over a bowl of shredded wheat when the children came running inside. All seven of them.

"Stanley's put up lights and he bought a Christmas tree!"

She calmly took a bite of cereal, chewed it, swallowed it, and washed it down with a sip of coffee. "He bought lights so he can show off. He probably wants to burn the tree in the fireplace, but none of that matters one whit to me. Stanley can eat a can of worms, for all I care."

Down to the last child, they all wheeled around and went running outside, shouting they were going to tell Stanley. When did her children become so enamored with Stanley?

It was a while later that the pack came charging into the house again, this time to tell her Stanley wasn't going to burn his Christmas tree in the fireplace. "He's decorating his tree and it was looking very nice," Amy said.

"He's got lots of bootiful decorations," Maudie added.

"That's good." Suddenly, she gave them a serious, mother-is-suspicious-about-something look. "And how do you know he's decorating it, and that it's looking very nice?"

She had no more than spoken the words when they grew very quiet, each of them suddenly interested in staring at the floor. She zeroed in on Katie because Katie was at the age it was easiest to intimidate. Giving her the tell-or-go-to-bed-with-no-supper look, she asked, "You've been spying again, haven't you?"

Katie nodded violently. "Yes . . . but Stanley said it was okay."

That did it.

She left her bowl of shredded wheat, not caring if it got mushy, and marched out of the house. A minute later she was banging on Stanley's front door.

When he opened the door, she did not give him a chance to say anything. She started in on him, berating him for everything from the sinking of the *Titanic* to the Vietnam War. "Do you know what I think of your interference?"

She didn't give him time to answer. "I'd like to know what makes you an authority on child-rearing. Just how many children have you raised? And don't think your medical degree makes you an expert. Books don't raise children."

She didn't give him a chance to say anything this time, either. "Do you have any idea what it's like to have your authority undermined? Don't you care how hard I've been trying to teach the children to respect other people's property, their rights? And what do you do, Mr. Author of Complaints? You tell them it's okay to peek in your windows. What are you using for brains? It's *not* okay for my children to peek in your windows. It's not okay for them to peek in *anyone's* windows. You should be ashamed of yourself, Stanley Levine. You really should. I'm a single, working mother with seven kids to raise. It's a full-time job just to keep them from killing each other. I have an investment in my children. You do not. When was the last time you came home late and saw fourteen white socks and seven pairs of brown shoes on the living room floor and stayed up another hour trying to figure which kid they belonged to? Have you ever tried working and taking care of seven kids with the chicken pox? Have you ever stared at a pot of gooey oatmeal at six in the morning when everyone is crying that they want pancakes, or pulled back the covers of your bed at two in the morning, only to be greeted by a sleepy garter snake? Do you know what it's like to explain heaven to a child, or to console them when they've just flushed their goldfish down the drain? And tell me, please, just when was the last time you found a gerbil in your underwear drawer? Being a mother is hard work. Being a single working mother is even harder. Being a mother is time-consuming and sometimes there aren't enough hours in the day, especially when I'm also responsible for their support, but I do the best I can. I may not have all the answers or meet all of their needs all of the time, but I can tell you one thing I don't need—a shrink with a balanced checkbook, a lot of free time, and a neurotic dog telling me how to raise my children. Now, before I go, do you have anything to say for yourself?''

She was so worked up and had so much adrenaline pumping she could have climbed Mt. Everest with one hand. And what was he doing? Looking quite relaxed and smiling at her, as if he was enjoying all of this. She fully expected him to say something philosophical like you made your bed, now lie in it. That is why it caught her completely off guard when he said, "That is, perhaps, one of the loveliest tirades I have ever heard. You have managed to encapsulate the bittersweetness of motherhood in one paragraph."

She was so shocked, all she could do was look at him. It was while she was looking at him that it occurred to her that something about Stanley was different. Gone were his frumpy old corduroy slacks and the run-over topsiders. Gone, too, was the shapeless sweater with the worn-slick suede patches on the sleeves. In fact, it was as if Stanley himself had disappeared and in his place was another man who looked like him.

This new man looked quite elegant, like something right out of *GQ,* or a Ralph Lauren ad, and his hair . . . No more shaggy, absentminded professor. Now his hair was clipped short, with the top left long and combed back. A miracle is what it was. It had turned Stanley into Hugh Grant.

"What are you looking at?"

"You. What have you done?"

"What do you mean?"

"You've changed. You aren't the same ner . . . uh, person who lived next door. I think that fall on your head did something to you, Stanley. It affected your personality in some way . . . or at least your taste in clothes."

"Maybe you're right. Perhaps I should have it checked."

"I wouldn't, if I were you."

"Like me better this way, do you?"

She frowned. "Where are your glasses?"

"In the drawer."

"What did you do? Have a cornea transplant?"

"Contacts. I got fitted for them a couple of weeks ago. Do you like them? You don't think I look better with my glasses, do you?"

"No, of course not. I've always thought you'd look much better without them . . . Uhhhh . . . Not that I've been sitting around thinking about you all the time . . . it was just a passing thought."

He was laughing again. "If I'd known that, I would have tossed them in the drawer a long time ago."

She wasn't really listening to what he said. She was too bowled over by the change in him. Stanley looking virile? Stanley with a personality and charm? Stanley laughing on a regular basis? She had never noticed how much laughter could change a person's countenance, or influence her feelings.

"What are you thinking?"

"Nothing. I just can't get over the transformation. Just look at you . . . you've changed . . . completely."

"For the better, I hope."

"Definitely for the better. Why, Stanley, you look positively male."

He gave her a wry grin. "Male enough to take you to dinner Friday night?"

"Well, I don't know. I'm still angry with you for undermining my authority."

"Then have dinner with me and I'll give you a full apology. Of course, I'd give it to you anyway, but over dinner would be nice, I think."

She had dinner with him.

They stayed at the table long after the dishes had been cleared away. They drank cappuccino and talked. Stanley gave her a formal apology for interfering with her child-raising. She accepted it, then he ordered a bottle of champagne.

"Champagne? I don't think we need champagne."

"One should always have champagne on a special occasion."

"What special occasion? My accepting your apology?"

"No, our engagement."

"Engagement? Have you lost your senses? We're not compatible and we're not engaged. You haven't even asked me to marry you."

"I'm asking you now."

"On the basis of one kiss? Are you out of your mind? I have a house full of kids. You hate kids. I have an assertive cat. You hate cats. I'm a Southern woman. You hate Southern women. Now I ask you, why would you want to marry into something when you detest everything about it?"

"Because I've changed my mind. I've decided I like kids . . . at least, your kids. As for cats, I can't say I'm crazy about all cats, but there's one particular cat who's aggressive as hell and has earned my respect. Concerning Southern women, I realize now that I spoke from ignorance. What I considered over-frosted hair that affected their brains was really gentility and manners. What I saw as passivity was really a quiet, gentle strength. What I thought to be fakery was really a love of heritage and tradition."

"I can't marry you, Stanley."

"Yes, you can. You just don't know it yet."

Chapter Seventeen

A few days before Christmas, Holly went to Atlanta to shop. As she drove there, she thought about Stanley. Since the night he asked her to marry him, he had kept his distance. Not that she blamed him. Poor guy. He was probably nursing his wounds.

Just because he was keeping his distance, that did not mean he had given up. He was doing everything he could to change her mind.

Her house looked like a florist. The kids were so enamored with Stanley, they had all but moved next door. Even ES and ER were seen to slip over to Stanley's for a visit now and then. She was feeling outnumbered, and wondered how long she could hold out, or if she really wanted to.

Once she reached Atlanta, she drove down Peachtree to the mall, since that would make it easier to shop by doing it all with one stop. It took longer than she thought. She hadn't realized it would take so long to buy Christmas presents for seven kids and two helpers. By the time she left Atlanta, it was later than she had planned to leave.

By the time she turned down Orchard Street, she saw the Christmas lights were turned on at both her house and Stanley's. Only there was something curious about Stanley's lights, something that looked different than before.

As she drove down the street, she kept her eye on Stanley's house, trying to figure out just what it was that was different. Suddenly, it hit her. He had something written in red letters that stretched across his entire roof.

From where she was, she couldn't make out what it said exactly, but as she drew closer the message became crystal clear.

> *Holly, make my Christmas complete*
> *Marry me*

She slammed on her brakes in her driveway and shoved it into gear so fast she almost tore the transmission out of the car. Then she marched over to his house and rang his doorbell. When he opened the door, she let him have it.

"Take those ridiculous lights down, right now."

"It's dark. What if I fell off the roof?"

"Then turn them off and take them down tomorrow."

"I like them."

"Stanley, what are you trying to do? Make me the laughingstock of the neighborhood? Do you want everyone talking about us? They probably think we're sleeping together. I wouldn't be surprised if the social workers didn't show up tomorrow and take my children away from me."

"I don't think they take children away because their mother received a proposal of marriage."

"Listen, I grew up here. I have friends in this town . . . friends of long standing. They'll think I've lost my mind. They'll think I'm living next door to a lunatic.

This is humiliating. It's embarrassing. People don't put lights on their roof and make declarations like that."

"They do at Christmas."

"They say Merry Christmas or Happy New Year. They do not say, Marry me."

"They do now."

"Aren't you the least bit embarrassed to do this?"

"Not in the least."

"Why not?"

"Holly, I've learned that you can't please everyone, that you must make decisions about what you value."

She was not ready to get psychological. Lights and psychology were two different things. That was the trouble with men and women. Here she was talking lights and he was answering psychology. It wouldn't work. "Stanley, I'm warning you. Take those lights down."

"When you agree to marry me."

"This is blackmail."

"You or the lights. I get one of them. So, what's it to be?"

"Give me one good reason why I should even consider marrying a psychiatrist who needs a psychiatrist."

"I can give you a dozen: Because I love you and all of your endearing, Southern ways. Because I've grown to care for the kids, the housekeeper, the nanny, and even that militant cat you should have named Sourpuss. And I can give you more: Because I would make you a good husband, and a father for the kids, and we both know they need a father. Because you like kissing me. And if you deny it, I'll take great pleasure in proving you wrong. Because I'll love you until the day I die, and lastly, because I'm damn good in bed."

"I have no knowledge of the latter."

"But you will."

She began backing up. "Stay away from me, Stanley Levine. Don't you dare lay a hand on me or I'll scream."

"No one will come. They all want us to get married. They won't come to your rescue."

She made a dash for the door, but he caught her just as she put her hand on the handle. He turned her toward him and kissed her soundly.

She resisted him for just a moment, then she moaned and melted against him, kissing him back with equal fervor. When at last he broke the kiss, she rested her head against his shoulder for some time, too confused and too weak to speak.

When she found her voice, which was sometime later, she whispered, "Are you going to seduce me?"

He chuckled. "No, I'm going to make you wait for it."

"If you think I'm going to change my mind and come begging, you've got another thought coming." She turned and opened the door, not bothering to close it behind her.

Later that night, when she had wrapped dozens of presents and put them under the tree, she crawled into bed, too exhausted to think.

She was restless and could not sleep. At last, she sat up in bed and realized why. Those damn twinkling lights on Stanley's roof. He was leaving them on all night, just to spite her. Well, he could leave them on until they melted a hole in his roof and she wouldn't change her mind.

She lay back down and pulled the covers up over her head, but that made her too hot, so she put them back the way they had been. She wasn't certain how long she lay in bed watching the colors blink on her bedroom wall before she finally drifted off to sleep.

The phone ringing just inches from her head woke her early the next morning.

"Hello." It was a groggy sound.

"Have dinner with me tonight."

"Turn your lights off."

"The lights stay on until you say yes."

She hung up on him.

That afternoon, the weather turned unseasonably warm. The snow had all melted and Stanley took advantage of the break in the weather to do some chores outside.

He was hosing off the driveway that ran between their two houses when he was seized by the urge to sing, so he broke into a shameful rendition of "Oh, Come All Ye Faithful."

He was really getting into the spirit of things when he heard a window open and looked up. Just as he did, Holly threw a Kleenex box at him. He caught it easily in one hand.

"I'll have dinner," she said, "if you promise never to sing another note."

Stanley felt wonderful. "You won't regret it."

"I regret it already, but the way I look at it, this is Christmas, the season of forgiveness and friendship."

"Why, Holly, that's wonderful."

"The Christmas season is over December thirty-first."

"Dinner at eight o'clock?"

She nodded. "Eight o'clock."

That night, after dinner, Stanley stopped by his house for dessert. Holly wore a skeptical expression when she stepped into the house and he closed the door behind them. The moment he shut the door, he took her into his arms. He kissed her while he backed her against the door. He kept on kissing her until she was weak at the knees, thankful for the support of the door.

His hands were caressing her, touching her gently in a manner that made her insane. Just enough to tease her, to arouse her and make her want more. And she did.

She realized that now. She wanted this, had wanted

it for some time. She kept kissing him and kissing him, hoping he would take the initiative, but he went just so far and no further. She could feel her desire and her frustration mounting.

"Is this dessert?" she whispered.

"It can be," he whispered back.

"What are the other choices?"

"Keep on kissing or stop and go home."

"Hmmm, kissing is okay. Going home is definitely out."

"Kissing it is, then." He kissed her again, paused a moment to lead her to the sofa, then kissed her again. Sometime during all the kissing, she found herself lying down. He lay partly over her, speaking between nibbling kisses. "This is better."

"Yes," she said, "it is. Much better." He was kissing her neck, her throat, her ears, her face. His hands were on her back, her breasts, between her legs. Everywhere he touched, she was on fire. He would make love to her now.

"It's much easier to kiss lying down than standing up," he said, his voice throbbing and low.

Kiss? Is that all they were going to do? Just kiss? Couldn't he tell she was primed and ready for more than kissing? What did she have to do? Draw him a map and hit him over the head with it? Well, if that's what it took . . . "Stanley?"

"Hmmmm?"

"Make love to me."

"Stubborn woman," he said, then with a chuckle, "Thank God. I don't think I could have kept this up a moment longer." He began stripping his clothes off, then helping her with hers.

He positioned himself above her, ready to come into her. She moved her legs apart to accommodate him. She could feel him against her now and she anticipated their joining. It had been so very long and she wanted him.

"I ought to paddle your backside."

She couldn't believe he was talking at a moment like this. "Why?"

"You should have asked me by now."

"Asked you what?"

"There's an AIDS explosion going on in the world, Holly. Haven't you ever heard of safe sex?"

"Yes, but I've been tested."

"You weren't worried about me?"

"You're a doctor. I thought . . ."

"Oh hell, I've been tested, and I can't talk about this anymore. Remind me to finish this conversation later."

She didn't get to reply, for he came into her quickly, with one powerful move. She was so ready for him that the shyness, the inhibition she normally felt was swept away. It was replaced by a desire to match him, to be his equal in every way.

Holly had made love many times in her three marriages, but it had not been like this. Never like this.

When it was over, and he held her against him, their breathing coming down and getting close to normal, she whispered to him, "You were right."

"About what?"

"You are good in bed."

"Does that mean you'll marry me?"

"No, it means I'll have to think about it. You don't marry for sex."

"I hadn't planned on it, nor would I expect you to marry for that reason. I had hoped you had come to care for me."

"It isn't that. I'm afraid, Stanley. I've been married three times."

"I know," he said softly, "but I won't ask you again. If you decide you want me, Holly, this time, you'll have to tell me."

One day passed. Then two. She couldn't believe it was possible to miss anyone as much as she missed Stanley. She knew she loved him, but they seemed to be at a stalemate. She was terrified of making another mistake. She wished Stanley would be forceful, that he would come over to her house and tell her she was going to marry him.

But he never came.

He left the lights on his roof, and she lay in her bed, watching the colors splash across her wall as a reminder of just how close he was. She wanted to go to him, but she couldn't just walk over there and tell him she had changed her mind. She didn't know why. She needed something to happen, something to prod her, something to give her a reason.

Things rocked on in the same torturous manner for another day. That night, she went to a movie with Heather. It was after ten when she turned down Orchard Street and was almost blinded. She had never seen so many lights. The entire street was lit up with such a glare she had to put her hand over her eyes to see. As she drove slowly down the street, every house she passed had something written on their roof:

HOLLY, MARRY THE GUY AND GIVE US PEACE

She stopped the Jeep in his driveway and left the door open as she ran up the steps to his house. She was laughing. She was crying.

She rang the doorbell. It seemed like a year before he opened the door. He looked wonderful, wearing just his boxer shorts and rumpled hair. God, how had she ever thought him a nerd?

"Hi."

He didn't say anything, nor did he invite her in.

"May I come in?"

"Do you think it's a good idea?"

"I think it might be the best idea I've ever had. I love you, Stanley."

He gave her a smiling look that said she took her own sweet time admitting it, then stood back and she stepped inside the house and into the circle of his arms.

"I love you," she said again.

"Enough to marry me?"

"More than enough."

Chapter Eighteen

They were married in Atlanta on the last day in December, because they thought it a fitting way to start the new year. When the party was over, some five hours after the wedding ceremony, Holly and Stanley spent the night in the Ritz Carlton. Early the next morning they caught a flight for a month-long honeymoon in Tahiti.

The children were all there to see them off. When Holly saw them at the airport, all lined up like little toy soldiers, wearing their matching red coats and their best smiles, she felt a twinge of regret and turning to him, she asked if he wouldn't want a child of his own.

Stanley looked at her and she knew he was thinking of all those girls. "A son would be nice."

He got another daughter.

They named her Holly Noel, because she was born the following Christmas Eve. But by the time she was born, Stanley didn't really care if he had a son or another daughter. He was convinced a house full of women wasn't all that bad.

And being the only man around wasn't so bad, either. He was loved and loved in return. Life was blissfully normal and things were the way they ought to be: Holly was his wife. He had a family. ER taught him to be mouthy. ES had him cursing fluently in Spanish.

And yet, if there was one thing about being normal that thrilled his very soul, it was that now, Plato was chasing Sweetie.

...

A Baby for Christmas
Lisa Jackson

Prologue

December 1995
Boston, Massachusetts

I'll have a blue Christmas without you . . .

"Oh, no, I won't!" Angrily, Annie McFarlane snapped off the radio. She wasn't about to let the sad lyrics of that particular song echo through her heart. It was the Christmas season, for heaven's sake. A time for merriment and joy, not the dull loneliness that caused her to ache inside.

She unwound a string of Christmas lights and plugged it into the socket. Instantly the dreary living room of her condominium was awash with twinkling bright color. Red, blue, yellow, and green reflected on the carpet and bare walls, giving a hint of warmth to a room littered with half-filled boxes and crates, evidence of the move across country she was planning. Pictures, mementos of her life as a married woman, clothes, knick-knacks, everything she owned was half-packed in the boxes strewn haphazardly through the condo.

Her throat tightened and she fought back another attack of hot, painful tears. "Don't do this," she reprimanded herself sharply. "He's not worth it. He never was."

So what if David had left her for another woman? So what if this was the first Christmas she would spend alone in her entire life? So what if she was truly and finally divorced, a situation she'd never wanted?

Women went through it all the time. So did men. It wasn't the end of the world.

But it felt like it. The weight on her shoulders and pain deep in her heart wouldn't listen to the mental tongue-lashings she constantly gave herself. "Get over it," she said aloud and was surprised that her words nearly reverberated in the half-empty rooms. Her dog, a mutt who looked like he had his share of German shepherd hidden somewhere in his genes, thumped his tail against the floor as he lay, head on paws, under the kitchen table.

"It's all right, Riley," she said, her words sounding as hollow as she felt.

Sleet slashed against the windows, the old Seth Thomas clock still mounted over the fireplace ticked off the seconds of her life, and the gas flames in the grate hissed steadily against ceramic logs that would never burn. Outside, the city of Boston was alive with the festivities of the holiday season. Brilliant lights winked and dazzled on garland-clad porches while bare-branched trees were ablaze in neighboring yards. Wreaths and pine-scented swags adorned doors and electric candles burned in most of the windows. Children in those other houses were too excited to sleep. Parents, frazzled but happy, sipped mulled wine, planned family dinners, and worried that their hastily bought, last-minute presents wouldn't bring a gleam of gladness to their recipients' eyes.

And here she was, stringing a single strand of lights

over a potted tree she'd bought at the local grocery store, knowing that tomorrow she would eat alone, put in some hours down at the local women's shelter, and come home to pack the rest of her things. She only wished that she'd been able to move before the holidays, but her timing—or, more precisely, David's timing— hadn't allowed for Christmas.

Three months ago she'd called her real estate agent about selling the condo, watched through her tears as David had carried his half of their possessions out the door, smiled bravely when he'd casually mentioned that Caroline, his girlfriend, was pregnant, and then had fallen apart completely as she'd reluctantly signed the divorce papers.

Annie had never felt more alone in her life. Her mother and stepfather were spending the holidays cruising up and down the west coast of Mexico; her sister Nola, forever the free spirit, was again missing in action, probably with a new-found lover. Annie remembered Nola's last choice, a tall, strapping blond man by the name of Liam O'Shaughnessy, whom Nola professed to adore for all of two or three weeks. Since O'Shaughnessy, there had been others, Annie supposed, but none she'd heard of.

Then there was Annie's brother, Joel, and his wife. They were spending Christmas at home in Atlanta with their three kids. Though invited to visit them, Annie hadn't wanted to fly down south with her case of the blues and spoil everyone's Christmas so she'd decided to stick it out here, alone in the home that she and David had shared, until she moved to Oregon after the first of the year.

Thank God the condo had sold quickly. She couldn't imagine spending much more time here in this lonely tomb, which was little more than a shrine to a marriage that had failed.

She fished in a box of handmade ornaments she'd

sewed and glued together only last year and placed a tiny
sleigh on an already-drooping bough. As she finished
looping a length of strung cranberries and popcorn
around the little evergreen, she had to smile. The forlorn little tree looked almost festive.

There would be life, a more satisfying life, after David.
She'd see to it personally. At least she still had Riley,
who was company if nothing else.

With a glimmer of hope as inspiration, she walked to
the kitchen, scrounged in a drawer for a corkscrew, and
realized that, as she'd given the good one to David, she
was forced to use the all-in-one tool they'd bought years
before for a camping trip. The screwdriver-can opener-
bottle opener was more inclined to slice the user's hand
than open a can or bottle, but it was the best implement
she could come up with at the moment.

She managed to open a bottle of chardonnay without
drawing any blood, then found one of the wine goblets
from the crystal she'd picked out seven years ago when
she'd planned her wedding to David. She'd been twenty-
three at the time, graduated from college as a business
major and had met David McFarlane, a witty, good-
looking law student, only to fall hopelessly in love with
him. She'd never thought it would end. Not even during
the horrid anguish and pain of her first miscarriage.
The second loss—during the fifth month—had been
no better, but the third, and final, when the doctor had
advised her to think seriously of adoption, had been
the straw that had broken the over-burdened back of
their union. David was the last son of his particular
branch of the McFarlane family tree and as such was
expected, as well as personally determined, to spawn
his own child, with or without Annie.

It was then, during the talks of surrogate mothers and
fertility clinics, that the marriage had really started to
crumble. Enter Caroline Gentry: young, nubile, willing,

and, apparently, if David were to be believed, able to carry a baby to term.

"What a mess," Annie said to herself as she carried her bottle and goblet into the living room. On the hearth, she tucked her legs beneath the hem of her oversized sweater and watched the reflection of the colored lights play in her wine. "Next year will be better." She held up her glass in a mock toast and her dog, as if he understood her, snorted in disdain. "I'm not kidding, Riley. Next year, the good Lord willin' and the creek don't rise, things will be much, much better." Riley yawned and stretched, as if tired of her pep talks to herself. She took a long swallow and closed her eyes.

No matter what happened, she'd get over this pain, forget about David and his infidelity, and find a new life.

And a new man, an inner voice prompted.

"Never," she whispered. She'd never let a man get close enough to her again to wound her so deeply. "I'll make it on my own, damn it, or die trying."

Chapter One

December 1996

Oh, the weather outside is frightful . . .

"Damn." Liam snapped off the radio and scowling, settled against the passenger window of the battle-scarred Ford.

"Not in the spirit of the season?" Jake Cranston snorted as he stared through the windshield of his car. "I guess jail will do that to you."

Liam didn't respond, just clamped his jaw tight. He'd been through hell and back in the past few weeks; he didn't need to be reminded of it. Not even from a friend. Tonight Jake was more than a friend; he'd turned out to be Liam's goddamned guardian angel.

Liam glared out the window to the dark night beyond. Ahead of them, red taillights blurred through the thick raindrops that the wipers couldn't slap away fast enough. On the other side of the median, headlights flashed as cars screamed in the opposite direction. Christ, he was tired. He needed a good night's sleep, a stiff drink, and a woman. Not necessarily in that order.

It seemed as if Jake had been driving for hours, speeding through this rainy section of freeway without getting anywhere, but the city lights of Seattle were beginning to glow to the north.

"Want to stop somewhere?" Jake, while negotiating a banked turn, managed to shake a cigarette from his pack of Marlboros located forever on the dusty dash of his Taurus wagon. He passed the pack to his friend and shoved the Marlboro between his teeth.

He thought about lighting up. It had been six years since his last smoke and he could use the relief. He was so damned keyed up, his mind racing miles a minute even though he was dead tired. He tossed the pack onto the dash again. "Just get me home, Cranston."

"Why the devil would you want to go there?" Jake punched the lighter.

"Gotta start somewhere."

"Yeah, but if I were you I'd put this whole thing behind me and start over."

"Not yet."

"You're well out of it." The lighter clicked. Jake lit up and let smoke drift from his nostrils.

"Not until my name is cleared." Leaning back in the seat, Liam tried to forget the nightmare of the past few months and the hell he'd been through. But the days of looking over his shoulder and knowing he was being followed, watched by men he'd once trusted, still struck a deep, unyielding anger in his soul.

It had all started four months ago on a hot August night in Bellevue. In the early morning hours, there had been a break-in at the company offices where Liam worked. At first the police thought it was a typical burglary gone sour; the security guard on duty that night, old Bill Arness, had been unfortunate enough to confront the crook and had been bashed over the head,

his skull crushed. Bill, a six-times grandfather with a
wide girth and quick smile, had never awakened, but
lingered in a coma for six weeks, then died before he
was able to give the name of his attacker. His wife had
never once left his side and the president of Belfry
Construction, Zeke Belfry, had offered a twenty-five-
thousand-dollar reward for anyone who had information that would lead to the arrest and conviction of
the perpetrator. Zeke, a law-abiding, holier-than-thou
Christian with whom Liam had never gotten along, was
personally offended that his company had been singled
out for any kind of criminal act and he wanted revenge.

Which he ultimately got.

Out of Liam O'Shaughnessy's hide.

Within a few months the police had decided the
break-in was an inside job. Records had been destroyed.
An audit showed that over a hundred thousand dollars
was missing, all of the money skimmed from construction jobs for which Liam had been the project manager.

The police and internal auditors had started asking
questions.

It had been nearly two months from the time of all
the trouble until the police had closed in on him, slowly
pulling their noose around his neck tighter and tighter
while he himself was working on his own investigation.
It was obvious someone had set him up to take a fall,
but whom?

Before he could zero in on all of the suspects, one
woman had come forward, a woman who held a personal
grudge, a woman who had driven the final nails in his
coffin. Nola Prescott, his ex-lover, had gone to the police
and somehow convinced them that Liam was involved
not only with the embezzling, but the death of old Bill
Arness as well.

So here he was with his only friend in the world,
trying to forget the sounds that had kept him awake at
night. The clang of metal against metal, the shuffle of

tired feet, shouts of the guards, and clank of chains still rattled through his brain. Prison. He'd been in prison, for Christ's sake. All because of one woman.

His teeth ground in frustration, but he forced his anger back. *Don't get mad, get even.* The old words of wisdom had been his personal mantra for the past few weeks. He'd known that eventually he'd be set free, that the D.A. couldn't possibly hold him without bail forever, that there wasn't a strong enough case against him because he hadn't done it.

"Okay, so what's the story?" he finally asked. "Why was I let go all of a sudden?"

"I thought you talked to your attorney."

"He just sketched out the details. Something about the prosecution losing their prime witness. Seems Nola chickened out. Didn't want to perjure herself."

Jake snorted and two jets of smoke streamed from his nostrils. "That's about the size of it. Nola Prescott recanted the testimony in her deposition."

Liam's guts churned. Nola. Beautiful. Bright. Secretary to one of the engineers at the firm. Great in bed, if you liked cold, unemotional, but well-practiced sex. No commitment. Just one body seeking relief from another. Liam had quickly grown bored and felt like hell after his few times in bed with her. Too much vodka had been his downfall. Their affair had been brief. "Why'd she change her mind?"

"Who knows? Maybe she got religion," Jake cracked and when Liam didn't smile, drew hard on his cigarette. He guided the Taurus onto the off-ramp leading to Bellevue, a bedroom community located north and east of Seattle.

"I think she might be protecting someone," Liam said, his eyes narrowing.

"Who?"

"Don't know. Maybe someone else she was involved with." He concentrated long and hard. "Someone at the company, probably. It would have been someone she was involved with six or seven months ago, before she left for her new job with that company in Tacoma."

"Christ, why didn't you tell this to the cops?"

"No proof. I'd look like I was just grasping at straws, but there's got to be a reason she set me up."

"You dumped her."

"So she accuses me of murder? That's even lower than Nola would go. She claimed to see me at the company that night. Why? She worked in another city."

"But still lived in the area."

"Too much of a coincidence, if you ask me." He stared at the streaks of raindrops on the windows. "It's just a matter of finding out who she was involved with." He drummed his fingers on the dash and thought of the possibilities—several names came to mind.

"Anyone you want me to check?" Jake offered.

"Yeah. Kim Boniface, one of her friends, but I wouldn't think she'd be covering for a woman. Then there's Hank Swanson, another project manager, Peter Talbott in accounting, and Jim Scorelli, an engineer who was always making a pass at her. Other than that,"—he shook his head, mentally disregarding rumors of financial difficulties of other friends and coworkers he knew at Belfry—"I can't think of anyone."

"I'll check."

"There's something else," Liam admitted, though he hated to bring up the subject. "I heard Nola was pregnant."

Jake's lips curled in upon themselves, the way they always did when he was weighing whether or not he should level with Liam. "So the rumor goes, but who knows? A woman like that—"

"Is it mine?"

The question hung in the smoky interior.

"How would I know?"

Liam squinted hard as the Taurus accelerated

through the hills surrounding Bellevue. "Just tell me if the kid was born late in November or early December."

"Look, O'Shaughnessy, I wouldn't open that can of worms if I were—"

"Is it mine?" he repeated.

"For Chrissakes, Liam, who cares?" Jake growled.

"I do."

"Don't do this." He cracked his window and flicked his cigarette outside onto the pavement where the burning ember died a quick death in the gathering puddles.

"Do what?"

"Develop some latent sense of nobility. You had a fling with the woman. A *short* fling. Later she testified against you, tried to get you locked up for something you didn't do. She's no good. Leave her alone."

Liam's neck muscles tightened in frustration. "I just want to know if the kid's got O'Shaughnessy blood running through its veins."

"Right now, you should concentrate on getting a job. Just because you're exonerated doesn't mean that Zeke Belfry's gonna welcome you back with open arms."

That much was true. Ever since the old man had retired and his son Zeke had become president of the company, things had changed at Belfry Construction. Liam and Zeke had clashed on several occasions before all hell had broken loose. He'd already planned to sell his house, cash in his company stock, and start his own consulting firm. He didn't need Zeke Belfry—or anyone else, for that matter.

Jake nosed the Taurus into a winding street of upscale homes built on junior acres. Liam's house, an English Tudor, sat dark and foreboding, the lawn overgrown, moss collecting on the split shake roof, the windows black. The other houses in the neighborhood were aglow with strings of winking lights, nativity scenes tucked in well-groomed shrubbery, and illuminated Santas and snowmen poised on rooftops. The lawns were mowed and edged, the bushes neatly trimmed, the driveways blown free of leaves and fir needles.

Welcome to suburbia.

He fingered his keys.

"Your Jeep's in the garage. Mail on the table."

"Where's Nola?" Liam wasn't giving up.

Jake pulled into the driveway and let the car idle in the rain, the beams of his headlights splashing against Liam's garage. "Don't know."

"What?"

"No one does."

"Now, wait a minute—"

"Let it go, Liam." Suddenly Jake's hand was on his arm, his firm fingers restraining his friend through the thick rawhide of his jacket.

"Can't do it. Where is she?"

"Really. No one knows. Not even the D.A. She recanted her testimony and disappeared. A week ago. Your guess is as good as mine."

"She's got family," Liam said, remembering. "A brother in the south somewhere, folks who follow the sun, and a sister in Boston . . . no, she moved. To Oregon." Liam snapped his fingers.

"No reason to drag her into this."

"Unless she knows where Nola is and if the kid is mine."

"I knew I shouldn't have told you." Jake slapped the heel of his hand to his forehead.

"You had to," Liam said, opening the car door as a blast of December wind rushed into the warm, smoky interior. "Thanks."

"Don't mention it."

Liam slammed the door shut and saw his friend flick on the radio before ramming the car into reverse. Jake rolled down the window at the end of the drive and laughed without a trace of mirth. "Oh, by the way, O'Shaughnessy. Merry Christmas."

* * *

Feliz Navidad, Feliz Navidad . . .

Annie hummed along with José Feliciano as she sat at her kitchen table and licked stamps to attach to her Christmas card envelopes. Marilyn Monroe, Elvis, and James Dean smiled up at her along with the more traditional wreaths, Christmas trees, or flags that decorated her rather eclectic smattering of stamps. Her home, a small cottage tucked into the low hills of western Oregon, was decorated with lights, fir garlands, pine cones, and a tree that nearly filled the living room. The cabin was warm and earthy from years of settling here in this forest. The pipes creaked, the doors stuck, and sometimes the electricity was temperamental, but the house was quaint and cozy with a view of a small lake where herons and ducks made their home.

Riley lay beneath the table, his eyes at half-mast, his back leg absently scratching at his belly.

Annie had been lucky to find this place, which had once been the home of the foreman of a large ranch. The main house still stood on thirty forested acres while the rest of the old homestead, the fields of a once-working farm, had been sliced away and sold into subdivisions that crawled up the lower slopes. The larger farmhouse, quaintly elegant with its Victorian charm, was empty now as the elderly couple who owned it had moved to a retirement center. It was Annie's job to see that the grounds were maintained, the house kept in decent repair, the remaining livestock—three aging horses—were fed and exercised and, in general, look after the place. For free rent, she was able to live in the cottage and run a small secretarial service from her home.

"I wanna wish you a Merry Christmas, I wanna wish you a Merry Christmas . . ." She sang softly to herself as the timer on the ancient oven dinged and she scooted back her chair to check the batch of Christmas cookies.

Outside, snow had begun to fall in thick flakes that were quickly covering the ground. Supposedly, according to the local newspeople, a storm was going to drop several inches of snow over the Willamette Valley before moving east. But there was no cause for concern— maybe a slick road or two, but for the most part the broadcasters were downplaying the hazards of the storm and seemed happy to predict the first white Christmas to visit western Oregon in years.

Annie planned to fly to Atlanta to spend the holidays with Joel, Polly, and her nephews. She'd come a long way from her dark memories of the past year, managing to shove most of her pain aside and start a new life for herself. Even the news of David's marriage and the birth of his son hadn't affected her as adversely as she'd thought it would, though her own situation sometimes seemed bleak. She wondered if she'd ever become a mother when she couldn't begin to imagine becoming some man's wife.

Well, as Dr. James had told her after the last miscarriage, "There's always adoption."

Could she, as a single woman?

The scents of cinnamon and nutmeg filled the kitchen as she slipped her fingers through a hot mitt and pulled a tray of cookies from the oven. She glanced out the window and saw snow drifting in the corners of the glass. Ice crystals stung the panes and a chill seeped through the old windows. A gust of wind whipped the snow-laden boughs of the trees and rattled the panes. The newspeople were certainly right about the storm, Annie thought, feeling the first hint of worry. She turned on an exterior light and mentally calculated that there were two inches of white powder on the deck rail.

If this kept up, she'd have a devil of a time getting

to the airport tomorrow. "It'll be all right," she told herself as she snapped off the oven.

Bam!

A noise like the backfiring of a car or the sharp report of a shotgun blast thundered through the house. Within seconds everything went dark.

"What in the world—?"

Riley was on his feet in an instant, barking wildly and dashing toward the door.

"It's all right, boy," Annie said, though she didn't believe a word of it. What had happened? Had a car run into a telephone pole and knocked down the electrical lines? Had a transformer blown?

It didn't matter. The result was that she was suddenly enveloped in total darkness and she didn't know when the electricity might be turned on again. Muttering under her breath, she reached into a drawer, her fingers fumbling over matches, a screwdriver, and a deck of cards until she found a flashlight. She flicked on the low beam and quickly lit several candles before peering outside into the total darkness of the hill. Though she was somewhat isolated, there were neighbors in the development down the hill, but no lights shone through the thick stands of fir and maple.

Alone. You're all alone.

"Big deal," she muttered as her eyes became accustomed to the darkness. She wasn't a scared, whimpering female. Shaking off a case of the jitters, she found her one hurricane lantern and lit the wick. "Okay, okay, now heat," she told herself as she opened the damper of the old river-rock fireplace, then touched one candle to the dry logs stacked in the grate. The kindling caught quickly and eager flames began to lick the chunks of mossy oak while Riley, not usually so nervous, paced near the front door. He growled, glanced at Annie, then scratched against the woodwork.

"That's not helping," Annie said. "Lie down."

Riley ignored her.

"Just like all males," she grumbled. "Stubborn, head-strong, and won't listen to sound advice." Bundling into boots, gloves, her ski jacket, and a scarf, she headed for the back porch where several cords of firewood had been stacked for the winter. She hauled a basket with her and after twenty minutes had enough lengths of oak and fir to see her through the night. The batteries on her transistor radio were shot, and the phone, when she tried to use it, bleeped at her. A woman's voice calmly informed her that all circuits were busy. "Perfect," she said grimly and slammed down the receiver.

I wanna wish you a Merry Christmas from the bottom of my heart . . . The lyrics tumbled over in her mind, though the music had long since faded. "Right. A Merry Christmas. Fat chance!"

As firelight played upon the walls and windows, she drew the curtains and dragged her blankets from the bedroom. She'd be warmer close to the fire and could handle a night on the hide-a-bed. In the morning she'd call a cab to drive her to the airport, but for now she needed to sleep. Riley took up his post at the door and refused to budge. He stared at the oak panels as if he could see through the hardwood and Annie decided her dog was a definite head case. "It's warmer over here," she said and was rewarded with a disquieting "woof," the kind of noise Riley made whenever he was confused.

"Okay, okay, so have it your way." Settling under her down comforter, she closed her eyes and started to drift off. She could still hear José Feliciano's voice in her mind, but there was something else, something different—a tiny, whimpering cry over the sound of Riley's whine. No, she was imagining things, only the shriek of the wind, tick of the clock, and . . . there it was again. A sharp cry.

Heart racing, she tossed off the covers and ran to

the front door where Riley was whining and scratching. "What is it?" she asked, yanking open the door. A blast of ice-cold wind tore through the door. The fire burned bright from the added air. Riley bounded onto the front porch where a basket covered with a blanket was waiting. From beneath the pink coverlet came the distinctive wail of an infant.

"What in the name of Mary ..." Leaning down, Annie lifted the blanket and found a red-faced baby, fists clenched near its face, tears streaming from its eyes, lying on a tiny mattress. "Dear God in heaven." Annie snatched the basket and, looking around the yard for any sign of whoever had left the child on her stoop, she drew baby, basket, and blankets into the house. "Who are you?" she asked as she placed the bundle on her table and lifted the tiny child from its nest.

With a shock of blond hair and eyes that appeared blue in the dim light, the baby screamed.

"Dear God, how did you get here?" Annie asked in awe. She immediately lost her heart to this tiny little person. "Hey, hey, it's all right. Shhh." *Who* would leave a baby on the porch in the middle of this storm? What kind of idiot would ... Still clutching the baby, she ran to the window and peered outside, searching the powdery drifts for signs of footprints, or any other hint that someone had been nearby.

Riley leaped and barked, eyeing the baby jealously.

"Stop it!" Annie commanded, holding the child against her and swaying side to side as if she were listening to some quiet lullaby that played only in her head. She squinted into the night and felt a shiver of fear slide down her spine. Was the person who left the baby lurking in the woods, perhaps watching her as she peered through the curtains?

Swallowing back her fear, she stepped away from the window and closer to the warmth of the fire.

The baby, a girl if the pink snowsuit could be believed,

quieted and her little eyes closed. Head nestled against Annie's breast, she made soft little whimpers and her tiny lips moved as if she were sucking in her dreams. Again Annie asked, "Who are you?" as she carried the basket closer to the fire to peer into the interior.

A wide red ribbon was wound through the wicker and several cans of dry formula were tucked in a corner with a small package of disposable diapers. Six cloth diapers, a bottle, two pacifiers, one change of clothes, and a card that simply read, "For you, Annie," were crammed into a small diaper bag hidden beneath a couple of receiving blankets and a heavier quilt. Everything a woman would need to start mothering.

Including a baby.

"I can't believe this," Annie whispered as again she walked to the window where she shoved aside the curtains and stared into an inky darkness broken only by the continuing fall of snowflakes. The moon and stars were covered by thick, snow-laden clouds, and all the electrical lights in the vicinity were out.

Annie picked up the phone again and heard the same message she'd heard earlier. "Great," she muttered.

As the wind raged and the snow fell in thick, heavy flakes, she realized that unless she wanted to brave the frigid weather and hike to the neighbor's house, she and this baby were alone. Completely cut off from civilization.

"I guess you're stuck with me," she said and worried about the baby's mother. Who was she? Had she left the child unattended on the stoop? What kind of mother was she? Or had the baby been kidnapped and dropped off? But by whom?

For you, Annie.

The questions chasing after each other in endless circles raced through her mind. She placed a soft kiss on the infant's downy blond curls and lay down on the couch, where she held the child in the warmth of her comforter. "I'll keep you safe tonight," she promised, bonding so quickly with the infant that she knew she was going to lose her heart. "Riley will keep watch."

The dog, hearing his name, woofed softly and positioned himself in front of the door, as if he truly were guarding them both. Annie closed her eyes and wondered when she woke up in the morning, if she'd be alone and discover that this was all just part of a wonderful dream.

Chapter Two

"Is this an emergency?" a disinterested voice asked on the other end of the line.

"Yes, no . . . I mean it's not life or death," Annie said, frustrated that after finally getting through to the sheriff's department she was stymied. "As I said, a baby was left on my porch last night and—"

"Who does the child belong to?"

"That's what I'm trying to find out." Annie glanced at the basket—and at Carol, the name she'd given the child upon awaking this morning and discovering last night's storm wasn't a nightmare, nor was the basket part of a dream.

"Are you injured?"

"No, but—"

"Is the baby healthy?"

"As far as I can tell, but her parents are probably sick with worry—"

"Look, lady, we've got elderly people without any heat, cars piling up on the freeways, and people stranded in their vehicles. Everyone here is pulling double shifts.''

''I know, but I'm concerned that—''

''You can come down to the station and fill out a report or we can send an officer when one's available.''

''Do that,'' Annie said as she rattled off her address. A part of her felt pure elation that she had more time alone with the infant and another part of her was filled with dread that she'd become too attached to someone else's baby.

''Deputy Kemp will stop by and I'll put calls into the local hospitals to see if a baby is missing. I'll also see that social services gets a copy of this message. A social worker or nurse will probably contact you in the next couple of days.''

''Thank you.''

''As I said, an officer will stop by as soon as he can, but I wouldn't hold my breath. It could be a day or two. We're shorthanded down here with all the accidents and power outages. He'll call you.''

''Thanks.''

Annie hung up and sighed loudly. The frigid northern Willamette Valley was paralyzed. Sanding trucks and snowplows couldn't keep up with the fifteen-inch accumulation and still the snow kept falling. Annie had no means of communication except for the phone and her driveway, steep on a normal day, was impassable. She was lucky in that she had plenty of food and a fire on which she could cook. She'd even managed to heat Carol's bottle in a pan of water she had warmed on the grate.

She'd been awakened in the middle of the night when the baby had stirred and fussed. It took a while, but she'd added water to the dry formula she'd mixed in the bottle, then waited as it heated. The baby had quieted instantly upon being fed and Annie had hummed Christmas carols to the child as she suckled hungrily.

"You're so precious," she'd murmured and the baby had cooed. She couldn't imagine giving her up. But she would have to. Somewhere little Carol probably had a mother and father who were missing her.

She fingered the note again, turning it over and studying the single white page decorated with a stenciled sprig of holly. Who had sent her the baby and cryptic message? Obviously someone who knew her and knew where she lived. Someone who trusted her with this baby. But who?

Was the child unwanted? Kidnapped? Stolen from a hospital? Taken from her cradle as her parents slept? Part of a divorce dispute? Her head thundered with the questions that plagued her over and over again.

She'd called the airport and found that Portland International was closed, all flights grounded. She'd tried to reach her brother in Atlanta, but all outside circuits had been busy and she figured Joel would eventually call her.

"So it looks like it's just going to be you and me," she told the infant as she changed her diaper and sprinkled her soft skin with baby powder. "You can have a bottle and I'll open a can of chili."

The child yawned and stretched, arching her little back and blinking those incredible crystal-blue eyes. "You're a cherub, that's what you are," Annie teased. She let her worries drift away and concentrated on keeping the fire stoked, the baby dry, clean, and fed, and allowing Riley outside where the snow reached his belly and clung to his whiskers.

Late in the afternoon while Carol was napping in her basket, Annie checked on the horses, then poured herself a cup of coffee and started writing notes to herself about the baby. The infant was less than a month old, Caucasian, with no identifying marks—no birthmarks or moles or scars—in good health. So who was she?

Though she tried to suppress it, an idea that the child might have been abandoned—legitimately abandoned—kept crossing her mind. Could it be possible? The note was addressed to her so . . . But why would someone who so obviously cared about the infant leave her in freezing weather? No, that didn't make sense—

"Stop it, McFarlane," she growled at herself as Riley lifted his head and stared at the door. He barked sharply, then jumped to his feet. "What is it?"

Bam! Bam! Bam!

Riley started barking like crazy as the person on the other side of the door pounded so hard that the old oak panels seemed to jump.

"Hush!" Annie hurried to the door. "Who is it?" she yelled through the panels, then smoothed away the condensation on the narrow window flanking the door so she could see outside.

She nearly gasped when she saw the man, a very big man—six feet two or three, unless she missed her guess. His face was flushed, his gaze intense, his long arms folded firmly across his chest.

Liam O'Shaughnessy. In the flesh.

"Oh, no—" she whispered and her stomach did a slow, sensual roll. Liam was the one man of all of Nola's suitors that Annie found sexy—too sexy.

And right now he was livid, his face red with fury— or the bite of the winter air. Blond hair, damp from melting snowflakes, was tousled in the wind. Wearing a suede jacket, jeans, and boots covered in snow, he was poised to pound on the door again when he caught sight of her in the window. His eyes, when they met hers, were as blue as an arctic sea and just as violent.

"Help me," she said under her breath.

Nervously, she licked her lips. Never in her life had she faced such a wrathful male. His jaw was square and set, his blond eyebrows drawn into a single unforgiving line. Power, rage, and determination radiated from him in cold, hard waves.

"Open the damned door or I'll break it down," he yelled as the wind keened around him and caused the snow-laden boughs of the fir trees near the porch to sway in a slow, macabre dance. "Annie McFarlane—do you hear me?"

Loud and clear, she thought, and swallowing against a mounting sensation of dread, she yanked on the door handle. Without waiting for a word of invitation, he stepped inside.

"Where is she?" he demanded, stomping snow from his boots.

"Who?"

"Your sister!"

"Nola?" Annie asked, remembering that he'd once been her sister's lover, but only for a little while, or so Nola had confided. Their brief affair had ended abruptly and badly. Nola had been heartbroken, but then she'd been heartbroken half a dozen times because she always fell for the wrong kind of guy.

"Nola isn't here."

He frowned, snow melting on the shoulders of his rawhide jacket as well as in his hair.

"What do you want with her? I thought you broke up—"

"There was nothing to break," he said swiftly. "But, it appears she and I have a lot to discuss."

"You do?" Why was he here, looking for her in the middle of this storm?

"So she isn't here, eh?" He seemed to doubt her and his restless gaze slid around the room, searching the shadowy nooks and crannies as if he expected to find Nola hiding nearby.

"No. I haven't seen her in months."

"Close relationship."

"It is—not that it's any of your business," she said,

bristling at his condescending tone. "Now, was there something else you wanted?"

His eyes narrowed suspiciously. "Just to find your sister. She seems to have disappeared."

"No, she hasn't. She's just . . . well, she takes off for little mini-vacations every once in a while."

"Mini-vacations?" His laugh was hollow and the corners of his mouth didn't so much as lift. "I'm willing to bet there's more to it this time."

"I doubt it."

"Then where is she?" His nostrils flared slightly. "Where does she go on these—what did you call them?—mini-vacations. That's rich."

"Look, I don't have any idea. Nola sometimes just takes off, not that it's any business of yours."

He snorted. "It's my business, all right."

"Sometimes Nola goes to the beach or the mountains—"

"Or Timbuktu, if she's smart." He wiped a big hand over his face as if he were dead tired. "If you want to know the truth, I really don't give a damn about Nola."

"But you want to find her?"

"*Have to* is more like it." He raked the interior of the cabin with his predatory gaze once more. "Her beautiful carcass could rot in hell for all I care."

That did it. Annie didn't need to take insults from him, or any other man, for that matter. "I think you should leave."

"I will. Once I get some answers."

"I don't have any—"

Carol coughed softly and O'Shaughnessy's head snapped around. Without a word he crossed the living room, tracking snow and staring down at the baby as if he were seeing Jesus in the manger.

"Yours?" he asked, but the tone of his voice was skeptical.

She shook her head automatically. There was no reason to lie, though she felt a wave of maternal protectiveness come over her. "I—I found her."

"What?" He touched Carol's crown with one long finger. The caress was so tender, his expression so awestruck, that Annie stupidly felt the heat of unshed tears behind her eyes. "Found her? Where?"

"On the front porch. Last night."

He looked up, pinning her with that intense, laser-blue gaze. "Someone left her?"

"Yes. I guess."

"Who?"

"I don't know."

"Nola." He scowled and picked up the basket. "Figures."

"You think my sister brought a baby here?" Annie laughed at the notion.

"Not just any baby," he said, his expression turning dark. "Her baby. And mine."

"What?" she gasped.

"You heard me."

"But . . . Oh, God." He couldn't be serious, but she'd never seen a man so determined in all her life. He glanced down at the beribboned basket. A muscle worked in his jaw and when he looked up again, the glare he shot Annie could have melted steel. "Listen, O'Shaughnessy, I don't know what you're talking about, what you're saying. I—you—we don't have any idea if Nola did this."

"Sure we do."

"Nola's never been pregnant."

"Give me a break."

"Really. I know my sister and I'm sure . . ." Her words faded away. What did she really know about Nola? When was the last time they'd talked besides a quick chat on the phone? The last time Annie had seen Nola had been months ago.

"You're sure of what?" he spat out.

"She would have told me about a baby." Or would she have? Nola knew how much Annie had wanted a child, how crushed and forlorn she'd been after each miscarriage . . . was it possible?

For you, Annie. Sweet Jesus, was the note in Nola's loopy handwriting? Her knees gave way and she propped herself against the back of the couch. As if he'd read her thoughts, he nodded grimly and reached for the basket.

No! "Wait a minute—" But he was already tucking the wicker holder under one strong arm.

She was frantic. He intended to take the baby away! Oh, God, he couldn't. Not now, not yet, not after Annie had already lost her heart to the little blond cherub.

"O'Shaughnessy, you can't do this."

"Sure I can." His face was a mask of sheer determination. "If you hear from Nola, tell her I'm looking for her, that we need to talk."

"No! You can't. I—I mean—" She threw herself across the room and placed her body squarely between him and the door. Fear and pain clawed at her soul at the thought of losing her precious little baby. "Don't leave yet."

"It's time. Give Nola the message."

"But the baby. You can't just take her away and—"

"I'm her father."

"But I don't know that. In fact, I don't know anything about you or the baby or—" Oh, God. In such a short time she'd come to think of the baby as her own even though the notion was impossible.

"Look, Annie, I won't hold you accountable as long as you don't give me any trouble, but tell Nola this isn't over. When I find her—"

"What? You'll what?" Her heart was racing, her head ached, and she knew she'd never let him take the child. She reached for the basket, brushing his sleeve with her hand. "You . . . you can't just barge in here and take the baby and leave."

"Can't I?"

"No!"

His face was etched in stone, his countenance without a grain of remorse. Without much effort he sidestepped her, brushed her body aside, and reached for the doorknob with his free hand. "Watch me."

Chapter Three

"You're not going anywhere with that baby, O'Shaughnessy." Annie wasn't letting the baby out of her sight. Not without a fight. She squeezed between him and the door again. Riley, the scruff of his neck standing on end, growled a low, fierce agreement. "How do I know she's yours?"

"She's mine, all right. Just ask your sister."

Annie glared up at him and felt the heat of his gaze, the raw masculine intensity of this giant of a man, but she wasn't going to back down. Not to him. Not to anyone. He seemed to think that Nola was really Carol's mother. But it couldn't be . . . or could it? Was it possible? Who else would know that she desperately wanted a baby, that she would care for an infant as if it were her own, that in her heart of hearts, she would love the child forever? "Now why don't you back up a minute, okay? You're trying to convince me that you and Nola—who, as I heard it, only dated you a short while—that you had a baby together."

"Looks like it." Blond eyebrows slammed together

and his jaw was hard as granite. But Annie wasn't going to let him buffalo her.

"Why didn't I hear anything about it?" she demanded.

"Why didn't I?"

"What?" She was having trouble keeping up with all the twists and turns in the conversation.

"You know your sister. Figure it out. Just like her to try and hide the kid here." He started to pull on the doorknob, but Annie pressed her back against the hard panels and put all her weight into holding the door closed. "Get out of the way."

"No! You just stop right there. I don't know that this baby has any connection to Nola."

"Sure."

"I *am* sure," she said, her anger elevating with her voice. "This child"—she jabbed at the basket swinging from his right arm with her finger—"was left on my doorstep in the middle of a storm and then you ... you—how did you get here?"

"It was tricky. I have four-wheel drive," he conceded. "And a lot of sheer grit."

That much was true. She didn't know much about him, but she believed that with his determination he could literally move mountains.

"Just listen for a second," he insisted, and she notched her chin up an inch. "I thought you knew all about her pregnancy."

"I haven't seen her in months. She was ... busy with something, something she wouldn't talk about."

A trace of doubt darkened his gaze. A musky scent of aftershave mingled with the smoky odor of burning wood. God, he was close. "But you knew Nola was going to have a baby."

Shaking her head, Annie sighed and rammed fingers of frustration through her hair. "Nola never said a word. For all I know, you could be lying."

"I *don't* lie."

"No, you just storm into a person's house and take what you want."

A muscle jumped in his jaw and every muscle in his body seemed tense, ready to unleash. His words were measured. "I don't know why Nola left the kid here, but—"

"You don't even know *if* she left the baby here."

He hesitated, his lips pursing in vexation. His gaze, icy-blue and condemning, narrowed on her. Obviously he was trying to size her up, to determine how much she really knew.

Annie swallowed hard and tried to ignore the rapid beating of her heart. "Didn't ... didn't you say you never *talked* to Nola?" she pressed. He was so close that the rawhide of his jacket brushed against her breast. "How do you know that this baby is hers—or yours, for that matter?"

"Who else's?"

"I don't know, but until I do, the baby stays."

His smile had all the warmth of the arctic sea and yet she had the fleeting thought that he was a hot-blooded man. Passionate. Bold. Fierce one second, tender the next. *"You're* going to stop me from taking her?" That particular thought seemed to amuse him.

"Damned straight."

"You're half my size."

"I—I don't think this is a matter of physical strength." She'd lose in a minute to a man who was hard and well-muscled, all sinew and bone. "But I won't give her up without a fight, O'Shaughnessy."

"It's a fight you're gonna lose."

"I don't think so." She tried to appear taller as she looked up at him and tossed her hair over her shoulders. "If I can't convince you, then I guess I'll just have to call the police. They already know about the baby, anyway. A deputy by the name of Kemp is supposed to come and take a statement from me after they check and find out if there are any missing infants in the area. He could be here any minute. So—why don't you and I just wait for him?" She folded her arms over her chest. "I'll even make the coffee."

"We don't need the police involved."

"They already are."

"Damn!" He shook his head. "That was a foolish move."

"It wasn't 'a move.' I just wanted to find out where she came from."

"Sure."

"I did."

"Doesn't matter. What's done is done." His muscles seemed to stiffen even more at the mention of the authorities and the lines of his face deepened. For some reason he didn't want the police involved and for the first time Annie felt a niggle of fear. Who was this man? What did she know about him other than he'd seen her sister a few times, dropped Nola when he'd gotten bored with her, then landed smack-dab in the middle of Annie's living room with some ridiculous story about Nola having a baby—*this* baby! None of it made any sense.

"Fine," he relented. Muttering something under his breath about headstrong women who didn't know when to back off, he crossed the short distance to the grouping of chairs and couch surrounding the fireplace and set the basket on the floor near a small table. Throughout it all, Carol slept peacefully.

Annie breathed a long sigh of relief. Now, at last, she was getting somewhere and, fool that she was, she felt that she didn't have anything to fear from Liam—well, other than the possibility that he might take the baby from her.

She settled onto one of the arms of the couch while he warmed the backs of his legs by the fire. "So, now, why don't you start over and tell me why you came here—you said something about looking for Nola.''

His jaw slid to one side and Annie was struck again at how sexy he was when he was quiet and thoughtful. "That's right. I need to find your sister. I just found out a couple of days ago that she'd been pregnant and had a baby—presumably mine, considering the timing. Jake found birth records. No father was listed, but I'm sure that the kid's mine."

Her heart plummeted. Obviously he'd done his homework and she knew in an instant that her short-lived chance at motherhood was over. "Who—who is Jake?"

"A friend."

"Oh."

"He's also a private detective."

Great. She'd hoped his farfetched story would prove wrong. "So you came here looking for Nola or information about her and just happened to stumble on the baby."

"Yep." He rubbed his jaw and avoided her gaze for a second, concentrating instead on the snow piling in the corners of the windowpanes. "There's another reason," he admitted.

"Which is?"

Leaning his hips against the side of the fireplace, he closed his eyes and pinched the bridge of his nose for a second as if he could ward off a headache. "Let's just say Nola and I have some unfinished business that doesn't involve the baby. I only found out about her''—he added as he cocked his head in the direction of the basket—"because Jake found out. I had no idea Nola was pregnant."

"She didn't tell you?" she asked, standing and walking to the basket to see that Carol was still sleeping.

"Nope."

"Why not?"

"Good question. One I can't wait to ask her, but let's just say that your sister and I aren't on the best of terms."

"Is that why you hired your friend?" What was Nola involved in? Normal, regular people didn't employ investigators—or even have their friends check up on old lovers. Or did they? Something was wrong here. Very, very wrong. He moved closer to her and she found herself so near this man she could barely breathe. The air in the little cottage seemed suddenly thick, the light through the windows way too dim.

"Nola lied. About a lot of things. Not just the baby."

"Such as?" Annie's heart was knocking, her breathing shallow as her gaze dropped from his to the contour of his lips, so bold and thin. Too much was happening, way too fast. She felt as if her life was spinning out of control.

"She set me up."

"For?"

He shrugged. "My guess is to get the blame off whoever she's protecting. She claimed she knew that before she left Belfry Construction, I was embezzling. One night, when she just happened to be driving by, she saw me go into the office. She concluded I'd gone to doctor the company books and was surprised by the security guard, so of course I killed him." He didn't elaborate, just stared at her with unforgiving eyes. "I didn't do it, Annie. I swear."

"But—but why would she lie?" Oh, God, what was he saying? Nola wouldn't . . . *couldn't* fabricate something so horrid. A man was dead. *Murdered* from the sound of it and Nola thought O'Shaughnessy was involved? "I—I think you'd better start from the beginning."

He did. In short, angry sentences he told her about his work, the projects he'd overseen, the discrepancy in the books, and Nola's suddenly recanted testimony that she'd known he was at the office that night. The problem was that he had been there, but when he'd left, Bill

Arness was very much alive. Liam had thrown a wave to the old man as he'd stepped off the elevator and Bill had locked the door behind him. He finished there; he didn't tell her about being watched by the police, eventually hauled into jail, fingerprinted, and booked, only to have the charges dropped. Hell, what a nightmare.

Annie stared at him with disbelieving eyes. "On top of all this—which is damned incredible, let me tell you— you're sure that you're the baby's father and Nola's her mother?"

"I wouldn't put Nola in the same sentence with *mother*." O'Shaughnessy glanced down at the basket as Carol uttered a soft little coo. The hard line of his jaw softened slightly and a fleeting tenderness changed his expression, but only for a moment. In that instant Annie noticed the wet streaks in his hair where snow had melted and the stubble of a beard that turned his jaw to gold in the dim fireglow. As he unbuttoned his coat and rubbed kinks from the back of his neck, Annie was nearly undone.

She had to think, to buy some time and sort this all out. Since he was bound and determined to take the baby with him, she had to entice him to stay. At least for a while. "Would you like something? I've got a Thermos of instant coffee I made on the fire this afternoon. It's not gourmet by any means, but I can guarantee that it's hot."

"That would be great." He shrugged out of his jacket and tossed it over the back of the couch as Annie hurried to the kitchen, twisted the lid of the Thermos, and quickly poured two cups. Her hands were trembling slightly, not out of fear exactly, but because she was a bundle of nerves around this man.

"So tell me again about last night," he suggested as she handed him a steaming mug. His gaze kept wandering back to the basket where the baby slept.

Quickly, she repeated her story of finding the baby, the note, seeing no one, not even footprints leading away from the porch, nothing. As she spoke, he sipped from his cup and listened, not interrupting, just hearing her out. ". . . So this morning, once I could get through, I started making calls. Everyone from the sheriff's department to social services and the hospitals around here, but no one seems to know anything about her."

"I do."

"You think. You really don't know that Carol—"

"Carol?"

"I named her, okay? The point is that there's no way to be sure she's your daughter."

The baby, as if sensing the tension building in the small room, mewled a small, worried whimper.

"Oh, great. See what you've done?" Disregarding the fact that he was a good foot taller than she and, if he decided, could stop her from doing anything, Annie hurried to the basket, gently withdrew baby and blankets, and held the tiny body close to hers. "It's okay," she whispered into the baby's soft curls and realized that the blond hair and blue eyes of this little sprite were incredibly like those of the irate man standing before her.

The baby cried again and Annie all but forgot about Liam O'Shaughnessy with his outrageous stories and damned sexy gaze. "She's wet and hungry and doesn't need to deal with all this . . . this stress."

"She doesn't know what's going on."

"I think that makes three of us!" Annie felt him silently watching her as she changed Carol's diaper, then warmed her bottle in a pan of water that had been heated in the coals of the fire.

"Here we go," she said softly as she settled into the creaky bentwood rocker and, as she fed the baby, nudged the floor with her toe. For the first time since O'Shaughnessy had pounded against her door, there was peace. The wind raged outside, the panes of the windows rattled eerily and a branch thumped in an irregular tempo against the worn shingles of the roof, but inside the cottage was warm, dry, and cozy. Even O'Shaughnessy seemed to relax a little as he rested one huge shoulder against the mantel and, while finishing his coffee, surveyed his surroundings with suspicious eyes.

"Okay," Annie finally said once Carol had burped and fallen asleep against her shoulder. "Instead of arguing with each other, why don't we figure out what we're going to do?"

"You think you can trust me?" he asked, trying to read her expression.

"I don't have much choice, do I?"

That much was true. He was here and definitely in her face. She couldn't budge him if she tried. Annie McFarlane was a little thing, but what she lost in stature she made up for in spirit. He cradled his cup in his hands and tried not to feel like a heel for barging in on her, for destroying her peace of mind, for intending to take away the baby that already appeared to mean so much to her.

"Nope, you don't."

"Great. Just . . . great."

Firelight played in her red-brown hair. High cheekbones curved beneath eyes that shifted from green to gold. Arched eyebrows moved expressively as she spoke with as sexy a mouth as he'd ever seen. A sprinkling of light freckles spanned the bridge of her nose and her hazel eyes were always alive, quick to flare in anger or joy.

What he knew of her wasn't much. She was divorced, had moved from somewhere on the East Coast, saw her sister infrequently, and did some kind of secretarial or bookkeeping work.

"Come on, O'Shaughnessy," she prodded as she carefully placed Carol into the basket. "Why would Nola lie to you and about you? Did she just want to get you into trouble?"

"A good question." He wasn't quite ready to tell her that he'd spent several days in a jail cell because of Nola and her lies. If he confided in her now he was certain she'd be frightened or, worse yet, call the police. There was no telling what she might do. Maybe she'd accuse him of trespassing or kidnapping if he insisted upon taking Carol—*Carol?*—with him. Good God, he was already giving the baby the name she'd put on the kid.

She looked up to find him staring at her. "How'd you find me? Wait, let me guess. Your friend the detective, right?"

"Jake's pretty thorough."

"I don't like my privacy invaded."

"No one does," he admitted, "but then, I don't like being lied to about my kid." *Or lied about.* He finished his coffee and tossed the dregs into the fire. Sparks sputtered and the flames hissed in protest. "So why did Nola leave the baby here for you without so much as a word? It seems strange."

"I—I don't know."

She was lying. He could smell a lie a mile away.

"Sure you do."

"It's personal, okay?"

"So's my daughter."

She stopped cold, took in a long breath, and seemed to fight some inner battle as the baby began to snooze again. "I don't know what your relationship was with Nola," she said. "As close as my sister and I are, we don't share everything and she . . . she's been distant lately." Clearing her throat, she stepped over to the makeshift bassinet as if to reassure herself that the baby was still there. "I've been wrapped up in my own life, settling here, rebuilding, and I guess Nola and I kind of lost touch. The last time I called her apartment, a recording told me the number was disconnected. No one in the family—not even my brother or mother—has heard from her in a few weeks."

"Isn't that unusual?"

"For Nola?" A smile touched her lips and she shook her head, "Unfortunately, no."

God, this woman was gorgeous. Her eyes were round and bright, a gray-green that reminded him of a pine-scented forest hazy with soft morning fog.

"I've got to find her."

"Why? What good would it do?"

He considered that for a second. "First, I want sole custody of my child." He saw the disappointment in her features and felt suddenly like the scum of the earth. "And then there's the little matter of my innocence in Bill Arness's death. I want to talk to good old Nola and find out why she wanted to set me up. I've been cleared, sort of, though I think I'm still a—what do they call it when they don't want to say *suspect*?—a 'person of interest' in the case. I want to talk to Nola, find out why she lied about the break-in at Belfry and—" He jerked his head toward the basket.

"—The baby," she finished for him. "You know, O'Shaughnessy, you make it sound as if my sister's involved in some major criminal conspiracy."

As the fire hissed in the grate and the wind whistled through the trees outside, Liam leveled his disturbing blue eyes at her. "Your sister's in big trouble."

"With you."

"For starters. I think the D.A. might be interested as well."

"Well, if you think I can help you find her, you'd better think again. She's a free spirit who—"

"Is running for her life, if she's smart."

The baby let out a wail certain to wake up the dead in the next three counties.

"Oh, God." Annie jumped up as if she were catapulted by an invisible device, then carefully extracted the little girl from beneath her covers as if she were born to be this child's mother.

Liam couldn't hear what Annie was saying as she whispered softly and rocked gently, holding the child close to her breast. As if a fourteenth-century sorceress had cast a quieting spell, the infant instantly calmed.

It was damned amazing. Could he work this magic with the kid? Hell, no! Could Nola? At the thought of that particularly selfish woman, he frowned and plowed stiff, frustrated fingers through his hair. What was he going to do?

Carol—if that's what the kid's name was—sighed audibly and a smile tugged at the corners of Annie's mouth. For an instant Liam wondered what it would be like to kiss her, to press his mouth against those soft, pliant lips and . . . He gave himself a quick mental shake. What was he doing thinking of embracing her, believing her, wanting to trust her, for crying out loud?

He cleared his throat. "Look, Annie, the bottom line is this: You have my daughter. I want her. And I'll do anything—do you hear me?—*anything* to gain custody of her."

"Then you'll have to fight me," Annie said, her chin lifting defiantly and her back stiffening. "You don't have any proof that Carol is yours."

She tried to look so damned brave as she held the child and pinned him with those furious hazel eyes. For a second his heart turned over for her. She obviously cared about the baby very much. No matter what her true motives were, she had strong ties to the child, probably a helluva lot stronger than Nola's. Nonetheless he was the kid's father and as such he had rights, rights he intended to invoke.

"She's mine, all right."

"Then you won't be adverse to a paternity test."

"For the love of Mike. It's not like you could take a maternity test, right?"

"I've already talked to the powers that be. I'm not claiming to be the baby's mother."

"Fine. No problem. I'll take any damned test." He glanced out the window and scowled at the snow piling over his footsteps. Though he'd been inside less than an hour, the marks made by his boots were nearly obscured. In all truth, there was a problem, a big one. His four-wheel drive rig had barely made it to the end of the driveway because of the packed snow and ice on the roads. Without chains, his wheels had slipped and spun, nearly landing him in the ditch. Though sanding crews had been working around the clock, the accumulation of snow and freezing temperatures had reduced the snow pack to ice. As it was, driving any distance was out of the question, especially with an infant and no safety car seat.

Annie cast him irritated looks as she attended to the baby. Finally, when the child's eyelids had drooped again, Annie carefully placed Carol into the basket. She tucked a blanket gently around the baby and smiled when the infant moved her tiny lips in a sucking motion. "She's so adorable," Annie said. "If she is your child, Mr. O'Shaughnessy, she's darned near perfect, and you're one very lucky man."

He couldn't agree more as he stared at the tiny bit of flesh that sighed softly in a swaddle of pink blankets. An unaccustomed lump filled his throat. He'd never expected any kind of emotional attachment to the baby, not like this. Sure, he'd felt obligated to take care of the kid—duty-bound to see that his offspring was financially and emotionally supported. He planned on hiring a full-time nanny to start with and then, as the kid grew, employ the best tutors, coaches, and teachers that money could buy. If he had to, he had supposed, he could even get married and provide a mother of sorts.

He glanced at Annie and felt a jab of guilt, though he didn't know why.

"However," Annie said, planting her hands on her hips, "if the blood tests prove that you're not her father, O'Shaughnessy, then you'll have a helluva lot of explaining to do. Not only to me, but to the police."

Chapter Four

The woman had him. No doubt about it. The last thing he wanted to do was get the police involved. She was smart, this sister of Nola's, and the firelight dancing in her angry green eyes made him think dangerous thoughts—of champagne, candlelight, and making love for hours.

"I've already told you I don't want to call the authorities. Not until I understand what's going on."

She lifted a finely sculpted eyebrow and desire, often his worst enemy, started swimming in his bloodstream. "And I've already told you," she said, poking a finger at his broad expanse of chest, "that I've talked to the police about the baby. I've got nothing to hide, so why don't you level with me?"

"I am."

Her hair shone red-gold in the dying embers of the fire. "I don't think so." Resolutely she crossed her arms under her chest, inadvertently lifting her breasts and causing Liam's mind to wander ever further into that dangerous and erotic territory. He couldn't seem to think straight when she was around; his purpose, once so honed and defined, became cloudy.

"I want you to help me find Nola."

"Why?"

"I need to talk to her and find out why she lied about the baby, why she lied about the break-in, why the hell she wanted to set me up for murder."

"If she did."

"She did, all right." Liam had no doubts. None whatsoever when it came to Nola Prescott. Annie was another story altogether. Her forehead wrinkled in concentration, but she didn't budge and he figured he should back off, at least a little. "Think about it and I'll do something about the heat in here, okay?" He didn't bother waiting for an answer, but threw on his jacket and walked outside. Firewood was already cut and stacked on the back porch, so he hauled in several baskets of fir and oak, restocking the dwindling pile on the hearth and adding more chunks to the fire.

Annie busied herself with the baby, feeding her, changing her, burping her, rocking her, cooing to her, and looking for all the world as if she were born to be a mother. *Idiot*, he told himself. *Don't be fooled. She and that sister of hers share the same blood.*

The phone jangled and they both jumped. Annie froze and just stared at the instrument, but Liam was quick and snagged the receiver before the person on the other end had a chance to hang up. "Hello?"

"Hello? Who is this?" a male voice demanded. Whoever the hell he was, he didn't sound happy. "I'm calling Annie McFarlane."

"Just a sec—"

Liam handed the phone to Annie and, without a word, took the baby. It was incredible how natural it felt to hold the kid, even though his hands were larger than the baby's head. Little Carol gurgled, but didn't protest as Annie, eyes riveted on him, placed the receiver to her ear.

"Hello?"

"Annie?" It was Joel, her brother. "For crying out loud, who was that?"

"A—a friend." Why she thought she had to protect O'Shaughnessy she didn't know, but somehow she thought it best not to tell her brother about his wild story and her plight.

"A *friend*? I don't know whether to be relieved or worried. I'm glad you're not pining over David, but from what the news here says, you're in the middle of one helluva storm. I've been trying to get through for hours."

"Me, too," she said and since she didn't offer any further explanation about O'Shaughnessy, Joel didn't pry.

"So you're okay?"

"All things considered." She watched Liam with the baby and her heart did a silly little leap. He was so big and the infant was so tiny, yet she sensed that this man who exuded such raw animal passion and fury would protect this child with his very life.

"Well, Merry Christmas."

"You, too."

"We all miss you."

"I know, but there's no way I can get to the airport." *Nor can I leave Carol.* At that particular thought her heart twisted painfully. How could she ever give up the baby?

"Yeah, I know." Joel sounded disappointed and they talked for a little while before she had the nerve to bring up their sister.

"You know, I haven't seen her since—geez, I can't remember when," Joel admitted, though there was some hesitation in his voice, a nervous edge that Annie hadn't heard earlier. "But then I didn't really expect to hear from her over the holidays. You know how it is with Nola—hit or miss. This year must be a miss."

"You don't have any idea where she is?"

"Nope. She did call, oh, maybe a month or so ago and said she was leaving Seattle, but that was it. No plans. No forwarding address. No damned idea where she'd end up. I can't imagine it, myself, but then I've got a wife and kids to consider." Annie could almost see her brother shaking his head at the folly that was his younger sister.

She noticed O'Shaughnessy studying her and turned her back, wrapping the telephone extension around herself and avoiding his probing gaze as she asked, "Do you know if she's been in any kind of trouble?"

"Nola? Always."

"No, no. I mean serious trouble."

There was a pause. "Such as?"

"Is it possible that she was pregnant?"

Another moment's hesitation and Annie knew the truth. "Joel?" Annie's heart was thundering, her head pounding, her hands suddenly ice-cold.

Her brother cleared his throat, then swore roundly. "I'm sorry, Annie, but Nola didn't want you to know." Annie closed her eyes and sagged against the kitchen counter. So it was true. At least part of O'Shaughnessy's story held up. Joel sighed. "Nola knew how badly you wanted a baby and with your miscarriages and the divorce and all, she thought—and for once I agreed with her—that you should be kept in the dark."

So the baby really was Nola's. "Did she say who the father was?" Annie's voice was barely a whisper.

"Nah. Some guy who was in and out of her life in a heartbeat. A real louse. She decided that the best thing to do was to . . . well, to terminate."

"No!"

"Annie, there's nothing you can do now. That was months ago. I tried to talk her into giving the kid up for adoption but she claimed she couldn't live with herself if she knew she had a baby out there somewhere with someone she didn't know raising it . . . I figured it was her decision.''

"When was this?"

"Seven—maybe eight months ago. Yeah, in the spring. End of March or early April, I think. You'd just confirmed that David was about to be a father—the timing was all wrong.''

"When . . . when was she due?"

"What does it matter?"

"When, damn it!"

"About now, I guess. No . . . wait. A few weeks ago, I suppose. I never asked her what happened. In fact, we never really talked again. I just assumed she did what she had to do and got on with her life.''

"Did she say who the father was?"

"No.''

"Just the louse.''

She rotated out of the phone line coils in time to notice Liam wince.

"Right.''

"Did she date anyone else?

"I can't remember. There was the guy with the Irish name—the father, I think.''

"O'Shaughnessy?"

"Right. That's the bastard.''

"No one else?"

"What does it matter, for crying out loud.''

"It matters, okay?"

"Well, let me think." He sighed audibly. "I can't think of anyone. Polly—" His voice trailed as he asked his wife the same question and there was some discussion. "Annie? Polly thinks there was another guy. Somebody named Tyson or Taylor or what?" Again his voice faded and Annie's heart nearly stopped beating. Liam was studying her so hard she could hardly breathe.

"Yeah, that's right. Polly seems to think the guy's name was Talbott."

"Peter Talbott?" Annie said and Liam's expression became absolutely murderous.

"Yeah, that's the guy."

"Good, Joel. Thanks."

"Are you okay?"

"Right as rain," she lied. The room began to swim. Annie's throat was dry. She brought up his kids and, for the moment, Joel's interest was diverted. Liam, however, seemed about to explode. His hands balled into angry fists and his eyes were dark as the night.

"Look, I'll see you after the first of the year," Joel finally said before hanging up. "And if I hear from Nola, I'll tell her you need to speak to her."

"Do that." She unwound the cord from her body and let the receiver fall back into its cradle. "So," she said in a voice she didn't recognize as her own. "It looks like part of your story is true. Joel knew about the pregnancy."

Liam's jaw tightened perceptively. "All of my 'story,' as you call it, is true, Annie. You've just got to face it." Carol was sleeping in his arms and Annie's heartstrings pulled as she saw the baby move her lips. Golden eyelashes fluttered for a second, then drooped over crystal-blue eyes.

"Here—let me put her down."

She took Carol from his arms and in the transfer of the baby, they touched, fingers twining for a second, arms brushing. As she placed the baby in her basket, Liam rubbed the back of his neck nervously, then shoved the curtains aside to view the relentlessly falling snow. He had to get out of the cozy little cabin with its built-in family. Not only was there a baby who had already wormed her way into his heart, but the woman who wanted to be the kid's mother had managed to get under his skin as well. It was too close—too comfortable—too damned domestic.

"So Talbott's the guy."

"Polly, my sister-in-law, seems to think Nola was involved with him."

"Figures," he said, conjuring up Talbott's face. Short and wiry, with blond hair, tinted contacts, and freckles, Pete was as ambitious as he was dogged. But Joel hadn't thought him a crook. Well, live and learn. "When's this gonna end?" he growled, staring through the frozen windowpanes. Anxious for a breath of fresh air and a chance to clear his head, he snatched up his jacket and rammed his arms through the sleeves. Snagging the wood basket from the hearth, he was out the door in an instant. Outside, the wind keened through the trees. Snow and ice pelted his face and bare head. He shoved gloves over his hands and wished he'd never given up smoking. A cigarette would help. Confronting Nola and Talbott would be even better.

What the hell was he going to do about the situation here? When he'd first stepped inside the cabin he'd planned to interrogate Annie, find out everything he could about Nola, grab his kid, and leave. Then he'd come face-to-face with the woman and damn it, she'd found a way to blast past his defenses, to put him off guard, to make him challenge everything he'd so fervently believed.

"Hell, what a mess!" He piled wood in the basket and headed back inside. As he entered, a rush of icy wind ruffled the curtains and caused flames to roar in the grate. Annie didn't say a word and he dumped the wood, then stormed outside, needing the exercise, having to find a way to expend some restless energy, wanting to grab hold of his equilibrium again.

Annie heated water for coffee and more formula and tried not to watch the door, waiting for O'Shaughnessy. Somehow she had to get away from him, to think clearly.

From the moment he'd barged into her life, she'd been out of control, not knowing what to do. She was certain that as soon as the storm lifted, he'd be gone. With Carol. Her heart broke at the thought, for though she told herself she was being foolish and only asking for trouble, she'd begun to think of the baby as hers. Hadn't the card said as much? *For you, Annie.* What a joke. Nobody gave a baby away. Not even Nola.

But the baby was here.

If Carol were truly Nola's child and if Nola had left the baby on Annie's doorstep—presumably to raise, at least for a while—then didn't she have some rights? At least as an aunt, and at most as the guardian of choice. *But what if the baby is really O'Shaughnessy's? What then? What kind of rights do you think you'll have if he's truly Carol's biological father? Face it, Annie, right now Liam O'Shaughnessy holds all the cards.*

He shouldered open the door, shut it behind him, and dropped a final basket of wood near the hearth. "That should get you through 'til morning."

"Me through? What about you?"

"I won't be staying."

Dear God, he hadn't changed his mind. He was leaving and taking Carol with him. Panic gripped her heart. "You don't have to go—"

"Don't worry, Annie," he said, his lips barely moving, his eyes dark with the night. "I won't rip her away from you. At least not tonight."

"Noble of you."

He snorted. "Nobility? Nah. I'm just looking out for my best interests. It's sub-zero outside and I don't think I could move the Jeep even if I tried. The kid's better off here, where it's warm."

So he did have a heart, after all. She should have been surprised, but wasn't. His gaze held hers for a breath-stopping second and she read sweet seduction in his eyes. Her blood thundered and she looked away, but not before the message was passed and she knew that he, too, wondered what it would feel like to kiss. Aside from the baby, they were alone. Cut off from civilization by the storm. One man. One woman. She swallowed hard.

"Carol will be safe here."

"I know." He dusted his gloved hands and reached for the door. "But I'll be right outside, so don't get any funny ideas about taking off."

"Outside?" She glanced at the windows and the icy glaze that covered the glass. "But it's freezing . . ."

"I don't think it would be a good idea if I slept in here, do you?"

The thought was horrifyingly seductive. "No—no—I, um . . . no, that wouldn't work," she admitted in a voice she didn't recognize. Sleeping in the same little house as O'Shaughnessy. Oh, God. She swallowed even though her mouth was dry as sandpaper.

"Yeah. I didn't think so." He crouched at the fire, tossing in another couple of logs before prodding them with the poker that had been leaning against the warm stones. Annie tried not to stare at the way his faded jeans stretched across his buttocks, or at the dip in his waistband where the denim pulled away from the hem of his jacket. However, her gaze seemed to have a mind of its own when it came to this man. Annie licked her lips and dragged her gaze back to the baby.

He dusted his hands together. "That should do it for a while. If it dies down—"

"I can handle it," she snapped.

His smile was downright sexy. "I know. Otherwise I wouldn't leave. I'll see ya in the morning." For the first time she noticed the lines around his eyes. "Think about everything I've said."

"I will." She didn't know whether she was relieved or disappointed. Relieved—she should definitely be relieved.

His smile wasn't filled with warmth. "I won't be far."

"But the storm—"

"Don't worry about me, Annie," he said, one side of his mouth lifting cynically. "I learned a long time ago how to take care of myself." He was out the door and Annie watched at the window where, despite the freezing temperatures and falling snow, he settled into his Jeep.

"Just go away. Take your incredible story and wild accusations and leave us alone," she muttered under her breath. But she couldn't help worrying about him just a little.

Chapter Five

"Come on, come on." Liam pressed the numbers from memory on his cellular phone, but the damned thing wouldn't work. He was too close to the hills or the signals were clogged because of the storm and the holidays. Whatever the reason, he couldn't reach Jake. "Hell." He clapped the cell shut and stared through the windshield as he tugged the edge of his sleeping bag more tightly around him. Nothing in this iced-over county was working.

And he needed to talk to Cranston, to report that he'd had a run-in with Nola's sister, found his kid, and suspected Peter Talbott of being the culprit in Bill Arness's murder. But he didn't want to use Annie's phone—not while she was in earshot.

Nola was involved. Up to her eyeballs. There was a reason she'd fingered him for a crime he didn't commit and it wasn't just vengeance because he'd broken up with her and unwittingly left her pregnant. Nope, it had something to do with Pete Talbott.

Liam glowered through the windshield. Ice and snow had begun to build over the glass, but he was able to see the windows of Annie's cabin, patches of golden light in an otherwise bleak and frigid night. Every once in a while a shadow would pass by the panes and he'd squint to catch another glimpse of Annie. His jaw clenched as he realized he was hoping to see her— waiting for her image to sweep past the window. Nola's sister. No good. Trouble. A woman to stay away from at all costs.

But he couldn't. Not just yet. His thoughts wandered into perilous territory again and he wondered what it would feel like to kiss her, to press his lips to hers, to run the tip of his tongue along that precocious seam of her lips, to reach beneath her sweater, let his fingers scale her ribs to touch her breasts and . . .

"Fool!" His jaw clenched and he pushed all kind thoughts of Annie out of his mind. So what if she was a package of warm innocence wrapped in a ribbon of fiery temper? Who cared if the stubborn angle of her chin emphasized the spark of determination of her green eyes? What did it matter that the sweep of her eyelashes brushed the tops of cheeks that dimpled in a sensual smile?

She was Nola's sister. Big-time trouble. The last woman in the world he should think about making love to. Besides, he had other things with which to occupy his mind, the first being to clear his name completely. Then he'd claim his daughter and then . . . then he'd deal with Annie. Just at the thought of her his blood heated and his cock started to swell.

"Down, boy," he muttered to the image glaring back at him in the rearview mirror. "That's one female who's off limits—way off. Remember it." But the eyes reflecting back at him didn't seem to be the least little bit convinced.

* * *

Jake Cranston wasn't a man who gave up easily, but this time he was more than ready to throw in the towel. Nola Prescott seemed to have vanished off the face of the earth. How could a woman disappear so quickly?

He'd checked with her friends and relatives, called people he knew who owed him favors on the police force and at the DMV, even spoken to the Social Security Administration, with no luck.

"Think, Cranston, think," he muttered under his breath as he walked from one end of his twelve-by-fifteen office to the other. It was a small cubicle crammed with files, a desk, and a computer that, tonight, was of no help whatsoever.

Not that it mattered. He'd done his part. Now it was up to Liam. He didn't doubt that O'Shaughnessy would handle the Nola Prescott situation his own way. But still he was puzzled. Where the hell was she?

It wasn't often anyone eluded him, but then he hadn't given up yet. Not really. Deep in his gut he felt that Liam still needed his help and he owed the man his life. Years ago O'Shaughnessy had been the first man on the scene of the hit and run. It had been his grit and brute strength that had helped pull Jake from the mangled truck seconds before it exploded in a conflagration that had lit up the cold winter night and singed the branches of the surrounding trees. The driver of the other car had never been caught, but Jake had discovered a friend for life in O'Shaughnessy.

Now the tables were turned. It was time for Jake to pay back a very big favor and he wouldn't quit until he did. Getting Liam out of jail had been a start. The next step was hunting down Nola Prescott, no matter that she'd gone to ground. He grunted and reached into the bottom drawer for his shot glass and a half-full bottle of rye whiskey. His personal favorite. He poured himself three fingers, tossed them back, and felt the familiar warmth blaze its way down his throat to his stomach. Wiping the back of his hand across his mouth, he felt a little better. Finding Ms. Prescott was only a matter of time.

Liam awoke with a start, his heart pounding crazily, the dream as vivid as if he were still locked away. The sound of metal against metal, keys clicking in locks, chains rattling—all receded with the dawn. He was in the Jeep in the middle of a damned forest. Would it never end? Cramped and cold, he rotated his neck until he felt a release and heard a series of pops. Now all he needed was coffee and lots of it.

Sunlight penetrated the stands of birch and fir, splintering in brilliant shards that pierced his eyes and did nothing to warm the frozen landscape. He shoved open the door and, boots crunching through the drifting snow, made his way to the cabin to see the kid again. And Annie. That woman was playing with his mind, whether she knew it or not.

He lifted a fist to pound on the door when it flew open and she stood on the other side of the threshold. Before he could enter she stepped onto the porch, the dog at her heels, then closed the door softly behind her. "Carol's asleep."

"So?"

"I don't want her disturbed." Her gloved hands were planted firmly on her hips and she stood in the doorway as if she intended to stop him from entering. Her determination was almost funny—tiny thing that she was.

"She's my daughter."

Dark eyebrows elevated as the mutt romped through the drifts, clumps of snow clinging to his hair. "Your fatherhood has yet to be determined."

"You still want a paternity test?"

"For starters."

"Not a problem."

Her eyes, so fierce, were suddenly a darker shade of hazel, more green than gold and not quite so certain. "Good," she said with more bravado than he expected. "I'll arrange it. When the roads are clear."

"Fair enough." She was bluffing. And scared. Of what? Him? He didn't think so.

"But for right now, we're not going to wake her up— she had a bad night." Annie hitched her chin toward the barn. "I've got to feed the horses. You can help."

"Can I?" He couldn't help baiting her.

"Yep." She didn't waste a second, but stepped off the porch and started breaking a trail in the knee-deep powder. The dog galloped in senseless circles before bounding up the ramp that led to a wide door on rollers. With all of her strength, Annie pushed. The thing didn't budge. Liam placed his hands above hers on the edge of the door. His body covered her as he put his weight into moving a door that was frozen closed.

"Great," she muttered and was close enough that the coffee on her breath tickled his nose, the back of her jacket rubbed up against the buttons of his, and her rump pressed against his upper thighs. Through the denim of his jeans he felt her heat and his damned cock responded, stiffening beneath his fly.

"It'll give." He ignored the scent of her perfume and the way his body was reacting to the proximity of hers. Again he threw his weight into the task and the ice gave way, rusty rollers screaming in protest, ice shattering as the door sped on its track. Annie tumbled forward and Liam's arms surrounded her, catching her before she slipped on the icy ramp.

"Whoa, darlin'," he said, surprised that an endearment had leapt so naturally to his lips.

"I'm . . . I'm okay." She twisted in his arms and her face was only inches from his, so near that he could see the sunlight playing in her eyes. His gut tightened and his mind spun to a future that would never exist, a time when she would be lying naked in his arms, bedsheets twined through her legs, moonlight playing upon her bare breasts. At the thought, his mouth was suddenly dry as a desert wind and he cleared his throat. Slowly, making sure she had her footing, he released her. Her gaze shifted to his lips for a second before she stepped into the musty interior of the barn and he followed with an erection that pressed hard against his jeans. Silently he cursed himself. Hadn't he spent the night convincing himself that Annie McFarlane was off-limits?

A soft nicker floated on air that smelled of dry hay, leather, and horse dung.

"Think I forgot you?" she said as she popped off the lid of a barrel of oats and, using an old coffee can, scooped up the grain that she poured into the mangers of three horses. Liquid eyes appraised him and large nostrils blew into the air as the animals buried their muzzles into the feed.

Annie reached into the pocket of her coat and, walking to a stack of hay bales piled into the corner, pulled out a small jackknife, opened the blade, and sliced the twine holding the first bale together. She glanced over to Liam. "You can make yourself useful by tossing down a few more of these from the hayloft." She went to work on the second bale and he climbed up a metal ladder.

Within minutes he'd dropped twelve bales and stacked them next to the dwindling pile near the stalls. Annie forked hay into the mangers and when he attempted to take the pitchfork from her hands to do the job, he was rewarded with a look that would melt steel. "I can handle this," she said.

"I just thought that—"

"That I was a female and since you were here you'd take over and give me a break. Thanks but no thanks. If you want to help out, grab a bucket and get them fresh water." She bit the edge of her lip. "You'll have to go back to the house, though, and use the faucets in the kitchen. I drained all the outside pipes just before the storm hit. Just be careful and don't wake—"

"—The baby. Yeah, I know." He grabbed a pail from a nail on the wall and trudged back to the cabin. He'd never met so prickly a woman and yet she was trusting him to be alone with his child.

He checked the makeshift bassinet as the bucket was filling and couldn't help but smile. The baby was indeed cutting a few z's. Barely moving, a blanket tucked all the way to her chin, Carol was lying there with such pure innocence that the little lump of flesh grabbed hold of Liam. How could something so perfect, so beautiful, have been conceived by an act of cold passion and grown in a womb devoid of love?

Despite Annie's warning, he pulled one of his gloves off with his teeth and touched a golden curl with the tip of his finger. The baby sighed quietly and in that barest meeting of callouses and perfect, baby-soft skin he felt a connection that wrapped around the darkest reaches of his heart and tied in a knot that could never be undone. Somehow, some way, no matter what, he would take care of this child.

With more effort than he would have imagined, he turned his thoughts to filling the pail over and over again until each animal had water enough for the day and the trail in the snow between the barn and the cabin was packed solidly.

Annie hung up the pitchfork and rubbed each velvet-soft nose as the animals ate, mashing their teeth together loudly and snorting.

"These belong to you?" he asked as she threw a winter blanket over the bay's back.

"No. I just care for them. They come with the house

and grounds. This guy is Hoss, then there's Little Joe," she said, pointing to a dapple gray, "and Adam, there, the sorrel gelding." At the mention of his name, Adam's ears flattened. "All named after characters on 'Bonanza.' "

"I got the connection."

"Yeah, great guys, but they could use a little exercise." With a glance to the window, she frowned. "I usually walk them later in the day, but they'll have to wait for anything more substantial, at least for a few more days." Her eyes found Liam's. "Like we all have to."

"I might be able to get the Jeep out today."

She swallowed hard. "And what then?"

"I find Nola."

"Just like that?" she asked skeptically as she snapped her fingers.

"It might take a little time, but I'll catch up with her."

"You make it sound like she's running from you."

"She is. She just doesn't realize how futile it is." He said it with a determination that made her shudder, as if he were stating an obvious fact.

Nervously, Annie rubbed the blaze running down Little Joe's nose, then wiped her hands on the front of her jeans before leaving the stall. Liam shouldn't be here. He was too male, too intense, too close. Emotions, conflicting and worrisome, battled within her. She was attracted to him, there was no doubt about it, but he was here for one reason and one reason only—his child. "I—I'd better check on the baby."

"She's fine."

"I'll see for myself—"

He grabbed her arm so quickly she gasped. Even through the denim of her jacket and sweater beneath, she felt the iron grip of his fingers, the hard strength of the man. "Be careful," he said through lips that barely moved.

"Of what? You?"

"Of getting too attached to the baby."

"Too late." Tossing her hair over her shoulders, she glared up at him. "I'm already attached to that little girl and you may as well know that you can't bully her away from me."

"She's not yours—"

"Or yours." She tried to pull away, to keep her distance from him, but he drew her closer to his body, close enough that she noticed the pores of his skin and the red-blond glimmer that gilded a jaw set in silent fury. "She's mine, all right."

Oh, God, was that her heart beating so furiously? His gaze dropped to her throat and she sensed her pulse quicken. She licked her lips, tried to back away and was suddenly lost as his lips found hers. She was trapped, her breath caught somewhere in her lungs, her knees turning weak as his arms surrounded her. She tried to protest, to tell him to go to hell, to back away and slap him hard across the jaw but instead she opened her mouth willingly, invitingly.

It had been so long, so damned long since a man had held her, kissed her, caused her blood to race.

But this is wrong. And dangerous. This is O'Shaughnessy. He only wants you so he can get close to the baby.

She wouldn't listen to that awful, nagging voice. No, right now, she just wanted to be held. While the world was snowbound and frigid, she was warm here in Liam's arms. She felt his tongue touch the tip of hers. A hot shiver of desire, wanton and needy, skittered down her spine. With a moan she sagged against him and his kiss deepened, his tongue searching and exploring, causing the world to spin.

He's only doing this to get close to Carol, to find Nola, to further his own interests. Wake up, Annie. He doesn't care one iota about you. He's using you.

"No!" She dragged her head from his, ignoring the

desire still singing through her veins. Breathing unevenly, she stepped back. "I mean, I can't . . . I won't . . . Oh, for the love of . . . just . . . just leave, would you?"

"That's what you want?" His lips tugged into a cynical, amused smile that sent her temper into the stratosphere.

"Yes. Just go!"

His teeth flashed white against his skin in a cynical I-don't-believe-you-for-a-second grin and it was all she could do not to slap him. "As I said, I—I'd better check on Carol." She tore out of the barn, gulped big lungfuls of crisp winter air, and hurried along the broken path to the cabin. Riley, barking madly at a startled winter bird, sprinted ahead of her.

She kicked off her boots on the porch and threw open the door. "How could you?" she muttered, berating herself as she saw her reflection in the iced-over windows. "I thought you were a smart woman." She pulled off her gloves, threw them on the back of her couch, ripped off her jacket, and closed her eyes. "Fool. Damned silly fool of a female!" What was she thinking, kissing O'Shaughnessy? No, *wanting* to kiss him, to touch him, to feel his body lying on top of hers . . . "Oh, for the love of Mike. Stop it!"

Thunk! The door banged open. A frozen blast of wind swept into the room, causing the fire to spark and the curtains to flutter as Liam stepped inside, his boots dripping on an old braided rug.

"You don't take a hint very well, do you?" she accused as he latched the door and they were again alone, away from the world, one man, one woman, and a sleeping infant. Her heart skipped a beat.

"You weren't serious." His eyes, blue as an August sky, held hers.

She cleared her throat and prayed her voice would remain steady. "About you leaving?" Why did she feel he could read her mind? "Believe me, O'Shaughnessy,

I've never been more serious in my life.'' She turned toward a mirror mounted near the kitchen door and grabbed a rubber band from her pocket with one hand while scraping her hair away from her face with the other. With a flip of her wrist she snapped the ponytail into place. "I think it would be best for all of us if you just opened the door and took off."

"Liar." He was across the room in an instant, standing behind her, strong arms wrapping firmly around her torso, splayed fingers against the underside of her breasts. "You don't want me to leave."

"You arrogant, self-serving, son of a . . . oooh."

His lips brushed against her nape. Warm and seductive, his breath wafted across her skin.

A nest of butterflies, long dormant, exploded in her stomach as his tongue traced the curve of her neck. "Don't lie to me, Annie. You want me as much as I want you."

Oh, Lord, he knew. Her body trembled at his touch and she hated herself for the weakness. Slowly he turned her into his embrace and as she stared into his eyes, he kissed her, long and hard, and with a desperation that cried out for more. She shouldn't do this, shouldn't let her body rule her mind, and yet as he sighed into her open mouth, she wrapped her arms around his neck, closed her eyes, and didn't argue as his hands found the hem of her sweater and his fingers skimmed the skin of her abdomen with feather-light touches that caused her breasts to ache and her mind to play with images of making love all night long.

"I—I can't," she said as his fingers traced her nipple through the silky fabric of her bra.

"Can't what?" he said, kissing the side of her neck and bending farther down as his hands caressed her breast.

I can't love you! her mind screamed, but she swallowed back the ridiculous words. "Do—do this—oooh."

He unhooked her bra deftly and scooped both her breasts into his palms.

"Liam, please—" she whispered, but her protest went unheeded and she closed her eyes against the wave of desire that rippled through her. Without hurry he kissed the flat of her abdomen, then moved ever upward, his tongue and lips and teeth touching her so intimately she thought she might die. "Liam," she whispered as he found her breast and began to suckle. Wet and warm, his mouth seemed to envelop her and all thoughts of stopping him vanished. Together they fell upon the worn couch and he pulled her sweater over her head before tossing away her bra and kissing her again.

"Sweet, sweet Annie. God, you're beautiful." He stared at her breasts for a heartbeat, touched them lightly, watched in fascination as her nipples tightened, then resumed his ministrations.

Desire pulsed through her blood, throbbing deep in her center, creating a core of desire that played games with her mind. The fire crackled and cast the room in a golden glow that vied with the sunlight slanting through icy windows as Liam kissed her.

Annie trembled and held him close, her fingers running through the thick, coarse strands of his hair, her body aching for more of his touch. *This is wrong, Annie. So wrong. Remember, he's only using you.* That horrid voice—her reason—nagged at her. *And there's pregnancy—you can't risk it. Or disease. What do you know of this man? What, really?*

His fingers dipped below the waistband of her jeans and a series of pops followed as the snaps of her fly gave way easily. The lace of her panties was a thin barrier to the heat of his hands and as he traced the V of her legs with his fingers, she began to move to a gentle rhythm that controlled her body and mind.

He nudged her legs apart with deft fingers and pushed her panties to one side. Gently he touched her, slowly prodding and retracting, just grazing that sensitive bud that palpitated with need. She cried out as he plunged ever deeper and her thoughts spun wildly in a whirlpool of desperate need that swirled ever faster . . .

She clung to him as he kissed her. Sweat broke out across her forehead and along her spine. She wanted more—all of him, to feel his body joined to hers. But she could only take what he was giving, that special touch that made her feel she was drowning in a pool of pleasure, gasping and panting and unable to breathe, yet still fighting him, knowing in her heart that this was wrong.

"Come on, Annie," he whispered against her ear. "Let go."

"I—I can't. Oh . . . oh, God."

"Sure you can, baby. Trust me."

With all of her heart she wanted to. Tears sprang to her eyes and yet desire reigned as he traced the tracks of her tears with his tongue while never letting up, his fingers continuing to work their own special magic.

He kissed her breast again and something deep inside of her gave way.

"That's it, girl."

Hotter and hotter, faster and faster she moved. A small moan escaped her. His lips found hers. His tongue delved deep into her mouth. He touched that perfect spot and she convulsed. With a soul-jarring jolt, her resistance shattered. Her body jerked. Once. Twice. Three times.

She heard a throaty, desperate cry and realized it was her own voice.

"For the love of God," she said, staring into his enigmatic eyes. Never had she felt so sated. Never had she been so pleasured. And never had she been so embarrassed.

Who was this man? Why had she let him touch her, kiss her, feel her most intimate regions?

As swift as a bolt of lightning, the reality of what she'd done shot through her. "Oh, no." She pushed him away, scrambled into her clothes, and with her face blushing a hot denial of her own wanton deeds, she climbed to her feet. "Look, this was wrong. All wrong."

"You don't believe that."

"Yes, yes, I do. And I just can't have sex with you. What about . . . about condoms and—"

"I've been tested," he said, climbing to his feet.

"But, I could get pregnant and . . . listen, the reason Nola left the baby with me is that I can't have children, can't seem to carry them to term and—"

He folded her into his arms and she let the tears run from her eyes. All this emotion. What could she do about him? For God's sake, she was falling in love with him. She let out a broken sob and the strength of his arms seeped into her bones. Sniffing, she pushed him away. "You . . . you have to leave."

"Annie, don't—"

"I mean it." She yanked the band from her hair and swiped at her eyes. Chin thrust forward defiantly, she added, "I don't know what I was thinking."

"You weren't." He was standing near the window, sunlight casting his body in relief. Good Lord, he was big. And strong. And powerful. *And dangerous. Don't forget dangerous, Annie. He just wants Carol and information about Nola.*

"Listen, O'Shaughnessy, you've got to go, to leave me alone—"

"So we're back to calling me O'Shaughnessy."

"Yes. No. Oh, I don't know." She shook her head, trying to clear the passion-induced cobwebs from her mind. "I just know that you've got to leave. Go do what it is you have to do. Find Nola, figure out this . . . break-in at the company—burglary, embezzlement, or whatever it is and find out about Carol, if she really is yours."

"Is there any doubt?"

Annie glanced at the infant. Golden hair, crystal-blue eyes, arched eyebrows, cheeks as rosy as her father's. She swallowed hard. No, Liam was right. There wasn't a whole lot of question as to the baby's paternity.

"I'll take her in for a blood test as soon as I can get to the hospital. With DNA and all, it should be pretty easy to figure out."

"A snap." He reached for his jacket and shoved one arm down a sleeve. "I'll be back," he promised.

She didn't doubt it for a minute, but she had no idea what to do about it. She glanced at the phone. If she had any brains at all, she'd call the police. Biting her lower lip, she heard the sound of his Jeep's engine roar to life, then the crunch and slide of tires as the vehicle tried to find traction.

Carol let out a tiny whimper and Annie picked her up in an instant. Heart in her throat, she held the tiny body close and felt Carol's breath against her breast— a breast Liam had so recently kissed. Annie's stomach slowly rolled in anticipation at the thought of his touch. "This is such a mess," she admitted to the baby. "Oh, Carol, I'm so sorry." She pressed her lips gently to the baby's soft, blond curls. "I love you so much."

And Liam—do you love him, too?

She snorted at the ridiculous thought. She didn't even know the man. And yet she was ready to make love to him. She should never, *never* have let him kiss her.

What could she do? What if Liam truly was Annie's father? What if he made good his promise and took the baby away from her? Tears stung her eyes as she thought about how long she'd wanted a child, how desperately she'd hoped that she could have one of her own and now this . . . this little one was in her arms and oh, so precious.

"I won't give you up," she whispered, though she knew deep in the blackest regions of her heart that her

words were only a silly, hopeless promise without any
meaning.

Carrying the child, she reached for the phone and
while propping the receiver between her ear and shoulder she bit her lip and dialed the number of the sheriff.

Chapter Six

Nola drew on her cigarette, waited for the nicotine to do its trick, then flicked the butt into the toilet of the Roadster Cafe. She studied her reflection in the cracked mirror in the tiny bathroom of the truck stop where she'd taken a job just two weeks earlier.

Her face was beginning to show signs of strain. With a frown, she sighed and brushed her bangs from her eyes. Dark roots were showing in the blond streaks she'd added to her hair. This wasn't the way it was supposed to have turned out. Not by a long shot.

She still looked good, or so she tried to tell herself as she applied a new layer of lipstick. Hardly any lines around her eyes and mouth—well, nothing permanent. Though she was younger than her sister by nearly two years, most people thought she was the eldest.

"Hard livin'," she muttered under her breath as she dabbed at the corner of her mouth with a finger to swipe away a little raspberry-colored gloss that had smeared. "But things'll be better." They had to be. She couldn't stand too much of this. Life on the run wasn't all it was cracked up to be. She was forever looking over her shoulder or spying someone she was certain she'd known in that other life. Was that only months ago? How had she gotten herself into this predicament?

"Love." She spat the word as if it tasted foul. And it did. Would she ever learn? Probably not.

Determined not to follow the dark path down which her thoughts invariably wandered, she tightened her apron around her waist and felt a glimmer of cold satisfaction that her figure was returning to its normal svelte proportions. Still a little thick around the middle, she was otherwise slim and her breasts were no longer swollen. Back to 36C. Nearly perfect despite the pregnancy. "Hang in there," she told the woman in the reflection, then felt close to tears yet again. God, when would this emotional roller coaster end?

Probably never.

Sniffing loudly, she wiped away any trace of tears from beneath her mascara-laden lashes. In the end it would be worth it and she consoled herself with the simple fact that everything she'd done—be it right or wrong— she'd done for love.

She ducked through swinging doors that opened to the kitchen, where the fry cook—a greasy-faced kid with bad skin and dishwater-blond hair—gave her the once-over. For some reason he thought he could come on to her.

Like he had a chance.

But then the kid didn't know who she was, or that she'd worked in much better jobs than this, making a decent salary in an office in a big city. For a second she longed for her old life back. Then she caught herself. She'd made her decision and there was no turning back. Not ever.

"I could use a little help up here," the other waitress yelled through the open window between the counter and the kitchen.

"On my way, Sherrie." Checking her watch as she passed through another set of swinging doors, Nola frowned. The call she'd been expecting was half an hour late. Worse yet, there was a customer using the pay phone—that same man she'd seen in here three days running—going on and on about the weather on the interstate. Great. Ignoring the nervous sweat that beaded between her shoulder blades and under her arms, she gathered up knives, forks, and spoons from the baskets at the busing station and began to wrap the utensils in wine-colored napkins.

Surely the guy couldn't talk all night.

"Hey, baby, how 'bout a refill?" At the counter, one of the customers, a trucker from the looks of him, was leaning over a nearly empty cup of coffee. The wedge of pecan pie she'd placed in front of him fifteen minutes earlier had disappeared, leaving only traces of nuts in a pool of melted ice cream. God, this place was a dive.

She plastered a smile on her face, the smile guaranteed to garner the best tips from these cheapskates, and reached for the glass pot of coffee warming on the hot plate. "Sure," she said. "On the house."

He chuckled and pulled at the ends of a scraggly red moustache. "Thanks, doll."

"Anytime," she lied as she glanced at the pay phone again. The guy had hung up and taken a table in the corner. Good.

Now, for the love of Jesus, call!

"Order up!" the cook shouted and rang a bell to catch her attention. She nearly jumped out of her skin and sloshed coffee onto her apron.

"Geez, Lorna, you're a bundle of nerves," Sherrie observed with a shake of her head. Her teased, over-sprayed black hair barely moved. "That's the trouble with you big-city girls. Jumpy. You got to learn to relax."

"I'll try." Wonderful. Now she was getting advice from a woman who raised chihuahuas according to the phases

of the moon and believed that space aliens had visited
her on the anniversary of her second husband's death.
Good-hearted to a fault, Sherrie Beckett was a woman
who could never hope to get out of this tiny town in
the southeastern corner of Idaho.

Nola, or Lorna, as she called herself in these parts,
grabbed the platter and carried the special—a hot turkey sandwich with mashed potatoes and canned cranberry sauce on the side—to the booth in the corner
where the man who'd been monopolizing the telephone
had settled with a copy of *USA Today* and a cigarette.
He barely glanced at her as she slid the plate in front
of him, but she had a cold impression that she'd seen
him somewhere before—somewhere other than this
podunk little town.

"Anything else?"

"This'll do just fine." He flashed her a disarming
grin, jabbed out his smoke, then turned to his meal.

Man, if she were paranoid she would believe that
she'd met him somewhere. But that was impossible. No
one knew where she was, not even any member of her
family. She'd chosen this wide spot in the road to hide
for a few weeks, just until things had cooled down; then,
after she heard from her accomplice, she'd split. For
Canada. From there the plan was to head to the
Bahamas.

And you'll never see your baby again.

Again the stupid tears threatened to rain. Shit, she
was a wimp. A goddamned Pollyanna in the throes of
postpartum trauma or whatever the hell it was. She had
to quit thinking about the baby. The little girl was safe.
With Annie. No one in the world would take better care
of her. So why the tears? It wasn't as if Nola had ever
really wanted a kid.

But she couldn't stop thinking about that little red-
faced bundle of energy that had grown inside her for
nine long, nervous months.

Oh, hell, the guy hadn't even taken a bite of his food and he was back on the phone, tying up the lines. She glanced out the window at the bleak, dark night. A single strand of colored bulbs connected the diner with the trailer park. Inside, a twirling aluminum tree was placed in a corner near the old jukebox. Familiar Christmas carols whispered through the diner, barely heard over the rattle of flatware, the clink of glasses, and the buzz of conversation in this truck stop.

I'm dreaming of a white Christmas . . .

Nola sighed and poured coffee in the half-filled cups sitting before patrons at the counter. *Yeah, well, I'm dreaming of a tropical island, hot sun, and enough rum to soak my mind so I forget about all the mistakes I made. For love.*

"Hey, could we get some service over here?" an angry male voice broke into her reverie.

"On my way," she said with a brightness she didn't feel.

"Well, make it snappy, will ya?"

And Merry Christmas to you, too, you stupid s.o.b. "Sure." She handed the three twenty-odd-year-old macho yahoos their plastic-coated menus and prayed that he would call—and soon. Before she lost what was left of her mind.

"Looks like you were right about Talbott. I'll be sure soon." Jake Cranston's voice crackled and faded on the cellular phone.

"You talked to him?" Liam's hand tightened over the steering wheel and he squinted against the coming darkness. Heavy snowflakes fell from the slate-colored heavens so quickly that the Jeep's wipers were having trouble keeping the windshield clear.

"Not yet, but it won't be long."

"How long?"

"Well, I found our missing link."

"Nola?" Liam couldn't believe his ears.

"Bingo."

"Where?"

"Southeastern Idaho. A remote spot."

"But how?"

"Clever detective work." There was a chuckle, then his voice faded again. " . . . Got a break . . . speeding ticket . . . checked with the Idaho . . . police . . . "

"I can't hear you. Jake?" But it was useless. He couldn't hear a thing. "Call me at Annie's cabin. The phone there works." He rattled off the number that he'd memorized several days earlier. "Jake? Did you get that? Oh, hell!" The connection fizzled completely and he hung up. He'd spent the last three days doing some investigating on his own, if you could call it that. With his four-wheel drive rig and chains, he was able to travel around the hilly streets that had been sanded, plowed, and then snowed and iced over again and again. The entire northern Willamette Valley was caught in the grip of a series of storms that just kept rolling in off the coast and dropping nearly a foot of snow each time. Emergency crews were working around the clock and electrical service had been restored to some of the customers, only to be lost by others.

Liam had spent as much time as he could tracking down the people he'd worked with at the construction company and the rest of the time, he'd been at Annie's cabin, keeping his distance while trying to learn everything she knew about her bitch of a sister. The damned thing of it was he kept finding excuses to hang out there, to get closer to her. The baby was the primary reason, of course, and the most obvious, but, whether he wanted to admit it or not, his emotions ran deep for the woman who had decided to become the kid's new mom.

She'd been nervous around him although he hadn't

touched her again and had resisted the compelling urge to crush her into his arms. He'd slept in the Jeep and dreamed about kissing her until dawn, making love to her until they couldn't breathe, holding her close until forever. He hadn't, because she was scared of him and the situation. Every time the phone had rung she'd jumped as if jolted by an electric shock. Twice he'd caught her looking out the window, staring down the drive as if she expected someone to appear.

Who?

Nola?

He'd begun to believe that she really didn't know if Nola was the mother of the baby, but something was keeping her worrying her lip and wringing her hands when she didn't think he was watching.

He turned into the drive and his headlights picked up fresh tracks in the snow. Someone had decided to visit Annie. Fear froze his heart. What if she'd decided to leave? To pack up the baby and take off? Had Nola sensed that Jake was on to her? He tromped on the gas past the main house and then, as he rounded the final corner to the cabin, he stood on the brakes. The Jeep shimmied and slid but stopped four feet from the back of a Sheriff's Department cruiser. Annie's Toyota truck was parked in front of the tiny garage, thirteen inches of snow undisturbed on the cab and bed.

What now? His hands, inside gloves, became clammy. For the first thirty-eight years of his life he'd respected the law and all officers thereof, but ever since his arrest and the days he'd spent in jail, detained on suspicion, his admiration had dwindled to be replaced by serious doubts. There were a dozen reasons the cops could be here—none of them good—but the worst would be if Annie or Carol were in some kind of trouble. Since there were no emergency vehicles screaming down the lane, Liam assumed that they were both all right.

No, this wasn't a medical emergency. The deputy was here because of him.

Bloody terrific.

He snapped off the engine, grabbed the two bags of groceries he'd bought in town, and stepped into the fresh snow. Whatever the problem was, he'd face it.

Annie heard the sound of the Jeep's engine and wished she could drop through the old floorboards. She'd called the Sheriff's Department three days earlier, explained about her predicament, and been told by a patient but overworked voice that they'd send someone out when they could. Other life-threatening emergencies were deemed more important than being visited by a man who claimed to be the father of a child who had been abandoned but was being cared for. Social Services would call back. The Sheriff's Department would phone when they were able, but she was told to be patient.

She'd regretted the call since she'd placed it and now, seated on the edge of the sofa, feeding Carol a bottle, she felt foolish.

" . . . It was a mistake," she said, not for the first time. "I shouldn't have bothered you."

"But the child's not yours." The deputy, fresh-faced and not more than in his mid-twenties, wasn't about to be put off. Determined to a fault, convinced that he was upholding every letter of the law, he scratched in his note pad and Annie gave herself a series of swift mental kicks for being so damned impulsive and calling the authorities.

Liam had returned and she'd never mentioned the call to him; instead she'd kept a distant and quiet peace with the man. He no longer frightened her and she nearly laughed when she remembered that she hadn't trusted him at first, that she feared for the baby's well-being. Since that first day she'd observed him with Carol and noticed the smile that tugged at his lips when he looked at his baby. His hands, so large and awkward while holding the infant, were kind and protective. No, as long as Liam O'Shaughnessy was around, the baby had nothing to fear.

"No, the baby isn't mine, but I have reason to believe that she is my sister's little girl. I've alerted the proper agencies and talked to Barbara Allen at C.S.D. She said they'd call when the storm passed."

"But this O'Shaughnessy was harassing you—"

"No."

"Trespassing?"

"No. He, um, just thinks the baby may be his. He's agreed to a paternity test and—"

Clunk! The door burst open and Liam filled the doorway. His eyes flashed blue fire as he set two full grocery bags on the table and kicked the door closed. "Is there a problem?"

"No." Annie was on her feet in an instant. Still carrying Carol, she stood next to Liam. "I was just explaining to Deputy Kemp how I found Carol—and about you."

"I'm her father."

The deputy scratched his chin. "So you came to claim her?"

"That's it."

"What about the mother?"

"Still looking for her. Annie's sister, Nola Prescott."

Deputy Kemp's eyebrows shot up to the brim of his hat and he started scratching out notes in his condemning little pad again. "The woman who accused you of breaking into the offices of the company where you worked, Belfry Construction, right? Where the night watchman ended up getting clobbered over the head and dying?"

"One and the same."

"You were hauled in for that one."

"Questioned and held. Charges were dropped." He saw Annie's eyes widen as she realized he'd spent time in jail.

"All because of Ms. Prescott's testimony—that she recanted."

Liam's nostrils flared slightly and he glared at Annie as if in so doing he could make her disappear. "Yep."

"Why would a woman you . . . well, you had a baby with want to send you to jail?"

"That's what I'd like to know." Every muscle in his body tensed and white lines around his lips indicated the extent of his ire. The stare he sent Annie would have melted nails. "When I locate Nola, believe me, I'll find out."

"The Seattle police don't seem to be very convinced that you weren't involved in the crime."

"They're wrong." Liam's lips were compressed into a razor-thin seam that barely moved when he spoke. "Was there anything else?"

"No." The deputy snapped his notebook closed and tipped his hat at Annie. "I'll be in touch."

"Thanks," she said weakly.

"And I'm sure C.S.D. will want to speak with you."

Liam followed him to the door and watched through the window as the cruiser skidded around his Jeep and slowly disappeared down the lane through the trees. Once satisfied that they were alone, he turned slowly, his irritation evident in the set of his jaw. "What was that all about?"

"I thought . . . I mean a few days ago when you came barging in here threatening to take Carol away and charging after Nola, I was scared and—"

"So you decided to turn me in?" he accused. "Damn it, woman, you're cut from the same cloth as that sister of yours!"

"No!"

"Both of you trying to set me up."

"Liam! No!"

Carol let out a whimper and Annie removed the nipple from her mouth and gently lifted her to her shoulder. Softly rubbing the baby's back, she sent Liam a look warning him not to raise his voice. He stalked to the window and stared outside while Annie, after burping and changing Carol, sat in the rocker and nudged the infant back to slumber.

Liam gave a soft whistle to the dog and stormed outside. Annie closed her eyes while rocking the baby. What a horrid predicament. With Carol smack-dab in the middle of it. As the rocker swayed she tried to sort out her life and came up with no answers. A few days ago, before the baby had been left on her doorstep, everything had been so clear, her days on a boring but regular track. Now she felt as if every aspect of her life was careening out of control. She loved Carol and was sure to lose her. She loved her sister, but was confused about Nola's intentions and she loved Liam . . . She stopped rocking. No way. She didn't love Liam O'Shaughnessy; she didn't even know the man, not really. What she felt for him was lust. Nothing more.

The baby let out a tiny puff of air and snuggled against her and Annie felt a tug on her heartstrings unlike any she'd ever felt before. *Precious, precious little girl, how am I ever going to bear to give you up?*

"I can't. I just can't," she whispered, her throat as thick as if she'd swallowed an orange. She thought to the future—first steps, learning to read, going off to school, soccer and T-ball, first kiss and high school prom. Oh, no, no, no! Annie couldn't not be a part of Carol's life. She blinked hard, realized she was close to tears, and finally, after Carol was asleep, placed the baby in her bassinet.

Sliding her arms through her jacket and wrapping a scarf around her neck, she walked outside where she donned her boots and gloves. She heard Liam before she saw him, the sound of an axe splitting wood cracking through the canyon. He was standing near the woodpile by the barn, the axe raised over his head. Gritting his teeth, he swung down and cleaved a thick length of fir into two parts, the split portions spinning to either side of the stump he used as a chopping block. Snowflakes clung to his blond hair and settled on the shoulders of his suede jacket. He reached down for another length of oak and set it in place.

"You want something?" he asked without turning. The axe was lifted skyward and came down with a thwack that split the wood easily as darkness fell.

"To explain."

"No need."

"But Liam—"

"So now it's 'Liam,' is it?" He slammed the axe down again, wedging the blade in the chopping block and turned to glare at her. "Just tell me one thing, Annie. What is it you expected to accomplish by drawing in the police?"

"I—I—just needed some peace of mind. You came in here like gangbusters, arguing and carrying on and threatening to take Carol away and I . . . I needed help."

He glanced at the sky and shook his head. "Did you get it? Peace of mind?"

"No." She shook her head.

"Me neither."

Swallowing back all of her pride, she lifted her head and stared him down. "Now it's your turn," she said. "You tell me just one thing."

"Shoot."

"What is it you want from me, Liam O'Shaughnessy?"

"Good question." His face softened slightly, the shadows of the night closing in. "I wish I knew."

She shivered, but not from the cold night air. No, her skin trembled from the intensity of his gaze and the way her body responded. She licked suddenly dry lips and willed her legs to move. "I . . . I'd better see about the horses."

"What is it you want from me?"

Like the icicles suspended from the eaves of the barn, his question seemed to hang in the air between them. *I want you to love me.* Oh, Lord, where did that wayward thought come from? She stopped short, her breath fogging in the frigid air. "I—I just want you to leave me alone."

His smile was as hard as the night. "I already told you what a lousy liar you are, so try again. What is it you want from me?"

"Nothing, Liam," she said and marched to the barn. She couldn't, wouldn't let him see how vulnerable he made her feel. Each day she'd snapped lead ropes to the horses' halters and walked them around the paddock for nearly an hour so that they trampled a path through the drifts, then returned them to their stalls with fresh water and feed and brushed the clumps of snow from their coats. They'd already been exercised for the day, but she walked into the barn and took in deep breaths of the musty air. From somewhere behind the oat bin, she heard the scurry of feet, a rat or mouse she'd startled.

She sensed rather than heard him enter. *Give me strength.*

"Annie."

Oh, God. She wrapped her arms around her middle, took a deep breath, and decided she had no choice but to meet him head-on. "Look, O'Shaughnessy—" Turning, she ran straight into him and his arms closed around her.

"No more lies," he said and she caught a glimpse of his eyes before his lips found hers in the darkness. She shouldn't do this, knew she was making an irrevocable mistake, but as his weight pulled her downward onto a mat of loose straw, she gave herself up to the silent cravings of her body. His lips were warm, his body strong, and she closed her mind to the doubts that nagged her, the worries that plagued her about this one enigmatic man.

She shivered as he opened her coat and slowly drew her scarf from around her neck, trembled in anticipation as he drew her sweater over her head and unhooked her bra, swallowed back any protest as he lowered his lips to her nipple and gently teased.

Warmth invaded that private space between her legs, and desire ran naked through her blood. Her fingers fumbled with the fastenings of his jacket and he shrugged out of the unwanted coat, tucking it beneath them, along with hers.

"I want you, Annie," he said as he threw off his sweater and her fingers traced the corded muscles of his chest and shoulders. His abdomen retracted as she kissed the mat of golden hair that covered his chest and he groaned in anticipation as she tickled his stomach with her breath.

"I want you, too," she admitted. "God forgive me, but I do."

His smile, crooked and jaded, slashed in the darkness. "It's not a sin, you know."

"I know," she agreed, but wasn't convinced. Only when his lips claimed hers again and his hands lovingly caressed her did she sigh and give up to the sorcery of his touch. His fingers tangled in her hair and he pressed urgent lips to her eyelids, the corner of her mouth, her throat, and lower still.

He skimmed her jeans over her hips and followed his hands with lips that breathed fire against her skin and through the sheer lace of her panties. She squirmed as he sculpted her buttocks, lifting her gently and kissing her with an intimacy that she felt in the back of her throat. Through the thin barrier he laved and teased until the barn with its smells of horses and grain disappeared into the shadows and she felt him pull away the final garment to reach deeper.

"Ooooh," she cried, wanting more, blind to anything but the lust that stoked deep in her soul. "Liam—"

"I'm here, love." In an instant he kicked off his jeans and was atop her, parting her knees with the firm muscles of his thighs, kissing her anxiously on the lips, breathing as if it would be his last.

She couldn't close her eyes, but watched in wonder as he made love to her, gasped and writhed, catching his tempo, following his lead, feeling as if her life would never be the same again.

"Annie," he cried as her mind grew foggy and she was swept on a current of sensations that brought heat to her loins and goose bumps to her flesh. "Oh, God, Annie." He threw back his head and squeezed his eyes shut. With a shudder, he poured himself into her and she convulsed, her body clamping around him, her mind lost somewhere in the clouds.

He collapsed against her and she willingly bore his weight. Dear God in heaven, how would she ever be able to give him up, to give this up? Her heart was pounding erratically, her breathing short and shallow.

You could get pregnant, Annie.

Would that be so bad? The thought of carrying Liam's child deep inside her was soothing rather than worrisome.

The doctor said you'd miscarry again, that you can't go to term.

But it was worth the risk.

Don't be a fool, Annie. Think!

Liam's arms tightened around her and he sighed into the curve of her neck, closing off all arguments with her rational mind. She knew he couldn't promise his undying love, realized that what she felt was not only one-sided but foolish as well, and yet she ached to hear the words that would bind him to her forever, inwardly cried to have him swear his undying love.

Slowly he lifted his head. Eyes still shining in after-glow, he pushed a stray strand of hair from her face. "There's something I want to tell you," he said, his voice still husky and deep.

Her heart did a silly little flip. "What's that, O'Shaughnessy?"

He winked at her and offered her that slightly off-center grin she found so endearing. "Merry Christmas, Annie McFarlane."

"To you, too, O'Shaughnessy."

"I think I've got a present for you," he added and his voice was rougher, more serious. She felt the first glimmer of despair.

"What's that?" she teased but saw that he was stone-cold sober.

He cleared his throat and plucked a strand of straw from her hair. Gazing into her eyes as if searching for a reaction, he said, "Jake found your sister."

"What?"

"That's right." He kissed her on the temple. "He's bringing Nola here sometime after the first of the year, after the storms have passed, and she's done dealing with the police and Peter Talbott."

Annie was stunned. The thought of seeing Liam with Nola and their baby, Carol, *her* baby, was overwhelming. "Good," she said without a trace of enthusiamsm. It had to happen sooner or later.

"Once we talk to Nola, we'll figure everything out."

Annie's heart seemed to dissolve. She was going to lose them—both Liam and Carol. She knew it as well as she knew that tonight was Christmas Eve.

Chapter Seven

"Will you marry me?"

Annie stopped dead in her tracks. They'd been walking from the main house back to the cabin, through the mud and slush still lingering in the forest. Liam was carrying a front pack with Carol sleeping cozily against him.

"Marry you?" Her voice seemed to echo through the forest.

Liam took her gloved hands in his and as rain drizzled through the fir and oak trees, he smiled down at her. "Carol needs a mother—someone who loves her."

Annie's heart plummeted. For a second she'd expected him to say that he loved her. In the past two weeks of being together, never once had he uttered those three wonderful words. "I—I—well, I told myself I'd never marry again." This was happening too fast— way too fast.

"I thought you wanted to be with Carol."

She bit her lip as she saw Carol's blond curls peeking

up through the top of the front pack. "I do, more than anything, but—"

His smile faded and he rubbed his jaw. "Look, Annie, I never thought I'd ever marry. I liked being a bachelor, but then I didn't realize that I was going to be a father, either. I'm glad about that. Ecstatic—and I want what's best for my daughter." He brushed a moist strand of hair from her eyes. "Carol couldn't have a better mother than you."

Her throat became swollen and he pressed a kiss to her temple. "Would it be so bad, married to me?"

No, she didn't think so. Though she'd barely known him for two weeks, she loved him. Foolishly and reverently. Maybe in time he would learn to love her and, if the truth be known, she couldn't imagine living her life without him. He'd proven himself, exonerating himself of the crime in Washington, refusing to prosecute Nola for her false claims against him, sticking by Annie through the holidays and helping her care for the main house, cabin, and livestock as the frozen countryside thawed, creating floods and mud slides. Also, more importantly, it was obvious that he was completely taken with his daughter.

They'd laughed together, fought a little, spent hours upon hours at each other's side only to make love long into the night. He'd helped clean the gutters, thaw the pipes, and repair the roof when icy branches had fallen on the old shingles. He'd exercised and fed the horses, shoveled the driveway, fixed her pickup that refused to start after being packed in snow for ten days, done the grocery shopping, and kept the fire stoked until the old furnace kicked in. He'd been a gentle lover, a concerned father, and, it seemed, a man determined to clear his name. He'd watched Carol as Annie had reconnected with her clients and worked on her word processor, but the bottom line was that he didn't love her. At least not yet.

"But . . . how? Where would we live? Wait a minute, this is all so fast." She held up a hand and he captured it in his larger one.

"We'll live here. I'm moving out of Washington anyway. I'll sell my house and start my own company, either in Portland or Vancouver. If it's money you're worried about—"

"No, no." She shook her head. Money was the last thing on her mind. In fact, she hadn't told him but she was three days late in her monthly cycle. Not a lot, but, considering that her periods came and went like clockwork, something to think about. Something very pleasant to consider.

"You can keep your job, or become a full-time mother. We'll buy a place of our own eventually, when the time is right."

"Are you sure?" Good Lord, she shouldn't even be contemplating anything so ludicrous.

Smiling, he used the finger of one gloved hand to smooth the worried furrow from her brow. "As sure as anything I've done lately. Come on, wouldn't you love to be Carol's mother?"

"You know I would," she admitted, wondering if she was about to make the mistake of her life. She'd suffered through one divorce and she wasn't about to go through another. If and when she married again, it would be for life. "What about Nola?" she asked, concern gnawing away at her optimism. "She'd be your sister-in-law."

Liam glanced to the gray sky and frowned. "As long as she doesn't live with us and doesn't interfere with Carol, it'll be okay."

"She accused you of murder."

His smile was cold as ice. "Don't worry about Nola, Annie. I can take care of your sister."

"I don't think anyone can take care of her." They hadn't seen Nola nor heard from her, though, according to Liam's friend Jake, she'd turned in her boyfriend, Peter Talbott, who had embezzled funds and killed Bill Arness when he was startled while doctoring the company books. Talbott had coached Nola into lying about Liam's participation in the crime, then skipped town, leaving Nola, who had been in love with him, alone to hold the bag. She'd gone to meet him somewhere in Idaho, but he'd never shown up and Jake had confronted her and convinced her to turn state's evidence against Talbott, who was already long gone, probably hiding out in Canada.

All that trouble seemed far away from their private spot here in the forest. Carol gurgled in the pack between them, a fine Oregon mist moistened their faces, and somewhere not too far off Riley was barking his fool head off at a rabbit or squirrel or some other creature hiding in the ferns and bracken.

She could be happy here with Liam and Carol, she thought, warmth invading her heart.

Hand in hand they walked back to the cabin where, despite the rumble of the furnace, a fire was burning and near her desk stacked with correspondence, the small Christmas tree still stood, draped in garlands and shimmering with tinsel. From the oven, the smell of pot roast and potatoes filled the air.

Liam carried Carol into the bedroom and placed her tiny body in the crib he'd purchased just two days earlier. The baby found her thumb and snuggled her little head against a gingham bumper as Annie adjusted her covers.

There was still so much to do. Social Services, upon learning that Liam was the father of the baby, had been lenient about Carol's situation. Marrying him would make the adoption all that much easier. And certainly Nola would comply. Though Annie hadn't spoken with her sister, she didn't doubt that Nola wanted her to care for the little girl. Liam had even gone through the formality of a paternity test, though the results wouldn't be confirmed for a few more days.

"Okay, Annie, what's it gonna be?" he asked and there was an edge to his voice she didn't recognize, a nervousness. He stood in the doorway of the bedroom, the firelight from the living room glowing behind him. "Will you marry me?"

"Yes." The word was out in an instant and Liam picked her up, twirling her in the small confines of the room. Startled, she gasped, then laughed. Carol let out a soft puff of a sigh. In the dim bedroom where only hours before they'd made love, she wrapped her arms around Liam's neck and kissed his cheek. "I'd love to marry you, Mr. O'Shaughnessy."

His smile was a slash of white as they tumbled onto the bed together. "We could fly to Reno tonight."

"Tonight?"

"Why wait?"

Yes, why? For years she'd wanted to become a mother. She thought of all the painful disappointments of her miscarriages, the guilt, the dull ache in her heart, the fear that she would never have a child. And now she had only to agree to marry the man she loved to become a mother. "All right," she finally agreed. "Tonight."

" . . . Mr. and Mrs. Liam O'Shaughnessy." The justice of the peace, a robust man of about sixty, rained a smile down on Liam, Annie, and Carol while his wife, dressed in polka dots, sat at the piano and played the wedding march.

"That's all there is to it?" Annie asked as she and Liam walked out of the small, neon-lit chapel and another couple took their places. Outside, the traffic raced by and a wind cut through the dusty streets of Reno.

"It's legal and that's all that matters." Liam took her arm as she shielded Carol from the noise and cold night air. The city was ablaze in lights; the crowds, oblivious to the frigid temperatures, wandered in and out of the hotels and casinos lining the main drag.

Annie followed Liam back to the hotel where they'd booked a room for the night. She remembered her last wedding six years earlier—a church with stained-glass windows, a preacher in robes, three bridesmaids, Nola as the maid of honor, a flower girl, and a ringbearer. Ribbons and rose petals, David's sister singing a love song, candles and organ music, and all for what? Nothing. A marriage that had turned to ashes all too soon.

This time there were no false promises, no stiff ceremony, nothing borrowed, blue, old, or new. *And no love?* her ever-nagging mind reminded her.

They took the elevator to the fifth floor where a roll-in crib was waiting for Carol and a bottle of chilled champagne waited in a stand packed in ice.

While Annie changed Carol and fed her a final bottle, Liam uncorked the champagne. Once the baby was fed, burped, and put to sleep, he poured them each a glass and touched the rim of his fluted goblet to hers.

"Here's to happiness," he said with a grin.

And love, she thought, but added, "And more children."

"More?" Blond eyebrows raised.

She nodded. "Maybe sooner than you thought."

"You're pregnant?"

"I'm not sure, but . . . well, I could be."

His smile grew from one side of his face to the other. He sipped from his glass, took her into his arms, and as champagne spilled between them, carried her to the bed. "I'd say congratulations are in order, Mrs. O'Shaughnessy."

"That they are, Mr. O."

He kissed her and Annie closed her eyes, refusing to listen to the doubts, to the worries, to the damned negative thoughts that had plagued her ever since she'd agreed to become Liam's bride. Tonight, on her wedding night, she would give herself to him. Nothing else mattered.

"This is a big mistake." Nola scratched both her arms with her fingernails and wished she was anywhere else but in this damned car with Jake Cranston. Some sappy country ballad was battling with static on the radio.

"You've made worse."

She rolled her eyes, but didn't argue. How could she? Without his help, the police in Seattle would have held her as an accomplice or material witness or whatever the hell else they could come up with in the Belfry break-in and murder of Bill Arness. She still felt cold inside when she thought about Bill. Guilt pressed a ten-ton weight on her chest. She had nothing to do with his death, but she had known that Peter was behind it. Even though Bill had surprised him at the computer and Peter had only meant to knock him out, the old man had died.

Peter Talbott.

Embezzler. Killer. Jerk. And so much more.

Tears burned behind Nola's eyelids. Jesus, she was an idiot. But she was going to see Annie again. And the baby. Her heart lightened at the thought.

Jake turned off the freeway and onto a two-lane road that wound through the hills surrounding Lake Oswego and West Linn. Metropolis one minute, cow country the next. He grabbed a pack of Marlboros from the dash and tossed it to her. "Light one for me, too."

"Thanks." She punched in the lighter, slipped a filter-tip into her mouth, and then, once the lighter popped out, lit up. "Here," she said in a cloud of nerve-calming smoke. She handed him the first cigarette, then shook a second from the pack.

Jake took the smoke and punched another button

on the radio. Country music faded and an old Bob Seeger tune met her ears.

Against the wind, I was runnin' against the wind . . .

Boy, and how, she thought, drawing hard on her cigarette and cracking the window. "He's gonna kill me."

"Who? Liam?" Jake snorted. "I doubt it. Not that he wouldn't have just cause."

"I know, I know. I was wrong, okay?"

"And lucky. Damned lucky that he's not got *you* up on charges."

"How could he? I'm his sister-in-law," she said, still hardly believing the news that Jake had given her only yesterday. According to Jake, Annie and Liam had gotten married over a week ago. "What a joke."

"It's no joke, believe me." Jake drove past a development, then turned onto a gravel road leading through a thicket of evergreens and scrub oak.

Nola's stomach clenched. What could she say to Annie? To Liam O'Shaughnessy? Oh, God. She took a long draw on her cigarette and noticed that her hands were cold as ice. This was no good—no damned good.

They passed a huge house with a peaked roof, turret, and dark windows, a gray Victorian that some people might think was quaint. Nola thought it looked like it had come right out of *Psycho*. "Annie lives here?" Nola asked, but Jake didn't stop and continued on the winding road to a much smaller house—a cottage of sorts—with a view of the lake and a barn nearby.

"She—well, they, I guess now, live here. Annie maintains the other house." He jabbed out his cigarette in the tray. "How close are you with your sister?"

"Sometimes closer than others," she said. "This hasn't been my best year."

"Amen." He cut the engine and reached across her to open her door. "Shall we?"

"If we must." She was already stepping out of the car

and couldn't stop the drumming of her heart at the thought of seeing her baby again. How much had she grown? Did she smile? Would she recognize the woman in whose womb she'd grown for nine months? Heart in her throat, Nola took one last drag from her Marlboro, then cast the butt onto the lawn where it sizzled against wet leaves. "Okay. It's now or never." She walked up the two steps to the front porch and pushed on a bell.

In an instant Annie, flushed face, sparkling eyes, and easy smile, opened the door. In her arms was a blond baby with wide blue eyes—a baby Nola barely recognized as her own.

"Nola." Annie's voice broke.

"Oh, God, Annie, I—I—!" Tears sprang to her eyes and ran down her face. She threw her arms around her sister and smelled the scent of baby powder mingling with Annie's perfume. Happiness and worry collided in her heart. How had she ever given the baby away? But how could she possibly consider keeping her? Besides, she'd made a promise . . . Sniffing loudly, she hugged her sister and looked up to see Liam O'Shaughnessy in the small home, his presence seeming to loom in the interior. He was staring at her with harsh blue eyes that held no mercy, not a speck of forgiveness. Her blood congealed and she stepped away from her sister. "Liam."

"Nola." His voice was harsh.

"Look, I owe you a big apology."

"Save it." His jaw was set. Uncompromising.

"No, hear me out. I wish you and Annie the best."

He snorted. "Can it."

"Jake Cranston," the man with Nola said. He held out his hand and shook Annie's in a firm, sure-of-himself grasp.

"My wife, Annie," Liam said.

"I assumed."

Annie, her insides a knot, ushered Nola inside.

Jake grabbed a kitchen chair, twirled it around, and straddled it. "I think you should listen to what your sister-in-law has to say, O'Shaughnessy."

"Fair enough." Liam skewered Nola with his gaze. "Shoot."

"I know you hate me," Nola said and Liam didn't say a word, not a syllable of denial even when Annie shot him a pleading look, silently begging him to be forgiving. Nola had, after all, given them Carol. Nola cleared her throat and, cheeks burning, added, "But I did what I thought I had to because . . . well, because I loved Peter."

"Great guy," Liam muttered.

"I thought he was and"—she held up a hand when she saw the protest forming on Liam's lips—"I was wrong. I know that now. I'm sorry for all the trouble and pain I caused you. I am. But I can't undo what's already been done."

"She explained everything to the authorities," Jake said. "I've got copies of her statement to the police in my briefcase."

Nola blinked back tears. "I just hope in time, you'll forgive me."

"Of course he will," Annie answered, but Liam didn't respond. She didn't blame him. Nola had put him through a living hell, but it was painful to witness the hardening of his jaw again, the harsh intensity of his gaze. Ever since the wedding he'd been more relaxed and their lives here, with Carol, had been stress-free.

Until now.

Annie put a hand on Nola's shoulder and her sister turned. She spied the baby again and tears trickled from her eyes. "Can I hold her?"

"If you tell me what leaving her here was all about." Annie couldn't put off the inevitable talk another second. The baby was what her life was all about, the reason she got up in the morning, the impetus for Liam to have met her and married her. Even though there was probably another child growing within her, Carol would always be special. Carol yawned as Annie handed her to her natural mother and Nola bit her lower lip.

"She's beautiful."

"Yes." Annie's voice was low and hoarse with emotion. "But how did you leave her on the stoop?"

"That was Peter's idea," Nola admitted, avoiding her sister's gaze. "I knew I couldn't take care of a baby, couldn't raise her and give her the security and stability she needed. So Peter brought her here."

"And left her in the freezing temperatures on the porch," Liam said.

"Annie was home—"

"What if she hadn't heard the baby cry?"

"Peter heard the dog. He was careful to stay near the bushes and brush his tracks away with a branch from a fir tree. But he waited in the shadows until Annie answered the door."

"You didn't come with him?" Liam asked.

Nola shook her head and swallowed hard. "I—I couldn't. It was too hard."

"Did you ever think of calling me?" Liam asked.

"You?" Nola shook her head. "Why?"

"You know a father has some rights."

Nola's eyebrows slammed together. "That's why I went along with Peter's plan."

"What?"

"Since he didn't think it was time for us to settle down with a baby, I told him about Annie and we decided—"

"Wait a minute." Annie's head was spinning. She was missing something. Something important. "Why would Peter have any say about it?"

"Because he's, what did you name her—Carol? I like that. Well, because he's Carol's father."

"Father?" Liam asked, his voice low, like rolling thunder far in the distance.

"Yeah. He and I . . . " She let the words fade away. "Wait a minute. You didn't think that . . . oh, my God, Liam, did you really think the baby was yours?" She laughed for a second before she turned and looked at the horror shining in Annie's eyes. "The baby's Peter's."

"No!" Annie cried.

"Yes."

"You're certain?" Liam demanded.

"Of course. I would know—"

"But you would lie."

"Not about this and I know, Liam. You and I were over before I conceived this baby." She said it with such conviction Annie didn't doubt her for a minute.

"Oh, dear God . . . " Annie's stomach turned sour. Bile rose up her throat. How could they have made such a horrendous mistake? Why hadn't they waited for the paternity tests? She'd been so certain—so sure Carol was Liam's flesh and blood.

"Talbott's?" Liam's eyes flashed like blue lightning.

"Yes. But he didn't want her and—oh, sweet Jesus, you really thought you were her father, didn't you?"

"I am," Liam said, his jaw tight, the cords of his neck strident. "Make no mistake, Nola, I'm Carol's father. Now and forever."

"But—"

"That's the way it is." He looked past his sister-in-law and his eyes sought Annie's. "And you, Annie Prescott McFarlane O'Shaughnessy, are Carol's mother."

"As long as Peter or I don't interfere," Nola said, lifting her chin. "Now that Peter's gone and I have no one, I could . . . I mean, biologically and legally, Carol's my daughter."

Annie let out a little squeak of protest, but then bit her tongue. What did she expect? That her sister would hand over the precious baby, that Nola wouldn't have second thoughts, that Peter Talbott, whoever he was, wouldn't exert his rights as the baby's father?

"I'll fight you," Liam said, his voice deadly as he advanced upon Nola. "If you try and take Carol away from Annie, I swear, I'll hunt you down and make your life a living hell. And I'll tell the court what a swell mother and role model you'd make. Don't forget I know you, Nola. Inside and out. Your fears and weaknesses and the fact that you abandoned your daughter, left her in freezing temperatures in a basket on a porch because it wasn't convenient for you to keep her. Then there's the lying to the court. I've been told I could press charges." He crossed the room in three swift strides to glare down at Nola who, despite her bravest efforts, cowered under the power of his gaze. "You've had quite a list of lovers, you've been involved in an embezzling scheme, you've never held a job for more than two years, and you disappear for months at a time. I don't know about you, but I think the court might find you unfit."

Nola swallowed hard. "You wouldn't dare—"

"Think about it," he warned.

"No, no, no!" Annie was fighting tears and shaking her head. "I—we can't do this. Carol is . . . " *Sweet, sweet baby, how can I give you up?* " . . . She belongs to Nola. And Peter." The floorboards seemed to shift beneath Annie's feet and somewhere deep inside there was a rending.

"Oh, God, not Pete." Nola waved her hands frantically on either side of her head. "He's useless. A criminal. A killer, for Christ's sake."

Annie's head was swimming; she held onto the back of the couch for support. Her blood pounded in her ears. She was losing the baby . . . no, no, no.

"And you were not only his lover, but his accomplice." Liam turned to Annie and his expression was unrelenting. "We are Carol's parents," he said.

"No." Her voice cracked and the absurdity of the

situation struck her. He'd only married her so that she would be Carol's mother. Her marriage was nothing more than a sham. Hollow. Empty. A fool's paradise. "We aren't Carol's parents legally, not yet and apparently not ever." She fought tears, blinking rapidly as she removed the wedding band that she'd worn for so few days. "Liam, I'm sorry." An ache burned through her.

"So am I, Annie," he said without a trace of warmth. "So am I."

The first pang struck her dead center and she thought it was just stress. The second was more painful and she gasped.

"Annie?" Liam's voice was edged in concern. The world started to go black. "Annie?" Again the pain and this time she felt the first ooze of blood, the fledgling life starting to slide from her. "Annie, are you okay?" Liam was standing over her and as she let go of the couch and started to sway, he caught her.

"She's bleeding," Nola said from someplace far away.

"Annie?" Liam's voice was strident, filled with terror, but she couldn't see him. "Call an ambulance—" Her eyes fluttered closed and a beckoning blackness enveloped her. The last thing she heard was Liam calling her name and there was something wrong with his voice—it sounded muffled and cracked. "Annie, hang in there. Oh, sweet Jesus, Annie!"

"Mr. O'Shaughnessy, why don't you go down to the cafeteria and get a cup of coffee? There's nothing you can do for her."

In the blackness, Annie heard the woman's voice as if from a distance. She tried to open her eyes, failed, and licked her lips—so dry.

"I'm staying." Liam's voice was firm. "She's my wife."

"I know, but—"

"I said, I'm not leaving her side, woman, so you can quit harping at me."

"Fine, have it your way. Sheesh. Newlyweds." Footsteps retreated and Liam let out his breath. "Come on, Annie, you can do it," he said as if she were running a marathon instead of just sleeping. "Come on, girl, don't you know that I love you?"

Love? Liam loved her?

"Don't let me down now. Show me some of that fighting spirit. I need you. Carol needs you."

Carol? Oh, yes, the baby.

Annie struggled, her eyes moving behind closed lids.

"She's waking up." Liam sounded surprised. "Annie, oh, thank God."

With an effort she forced her eyes to open, then winced at the light. "Where—?"

"You're in the hospital," Liam said as she focused on him and saw tears shining in his eyes. "And you're fine."

"Fine?"

"Everything's going to be all right, darling," he said, taking her hands and holding them in his as he sat near the hospital bed. "Nola's signed the papers, Peter's agreed that you and I are to be Carol's parents. Nothing's going to stop us now."

She smiled as a nurse entered the room. "Well, look who finally decided to wake up. How're you feeling, honey?" She rounded the bed, blood-pressure cuff ready.

Annie managed to hold up a hand and move it side to side.

"So-so? Don't worry about that—you'll be dancing a jig in no time." The nurse, a round little woman of about forty, slipped the cuff up Annie's arm. She took Annie's blood pressure, pulse, and temperature, admonished her to drink as much water as possible, and promised that food would arrive shortly.

"See, the red carpet treatment," Liam said, smiling down at her. "You had me worried for a while there, you know."

"What happened?"

"You fainted," he said, stroking the side of her cheek.

"Is that all?"

"No." Sighing, he held her gaze with his. "You were pregnant, Annie. And you lost the baby."

"No!" she cried and tears filled her eyes. Another child lost. Liam's baby.

"The doctor says we can try again. But that's up to you." Liam cupped her face in his big hands. "We still have Carol, Annie. And each other. That's more than most people have." He swallowed hard and pressed a kiss to her lips. She felt him tremble. "I love you, Annie O'Shaughnessy," he vowed, "and you just gave me the scare of my life. Don't ever do it again."

His words were like gentle rain, erasing some of the pain. "I won't, " she promised, "and I love you, Liam, more than you'll ever know."

Again he kissed her and for the first time she felt she really was his wife.

Epilogue

Nearly a year later

"... *I'm telling you why, Santa Claus is coming to town* ..."
Annie sang off-key as she hung the stocking on the mantel of her new home, the old Victorian house that overlooked the little cottage where she'd first discovered Carol on her stoop. Outside, the Oregon rain peppered the mullioned windows and inside Carol was taking her first few steps, grinning widely and walking like a drunken sailor from the table to the chair and back again.

The rooms were decorated haphazardly. Some of her furniture, a little of Liam's, and the rest having come with the house, but a tree stood in the parlor, strung with popcorn, cranberries, and twinkling lights, which Carol found absolutely fascinating.

The front door burst open and Liam, smelling of pine and leather, wiped the dampness from his face. "All done," he said and flipped a switch. Through the window Annie spied thousands of lights ablaze in the surrounding forest.

"Oooh!" Carol said, toddling to the window and staring outside.

"Daddy did a good job, didn't he?" Annie asked and Liam laughed, crossing the room and snagging Carol from the floor. With a squeal she landed on his shoulders and Annie laughed, her life complete. She still had her secretarial business, but she was working less and less with the demands of being a wife and mother. Liam, on the other hand, was so busy with his consulting firm in Portland that he was thinking of taking on a partner.

"Where's Jake?" Liam asked as he bussed his wife's cheek. Carol, still atop his broad shoulders, giggled.

"Sleeping, as usual."

"Let's wake him up."

"Let's not," Annie said, shaking her head. "Liam O'Shaughnessy, if you so much as breathe on that baby, I'll—" But it was no use, Liam was already climbing the stairs to the nursery, a small room off the master bedroom. Annie followed him and watched as he stared down in wonder at his son.

As if the baby sensed he was the center of attention, he opened his eyes and cooed. "And your mother didn't want you to wake up," Liam said as Annie picked up her son and felt him snuggle against her breast. Jake Liam O'Shaughnessy had been born on December seventh and the only problem Annie had experienced during the nine months of her pregnancy was an incredible craving for cherry vanilla ice cream.

Nola was working in Detroit and was engaged to a lawyer, Joel and Polly had promised to visit after the new year, and Annie's mother and stepfather promised to fly to Oregon once they'd returned from a trip to Palm Springs.

Life had become routine and nearly perfect. Riley barked at the back door as the little family hurried down the stairs. The smell of cinnamon cookies and gingerbread hung heavy in the air.

In the kitchen, Annie opened the door and the dog bounded in. Liam placed Carol in her high chair and offered her a cookie.

"You spoil her," Annie admonished.

"And you don't?"

"No, I spoil her rotten."

Liam reached into the cupboard and withdrew a bottle of Pinot Noir. "I think it's time for a toast," he said, opening the bottle as Annie held her son and Jake blinked up at her.

"To?"

"Us." He poured two stemmed glasses, then handed her one. "To the family O'Shaughnessy. Long may it prosper."

"Hear, hear." She touched the rim of her glass to his.

"And to the most beautiful woman in the world. My wife."

Annie blushed. "Here's to you, Mr. O. The most unlikely husband in the world, and the best."

They drank, then kissed, then found a way to personally wish each other the merriest Christmas ever.